P9-DHG-681

DOVER·THRIFT·EDITIONS

Death in Venice

THOMAS MANN

Translation and Commentary by
STANLEY APPELBAUM

82998
NJ-SP HS

No. Judson-San Pierre H.S
900 Campbell Drive
No. Judson, IN 46366

DOVER PUBLICATIONS, INC.
New York

82998

DOVER THRIFT EDITIONS

EDITOR: STANLEY APPELBAUM

Copyright

Copyright © 1995 by Dover Publications, Inc.
All rights reserved under Pan American and International Copyright Conventions.

Bibliographical Note

This Dover volume, first published in 1995, contains a new English translation of "Der Tod in Venedig" (translated from a standard edition of the German text; see "Note" for original German publication), plus three sections written by the translator/editor specially for the present edition: "Note," "A Word About the Translation" and "Commentary."

Library of Congress Cataloging-in-Publication Data

Mann, Thomas, 1875–1955.
   [Tod in Venedig. English]
   Death in Venice / Thomas Mann ; translation and commentary by Stanley Appelbaum.
      p.   cm. — (Dover thrift editions)
   ISBN 0-486-28714-9 (pbk.)
   I. Title   II. Series.
PT2625.A44T26   1995
833'.912—dc20
                                                 92-2967
                                                     CIP

Manufactured in the United States of America
Dover Publications, Inc., 31 East 2nd Street, Mineola, N.Y. 11501

Contents

Note

THOMAS MANN (1875–1955), Nobel laureate for literature in 1929, gained his undoubted eminence among twentieth-century authors only slowly, his unflagging industry bolstering his unusual brilliance. At the beginning of 1911, the year in which he began writing his most famous short story (or novella), "Der Tod in Venedig" (Death in Venice), his health was poor and his career development sluggish. Nothing he had published since his youthful autobiographical novel *Buddenbrooks* (1901) had been received with such universal acclaim (some critics still maintain it is his very best work), and only one novel, not usually included in the canon of his major writings, had appeared in the interim: *Königliche Hoheit* (Royal Highness), in 1909. He had planned but abandoned several other long works, but had published almost nothing but short stories, outstanding among them "Tristan" and "Tonio Kröger" (both 1903). Convinced that he needed to make a mark with a new piece that would appeal to current tastes, he poured all his mastery into "Death in Venice," and circumstances came obligingly to the aid of genius.

Mann had already been considering a story about an elderly writer's undignified love affair, and had planned to use as a subject the real-life infatuation of the septuagenarian Goethe for a teenager. But his own vivid experiences while vacationing on Brioni and in Venice in May and June of 1911 redirected his thoughts and produced the masterpiece we now possess. Intensely autobiographical, "Death in Venice" combines the traditional German love-death theme complex (Novalis, Wagner) with Mann's own preoccupations about the life of creative artists, whom he regularly portrayed as people psychologically torn between bourgeois and bohemian selves, doomed by their own nature to a disintegration that manifested itself as physical illness.

The story was written between July 1911 and July 1912, and was first published in two issues of the Berlin magazine *Die Neue Rundschau* (The New Review), a house organ of Mann's publisher S. Fischer: October and November, 1912 (Vol. 23, Nos. 10 and 11). Later in 1912 it was published in a limited luxury edition by Hans von Weber's Hyperionverlag in Munich. Its first trade publication in book form was by S. Fischer, Berlin, 1913.

The present translation, faithful and absolutely complete, was prepared specially for this Dover Thrift Edition. The text of the story has been kept entirely free of numerical or other references to annotations; however, readers, particularly those not comfortably familiar with Greek mythology and philosophy, so integral to the narrative, are urged to consult the Commentary at the back of the book. Not primarily intended as interpretative analysis, this Commentary concentrates on factual explanations that may very well enhance the user's enjoyment. Preceding the Commentary are a few remarks about the nature of this new translation.

First Chapter

GUSTAV ASCHENBACH (or von Aschenbach, as his name read officially since his fiftieth birthday), on a spring afternoon of that year 19 — which for months posed such a threat to our continent, had left his apartment in the Prinzregentenstrasse in Munich and had gone for a rather long walk all alone. Overstrained by the difficult and dangerous labor of the morning hours, which precisely at this moment called for extreme circumspection, discretion, forcefulness and exactitude of the will, even after the noon meal the writer had been unable to restrain the continued operation of the productive machinery within him — that *motus animi continuus* in which, according to Cicero, the nature of eloquence consists — and had not found the relieving slumber that, with the increasing tendency of his strength to wear out, was so necessary to him once in the course of the day. And so, soon after tea, he had sought the outdoors, in hopes that the fresh air and activity would restore him and help him have a profitable evening.

It was the beginning of May and, after weeks of cold and damp, a spurious midsummer had set in. The English Garden, although its trees still bore only a few leaves, had been as muggy as in August, and in the vicinity of the city it had been full of carriages and strolling people. At the Aumeister, to which increasingly quiet paths had led him, Aschenbach had for a short while glanced at the crowd in that popular outdoor restaurant, alongside which several fiacres and private carriages were stationed; from there, as the sun was setting, he had taken a homeward route outside the park across the open meadow; and now, since he felt tired and a storm was threatening over Föhring, he was waiting at the Northern Cemetery for the streetcar that would bring him directly back to the city.

By chance he found the stop and its surroundings free of people. Neither on the paved Ungererstrasse, whose tracks stretched lonely and

1

gleaming toward Schwabing, nor on the Föhringer Chaussee, was any conveyance to be seen; behind the fences of the stonecutters' establishments, where the crosses, memorial tablets and monuments available for sale constitute a second, unpopulated burial place, nothing was stirring; and the Hall of Last Rites opposite, with its Byzantine-style architecture, lay silent in the reflected glow of the departing day. Its facade, adorned with Greek crosses and hieratic paintings in bright colors, also features symmetrically arranged inscriptions in gold lettering, selected religious phrases concerning the life beyond, such as "You are entering into the dwelling place of God" or "May the eternal light shine for them"; and for a few minutes, as he waited there, he had found some serious amusement in reading off these formulas and allowing his mind's eye to become absorbed in their diaphanous mysticism — when, coming out of his reveries, he noticed in the portico, above the two apocalyptic beasts that guard the monumental staircase, a man whose somewhat unusual appearance gave his thoughts a totally new direction.

Now, whether the man had been inside the Hall and had stepped outside through the bronze portal, or whether he had ascended unnoticed from outdoors, remained uncertain. Aschenbach, without dwelling on the question particularly, inclined toward the first assumption. Moderately tall, thin, beardless and conspicuously snub-nosed, the man was redheaded and had the milky, freckled skin peculiar to that physical type. He was clearly not of Bavarian ancestry: at least, the broad, straight-rimmed bast hat that covered his head lent his appearance the stamp of foreignness, of having come from far away. To be sure, he was also wearing the locally common rucksack buckled around his shoulders and a yellowish belted outfit that seemed to be of loden, and he was carrying a gray rain-cape over his left forearm, which he held akimbo against his side; in his right hand was a walking stick fitted with an iron tip, which he leaned against the ground at an angle and in the crook of which he rested his hip as he stood there with his feet crossed. His head raised, so that his Adam's apple stuck out, prominent and bare, against the scrawny neck protruding from his loose sport shirt, he peered sharply and searchingly into the distance with colorless, red-lashed eyes between which, as a most unusual counterpart to his short, turned-up nose, stood two energetic vertical furrows. In this way — and perhaps his elevated and elevating standpoint contributed to the impression — his bearing was somewhat like that of a lord surveying his domain, with an element of boldness or even savagery; for, whether it was because, dazzled, he was grimacing into the sinking sun, or whether his features were permanently deformed, his lips seemed too short; they were drawn all the way back, so that his long, white teeth, exposed up to the gums, were visible between them.

It is very possible that Aschenbach, in his half-distracted, half-inquisitive examination of the stranger, had showed some lack of etiquette, for suddenly he noticed that the man was returning his gaze, and so hostilely, looking him so directly in the eye, with so obvious an intention to push the matter to extremes and force his opponent to avert his gaze, that Aschenbach, embarrassed, moved away and began walking along the fences, deciding casually to pay no further attention to the person. The next minute, he had forgotten him. But whether the wayfaring aspect of the stranger's appearance had stirred his imagination, or whether some other physical or mental influence was at work, he was most surprisingly conscious of an odd expansion within himself, a kind of roving unrest, a youthfully ardent desire for faraway places, a feeling so intense, so new or at least unaccustomed and forgotten for so long, that he stopped short as if rooted to the spot, his hands clasped behind him and his eyes fixed on the ground, in order to examine the nature and purpose of this sensation.

It was an urge to travel, nothing more; but it presented itself in the form of a real seizure, intensified to the point of passionateness; in fact, it was like a delusion of the senses. His desire was clairvoyant; his imagination, which had not yet come to rest since his hours of work, summoned up a representative sampling of all the wonders and terrors of the variegated earth, all of which it attempted to visualize at one and the same time: he saw, saw a landscape, a tropical swampy region under a vapor-laden sky, damp, luxuriant and uncanny; it was like the portrait of a primitive world of islands, morasses and silt-laden rivers. From lusty fern clusters, from bottoms in which grew thick, waterlogged plants with outlandish blossoms, he saw hairy palm trunks rising near and far; he saw strangely misshapen trees sinking their roots through the air into the soil, into stagnant waters that reflected the green shade, where amid floating flowers as white as milk and as large as platters, birds of an exotic species, with hunched shoulders, with monstrous beaks, stood in the shallows and gazed off to the side, motionless; between the knotty, tubular stalks of the bamboo thicket he saw the eyes of a crouching tiger sparkle — and he felt his heart pounding with fright and a puzzling desire. Then the vision receded; and, shaking his head, Aschenbach resumed his promenade beside the fences of the gravestone-cutting workshops.

Ever since he had had at his disposal the means to enjoy the advantages of world travel whenever he wished, and perhaps even before that, he had looked upon traveling merely as a health measure that had to be taken now and again, even if contrary to his plans and inclinations. Too occupied with the tasks set for him by his own ego and by the European spirit he represented, too burdened with the obligation to create and too undisposed to diversions to be a proper admirer of the colorful outside world, he had been perfectly satisfied with the view of the earth's surface that anyone can acquire without venturing far away from his own circle of interests, and he had never even been tempted to leave Europe. And now, most of all, when his life was slowly approaching its close and he could no longer dismiss as a mere fancy his fear, shared by every artist, that he might not complete his life's work, that his clock might run down before he had accomplished what was in him and had given all of himself, his external existence had been confined almost exclusively to the beautiful city that had become his home and to the simple country villa which he had built for himself in the mountains and where he spent the rainy summers.

And thus the emotion that had now come over him so belatedly and so suddenly was quickly tempered and rectified by his reason and by the self-discipline he had practiced from his youth. He had made up his mind that, before moving to the country, he would complete up to a given point the book he was now living for, and the thought of an aimless trip that would call him away from his work for months seemed too lax and counterproductive; it was not to be considered seriously. And yet he knew all too well from what cause the temptation had so unex-pectedly arisen. It was an urge to escape, he admitted it to himself, this longing for the distant and new, this desire for liberation, for unburden-ing and oblivion — an urge to leave behind his work and the everyday venue of a rigid, cold and passionate servitude. Of course he loved this servitude and by this time almost loved the enervating, daily renewed battle between his tenacious and proud will, which had stood the test so often, and this growing weariness, which no one must know about and which his writings must not reveal in any way, by any indication of loss of power or reduced pace. But it seemed sensible not to exaggerate, not to stifle such an intensely emerging need out of stubbornness. He thought about his work, thought about the passage at which he had had to abandon it again today, as he had yesterday, a passage that seemingly could not be made right either by patient application or by some bold stroke. He reviewed it once more, tried to break through the obstruction or dissolve it and, with a shudder of repulsion, gave up the assault. No unusual difficulty was involved; instead, he was being paralyzed by a scruple born of aversion, taking the form of a fastidious dissatisfaction that could no longer be dispelled by any means. To be sure, ever since he was a young man this kind of dissatisfaction had meant to him the essence and inmost nature of talent; and it was for its sake that he had curbed and chilled his emotions, because he knew that emotions tend to be satisfied with a happy approximation and with less than perfection. Were his enslaved emotions now taking their toll by abandoning him, by refusing to further his art and lend it wings, by taking away with them all his delight in form and expression? Not that what he produced was bad: his years of experience at least gave him the advantage of feeling comfortably sure of his mastery at every moment. But while the nation honored his status as a master, he himself had no joy of it, as if his work lacked those tokens of fiery, playful spontaneity which were a result of joy and in turn created the joy of his readers more than any depth of substance could—tokens that were thus an important asset. He was afraid of the summer in the country, alone in the little house with the maid who prepared his food and the manservant who brought it to the table; he was afraid of the familiar faces of the mountain peaks and slopes that would once again surround his discontented dullness. And so a parenthesis was necessary, a bit of impromptu existence, some loafing, an exotic atmosphere and an influx of new blood, if the summer was to be bearable and productive. Travel, then—he was satisfied with the idea. Not very far, not all the way to the tigers. One night in a sleeper and a siesta of three or four weeks at some well-known holiday resort in the charming south of Europe.

That is what he was thinking while the clatter of the electric streetcar approached down the Ungererstrasse, and as he boarded the car he determined to devote that evening to studying maps and timetables. On the platform of the car it occurred to him to look around for the man in the bast hat, his companion during that wait which had proved to be so momentous. But the man's whereabouts were unclear to him; he could not be located either where he was previously standing or further down the streetcar stop or in the car itself.

Second Chapter

THE AUTHOR of the clear, powerful prose epic on the life of Frederick of Prussia; the patient artist who with untiring industry wove the novelistic tapestry called *Maya*, with its numerous characters, in which so many human destinies were gathered together to illustrate a grand idea; the creator of that forceful story entitled "A Miserable Man," which demonstrated to an entire generation of grateful young people the possibility that moral determination could transcend the profoundest knowledge; finally (and this concludes the brief characterization of the works of his maturity), the writer of the passionate treatise *Intellect and Art*, a book whose power of organization and syllogistic eloquence led serious reviewers to place it immediately alongside Schiller's disquisition on "naive" and "sentimental" literature — Gustav Aschenbach — was born in L., a district town in the province of Silesia, as the son of a senior legal official. His forebears had been officers, judges, bureaucrats, men who had led their disciplined, respectable and frugal lives in the service of king and state. Deeper intellectuality had embodied itself among them on one occasion, in the person of a preacher; more swiftly flowing and sensual blood had entered the family in the previous generation through the writer's mother, daughter of a Bohemian orchestra conductor. It was from her that he derived the signs of foreign ancestry in his appearance. The marriage of sober official conscientiousness with darker, more ardent impulses produced an artist, this particular artist.

Since his entire nature was bent on fame, he proved to be, if not exactly precocious, then at least, thanks to the decisiveness and pithiness of his personal accent, ready and able to confront the public at an early age. Hardly out of high school, he had made a name for himself. Ten years later he had learned how to uphold his reputation and be a good steward of his fame without rising from his desk, by means of his correspondence (although the letters had to be short, for many claims are made on the time of a successful and trustworthy author); he had learned how to appear benevolent and significant. The forty-year-old, exhausted by the exertions and vicissitudes of his own work, had to cope daily with mail that bore the postage stamps of every imaginable country.

As far removed from the banal as from the eccentric, his talent was such as to win both the trust of the broad public and, at the same time, the admiring, demanding sympathy of the fastidious. Thus, from his youth onward already obligated on all sides to achieve — and to achieve the extraordinary — he had never known idleness, never known the carefree recklessness of the young. When, at about the age of thirty-five, he fell ill in Vienna, a shrewd observer said of him at a social gathering: "You see, for years now Aschenbach has only lived like this" — and the speaker closed the fingers of his left hand into a tight fist — "never like this" — and he let his open hand dangle at ease from the armrest of the chair. That was correct; and what made it all so brave and so moral was that his constitution was by no means robust and, though called upon for constant exertion, was not really born for it.

Medical consultants had kept the boy from attending primary school and had insisted on home tutoring. He had grown up solitary, without comrades, and yet had had to learn early on that he belonged to a lineage in which it was not talent itself that was rare, but the physical basis which talent needs in order to be fulfilled—a lineage that is accustomed to give the best of itself early and in which ability seldom lasts until old age. But his favorite phrase was "see it through"; he considered his novel about Frederick the Great to be the very apotheosis of this command, which he looked upon as the quintessence of the virtue that remains active in spite of suffering. Moreover, he wished ardently to live to an old age, for he had always maintained that only that artistry could be called truly great and comprehensive, yes, truly worthy of honor, which had the good fortune to be appropriately productive at all stages of human existence.

Therefore, since he had to bear on slender shoulders the tasks his talent laid upon him, but nevertheless wanted to go far, he was in urgent need of discipline—and fortunately discipline was his inborn inheritance from his father's side. At forty, at fifty—just as he had in years past, at an age when others are spendthrift daydreamers, blithely postponing the execution of great plans—he began his day early with jets of cold water over his chest and back, and then, a pair of tall wax candles in silver sticks shining over his manuscript, for two or three fervently conscientious morning hours he would sacrifice upon the altar of art the strength he had garnered during his sleep. It was pardonable, in fact it signified the true victory of his morality, if those ignorant of his habits thought that the world of *Maya*, or the epic mass of copy in which Frederick's heroic life unfolded, was the product of robust strength and an unlimited store of breath, whereas on the contrary their greatness was the result of patient amassment of material in short daily stints dependent upon hundreds of individual acts of inspiration, and they were that excellent throughout, and in every detail, only because their creator had held out for years under the strain of a single lengthy work with a continuity of willpower and a tenacity similar to those that conquered his native province, and had devoted none but his hours of greatest strength and dignity to the actual composition of these books.

In order for a significant production of the intellect to make a broad and deep impact immediately, there has to be a secret relationship, in fact a congruence, between the personal destiny of its creator and the general destiny of the generation in which he lives. People do not know why they confer fame on a work of art. Far removed from connoisseurship, they imagine they have discovered a hundred merits in it in order to justify such great sympathy; but the real reason for their approval is something imponderable, it is a natural bond of shared feelings. Aschenbach had once stated outright, in an inconspicuous passage, that nearly every great thing that exists exists "in despite," and was brought to completion despite distress and torment, poverty, abandonment, physical weakness, vice, passion and a thousand obstructions. But that was more than an observation, it was a record of experience; indeed, it was the formula for his life and fame, the key to his oeuvre; and so is it any wonder that it also informed the moral nature and the external behavior of his most characteristic protagonists?

At an early stage in the author's career, a clever analyst had written, in regard to the new type of hero he preferred, a type recurring in numerous individual incarnations in his work, that it was the concept "of an intellectual and youthful masculinity that grits its teeth in proud modesty and stands by calmly while its body is pierced by swords and spears." That was elegant, witty and correct, despite its apparently too passive formulation: because composure beneath blows of fate, graciousness in the midst of torment, does not signify mere endurance; it is an active achievement, a positive triumph, and the figure of Saint Sebastian is the most beautiful symbol, if not in all of art, then at least in the type of art we are discussing. When you looked into this fictional world of Aschenbach's, you saw the elegant self-control that conceals the sapping of strength and biological decay from the eyes of the world up to the last minute; you saw yellowed ugliness, handicapped in its appeal to the senses, but nevertheless able to kindle its smoldering lust into pure flame and even to rise to dominance in the realm of beauty; you saw the pallid weakness that from the glowing depths of the spirit derives the strength to humble an entire haughty nation at the foot of the Cross, at *its* feet; you saw charming composure in the empty and severe service of form; you saw the false, dangerous life, the rapidly enervating yearning and art of the born deceiver. When you considered all of these destinies, and so many similar ones besides, you could easily imagine that the only kind of heroism that existed at all was the heroism of weakness. But, in any case, what kind of hero could be more suited to our era than this? Gustav Aschenbach was the poet of all those who labor on the brink of exhaustion, of the overburdened, of those already worn out, of those still holding their heads up, of all those moralists of achievement who, puny of body and short of means, acquire the effects of greatness at least for a time through an exaltation of the will and wise stewardship of their resources. They are many, they are the heroes of the age. And they all recognized themselves in his work, they found themselves affirmed, exalted and extolled there, they were grateful to him, they proclaimed his name.

He had been young and raw when the era was young and raw, and, taking its bad advice, he had publicly stumbled, had made mistakes, had compromised himself, had committed offenses against tact and prudence in word and deed. But he had acquired the dignity which, as he asserted, every great talent has an inborn drive and impulse to obtain; indeed, one may say that his entire development had been a conscious and defiant ascent toward dignity, leaving behind all obstructions caused by doubt and irony.

Lively, three-dimensional descriptions, calling for no intellectual commitment, give delight to the bourgeois masses, but passionate, absolutistic youth is only captivated by works of a problematic nature; and Aschenbach had been as problematic and absolutistic as any youngster. He had been an addict of the intellect, had overexploited knowledge, had ground up seed-corn for bread, had divulged secrets, had cast suspicion on talent and had betrayed art — yes, at the same time that his word-pictures were entertaining, uplifting and enlivening his more naive readers, this youthful artist had kept the twenty-year-olds agog with his cynical remarks on the questionable nature of art and even the role of the artist.

But it seems there is nothing to which a noble and skillful mind becomes indifferent and numb more quickly and more thoroughly than the acrid and bitter appeal of knowledge; and assuredly the most gloomily conscientious thoroughness of a young man is shallowness itself when compared to the deep determination of a man who has attained the status of a master, when he wishes to disavow learning and scholarship, to reject it, to trample it with his head held high, if it tends in the slightest to paralyze, discourage or debase willpower, action, the emotions and even the passions. How else could the famous story "A Miserable Man" be interpreted than as an outburst of disgust with the indecent psychological leanings of the era as embodied in the figure of that weak and foolish semi-scoundrel who fraudulently acquires a destiny by driving his wife into the arms of a beardless youth out of helplessness, out of depravity, out of an ethical caprice, and who believes that it is his profundity that permits him to commit despicable actions? The powerful phrasing in which vileness was here vilified announced a turning away from all moral skepticism, from all sympathy with the abyss, a renunciation of the laxity of the sympathy-motto "To understand everything is to forgive everything." What was here prepared, in fact already accomplished, was that "miracle of reborn naïveté" that the author mentioned expressly somewhat later in one of his dialogues, not without a mysterious emphasis. Strange connections! Was it an intellectual consequence of this "rebirth," of this new dignity and severity, when at about the same time one could observe an almost immoderate strengthening of his feeling for beauty, that noble purity, simplicity and evenness of form that henceforth lent his productions such a striking, indeed conscious, stamp of mastery and classicism? But a moral determination which transcends learning, which transcends the knowledge that dissolves and obstructs — does that not signify in its turn a naive simplification, a moral oversimplification of the world and the psyche, and thus also a strengthening of the tendency toward evil, the forbidden and the morally impossible? And does not form possess a double face? Is it not moral and amoral at the same time — moral inasmuch as it is the result and expression of discipline, but amoral and even immoral to the extent that by nature it contains within itself an indifference to morality and indeed essentially strives to make morality bow before its proud and sovereign scepter?

However that may be: a development is a destiny; and how could a development attended with the approval and the massive confidence of a broad public fail to run a different course from one that is accomplished without the glory and obligations of fame? Only eternal bohemians find it boring, and are inclined to mock, when a great talent outgrows the chrysalis of libertinism, becomes accustomed to perceive the dignity of the intellect articulately, and assumes the courtliness of solitude — a solitude that, once full of ill-advised, strongly individual sufferings and struggles, has attained power and honors among men. Besides, how much sport, defiance and pleasure there is in the self-making of a talent! With time, an element of official pedagogy entered into Gustav Aschenbach's productions; in later years his style dispensed with forthright audacities, with subtle new nuances; he transformed himself into the exemplary established author, the polished traditionalist, conservative, formal, even formulaic; and, as the story about Louis XIV goes, the aging man banished all vulgar words from his vocabulary. It was then that the Board of Education included selected pages from his works in compulsory primary-school readers. It was in conformity with his own views, and he did not decline, when a German ruler, immediately after ascending the throne, bestowed a personal title of nobility on the author of *Frederick the Great* on the occasion of his fiftieth birthday.

After some years of unrest, some trial sojourns here and there, he presently selected Munich as his permanent place of residence and lived there as an honored bourgeois, an honor granted to intellect in special individual cases. The marriage he had contracted while still young with a girl from a family of scholars was cut short by death after a brief term of happiness. A daughter, herself already married, had remained to him. A son, he had never possessed.

Gustav von Aschenbach was somewhat shorter than average height, dark-haired, clean-shaven. His head seemed a little too large for his almost dainty body. His hair, brushed back, thin at the crown, very full and quite gray at the temples, framed a brow that was tall and so fissured it appeared to be scarred. The gold bridge of his rimless glasses cut into the root of his thick, nobly curved nose. His mouth was large, often limp, often suddenly narrow and tensed; his cheeks were thin and furrowed, his well-developed chin had a gentle cleft. Significant destinies seemed to have left their mark on his head, which usually leaned sideways as if in pain; and yet it was art that had here undertaken that task of forming the features which is usually the work of a difficult, agitated life. Beneath this brow had been born the brilliant dialogue of the conversation about war between Voltaire and the King; these eyes, gazing wearily and profoundly through the glasses, had seen the bloody inferno of the military hospitals of the Seven Years' War. Yes, even on a personal basis art is an enhancement of life. It makes you more deeply happy, it wears you out faster. It engraves on the face of its servant the traces of imaginary, intellectual adventures, and with time, even when his external existence is one of cloisterlike calm, it makes him spoiled and fastidious, producing a weariness and nervous curiosity that could hardly be generated by a lifetime full of extravagant passions and pleasures.

Third Chapter

SEVERAL MATTERS of a worldly and literary nature still detained him, though so eager to travel, for some two weeks after that walk in Munich. Finally he gave orders to prepare his country house for occupancy within four weeks, and on a day between the middle and end of May took the night train to Trieste, where he remained only twenty-four hours and boarded a ship for Pola on the following morning.

What he sought was a place that would be exotic, outside his everyday frame of reference, and yet easily reached; and so he went to an island in the Adriatic, situated not far from the coast of Istria, which had been famous for the last few years. It had a colorfully ragged local population, speaking a language totally unknown to him, and beautifully eroded cliff scenery on the side open to the sea. But rain and a leaden atmosphere, the provincial and self-contained Austrian guests in the hotel, and the lack of the restful intimate rapport with the sea that only a gentle, sandy beach affords, vexed him, and kept him from feeling he had found the spot he had really intended; an inner compulsion to move on — it was still not clear to him where to — troubled him; he studied ship connections, he gazed around questingly, and all at once, surprising and at the same time self-evident, he saw his goal before him. If you wanted to reach someplace overnight that was incomparable, different as a fairy tale, where would you go? But that was obvious! What was he doing here? He had come to the wrong place. *That* is where he had wanted to go. He lost no time in terminating his abortive visit. A week and a half after his arrival on the island, in the early morning haze, a swift motor launch carried him and his luggage back across the waters to the naval base, where he went on land only long enough to ascend a plank gangway onto the damp deck of a ship that lay under steam and was heading for Venice.

It was an old vessel of Italian registry, antiquated, sooty and gloomy. In a cavelike, artificially illuminated inner cabin, into which, immediately upon boarding, Aschenbach was ushered by a courteously grinning hunchbacked and dirty sailor, there sat behind a table, with hat pushed down crookedly over his forehead and a cigarette butt in the corner of his mouth, a goateed man with the face of an old-time circus manager, who, with a professional manner that was grotesquely easygoing, took down the particulars of the travelers and issued them their tickets. "To Venice!" he repeated Aschenbach's request, stretching out his arm and thrusting his pen into the viscous bottom of a tilted inkwell. "First class to Venice! At your service, Sir." And he wrote in a large scrawl, sprinkled blue sand onto the paper out of a box, let it run off into a clay bowl, folded the paper with yellow, bony fingers and began writing again. "A well-chosen destination!" he chattered meanwhile. "Ah, Venice! A splendid city! A city of irresistible attraction for an educated man, not only for its history but also for its present-day charms!" The smooth rapidity of his movements and the empty talk with which he accompanied them had something stupefying and distracting in them, as if he were afraid the traveler might still falter in his resolve to visit Venice. He took the fare hurriedly, and with the dexterity of a croupier dropped the change onto the stained cloth covering of the table. "Enjoy yourself, Sir!" he said with a bow like an actor's. "I am honored to be of assistance to you . . . Gentlemen!" he immediately called with his arm raised, carrying on as if his business were as brisk as could be, even though there was no one else there in need of his services. Aschenbach went back on deck.

With one arm leaning on the railing, he observed the idlers loitering on the quay to watch the departure of the ship, and he studied the passengers on board. Those sailing second class, men and women, were squatting on the foredeck, using boxes and bundles as seats. A group of young people were the passengers on the main deck, apparently business clerks in Pola who, in a spirited mood, had joined together for an excursion to Italy. They made a great ado about themselves and their undertaking; they were chattering, laughing, complacently enjoying their own gesticulations; and, leaning over the railing, they were calling out glib jeers to their comrades who, briefcases under their arms, were walking along the harbor street on business and who menaced the holidaymakers with their thin walking sticks. One of these passengers, in a light yellow summer suit of an extravagantly stylish cut, red tie and jauntily uptilted Panama hat, outdid all the rest in jollity with his squawky voice. But scarcely had Aschenbach taken a closer look at him, when with a sort of terror he realized that the youthful impression was spurious. This was an old man, there could be no doubt. Wrinkles surrounded his eyes and mouth. The faint crimson of his cheeks was rouge; the brown hair beneath the straw hat with its colorful band was a wig; his neck was scraggy and sinewy; his little stuck-on mustache and the tiny beard on his chin were dyed; the complete set of yellow teeth, which he displayed as he laughed, was a cheap denture; and his hands, with signet rings on both index fingers, were those of an old, old man. With a feeling of horror Aschenbach watched him and his intercourse with his friends. Didn't they know, didn't they notice, that he was old, that it was wrong for him to be wearing their dandified, colorful clothing, wrong to be playing the part of one of them? As it seems, they put up with him in their midst as a matter of course and of habit, treated him as one of themselves, returned his teasing pokes in the ribs without repugnance. How was that? Aschenbach covered his forehead with his hand and closed his eyes, which were hot, since he had slept too little. He felt as if things were not going normally, as if a dreamlike alienation, a deformation of the world into oddness, was beginning to gain ground, and that perhaps he could interrupt this by shutting off his vision for a while and then looking around again. At that moment, however, he felt a sensation of floating and, looking up with irrational terror, he noticed that the heavy, gloomy body of the ship was slowly freeing itself from the walled-in shoreline. Inch by inch, with the forward and backward motion of the engine, the strip of dirty, glittering water between the quay and the side of the ship was broadening, and after clumsy maneuvers the steamer turned its bowsprit toward the open sea. Aschenbach walked over to the starboard side, where the hunchback had set up a deck chair for him and a steward in a stained dress coat asked if there was anything he wished.

The sky was gray, the wind damp. The harbor and the islands had been left behind, and all sight of land was soon lost from view in the haze. Flakes of coal dust, swollen with moisture, fell onto the swabbed deck, which would not dry. After only an hour a sailcloth awning was spread since it was beginning to rain.

Wrapped up in his coat, a book on his lap, the traveler rested, and the hours went by without his noticing. It had stopped raining; the awning was removed. The horizon was fully visible. Under the murky dome of the sky the enormous disk of the barren sea extended all around. But in empty, undifferentiated space our senses lack the means to measure time as well, and we daydream in a measureless realm. Odd, shadelike figures, the old fop, the goateed man from inside the ship, passed with undefined gestures and confused dream words through the mind of the resting man, and he fell asleep.

At noon he was asked to go down for a meal to the corridorlike dining room, onto which the doors of the cabins opened; he dined at the head of the long table, at the foot of which the business clerks, including the old man, had been carousing with the jolly captain since ten o'clock. The meal was wretched, and he finished it quickly. He had an urge to go outdoors, to look at the sky: to see if it might not be trying to clear over Venice.

He had never doubted that this would be the case, for the city had always received him in bright sunshine. But sky and sea remained dull and leaden, from time to time a misty rain fell, and he had to resign himself to arriving at a different Venice by the sea route from any he had yet encountered when approaching by land. He stood by the foremast, gazing into the distance, awaiting a view of land. He thought about the melancholy but enthusiastic poet who had in the past seen the domes and bell towers of his dream rising from these waters; he repeated silently a portion of the words that, inspired by awe, happiness and sorrow, had been shaped into measured song; and, effortlessly stirred by a feeling that had already attained form, he examined his earnest, weary heart to see whether a new rapture and entanglement, a belated adventure of the emotions, might perhaps still be in store for the traveling idler.

Then the flat coastline emerged on his right, fishing boats animated the sea, the island of sea-baths appeared; the steamer left it behind on the left, glided at reduced speed through the narrow strait that is named after it, and came to a full stop on the lagoon, in view of lodgings picturesque in their wretchedness; the medical-service boat had to be awaited.

An hour passed before it appeared. He had arrived and had not arrived; no one was in a hurry, yet everyone was nervous with impatience. The young people from Pola, probably also attracted patriotically by the military bugle calls that resounded over the water from the vicinity of the Public Gardens, had come on deck and, animated by Asti, were drinking toasts to the bersaglieri who were drilling there. But it was repulsive to see to what a state the spruced-up old man had been reduced by his spurious association with youth. His old brain had been unable to hold the wine the way the sturdy youngsters did; he was pitifully drunk. With dulled eyes, a cigarette between his trembling fingers, he tottered on one spot, keeping his balance only with difficulty, jerked forward and backward by his drunkenness. Since he would have fallen at the first step, he did not dare to move away from the place where he stood, but exhibited pathetic high spirits, buttonholed everyone who approached him, babbled, winked, giggled, lifted his ringed, wrinkled index finger in stupid raillery and licked the corners of his mouth with the tip of his tongue in a hideously suggestive manner. Aschenbach gave him black looks, and once again a feeling of giddiness came over him, as if the world were showing a slight but uncontrollable inclination to deform itself into the odd and the grotesque: a feeling, however, that the circumstances kept him from indulging in, since just then the pounding activity of the engine resumed and the ship once more pursued its progress — interrupted so close to its destination — through the Canale di San Marco.

And so he saw it again, that most amazing landing place, that dazzling composition of fantastic architecture which the Republic presented to the reverent gaze of approaching seafarers: the weightless splendor of the Palace, the Bridge of Sighs, the columns with lion and saint on the bank, the ostentatiously projecting side of the fairy-tale temple, the view through to the gateway and the giant clock; and, as he gazed, he reflected that to arrive by land, at the Venice railroad station, was like entering a palace through a back door, and that the only proper way to approach that most improbable of cities was that by which he had now come, by ship, across the open sea.

The engine stopped, gondolas crowded up, the gangway was lowered, customs officials climbed on board and perfunctorily attended to their duties; the debarkation could begin. Aschenbach let it be known that he wished a gondola that would take him and his luggage to the landing place of those small steamers that shuttle between the city and the Lido; for he intended to take up residence by the sea. His plan is found good, his request is loudly transmitted to water level, where the gondoliers are quarreling among themselves in the local dialect. He is still hindered in his descent, hindered by his trunk, which is just now being tugged and dragged down the ladderlike gangway with great effort. Thus for some minutes he finds it impossible to escape the importunities of the horrible old man, whose intoxication spurs him on unconsciously to address a formal leavetaking to the stranger. "We wish you a very happy stay," he bleats while bowing. "We hope you think of us kindly! Au revoir, excusez and bonjour, your Excellence!" His mouth waters, he shuts his eyes, he licks the corners of his mouth, and the dyed tuft of beard beneath his senile lip bristles up. "Our compliments," he babbles, two fingertips alongside his mouth, "our compliments to your darling, to your dearly beloved, the most beautiful darling . . ." And suddenly his upper denture falls out of his jaw onto his lower lip. Aschenbach was able to get away. "To the darling, the sweet darling," he heard behind him, in cooing, hollow, slurred tones, while, holding onto the rope handrail, he descended the gangway.

Who could avoid experiencing a fleeting shudder, a secret timidity and anxiety upon boarding a Venetian gondola for the first time or after a long absence? The strange conveyance, handed down without any change from ages of yore, and so peculiarly black — the only other thing that black is a coffin — recalls hushed criminal adventures in the night, accompanied only by the quiet splashing of water; even more, it recalls death itself, the bier and the dismal funeral and the final taciturn passage. And have you observed that the seat in such a boat, that armchair painted black like a coffin and upholstered in a dull black, is the softest, most luxurious and enervating seat in the world? Aschenbach noticed this when he sat down at the gondolier's feet opposite his luggage, which was arranged neatly at the prow. The oarsmen were still quarreling, in rough, incomprehensible tones, with threatening gestures. But the particular calm of the City on the Waters seemed to absorb their voices softly, to disembody them and scatter them over the waves. It was hot here in the harbor. Lulled by the tepid breath of the scirocco, resting on pillows and cradled by the yielding element, the traveler closed his eyes in enjoyment of an indolence that was as unaccustomed as it was sweet. "The ride will be a short one," he thought; "I wish it would last forever!" A gentle rocking indicated that he was drifting away from the crowd and the babel of voices.

How calm, and calmer still, his surroundings became! Nothing could be heard but the splashing of the oar, the muffled lapping of the waves against the prow of the boat — which projected above the water steep, black and armed at the tip like a halberd — and, as a third added component, the sound of speech, of muttering — the whispering of the gondolier, who was talking to himself between his teeth, in short spurts, in tones that were forced from him by the effort of his arms. Aschenbach looked up, and with a touch of consternation noticed that the lagoon was widening around him and that he was heading for the open sea.

Therefore it occurred to him that he should not relax too much but should give some attention to the execution of his orders.

"I said, to the steamer landing," he said with a half-turn backward. The muttering ceased. He received no answer.

"I said, to the steamer landing!" he repeated, turning all the way around and looking up into the face of the gondolier, who, standing behind him on a raised board, towered against the livid sky. He was a man of disagreeable, even brutal features, dressed in blue like a sailor, around his waist a yellow sash and on his head, at a reckless angle, a shapeless straw hat with its weave beginning to come undone. His facial type, the curly blond mustache beneath his short, turned-up nose, seemed to rule out Italian ancestry. Although rather slight in build, so that he might have been thought not especially suited to his trade, he plied the oar with great energy, putting his whole body behind each stroke. A few times the exertion made him draw back his lips, baring his white teeth. Wrinkling his reddish eyebrows, he looked past Aschenbach into the distance while replying in a determined, almost rude tone:

"You are riding to the Lido."

Aschenbach countered:

"Of course. But I only wanted the gondola to take me as far as San Marco. I wish to use the vaporetto."

"You cannot use the vaporetto, Sir."

"And why not?"

"Because the vaporetto doesn't transport luggage."

That was true; Aschenbach remembered. He kept silent. But the man's surly, arrogant behavior, so different from the way strangers are normally treated by the locals, seemed intolerable. He said:

"That's my business. Maybe I want to store my luggage. Please turn back."

Silence ensued. The oar splashed, the water lapped dully against the bow. And the talking and muttering resumed: the gondolier was talking to himself between his teeth.

What was to be done? Alone on the waters with the strangely uncompliant, weirdly stubborn man, the traveler saw no way to enforce his orders. Anyway, how comfortably he could rest if he didn't get excited! Had he not wished for the ride to last a long time — forever? It was wisest to let things take their course and, most of all, it was extremely pleasant. A spellbinding indolence seemed to emanate from his seat, from the low armchair upholstered in black, so gently rocked by the oar strokes of the self-willed gondolier behind him. The idea that he had fallen into the hands of a criminal crossed Aschenbach's mind in a dreamy way, but was powerless to arouse his thoughts to active resistance. More distressing was the possibility that all of this was merely a ruse to mulct him. A kind of sense of duty or pride, a sort of recollection that one ought to prevent such a thing, gave him the strength to bestir himself once more. He asked:

"What do you charge for the ride?"

And, looking past him, the gondolier answered:

"You will pay."

It was clear what the answer to that should be. Aschenbach said mechanically:

"I won't pay a thing, nothing at all, if you take me where I don't want to go."

"You want to go to the Lido."

"But not with you."

"I'm giving you a good ride."

"That's true," thought Aschenbach, and relaxed again. "That's true, you're giving me a good ride. Even if you have an eye on my cash and send me down to the house of Aides with a blow of the oar from behind, you will have given me a good ride."

But nothing of the sort happened. In fact, company arrived, a boatload of musical highwaymen, men and women, who sang to the accompaniment of guitar and mandolin, sailing importunately right alongside the gondola and breaking the stillness over the waters with their mercenary poetry for foreigners. Aschenbach threw money into the hat they held out. Then they fell silent and sailed away. And the whispering of the gondolier became audible again, as he spoke to himself in fits and starts.

And so they arrived, rocked by the wake of a steamer headed for the city. Two policemen, their hands clasped behind them, their faces turned toward the lagoon, were walking to and fro on shore. Aschenbach stepped out of the gondola at the landing stage, assisted by one of the old men with a grappling hook who are stationed at every landing place in Venice; and, since he had no small change, he crossed over the way to the hotel that adjoined the steamer landing to get some there and pay the oarsman the amount he thought appropriate. He is attended to in the lounge, he comes back, he finds his luggage on a wagon by the dock, and gondola and gondolier have disappeared.

"He took himself off," said the old man with the grappling hook. "A bad man, a man without a license, Sir. He is the only gondolier who has no license. The others phoned here. He saw that he was expected. So he took himself off."

Aschenbach shrugged his shoulders.

"You had a free ride, Sir," said the old man and held out his hat. Aschenbach threw in some coins. He gave directions to take his luggage to the Hôtel des Bains and followed the wagon through the broad street, the street of white blossoms, which, lined with taverns, bazaars and boardinghouses on both sides, runs straight across the island to the beach.

He entered the spacious hotel from the back, through the garden terrace, and made his way across the extensive lounge and the lobby into the office. Since he was expected, he was received with attentive care. A manager, a short, quiet man of flattering courtesy with a black mustache and a French-style frock coat, accompanied him in the elevator to the second floor and showed him his room, a pleasant place with cherry-wood furniture. It had been decorated with flowers of a heady fragrance and its tall windows looked out upon the open sea. He walked over to one of them after the hotel employee had withdrawn and, while his luggage was being brought in behind him and stowed away in the room, he looked out at the beach, nearly devoid of people since it was afternoon, and at the sunless sea, which was at high tide and was sending long, low waves against the shore at calm, even intervals.

The observations and encounters of a solitary, taciturn man are vaguer and at the same time more intense than those of a sociable man; his thoughts are deeper, odder and never without a touch of sadness. Images and perceptions that could be dismissed with a glance, a laugh, an exchange of opinions, occupy him unduly, become more intense in the silence, become significant, become an experience, an adventure, an emotion. Solitude produces originality, bold and astonishing beauty, poetry. But solitude also produces perverseness, the disproportionate, the absurd and the forbidden. — Thus the phenomena of his journey here, the awful old dandy with his drivel about the darling, the outcast gondolier who had been bilked of his money, were still unsettling the traveler's mind. Although easily explained rationally and providing no really solid matter for contemplation, nevertheless these phenomena were thoroughly peculiar in nature, it seemed to him, and were unsettling precisely because of this contradiction. Meanwhile he looked at the sea in greeting and was glad to know that Venice was so close and easily reached. Finally he turned away, washed his face, gave the chambermaid some instructions with a view to making his comfort complete, and let the green-garbed Swiss who operated the elevator take him down to the ground floor.

He took his tea on the terrace facing the sea, then descended to the seaside promenade and walked down it a good distance in the direction of the Hotel Excelsior. When he returned, he thought it was already time to change for dinner. He did this slowly and precisely, as was his habit, since he was accustomed to work while dressing, but nevertheless he found that he was a little too early when he reached the lounge, where he found a good number of the hotel guests assembled, strangers to one another and playing a role of mutual indifference, but all of them eagerly awaiting the meal. He picked up a newspaper from the table, settled into a leather armchair and observed the crowd, which differed from that in his previous hotel in a way that pleased him.

A broad horizon opened up, tolerant and widely comprehensive. The sounds of the major languages mingled in hushed tones. The universally accepted evening dress, a uniform of civilization, created an outward unity among the different varieties of humanity, conferring respectability upon them. Here were to be seen the dry, long face of the American, the large Russian family, English ladies, German children with French *bonnes*. The Slavic element seemed to prevail. In his immediate vicinity Polish was being spoken.

A group of adolescents and young adults under the care of a governess or paid companion were gathered around a small wicker table: three girls who seemed to range in age from fifteen to seventeen and a long-haired boy of perhaps fourteen. With astonishment Aschenbach observed that the boy was perfectly beautiful. His face, pale and charmingly secretive, with the honey-colored hair curling around it, with its straight-sloping nose, its lovely mouth and its expression of sweet and divine earnestness, recalled Greek statues of the noblest period, and, along with its extremely pure perfection of form, it was of such unique personal charm that the onlooker thought he had never come across anything so felicitous either in nature or in art. Also in evidence was an obviously fundamental contrast between the pedagogical viewpoints that seemed to govern the clothing and the general deportment of the siblings. The attire of the three girls, the oldest of whom could be considered grown-up, was austere and chaste to the point of spoiling their looks. A uniform conventlike garb, slate-colored, knee-length, sober and intentionally unbecoming in style, with white turndown collars as the only bright accent, suppressed and negated any pleasure that their figures might afford. Their hair, smooth and plastered down close to their head, made their faces seem as empty and inexpressive as a nun's. No doubt, a mother was behind this, to whom it never even occurred to apply to the boy the pedagogical severity she apparently felt was imperative for the girls. Softness and tenderness obviously presided over his existence. They had refrained from subjecting his beautiful hair to the shears; like that of the Boy with a Thorn, it curled over his forehead and ears and was even longer at the back of his neck. The laces, bows and embroidery on his English sailor suit, with its puffy sleeves that narrowed below and closed tightly around the delicate wrists of his still childlike but slim hands, gave his delicate figure a rich and pampered appearance. He sat in semiprofile opposite his observer, one foot, shod in black patent leather, placed in front of the other, an elbow leaning on the armrest of his wicker chair, his cheek pressed against his closed hand, in an attitude of decorous indolence and completely free of the rigidity, almost like that of an underling, to which his sisters appeared to be accustomed. Was he ill?—because the skin of his face stood out white as ivory against the darker gold of the encircling curls. Or was he merely a mollycoddled favorite, enjoying capriciously prejudiced love? Aschenbach was inclined to believe the latter. Inborn in nearly every artist's nature is a voluptuous, treacherous tendency to accept injustice if it creates beauty and to grant sympathy and homage to aristocratic preferences.

A waiter made the rounds announcing in English that dinner was served. Little by little the guests disappeared through the glass door into the dining room. Latecomers, arriving from the lobby or the elevators, walked by. The waiters had begun serving inside but the young Poles still lingered around their little wicker table, and Aschenbach, comfortably ensconced in a deep armchair and, moreover, with beauty before his eyes, waited along with them.

The governess, a short, stout, red-faced woman, not quite a lady, finally gave the signal to rise. With raised eyebrows she shoved her chair back and bowed as a tall woman, dressed in light gray and very richly adorned with pearls, entered the lounge. This woman's attitude was cool and dignified; the style in which she wore her lightly powdered hair and the cut of her dress exhibited that simplicity which always governs taste when piety is considered a component of aristocratic elegance. She might have been the wife of a German government official of high rank. The only thing in her appearance that bespoke imagination and luxury was her jewelry, which was indeed almost priceless and consisted of earrings and a very long three-strand necklace of quietly gleaming pearls as big as cherries.

The siblings had stood up quickly. They bent down to kiss the hand of their mother, who, with a reserved smile on her well-cared-for but somewhat weary and sharp-nosed face, gazed over their heads and addressed a few words in French to their governess. Then she walked to the glass door. The siblings followed her, the girls in the order of their ages, after them the governess, last the boy. For some reason he turned around before crossing the threshold and, since no one else was left in the lounge, his peculiarly hazy-gray eyes met those of Aschenbach, who, his newspaper on his knees, lost in contemplation, was watching the group.

What he had seen had certainly not been remarkable in any way. They had not gone to eat before their mother, they had waited for her, had greeted her respectfully and had observed the customary forms when entering the dining room. But all of that had been performed so distinctively, with such a cachet of good breeding, dutifulness and self-esteem, that Aschenbach felt peculiarly touched. He hesitated a few moments more, then he, too, walked over into the dining room and was shown to his own small table, which he noticed, with a brief feeling of regret, was located very far from that of the Polish family.

Weary and yet mentally agitated, he spent the protracted mealtime considering abstract, in fact transcendental matters; he reflected on the mysterious combination of regularity and individuality that is requisite for the creation of human beauty; this led him to general problems of form and art; and finally he concluded that these thoughts and discoveries of his resembled those apparently felicitous inspirations in dreams which, when you are fully awake again, prove to be totally insipid and worthless. After dinner he lingered in the hotel park, enjoying its evening fragrance, smoking, sitting and strolling about; then went to bed early and spent the night in a slumber that remained deep but was variously enlivened by dream images.

The weather did not improve the next day. The wind blew from the land. Beneath a livid, overcast sky the sea lay in a dull calm, as if shrunken, with an uninterestingly close horizon, and it had receded so far from the beach that several tiers of long sandbars were left exposed. When Aschenbach opened his window, he thought he could smell the putrid odor of the lagoon.

He became depressed. At that moment he was already thinking about leaving. Once, years before, after weeks of clear spring skies, this type of weather had afflicted him here, affecting his health so badly that he had had to abandon Venice like a fugitive. Wasn't the same feverish discomfort, the same pressure on his temples, the same heaviness of his eyelids, already setting in again? To move to yet another locale would be a nuisance; but if the wind didn't shift, he couldn't stay here. As a security measure, he didn't unpack everything. At nine o'clock he breakfasted in the smaller room reserved for that purpose, located between the lounge and the main dining room.

In this room there prevailed that solemn silence which is part of the pride of large hotels. The waiters moved about quietly. A rattling of tea things, a half-whispered word, was all that one heard. In a corner, obliquely opposite the door and two tables away from his, Aschenbach noticed the Polish girls with their governess. Very erect, their ash-blond hair freshly plastered down, their eyes red-rimmed, in stiff dresses of

blue linen with small white turndown collars and cuffs, they sat there
and passed around a glass of preserves. They were nearly finished with
their breakfast. The boy was not present.

Aschenbach smiled. "Now, little happy-go-lucky Phaeacian!" he
thought. "It appears that, unlike the others, you have the privilege of
staying in bed as long as you like." And suddenly cheering up, he silently
recited the verse: "Adornment frequently changed and heated baths and
repose."

He breakfasted unhurriedly and received some forwarded mail from
the porter, who entered the room with his braided cap in his hand;
smoking a cigarette, he opened one or two letters. And so it happened
that he was still present at the entrance of the late riser, whom those at
the other table had been waiting for.

He entered through the glass door and walked diagonally across the
silent room to his sisters' table. His gait, not only in the way he held his
torso but also in the way he bent his knees and planted his feet, in their
white shoes, on the floor, was of extraordinary grace, very light, simultaneously gentle and proud, and was made even more beautiful by the
childlike bashfulness with which, twice along the way, turning his head
to take in the room, he raised his eyes and lowered them again. Smiling,
pronouncing a subdued phrase in his soft, blurry language, he took his
seat, and especially now, as he turned his full profile toward his observer,
Aschenbach was once more amazed, in fact frightened, by the truly
godlike beauty of this human child. Today the boy was wearing a
lightweight washable tunic outfit of blue-and-white striped cotton, with
a red silk bow on the chest, closed at the neck with a simple white stand-
up collar. But on this collar, which did not even match the character of
the outfit particularly elegantly, rested the blossom of his head in incomparable loveliness — the head of Eros, with the yellowish luster of Parian
marble, with sharply defined, grave eyebrows, with temples and ears
darkly and softly covered by the curly hair that intersected them at right
angles.

"Good, good!" thought Aschenbach with that professionally cool
approval in which artists sometimes cloak their rapture and ecstasy
when face to face with a masterpiece. And he also thought: "To tell the
truth, if the ocean and the beach weren't waiting for me, I'd stay here as
long as you stay!" But, as it was, he did go; he passed through the lounge,
courteously greeted by the staff, descended the broad terrace and proceeded straight across the boardwalk to the partitioned private beach for
hotel guests. He was shown to his rented cabana by the barefoot old
man, who, dressed in linen trousers, a sailor's tunic and a straw hat, was
employed there as a bath attendant; he had his table and chair brought

out onto the sandy wooden deck and settled down comfortably in the reclining chair, which he had drawn closer to the sea, moving it onto the waxy-yellow sand.

The view of the beach, this sight of civilized people enjoying themselves lightheartedly and sensuously by the brink of the liquid element, entertained and delighted him as much as it ever had. The gray, level sea was already animated with wading children, swimmers and colorful figures lying on the sandbars with their arms tucked under their heads. Others were rowing in small keelless boats painted red and blue, and laughing as they capsized. In front of the long row of cabanas, on the decks of which people sat as if on small verandas, there was playful activity and indolently protracted repose, visits and conversation, people in elegant morning wear alongside others scantily clad, who were enjoying the liberties of the place in impudent comfort. Out in front, on the damp, firm sand, individuals were strolling in white robes or in loose, bright-colored wrappers. On the right, a complicated sand castle, constructed by children, was decked all around with small flags in the colors of all nations. Vendors of shellfish, pastries and fruit were kneeling with their wares spread in front of them. On the left, in front of one of the row of cabanas that formed a right angle with the others and with the sea, and served as a boundary on this side of the beach, a Russian family was camping out: men with beards and large teeth, flaccid, indolent women, a Baltic spinster who, seated by an easel, was painting the sea while exclaiming in despair, two good-natured homely children, an old servant woman in a kerchief with the delicately submissive manners of a serf. They lived there, grateful for their pleasure, tirelessly calling out the names of their disobedient romping children, indulging in long humorous conversations, by means of the few Italian words they knew, with the witty old man from whom they bought candy, kissing one another on the cheeks and paying no heed to any observer of their very human community.

"Well, I'll stay," thought Aschenbach. "Where would it be better?" And with his hands folded on his lap, he let his eyes stray at random over the distant reaches of the sea; he let his gaze drift away, grow blurred, glaze over in the monotonous haze of that wilderness of space. He loved the sea for deep-seated reasons: because of the hard-working artist's yearning for repose, his desire to take shelter in the bosom of undifferentiated immensity from the demanding complexity of the world's phenomena; because of his own proclivity — forbidden, directly counter to his life's work, and seductive for that very reason — for the unorganized, immoderate, eternal: for nothingness. To take rest in perfection is the desire of those who strive for excellence; and is not nothingness one form of perfection? But as he was now daydreaming so deeply, the horizontal line of the shore was suddenly intersected by a human figure, and, when he summoned his gaze back from unbounded space and focused his eyes again, it was the beautiful boy who, coming from the left, was walking by in front of him on the sand. Barefoot, ready for wading, his slender legs bare to above the knees, he was walking slowly but with a step as light and proud as if he were thoroughly accustomed to go about without footgear, and he looked around toward the cabanas in the right-angled row. But scarcely had he noticed the Russian family, which was living its own life there in grateful harmony, when a storm-cloud of angry contempt covered his face. His forehead darkened, his mouth was raised up, an embittered twist of his lips to one side creased his cheek, and his eyebrows were so heavily wrinkled that his eyes seemed sunken beneath their pressure and, looking out from under, maliciously and blackly, spoke the language of hatred. He looked at the ground, looked behind him once more menacingly, then jerked his shoulder in a violent expression of disparagement and aversion and left his enemies behind him.

A kind of delicacy or alarm, something like deference and shame, caused Aschenbach to turn aside as if he had seen nothing; for, as a serious chance observer of this passion, he was loath to make use of what he had seen, not even in his own thoughts. But he was exhilarated and shaken at the same time — in a word, he was in bliss. Through this childish fanaticism directed against that totally good-natured segment of life, what had been as inexpressive as a god was placed within a human relationship; a precious artefact of nature, which had served only as a feast for the eyes, now appeared worthy of a deeper rapport; and the figure of the adolescent, already significant for its beauty, was now set off against a background that made it possible to take him seriously beyond his years.

His glance still averted, Aschenbach listened to the boy's voice, to his clear, somewhat weak voice, with which from a distance he was already trying to greet his playmates, who were busy around the sand castle, and to announce his presence to them. They answered him, calling out his name or a nickname several times, and Aschenbach listened to them with a certain curiosity but could not make out anything more precise than two musical syllables like "Adgio" or, even more frequently, "Adgiu," with a u-sound at the end that was prolonged as they called to him. He enjoyed the sound of the name, found that its euphony suited the boy himself, repeated it silently, and contentedly turned to his letters and papers.

With his little portable writing case on his knees, he began to dispose

No. Judson-San Pierre H.S
900 Campbell Drive
No. Judson, IN 46366
82998

of this and that piece of correspondence, using his fountain pen. But after only a quarter of an hour he thought it was a pity to dismiss the situation, the most enjoyable he knew of, from his mind that way and to let it slip by while indulging in indifferent pursuits. He threw the writing materials aside, he resumed his inspection of the sea; and before long, distracted by the voices of the youngsters at the sand castle, he turned his head, which was resting comfortably against the back of the chair, to the right in order to look once more at the doings of the exquisite Adgio.

He located him at first glance; the red bow on his chest could not be missed. Occupied along with others in laying an old plank as a bridge across the damp moat of the sand castle, he was giving directions for carrying out this task with shouts and waves of his head. There were about ten comrades with him, boys and girls, some his age and a few younger, chattering confusedly in several languages, Polish, French and some Balkan tongues. But it was his name that was most often heard. Obviously he was sought after, courted, admired. One boy especially, also a Pole, a stocky lad who was called something like "Jaschu," with black, pomaded hair and a belted suit of linen, seemed to be his chief vassal and closest friend. After this working session on the sand castle was over, they walked down the beach with their arms around each other, and the lad called "Jaschu" kissed the beautiful boy.

Aschenbach was tempted to shake a warning finger at him. " 'I advise you, however, Critobulus,' " he thought, smiling, " 'go traveling for a year! For you will need at least that much time to recover.' " And then he breakfasted on large, perfectly ripe strawberries that he bought from a vendor. It had become very hot, even though the sun was unable to penetrate the layer of haze in the sky. Indolence fettered the spirit while the senses enjoyed the immense, soothing pleasure of the calm sea. To guess, to inquire what name it was that sounded more or less like "Adgio" seemed to the earnest man a suitable and completely engrossing task and occupation. And with the help of some recollections of Polish he ascertained that the name must be "Tadzio," the short form of "Tadeusz," which became "Tadziu" in direct address.

Tadzio was swimming. Aschenbach, who had lost sight of him, now made out his head and his arm, which he thrust forward in a paddling motion, far out at sea; for the sea was probably shallow for a good distance. But his people already seemed to be worrying about him, women's voices were already calling to him from the cabanas, once more exclaiming that name which dominated the beach almost like a watchword and which, with its soft consonants and its prolonged *u*-sound at the end, had in it something sweet and savage at the same time: "Tadziu! Tadziu!" He came back; he ran through the waves, beating the resistant water into foam with his legs, his head thrown back; and to see how that living figure, lovely, acrid as new wine in its foretaste of masculinity, with dripping curls and beautiful as a delicate god, coming from the depths of sky and sea, arose and escaped from the watery element — the sight inspired mythic ideas, it was like a poetic message telling of primordial times, the origin of form and the birth of the gods. With eyes closed, Aschenbach listened to this chant intoning within him, and again he felt that this place was good and he would stay.

Later Tadzio, resting from his swim, lay on the sand wrapped in a white robe drawn under his right shoulder, his head nestled on his bare arm; and even when Aschenbach was not looking at him but was reading a few pages of his book, he almost never forgot that the boy was lying there and that, with no more trouble than a slight turn of his head to the right, he could catch sight of that admirable object. He almost felt as if he were sitting there to guard him as he rested — occupied with his own business and yet constantly vigilant on behalf of that noble human figure there on the right, not far from him. And his heart was filled and stirred by a paternal kindness, by the emotional attraction that a man who through self-sacrifice creates the beautiful in his mind feels toward one who possesses beauty itself.

After noon he left the beach, returned to the hotel and took the elevator up to his room. There he lingered for some time in front of the mirror, looking at his gray hair and his weary, pinched face. At that moment he thought about his fame, he recalled that many people recognized him on the street and looked at him with respect because of his apt and graceful writings; he summoned to mind all the outward signs of professional success that he could think of, and even remembered his ennoblement. Then he went down to the dining room for lunch and ate at his table. When the meal was over and he stepped into the elevator, youngsters who were also coming from lunch crowded after him into the little floating chamber, and Tadzio got on, too. He stood very close to Aschenbach, for the first time so close that the latter perceived and observed him not as a work of art that one views at a given distance, but with precision, studying the details that made him human. Someone addressed the boy and, while still replying with an indescribably sweet smile, he got off again, at the first floor, walking backwards with his eyes cast down. Beauty makes one bashful, thought Aschenbach, and reflected very seriously why this should be so. He had noticed, however, that Tadzio's teeth were not that fine: a little jagged and pale, lacking the glow of health, strangely brittle and transparent, like those of some anemic people. "He is very delicate, he is sickly," thought Aschenbach. "He probably won't live to a ripe old age." And he avoided accounting to himself for the feeling of satisfaction or consolation which accompanied that thought.

He spent two hours in his room and in the afternoon took the vaporetto across the ill-smelling lagoon to Venice. He got off at San Marco, had tea in the square and then, in conformity with his local daily routine, began strolling through the streets. But it was this walk that resulted in a total shift in his mood and his resolutions.

The narrow streets were unpleasantly sultry; the air was so thick that the odors emanating from homes, stores and cookshops — olive oil, clouds of perfume and many others — hung like wisps of smoke without being dispersed. Cigarette smoke remained in place and drifted away only slowly. The jostling in narrow passages annoyed him instead of amusing him as he strolled. The longer he walked, the more tormented he became by the horrible state of health that the sea air can cause in conjunction with the scirocco, a state of excitement and prostration at the same time. He broke out into a distressing sweat. His eyes no longer performed their duty, he felt a tightness in his chest, he was feverish, the blood pounded in his head. He fled from the crowded shopping streets across bridges into the haunts of the poor. There he was importuned by beggars, and the foul effluvia of the canals made breathing a torture. On a quiet square, one of those spots deep within Venice that give the impression of being forgotten under an evil spell, he rested by the rim of a fountain, dried his forehead and realized that he had to go away.

It was now proven for a second time, and this time definitively, that in this kind of weather the city was extremely harmful to him. To stay on out of stubbornness seemed to make no sense; the prospect of a shift in the wind was quite uncertain. He had to make up his mind right away. To go back home now was out of the question. Neither his summer nor his winter quarters were ready for occupancy. But this was not the only place offering the sea and a beach, and elsewhere these were to be found without the unpleasant addition of the lagoon and its fever-bearing vapors. He remembered a small sea-bath not far from Trieste that people had mentioned to him in glowing terms. Why not go there? And without delay, so that this new change of locale was still worth the trouble. Now fully decided, he stood up. At the nearest gondola landing he boarded a boat and made his way to San Marco through the gloomy labyrinth of the canals, under ornamental marble balconies flanked by statues of lions, around greasy corners of walls, past mournful palace facades that reflected large commercial signs in the garbage-strewn rocking water. He had difficulty getting there because the gondolier, who was in collusion with lace factories and glass workshops, tried everywhere to make him get out, look at the merchandise and make purchases; and whenever the bizarre ride through Venice began to exert its magic, the moneygrabbing businesss mentality of the fallen Queen did its part to bring him back to reality in a painful way.

Back at his hotel, even before dinner he explained in the office that unforeseen circumstances compelled him to leave early the next morning. Accepting their regrets, he paid his bill. He dined and spent the warm evening reading newspapers in a rocking chair on the rear terrace. Before going to bed he made his luggage all ready for departure.

His sleep was not of the best because the imminent new journey troubled him. But when he opened his windows in the morning, the sky was still just as overcast, yet the air seemed fresher and—he already began to regret his decision. Had this cancellation not been overhasty and mistaken, the reflex of a bad state of health, which was no proper guide for his actions? If he had delayed it a little while, if he had not been so quick to despair, if he had patiently tried to adjust to the air of Venice, or had waited for an improvement in the weather, then he would now have before him, instead of this wear and tear, another morning on the beach just like yesterday's. Too late. Now he had to keep on wanting what he had wanted yesterday. He got dressed and at eight he rode down to the ground floor for breakfast.

When he entered the auxiliary dining room, it was still free of hotel guests. A few arrived while he sat waiting for his order. The teacup at his lips, he saw the Polish girls come in with their escort: severe, fresh from sleep, with red-rimmed eyes, they walked to their table in the corner by the window. Immediately afterward the porter approached him with cap in hand and told him that all was ready for his departure. The automobile was waiting to take him and other travelers to the Hotel Excelsior, from which point the motor launch would transport them through the company's private canal and continue on to the railroad station. Time was pressing, the man said. — Aschenbach felt that this was far from being the case. There was still more than an hour before his train left. He was annoyed by the habit, common among hotelkeepers, of clearing departing guests out of the building early, and he informed the porter that he wished to eat his breakfast in peace. The man withdrew hesitatingly, only to show up again five minutes later. It was impossible for the car to wait any longer. Then it could leave and take along his trunk, Aschenbach replied, irritated. He himself would take the public steamer at the appropriate time; he begged them to leave the worry over his departure to him. The employee bowed. Aschenbach, glad that he had fended off the annoying reminders, ended his light meal without haste; in fact, he even had the waiter still hand him a newspaper. There was very little time left when he finally got up. It just so happened that at that very moment Tadzio came in through the glass door.

On his way to his family's table he crossed the path of Aschenbach, who was leaving; in front of the gray-haired, lofty-browed man he modestly cast his eyes down, then, in his charming fashion, at once looked up at him again with wide, tender eyes, and walked on by. "Adieu, Tadzio!" thought Aschenbach. "I didn't have long to look at you." And — contrary to his custom — actually shaping his thoughts into uttered words and muttering them to himself, he added: "God bless you!" Then he went through the routine of departure; he handed out tips; he was seen off by the small, quiet manager in the French frock coat, and left the hotel on foot, as he had come; followed by the bellhop who carried his hand luggage, he walked down the broad street, white with blossoms, that ran straight across the island to the steamer landing. He arrived there, took a seat — and what ensued was a lugubrious, painful journey through all the depths of regret.

It was the familiar ride across the lagoon, past San Marco, up the Grand Canal. Aschenbach sat on the round bench at the bow, his arm leaning on the railing, his hand shading his eyes. The Public Gardens were left in the distance, the Piazzetta disclosed itself once more in its princely charm and was left behind, next came the long series of palaces, and as the watery thoroughfare made a bend, the splendid marble curve of the Rialto Bridge came into view spanning the canal. The traveler looked and there was conflict in his heart. The atmosphere of the city, that slightly foul odor of sea and swamp, from which he had been in such a hurry to escape — he now breathed it in in deep, tenderly painful drafts. Was it possible that he hadn't known or considered how dear all this was to him? What in the morning had been a half-regret, a slight doubt about the correctness of his actions, now became a grief, a real ache, a distress of the soul, so bitter that more than once it brought tears to his eyes, a distress that he told himself he couldn't possibly have foreseen. Obviously, what he found so hard to bear, and at moments completely intolerable, was the thought that he would never see Venice again, that this was a permanent farewell. For, since it had proved for the second time that the city made him sick, since for the second time he had been forced to leave it posthaste, he would have to look on it henceforth as a place where it was impossible and forbidden for him to stay, a place he just wasn't up to and which it would be pointless to visit again. Yes, he felt that, if he left now, shame and defiance would surely prevent him from ever seeing the city he loved again, after he had twice broken down physically there; and this contention between his soul's inclinations and his body's capabilities suddenly seemed so weighty and important to the aging man, his physical defeat so shameful, to be combated at all costs, that he could not understand the frivolous submissiveness with which yesterday, without a serious struggle, he had decided to bear and acknowledge that defeat.

Meanwhile the steamer is approaching the railroad station, and his pain and perplexity are escalating to the point of bewilderment. For the tortured man departure seems impossible, but turning back no less so. Thus, totally at war with himself, he enters the station. It is very late, he hasn't a moment to lose if he wants to catch his train. He wants to and he doesn't want to. But time presses, it lashes him onward; he hastens to buy a ticket and in the tumult of the hall he looks around for the employee of the hotel company who has his post here. The man turns up and announces that the large trunk has been sent on ahead. Already sent on? Yes, just as ordered — to Como. To Como? And from the hasty interchange of the conversation, from the angry questions and embarrassed answers, it is revealed that much earlier, back at the luggage desk of the Hotel Excelsior, the trunk, together with other people's luggage, had been shipped in a totally wrong direction.

Aschenbach had difficulty in maintaining the facial expression that was the only understandable one in these circumstances. An adventurous joy, an unbelievable gaiety sent an almost convulsive thrill through his heart. The employee dashed away to see if the trunk could still possibly be stopped; he returned, as was to be expected, with nothing accomplished. Then Aschenbach declared that he did not wish to travel without his luggage, but was determined to turn back and await the arrival of the trunk in the Hôtel des Bains. He asked whether the company's motor launch was outside the railroad station. The man assured him it was right outside the door. With Italian volubility he persuaded the ticket seller to take back the ticket that had been paid for, he swore that a telegram would be sent, that no expense would be spared nor anything left undone to retrieve the trunk quickly; and thus the strange situation presented itself that, twenty minutes after his arrival at the railroad station, the traveler was once more on the Grand Canal on his way back to the Lido.

A peculiar, unbelievable, embarrassing, comic, dreamlike adventure: to be turned around and sent back by fate; to revisit sights, within the same hour, of which one has just taken leave forever in deepest melancholy! Foam in front of its bow, veering between gondolas and steamers with amusing adroitness, the zealous little vessel sped toward its destination, while its sole passenger hid his anxious but merry excitement, like that of a boy who has run away, beneath a mask of vexed resignation. From time to time his breast was still shaken by laughter over this mishap which, he told himself, could not have befallen even a Sunday's child more opportunely. He would have to give explanations, undergo stares from surprised faces — then, he told himself, everything would be all right again; then a misfortune would be prevented, a grievous error set right, and everything he thought he had left behind him would be offered to him again, would be his again as long as he liked . . . Besides, was he deluded by the speed of the journey or, as an added attraction, was the wind really now blowing from the sea?

The waves beat against the concrete-covered walls of the narrow canal that extends through the island to the Hotel Excelsior. A motor bus awaited the returning man there and led him above the rippled sea on a straight road to the Hôtel des Bains. The small, mustached manager in the tailed frock coat came down the outside stairs to greet him.

With quiet flattery he regretted the incident, calling it extremely painful for himself and for the establishment, but with conviction he approved Aschenbach's decision to wait for the trunk here. To be sure, his old room was occupied, but another one just as good was immediately available. "Pas de chance, monsieur," said the Swiss elevator operator with a smile as they glided up. And so the fugitive was given new quarters, in a room that resembled the previous one almost completely in its situation and furnishings.

Tired out, numbed by the hubbub of this strange morning, he distributed the contents of his handbag in the room and then settled down in a reclining chair by the open window. The sea had taken on a pale-green shade, the air seemed clearer and fresher, the beach with its cabanas and boats seemed more colorful, although the sky was still gray. Aschenbach looked out, his hands folded on his lap, contented to be back again, but shaking his head in discontentment at his flightiness, at his lack of knowledge of his own wishes. He sat there like that for about an hour, resting in a reverie untroubled by thoughts. At noon he caught sight of Tadzio, wearing a striped linen suit with a red bow; coming from the sea, he was returning to the hotel through the beach barrier and along the boardwalks. From his lofty vantage point Aschenbach recognized him at once, before he had really taken a hard look, and was about to formulate some such thought as: "Well, Tadzio, here you are again, too!" But at that moment he felt this casual greeting die away and grow silent in the face of the truth that was in his heart; he felt the enthusiasm in his blood, the joy and pain in his soul, and realized that it was for Tadzio's sake that the departure had been so hard on him.

He sat completely still, altogether unseen, in his lofty place and looked inside himself. His features were alert, his eyebrows rose, a smile of attentive, inquisitive intelligence tightened his lips. Then he raised

his head and with his two hands, which were hanging down limply over
the armrests of the chair, he made a slow turning and lifting motion,
bringing the palms upward, as if he were opening his arms and holding
them out. It was a gesture that bespoke an open welcome, a calm
acceptance.

Fourth Chapter

DAY AFTER DAY now the god with the glowing cheeks, nude, steered his
fiery team of four through the regions of the sky, his yellow tresses
floating behind him in the east wind that was also vigorously blowing. A
whitish silky sheen covered the expanse of the indolently rolling *pontos*.
The sand burned. Beneath the silvery, glittering blue of the aether, rust-
colored canvases were spread in front of the cabanas, and in the sharply
outlined patch of shade that they afforded people spent the morning
hours. But the evening was also delicious, when the plants in the park
emitted a balmy fragrance, the heavenly bodies up above went through
the paces of their round dance, and the murmuring of the benighted sea,
quietly rising, cast a spell over the soul. Such an evening carried with it
the happy assurance of a new sunshiny day of casually organized leisure,
a day adorned with countless, frequently occurring opportunities for
delightful chance events.

The guest who had been detained here by such an obliging mishap
was far from considering the reacquisition of his belongings as any
reason for a new departure. For two days he had had to make do without
a few items and had had to show up for meals in the main dining room
wearing a traveling suit. Then, when the misdirected luggage was finally
brought to his room again, he unpacked completely, filling the wardrobe and the drawers with his possessions. Resolved to remain for a
momentarily unspecified time, he was pleased that he could spend the
hours on the beach in a silk suit and once again appear at his table at
dinnertime in proper evening clothes.

The comfortable regularity of this existence had already cast its spell
over him; the soft, bright gentleness of this way of life had quickly
bewitched him. Indeed, what a fine place this was to stay, combining
the attractions of a well-ordered bathing establishment on a southern
beach with the handy, easy accessibility of that strange but wonderful
city! Aschenbach did not like pleasure. Whenever and wherever he had
to leave off work, to take a rest, to have a good time, he soon felt the

restless and reluctant desire — and this had been the case in his younger years especially — to return to his noble labors, the sober, hallowed servitude of his normal routine. Only this one spot enchanted him, relaxed his willpower, made him happy. Sometimes in the mornings, beneath the canvas shade in front of his cabana, daydreaming as he gazed at the blue of the southern sea, or in the warm evenings as well, while he leaned on the cushions of the gondola that brought him from St. Mark's Square, where he had stayed late, homeward to the Lido beneath the wide, starry sky — the colored lights, the melodious strains of the serenade fading into the distance — he would remember his country house in the mountains, the locale of his summertime struggles, where the low clouds passed through the garden, fearful storms blew out the house lights in the evening, and the ravens he used to feed rocked in the tops of the spruces. Then he really felt as if he had been carried off to an Elysian land, to the ends of the earth, where the easiest possible life is the lot of mankind, where there is no snow and no winter, no storm and no driving rain, but always Oceanus makes a gently cooling breeze spring up, and the days flow by in blissful idleness, effortless, free from battle and consecrated solely to the sun and its festivals.

Often, almost constantly, Aschenbach saw the boy Tadzio; because of the confined space and the uniform life-style of one and all at the hotel, the beautiful boy was close to him all day long with only brief intervals. He saw him, met him everywhere: in the public areas of the hotel, on the refreshing boat rides into town and back, amid the pomp of the Square itself and often at odd times as well, on this street or that, as chance would have it. Chiefly, however, and with the most happy regularity, the mornings on the beach afforded him extended opportunities to devote adoration and study to the lovely apparition. Yes, it was this firmly established good fortune, this regular daily renewal of favorable circumstances, that filled him with so much contentment and enjoyment of life, that made his stay here dear to him and that made each sunny day link up with the next in such obliging continuity.

He rose early, as he was otherwise wont to do when the pressure of work assailed him, and was one of the first on the beach, when the sunshine was still mild and the sea lay in a white dazzle, dreaming its morning dreams. After a courteous greeting to the guard at the barrier, and a warm greeting to the barefoot graybeard who had prepared his place, had spread out the brown canvas and had moved the cabana furniture out onto the deck, he sat down. He then had three or four hours before him, during which the sun climbed to the zenith, becoming terribly strong, the sea turned a deeper and deeper blue, and he could look at Tadzio.

He saw him coming, from the left, along the shoreline, saw him emerge between the cabanas from behind, or else he suddenly discovered, not without a shock of happy surprise, that he had missed his arrival and that Tadzio was already there, and, in the blue-and-white bathing suit that was now the only outfit he wore on the beach, had already resumed his usual activities in the sun and the sand, that charmingly trivial, idly roving life which was both playful and restful: sauntering, wading, digging, playing tag, camping and swimming. Meanwhile the women on the deck watched over him and called out to him, shouting his name at a high pitch — "Tadziu! Tadziu!" — and he would come running to them with eager gestures, to narrate an experience and to show them what he had found or caught: shells, sea horses, jellyfish and sideways-scuttling crabs. Aschenbach didn't understand a word he was saying and, even if the boy's conversation was really as humdrum as could be, to *his* ears it was a blur of euphony. Thus the foreignness of the boy's speech elevated it to the status of music, a frolicsome sun lavishly shed its glow over him, and the sublime deep perspective of the sea provided a constant foil and background for him whenever he appeared.

Soon the observer knew every line and pose of that body which was so elegant, which offered itself so freely; with joy he greeted anew each already familiar detail of his beauty; there was no end to his admiration, his delicate sensual pleasure. The boy was called over to say hello to a guest who was paying his respects to the women at the cabana; he ran up, perhaps all wet as he emerged from the water, tossed his curls and, as he held out his hand, standing on one leg, the other foot resting on the tips of the toes, he performed a charming twist and turn of the body; he was filled with graceful attention, bashful in his amiability, eager to please out of his sense of a nobleman's duty. He lay outstretched, the bath towel wound across his chest, his delicately chiseled arm leaning on the sand, his chin in the hollow of his hand; the boy called "Jaschu" squatted beside him and flirted with him, and nothing could be more bewitching than the smile of eyes and lips with which the one thus honored looked up at his underling, his servant. He stood by the edge of the sea, alone, apart from his family, quite close to Aschenbach, erect, his hands clasped behind his neck, slowly rocking on the balls of his feet, daydreaming as he stared into the blue, while small waves ran up and bathed his toes. His honey-colored hair curled close to his temples and down his neck; the sun illuminated the down at the top of his spine; his finely delineated ribs, his well-formed chest were readily visible through the scanty covering of his torso; his armpits were still as smooth as a statue's; his knee hollows shone, and their bluish veins made his body look as if it were formed of some more pellucid material. What breeding, what precision of thought were expressed in this outstretched body, perfect in its youthfulness! But the severe and pure will, which, operating obscurely, had managed to bring this godlike image into the light of day — was it not well known and familiar to him, the artist? Was it not operative in him as well when, full of sober passion, he liberated from the marble block of language the slender form which he had seen in his mind and which he presented to the world as an icon and mirror of intellectual beauty?

Icon and mirror! His eyes embraced the noble figure standing there by the edge of the blue, and in a rising wave of rapture he felt that as he looked he understood beauty itself, form as divine thought, the one, the pure perfection, which dwells in the mind, and of which a human image and metaphor, slender and lovely, was offered here for worship. This was Aschenbach's delirium, and the aging artist welcomed it unhesitatingly — yes, greedily. His mind was in labor pains; his cultural baggage was all helter-skelter; his memory cast up ancient thoughts that had been taught to him as a youth but had never yet been brought to life by his own ardor. Did not books state that the sun redirects our attention from intellectual to sensory things? It was said to numb and bewitch the understanding and the memory in such a way that, from sheer pleasure, the soul totally forgets its true condition and attaches itself with awe-struck admiration to the most beautiful of the objects that the sun shines on; yes, only with the aid of a physical body can it then raise itself to the contemplation of higher things. Truly, Amor behaved like mathematicians, who show tangible images of ideal forms to children who are still incapable of abstract thinking. Similarly, in order to render intellectual concepts visible to us, the god was wont to employ the physical attractions of youthful human beings, adorning them with all the reflected glow of beauty to make them an implement for anamnesis; when we see them, we are smitten with pain and hope.

These were the thoughts of the man kindled with enthusiasm; these were the feelings of which he was capable. And out of the intoxication of the sea and the blaze of the sun a charming picture was woven in his mind. It was the old plane tree not far from the walls of Athens; it was that place of sacred shade filled with the fragrance of the agnus-castus bush blossoms, adorned with votive images and pious offerings in honor of the nymphs and Achelous. The crystal-clear brook flowed over smooth pebbles at the foot of the widely branching tree; the cicadas were chirping. But on the grassy bank, which sloped gently so that even when recumbent one could hold one's head erect, there lay two men, sheltering here from the heat of the day: an older man and a young one, an ugly man and a handsome one, the wise man alongside the charming one. And amid the compliments and witty sallies of his courtship, Socrates instructed Phaedrus about desire and virtue. He spoke to him of the burning awe from which the man of feeling suffers when his eye catches sight of a metaphor of eternal beauty; he spoke to him of the lusts of the profane and bad man, who cannot conceive of beauty when he sees its image and is incapable of reverence; he spoke of the sacred fear that assails the noble man when a godlike countenance, a perfect body, comes into view — how he then trembles, and is beside himself, and scarcely dares to look, and honors the one who possesses the beauty, yes, would even sacrifice to him, as he might to the statue of a god, if he were not afraid of seeming like a fool in the eyes of men. "For beauty, dear Phaedrus, beauty alone, is charming and visible at the same time; remember this: it is the only form of intellectuality which we perceive with, and can tolerate with, our senses. Otherwise, what would become of us if the godhead, if reason and virtue and truth were to make themselves directly known to our senses? Would we not perish and burn up from love just as Semele once burned in the presence of Zeus? Thus, beauty is the path taken by the man of feeling to attain the intellectual — only the path, only a means, young Phaedrus" . . . And then that crafty wooer made his subtlest pronouncement: that the lover is more divine than the beloved, because the god dwells in the former but not in the latter — perhaps the most delicate and ironical thought that has ever occurred to man, the original source of all the roguishness and most secret lust of desire.

An author finds great joy in the idea that can be totally transformed into emotion, and the emotion that can be totally transformed into an idea. Just such a throbbing idea, such a precise emotion, was then in the possession and service of that solitary man: the idea that nature trembles with rapture when the intellect bows in homage to beauty. He suddenly felt a desire to write. To be sure, Eros is said to love idleness, and to have been made for nothing else. Yet, at this point in his crisis, the afflicted man's excitement was directed toward creativity. The immediate occasion hardly mattered. A new query, an incitement to writers to take a personal stand on a certain important, burning issue of culture and taste, had made the rounds of the intellectual world, and a copy of this solicitation had reached Aschenbach on his vacation. The matter involved was familiar to him, it was part of his experience; his urge to shed light on this issue with the splendor of his style was suddenly irresistible. Moreover, he desired to do this work in Tadzio's presence, to take the boy's form as a model for his writing, to adapt his style to the lines of that body, which seemed godlike to him, and to transfer his physical beauty to the intellectual sphere, just as the eagle once bore the Trojan shepherd off into the aether. Never had he felt more sweetly the pleasure of words, never had he been so conscious that Eros dwells in the word, as during the dangerously delicious hours in which, seated at his rough table beneath the canvas, in view of his idol and with the music of his voice in his ears, he modeled his little essay on Tadzio's beauty — that page and a half of choice prose whose purity, nobility and pulsating emotional tension were before long to excite the admiration of many. It is certainly a good thing that the world can see only finished works of art without knowing their origins, the conditions for their existence; for knowledge of the sources from which the artist derived his inspirations would often confuse and frighten away his public, thus vitiating the effects of his outstanding achievement. Strange hours! Strangely enervating labor! Oddly productive intercourse between the mind and a body! When Aschenbach put his work safely away and left the beach, he felt exhausted, indeed shattered; his conscience seemed to be accusing him as if he had committed some excess.

It was the next morning that, on the point of leaving the hotel, as he stood on the outer staircase, he noticed that Tadzio, already heading for the sea — alone — was just approaching the barrier of the beach. It was an obvious wish, an uncomplicated idea — and one that obtruded itself — to take advantage of the opportunity and introduce himself in an easygoing, cheerful way to the boy who all unawares had caused him so much exaltation and agitation, to talk to him, to enjoy his answer and the look in his eyes. The beautiful boy was walking at a saunter, it was easy to catch up with him, and Aschenbach accelerated his pace. He comes up to him on the boardwalk behind the cabanas, he wants to put his hand on his head, on his shoulder, and some phrase, a friendly expression in French, is already on his lips, when he feels that — partly perhaps because of his rapid walk — his heart is beating like a hammer; that, being so short of breath, he will only be able to speak in a choked voice, stammeringly; he hesitates, he tries to pull himself together, he suddenly fears that he has already been walking too long directly behind the beautiful boy, he fears that the boy will notice it, will look around questioningly; he tries once more, he gives up, he renounces his objective and walks past with downcast head.

"Too late!" he thought at that moment. "Too late!" But was it too late? The step he had failed to take might very possibly have led to a good result, to relief, to happiness, to a beneficial sobering. But the truth probably was that the aging man did not wish to be sobered, that the intoxication was too precious to him. Who can unriddle the essence and characteristics of the artistic temperament? Who understands the deep-lying instinctive fusion of discipline and dissoluteness on which it is founded? For the inability to wish for beneficial sobering is tantamount to dissoluteness. Aschenbach was no longer disposed toward self-criticism; his taste, the frame of mind that went with his age, his self-esteem, maturity and late-won simplicity of style made him disinclined to analyze motives and to decide whether he had failed to carry out his intentions because of conscience or because of negligence and weak-ness. He was confused, he was afraid that somebody, even if only the beach guard, might have noticed his chase and his comedown, he was very much afraid of looking ridiculous. Moreover, he joked to himself about his comically holy fear. "Dumbfounded," he thought, "as dumb-founded as a fighting cock that droops his wings in fear during the fight. Truly, it's the god who, when we view something lovely, quenches our courage in this way and humbles our proud mind so drastically . . ." He played with his thoughts, daydreamed, and was far too proud to fear the presence of an emotion.

By this time he was no longer keeping track of the passing of the leisure time he had granted himself; he never even thought about going home. He had sent for plenty of money. His only concern was the possible departure of the Polish family; but he had learned clandes-tinely, through casual questions put to the hotel barber, that they had registered only shortly before his own arrival. The sun tanned his face and hands, the stimulating salt air made him strong enough for emo-tions, and just as he had formerly been accustomed to expend imme-diately on some manuscript all the refreshment he received from sleep, nourishment or nature, so now he allowed all his daily strengthening by sunshine, leisure and sea air to be devoted, magnanimously but uneco-nomically, to mental intoxication and sentiment.

His sleep was irregular; the deliciously uniform days were separated by brief nights filled with pleasing disquiet. He retired early, it is true, because at nine, when Tadzio had vanished from the scene, the day seemed over to him. But around the first morning light he would be awakened by a feeling of awe that penetrated him gently; his heart would recollect his adventure; he could no longer abide staying in bed; he would get up and, lightly clad to fend off the morning chill, he would sit down by the open window to await the rising of the sun. This marvelous event filled his soul, which had been consecrated by sleep, with piety. Sky, earth and sea still lay in the ghostly, glassy pallor of dawn; a vanishing star still drifted in the featureless heavens. But a breeze sprang up, a winged announcement from unapproachable dwelling places that Eos was leaving her husband's side; and in the furthest reaches of sky and sea could be seen that first, sweet blush which indicates that the created world is becoming perceptible to the senses. The goddess approached, the seducer of youths, she who abducted Clitus and Cephalus and defiantly, to the envy of all the Olympians, enjoyed the love of the handsome Orion. A strewing of roses began there at the edge of the world, an inexpressibly lovely shining and blossoming; childlike clouds, transfigured, illuminated, floated like ministering Amorets in the pink and bluish fragrance; purple fell upon the sea, which, in its rolling, seemed to carry it onward; golden spears flashed from down below up to the heights of heaven; the glow became a blaze; soundlessly, with godlike, superhuman power, heat, ardor and flickering flames shot skyward, and with rapacious hooves her brother's sacred racers rose above the earth. Irradiated by the splendor of the god sat the solitary, wakeful man; he closed his eyes and let the glory kiss his eyelids. Emotions from the past, early, delicious afflictions of the heart, which had been dissolved in the strict discipline that was his way of life, and were now returning so strangely metamorphosed — he recognized them with a confused, puzzled smile. He reflected, he dreamed; slowly his lips shaped a name, and, still smiling, with face turned upward, with hands folded on his lap, he dozed off again in his armchair.

But the day that had begun with such fiery solemnities remained mysteriously exalted and mythically transformed. Whence came the breeze, from what source, that suddenly, so gentle and significant, like an inspiration from on high, played around his temples and ears? White, feathery clouds hung in the sky in widely scattered groups, like grazing flocks of the gods. A stronger wind sprang up, and Poseidon's steeds dashed forward, rearing — bulls as well, belonging to him of the bluish tresses, lowering their horns in a bellowing charge. But between the rocky boulders of the more remote beach the waves dashed upward like leaping goats. A sacredly distorted world full of Panic life enfolded the bewitched man, and his heart dreamed gentle fables. Often, when the sun went down behind Venice, he sat on a bench in the park to watch Tadzio, who, dressed in white with a sash of some bright color, was enjoying himself playing ball on the rolled gravel court; and it was Hyacinth whom he thought he saw, Hyacinth, who was fated to die because two gods loved him. Yes, he felt Zephyr's painful jealousy of his rival, who forgot his oracle, his bow and his cithara so that he could constantly sport with the beautiful boy; he saw the discus, directed by cruel jealousy, striking the lovely head; turning pale himself, he caught the limp body, and the flower that blossomed from the sweet blood bore the inscription of his unending lament . . .

Nothing is stranger or more ticklish than a relationship between people who know each other only by sight, who meet and observe each other daily—no, hourly—and are nevertheless compelled to keep up the pose of an indifferent stranger, neither greeting nor addressing each other, whether out of etiquette or their own whim. Between them there exists a disquiet, a strained curiosity, the hysteria of an unsatisfied, unnaturally repressed need for recognition and exchange of thoughts— and also, especially, a sort of nervous respect. For, one person loves and honors another only as long as he is unable to assess him, and yearning is a result of a lack of knowledge.

Some kind of relationship and acquaintance had inevitably to develop between Aschenbach and young Tadzio, and with penetrating joy the older man was able to ascertain that his friendly feelings and attention were not altogether unreciprocated. For instance, what induced the beautiful boy, when he appeared on the beach in the morning, no longer to use the boardwalk in the rear of the cabanas, but, when sauntering to his family's cabana, to go only the front way, through the sand, past Aschenbach's place and sometimes quite close to him, almost grazing his table and chair? Was this the effect of the attraction and fascination of a superior emotion on its tender, carefree object? Daily Aschenbach awaited Tadzio's entrance, and at times he acted as if he were busy when it took place, and let the beautiful boy walk by apparently unnoticed. But at other times he looked up and their eyes met. They were both as serious as possible when that happened. Nothing in the cultivated and dignified face of the older man betrayed an inner agitation; but in Tadzio's eyes there was an inquiry, a pensive question; his gait became hesitant, he looked down at the ground, looked up again charmingly, and when he had walked by, something in his bearing seemed to indicate that only good manners kept him from turning around.

Once, however, one evening, things went differently. The Polish siblings and the governess had failed to show up for the main meal in the large dining room—Aschenbach had noted this with concern. After the meal, very uneasy about their whereabouts, he was walking in his evening dress and straw hat in front of the hotel, at the foot of the terrace, when suddenly he saw the nunlike sisters and the governess and, four steps behind them, Tadzio, emerge into the light of the arc lamps. Obviously they were coming from the steamer landing after dining in the city for some reason. It had probably been cool on the water; Tadzio was wearing a dark blue sailor's jacket with gold buttons and a matching cap. Sunshine and sea air did not tan him; his skin was just the same yellowish marble color it had been from the outset; but today he seemed paler than usual, either because of the coolness or because of the bleaching effect of the lamps' moonlight. His fine, regular eyebrows were more distinct, his eyes were very dark. He was more beautiful than words can say, and Aschenbach felt painfully, as he had often done, that words are able to praise physical beauty but not to reproduce it.

He had not expected this precious appearance, it came unhoped-for; he had not had time to settle his features into an expression of dignified calm. Joy, surprise and admiration were allowed to be freely depicted there when his eyes met those of the boy whom he had missed—and at that second Tadzio smiled: smiled at him in a communicative, familiar, charming and unconcealed way, with lips that only slowly opened into a smile. It was the smile of Narcissus bending over his reflection in the water, that profound, enchanted, long smile with which he holds out his arms to the mirror image of his own beauty—a very slightly twisted smile, twisted by the hopelessness of his endeavor to kiss the lovely lips of his reflection, coquettish, curious and quietly tormented, deluded and deluding.

He who had received this smile dashed away with it as with some fatal gift. He was so shaken that he was compelled to flee the light of the terrace and the front garden, and with hasty steps he sought the darkness of the park in the rear of the hotel. Oddly indignant and tender admonitions were wrung from him: "You shouldn't smile like that! Listen, no one should smile at someone else that way!" He threw himself onto a bench; beside himself, he inhaled the nighttime fragrance of the plants. And, leaning back, with arms dangling, overcome and repeatedly shuddering, he whispered the standard formula of longing—impossible in this case, absurd, perverse, ludicrous and yet even here still sacred and respectable: "I love you!"

Fifth Chapter

IN THE FOURTH week of his stay on the Lido, Gustav von Aschenbach made some peculiar observations concerning the outside world. First of all, it seemed to him as if, with the season still approaching its height, the number of guests at his hotel was decreasing rather than the reverse; it seemed in particular as if there was progressively less German being spoken around him, so that, finally, in the dining room and on the beach, only foreign words met his ear. Then one day, while conversing with the barber, whom he now frequently visited, something in the conversation took him aback. The man had mentioned a German family that had just departed after a short stay, and in a chatty, flattering way added: "But you stay on, Sir; you have no fear of the disease." Aschenbach looked at him. "Of the disease?" he repeated. The babbler fell silent, acted busy, disregarded the question. And when it was put again more insistently, he declared that he knew nothing about it and tried to distract his listener with an embarrassed torrent of speech.

That was at noon. In the afternoon Aschenbach took a boat to Venice — the wind was calm and the sun beating down strongly — for he was driven by the mania to follow the Polish siblings, whom he had seen taking the path to the steamer landing with their escort. He did not find his idol at San Marco. But at tea, seated at his little round iron table on the shady side of the square, he suddenly noticed a peculiar smell in the air, a smell he now recalled he had been perceiving for days without being fully conscious of it — a sickly-sweet medicinal smell that made one think of poverty, sores and dubious cleanliness. He analyzed and recognized it pensively, finished his snack and left the square on the side opposite the cathedral. In that narrow space the smell was stronger. At street corners, printed notices were posted in which the city fathers warned the population, because of certain disorders of the gastric system that were only to be expected in this type of weather, not to eat oysters and mussels or drink canal water. The euphemistic nature of the message was obvious. Groups of people were standing silently together on bridges and squares; and the foreigner stood among them, searching and pondering.

He asked a shopowner, who was leaning in his doorway under an arch among strings of coral and fake amethyst jewelry, for information about the distressing smell. The man surveyed him with heavy eyes and hastily became more alert. "A temporary measure, Sir!" he answered, gesturing. "A police order one surely must concur with. This weather is oppressive, the scirocco isn't good for the health. In short, you understand — perhaps an exaggerated caution . . ." Aschenbach thanked him and moved on. Even on the steamer that took him back to the Lido he now noticed the smell of the germicide.

Back at the hotel, he immediately went to the periodical table in the lounge and looked through the papers. In the non-German ones he found nothing. The ones from home reported rumors, cited fluctuating statistics, reprinted official denials and cast doubts on their truthfulness. That explained the departure of the German and Austrian element. The citizens of the other nations obviously knew nothing, suspected nothing,

DISCARD

were not yet worried. "They want people to keep quiet!" thought Aschenbach in his excitement, throwing the papers back on the table. "They want people to cover this up!" But at the same time his heart was filled with contentment about the adventure into which the outside world was about to enter. For passion, like crime, is not a friend of routine law and order or of the public welfare, and must welcome every weakening of the framework of society, every confusion and affliction of the world, because it can detect a remote chance to profit by it. Thus, Aschenbach felt a hidden satisfaction with the events in the dirty alleys of Venice that were being covered up by the authorities — this criminal secret of the city which coincided with his own dark secret, and which he too was so very anxious to keep. For, deeply in love, he worried only that Tadzio might go away, and he realized, not without a shock, that he would not know how to go on living should that occur.

Of late it was not enough for him to be near the beautiful boy and to see him, merely as a result of daily routine and lucky chance; he pursued him, he lay in wait for him. On Sundays, for example, the Poles never showed up on the beach; he guessed that they went to Mass at St. Mark's, he hurried there and, stepping out of the heat of the square into the golden twilight of the sanctuary, he found the boy he had missed bending over a prie-dieu, at worship. Then he stood in the background, on the fissured mosaic floor, amid people kneeling, muttering, crossing themselves, and the splendor of the low, broad Oriental temple weighed luxuriantly on his senses. Down in front, the heavily adorned priest walked, gesticulated and sang; incense rose up, clouding the weak little flames of the altar tapers; and with the stuffy, sweet odor of sacrifice a different odor seemed to mingle quietly: the smell of the sick city. But through the vapor and the sparkle of lights Aschenbach saw how the beautiful boy down there in front turned his head, sought him out and caught sight of him.

Then, when the crowd poured out through the opened portals onto the gleaming square with its swarming pigeons, the deluded man hid in the vestibule, he concealed himself, he waited in ambush. He saw the Poles leave the church, saw how the siblings ceremoniously took leave of their mother, who turned toward the Piazzetta on her way home; he ascertained that the beautiful boy, the nunlike sisters and the governess were taking the righthand path through the gateway of the Clock Tower into the Merceria, and, after giving them a brief head start, he followed them, followed them secretly on their walk through Venice. He had to stand still when they lingered, had to take refuge in cookshops and courtyards to let them pass when they turned back; he lost them, sought them, heated and exhausted, across bridges and in filthy dead-end lanes, and endured minutes of mortal pain when he suddenly saw them coming toward him in a narrow passage where it was impossible to move out of their way. And yet it could not be said that he was suffering. His head and heart were drunk, and his steps followed the directions dictated by the demon who takes pleasure in trampling human reason and dignity beneath his feet.

At some point Tadzio and his family then took a gondola, and Aschenbach, who, while they were boarding, had been hiding behind part of a building that jutted out, or behind a fountain, did the same shortly after they had put off from shore. He spoke quickly and in muffled tones when, promising the oarsman a large tip, he instructed him to follow the gondola that was just turning the corner — but unobtrusively and at a distance — and he shuddered when the man, with a pander's villainous alacrity, assured him in the same tone of voice that he would serve him well and conscientiously.

Thus he floated and rocked, leaning on soft, black cushions, following the other black, high-prowed boat, to the wake of which his passion chained him. At moments he lost sight of it; then he felt sorrow and unrest. But his guide, as if well versed in such assignments, was constantly able — thanks to sly maneuvers, quick crisscross movements and shortcuts — to make the object of his desire visible to him again. The air was still and odorous, the sun blazed strongly through the vapor that colored the sky a slate gray. Water lapped gurgling against wood and stone. The call of the gondolier, half warning and half greeting, was answered from afar out of the stillness of the labyrinth as if by some odd prearranged agreement. From small gardens, situated at a height, clusters of flowers, white and purple, smelling of almonds, hung down over crumbling walls. Arabic window enframements could be seen in the murk. The marble steps of a church descended into the water; a beggar, squatting there, attesting to his destitute state, held out his hat and showed the whites of his eyes as if he were blind; a dealer in antiques, standing in front of his wretched shop, invited the passerby with cringing gestures to stop and look around, in hopes of cheating him. That was Venice, the obsequious and untrustworthy beauty — this city, half fairy tale, half tourist trap, in whose reeking atmosphere art had once extravagantly luxuriated, and which had inspired composers with music that gently rocks you and meretriciously lulls you to rest. The adventurer felt as if his eyes were drinking in this luxuriance, as if his ears were being wooed by these melodies; he also recollected that the city was sick and was disguising the fact so it could go on making money; and he was more unbridled as he watched for the gondola that glided ahead of him.

Thus, in his confusion, he knew and cared about nothing but the unremitting pursuit of the object that set him aflame; he wished only to dream of him when he was absent and, after the fashion of lovers, to speak tender words to his mere phantom. Solitude, his strange surroundings and the joy of a deep, belated intoxication encouraged and persuaded him to let himself be carried away, to commit the most embarrassing actions without timidity or shame. Even this had occurred: once, coming back from Venice late in the evening, he had stopped by the beautiful boy's door on the first floor of the hotel, had leaned his forehead on the jamb, lost in rapture, and had been unable to tear himself away for some time, running the risk of being discovered and caught in such an insane situation.

And yet there were still some moments when he paused and came halfway to his senses. "Where am I heading?" he then thought, in dismay. "Where am I heading?" Like every man in whom inborn merits instill an aristocratic interest in his ancestry, he was accustomed to think about his forebears whenever he had achieved anything or enjoyed any success in his life; he was accustomed to assure himself in his mind of their approval, their satisfaction, the esteem they could not help but feel. He thought about them again in this case, now that he was involved in such an inadmissible experience, caught up in such exotic extravagances of emotion; he thought of the dignified severity, the respectable manliness, of their character, and he smiled grimly. What would they say? But indeed, what would they have said about his entire life, which had deviated from theirs to the point of degeneracy, this life lived under the spell of art, this life about which he himself, with the bourgeois mentality of his fathers, had as a young man published such mocking judgments, and which nevertheless was fundamentally so similar to theirs? He too had served, he too had been a soldier and warrior, like many of them — for art was a war, an exhausting struggle, which people nowadays were unable to keep up for very long. A life of self-conquest, a life "in despite of things," a harsh, persevering and abstemious life, which he had shaped into a symbol of the delicate heroism suited to the times — he was entitled to call this life a manly and brave one, and it seemed to him as if the eros that had seized hold of him was in some way particularly appropriate and fitting for a life like his. Had not this kind of eros been held in special regard among the bravest nations? Yes, was it not said that it flourished in their cities just because of bravery? Numerous military heroes of ancient times had willingly borne its yoke, for no humiliation counted if it was decreed by the god, and actions that would have been blamed as signs of cowardice if they had been committed for any other purpose — prostrating oneself before others, swearing oaths, making fervent supplications and acting like a slave — such actions were not considered shameful for a lover, but instead even won him praise.

The deluded man's mind was set in this pattern; in this way he attempted to defend his actions, to uphold his dignity. But at the same time he constantly turned his attention, in an obstinately inquisitive manner, to the unsavory events inside Venice, to that adventure of the outside world which mysteriously coincided with the adventure of his heart, and which nourished his passion with vague, lawless hopes. Obsessed with gaining new, reliable information about the state and progress of the disease, he leafed through the papers from home in the city coffee shops; for several days now they had disappeared from the periodical table in the hotel lounge. The articles alternated between assertions and retractions. The number of cases of sickness and of death was said to mount up to twenty, forty, even a hundred and more; and, immediately afterward, the very existence of the epidemic was either categorically denied, or was at least said to be a matter of isolated cases brought into the city from outside. There was a scattering of serious warnings and protests against the dangerous game being played by the Italian authorities. There was no way of gaining any certainty.

And yet, in his solitude, Aschenbach felt he had a particular right to be let in on the secret and, even though excluded, he found a bizarre satisfaction in approaching people in the know with insidious questions, and forcing those partaking in the conspiracy of silence to tell an outright lie. One day at breakfast in the main dining room, he had it out in this way with the manager, that small, gently walking person in the French frock coat, who, passing among the tables greeting the guests and superintending the service, stopped at Aschenbach's table as well for a few words of conversation. "Why," asked the guest in an indolent, casual manner, "why in the world have they been disinfecting Venice for some time now?" The man of intrigue replied, "It is a police measure dutifully intended to counteract at an early stage all sorts of conditions injurious or disruptive to public health that might be caused by the sultry and unusually hot weather." "The police are to be congratulated," Aschenbach replied; and, after exchanging a few meteorological remarks, the manager excused himself.

That same day, in the evening, after dinner, it so happened that a small troupe of street singers from the city came to perform in the front garden of the hotel. Two men and two women, they stood by the iron post of an arc lamp and held their brightly lit faces up to the terrace, where the hotel guests were sitting with coffee and cold drinks, ready to put up with the typically local entertainment. The hotel staff, elevator operators, waiters and office clerks, appeared as listeners at the doors to the lounge. The Russian family, eager for pleasure and punctilious in their pursuit of it, had had wicker chairs carried down into the garden, in order to be closer to the musicians, and sat there gratefully in a semi-circle. Behind the family stood their old female serf, wearing a turban-like headdress.

Mandolins, guitars, an accordion and a squeaky fiddle were industriously plied by the mendicant virtuosos. Instrumental executions alternated with vocal numbers, in which the younger woman added her harsh, piping voice to the tenor's sugary falsetto in a yearning love duet. But beyond a doubt the real talent and head of the organization was the other man, the proprietor of the guitar, whose role was a kind of baritone buffo; he had almost no voice, but was histrionically gifted and possessed remarkable power as a comedian. Often, with his large instrument under his arm, he would break away from the group and push his way toward the "footlights," gesticulating; there his tomfoolery was rewarded with encouraging laughter. The Russians especially, in their "orchestra seats," were obviously delighted by so much southern animation and, with applause and cheers, exhorted him to behave even more boldly and self-assuredly.

Aschenbach sat by the balustrade, from time to time cooling his lips with the ruby-red mixture of pomegranate juice and soda that sparkled in the glass in front of him. His nerves eagerly drank in the tootling sounds and the vulgar, languishing melodies, because passion deadens one's taste and, with all seriousness, condescends to enjoy offerings that a clear mind would either take as a joke or indignantly reject. Watching the buffoon's antics, his face had become distorted into a fixed smile that was already becoming painful. He sat there with indolent body, while his mind was fully occupied with something demanding his closest attention: six paces away from him, Tadzio was leaning on the stone railing.

He stood there in the belted white suit he sometimes wore to dinner; with his inevitable, inborn gracefulness, he was leaning his left forearm on the rail, his feet were crossed and his right hand was resting on his hip; he was looking down at the mountebanks with an expression that was barely a smile, merely one of vague curiosity, a courteous acknowledgment of their efforts. At times he stood up straight and, expanding his chest, with a lovely action of both arms, he pulled his white blouse down through his leather belt. But at other times — and the aging man observed this triumphantly, with his reason reeling and with a touch of terror — now hesitantly and cautiously, now quickly and suddenly as if to take him by surprise, the boy would look over his left shoulder toward the place where his lover sat. Aschenbach did not look right into his eyes, for a shameful anxiety compelled the misguided man to keep his eyes rigidly under control. Farther back on the terrace sat the women who kept guard over Tadzio, and things had come to such a pass that the amorous man had to avoid being too noticeable and arousing suspicion. Yes, several times, on the beach, in the hotel lounge and on the Piazza San Marco, he had had occasion to observe, with a sort of torpor, that they were calling Tadzio away when he and the boy were close together, that they were intentionally keeping Tadzio at a distance from him — and he had been forced to acknowledge this as a terrible insult, which made his pride writhe in hitherto unknown torment, and which his own conscience prevented him from challenging.

Meanwhile the guitarist had begun a solo song to his own accompaniment, a many-stanzaed, trashy hit that was the rage of the moment all over Italy; every time its refrain came around, the entire company joined in with their voices and all the musical paraphernalia; he was quite good at performing this number in a graphic, dramatic fashion. Slight of build and with a thin, emaciated face, at a distance from his companions, with his shabby felt hat pushed so far back that a tuft of his red hair stuck out under the brim, he stood on the gravel in a posture of impudent bravura and, in an insistent parlando, to the dull rumble of the strings, he hurled his jokes up to the terrace, while his artistic exertions made the veins stand out on his forehead. He didn't look like a native Venetian, but more like a Neapolitan comedian, half pimp and half entertainer, brutal and reckless, dangerous and amusing. Through his facial expressions, through the movements of his body, through his way of winking suggestively and licking the corners of his mouth licentiously, the song, whose words were merely nonsensical, became, as he sang it, salacious and vaguely offensive. From the soft collar of his sport shirt, which did not go with his otherwise more formal clothing, projected his scrawny neck with a conspicuously large and naked-looking Adam's apple. His pale, snub-nosed face, whose beardless features made it hard to calculate his age, was wrinkled as if from grimacing and vice, and the grinning of his mobile mouth was an odd match to the two furrows which, defiant, dominating, almost savage, could be seen between his reddish eyebrows. But the solitary man really started to observe him closely after he noticed that this suspicious figure also seemed to bring along its own suspicious atmosphere: that is, every time the refrain returned, the singer, playing pranks and waving his hand in greeting, would set out on a grotesque circular march that led him right below Aschenbach's seat, and every time this happened a strong odor of carbolic acid would drift up to the terrace from his clothing and his body.

When the song was over, he began to collect money. He started with the Russians, who were seen to give freely, and then he proceeded up the stairs. Impudently as he had behaved during the performance, up here he was humble. Arching his back in low bows, he slinked between the tables, and a smile of cunning obsequiousness bared his large teeth, although the two furrows were still there, menacing, between his red eyebrows. The guests surveyed the foreign-looking fellow with curiosity and with some repugnance as he collected his livelihood; they threw coins into his felt hat with the tips of their fingers, taking care not to touch him. Elimination of the physical distance between an actor and his respectable onlookers, no matter how much the latter enjoyed the performance, always produces a certain embarrassment. He felt this and tried to excuse himself by means of groveling. He came up to Aschenbach and with him came the odor, which no one else around seemed to pay any mind to.

"Listen!" said the solitary man in muffled tones and almost mechanically. "Venice is being disinfected. Why?" The comedian answered hoarsely: "Because of the police! It's the regulations, Sir, with this heat and the scirocco. The scirocco puts pressure on you. It isn't good for the health . . ." He spoke as if surprised that anyone could pose such questions, and he demonstrated with the flat of his hand how much pressure the scirocco exerted. "So, then, there's no disease in Venice?" asked Aschenbach very quietly, between his teeth. The muscular features of the prankster settled into a grimace of humorous helplessness. "A disease? But what kind of disease? Is the scirocco a disease? Are our police perhaps a disease? You must be joking! A disease? No, no! A preventive measure, you surely understand! A police ordinance to counteract the effects of the oppressive weather . . ." He gesticulated. "Fine," said Aschenbach, once again curtly and quietly, and quickly dropped an inappropriately large coin into the hat. Then he dismissed the man with a signal of the eyes. He obeyed, grinning and bowing. But he had not yet reached the stairs when two hotel employees pounced on him and, their faces close to his, started to cross-examine him in whispers. He shrugged his shoulders, gave assurances, swore that he had been discreet; this was clearly seen. When they let him go, he returned to the garden and, after a brief conference with his companions, he stepped out under the arc lamp once more for a song of thanks and farewell.

It was a song that the solitary man did not recall ever hearing before, a saucy popular number, in an incomprehensible dialect, rigged out with a laughing refrain in which the troupe joined at the top of their voice at regular intervals. At these moments there were no longer any words or instrumental accompaniment, and nothing remained but laughter that was somehow rhythmically organized but treated in a very naturalistic manner; the soloist, especially, with great talent, was able to make this laughter seem deceptively lifelike. Now that the artistic distance between him and his distinguished public was restored, all of his impudence had returned, and his artificial laughter, brazenly directed upward at the terrace, was one of mockery. When approaching the end of the words in each stanza, he already seemed to be struggling with an uncontrollable urge to laugh. He sobbed, his voice wavered, he pressed his hand to his mouth, he twisted his shoulders, and, at the proper moment, the unruly laughter broke forth from him, howling and explosively, with such verisimilitude that it had a contagious effect; as the spectators became infected, an unmotivated hilarity, which fed only on itself, spread through the terrace as well. But this very event seemed to redouble the singer's exuberance. He bent his knees, he slapped his thighs, he held his sides, he was convulsed; he was no longer laughing but screaming; he pointed upward as if there were nothing funnier than the laughing audience up there, and finally everyone in the garden and on the veranda was laughing, even the waiters, elevator operators and hotel servants in the doorways.

Aschenbach was no longer relaxing in his chair; he sat upright as if trying to defend himself or run away. But the combination of the laughter, the hospital odor drifting up to him, and the nearness of the beautiful boy cast a dreamy spell over him that enveloped his head and his mind, a spell he could neither shatter nor flee. Amid the general animation and distraction, he was daring enough to look in Tadzio's direction, and as he did, he noticed that the beautiful boy, who returned his gaze, remained equally serious, just as if he were modeling his own behavior and expression on the older man's — as if the general mood of hilarity had no power over him since the other man was resisting it. This childlike compliance, indicative of a relationship between them, was so disarming and overwhelming that only with difficulty did the gray-haired man keep from hiding his face in his hands. It had also seemed to him as if Tadzio's occasional straightening up and deep breathing were indicative of a shortness of breath, a tightness in the chest. "He is sickly, he probably won't live to a ripe old age," he thought once again with that objectivity which, strangely, sometime breaks through the spell of intoxication and longing; and his heart was filled with real concern, together with unwarranted satisfaction.

Meanwhile the Venetians had concluded and were departing. They were accompanied by applause, and their leader did not neglect to spice his exit with more jokes. His bows, the kisses he blew to the audience, were laughed at, and so he indulged in more of them. After his companions were already outside, he still pretended to run backwards into a lamppost, hurting himself, and then crawled to the main gate as if doubled up in agony. There, finally, he suddenly threw off the mask of the humorous victim of fate; he straightened up — in fact, bounced up like rubber — impudently stuck out his tongue at the guests on the terrace, and slipped away into the darkness. The audience dispersed; for some time Tadzio had not been standing by the balustrade. But, to the annoyance of the waiters, the solitary man still sat for quite some time next to his table and what remained of his pomegranate drink. The night moved on, time wore away. In his parents' house, many years ago, there had been an hourglass; suddenly he saw the fragile, significant little instrument once more, as if it stood before him. Soundlessly, the fine, rust-colored sand slipped through the narrow waist of the glass, and when it had nearly run out of the upper globe, a small, whirling eddy had formed there.

On the very next day, in the afternoon, the stubborn man continued to tempt the outside world, and this time with the greatest possible success: from St. Mark's Square he entered the British travel agency located there, and, after changing some money at the till, he assumed the expression of a distrustful foreigner, and addressed his troublesome question to the clerk who was waiting on him. This was an Englishman in a woolen suit, still young, with hair parted in the middle, with eyes set close together and with that sedate honesty of character which strikes one as so different and peculiar when encountered in the scoundrelly, supersubtle south of Europe. He began: "No cause for concern, Sir. A measure without serious significance. Such arrangements are frequently made to prevent the unhealthful effects of the heat and scirocco . . ." But, opening his blue eyes wider, he encountered those of the stranger, weary and somewhat sad, which were directed at his lips with a look of mild contempt. Then the Englishman blushed. "That," he continued in a low voice and with some animation, "is the official explanation, which people here think it good to stick to. But I tell you that there is something else behind it." And then, in his honest and comfortable language, he told the truth.

For several years, Indian cholera had shown an increasing tendency to spread abroad and travel. Engendered in the hot swamps of the Ganges delta, arising from the mephitic exhalations of that wilderness of primordial world and islands, luxuriant but uninhabitable and shunned by man, in whose bamboo thickets the tiger crouches, the epidemic had raged throughout Hindustan unremittingly and with unusual violence, had spread eastward to China, westward to Afghanistan and Persia, and, following the main caravan routes, had brought its horrors as far as Astrakhan and even Moscow. But while Europe trembled in fear lest the phantom might enter its territory from that point, and by land, it had been carried across the sea by Syrian merchants, had appeared in several Mediterranean ports simultaneously, had raised its head in Toulon and Málaga, had shown its mask repeatedly in Palermo and Naples, and seemed to be a permanent fixture throughout Calabria and Apulia. The north of the peninsula had been spared. But in the middle of May of this year the fearful vibrios had been discovered in Venice twice in the same day, in the emaciated, blackened corpses of a cargo-ship crewman and a female greengrocer. The cases were kept secret. But a week later there were ten, there were twenty, thirty, and in different neighborhoods. A man from the Austrian provinces, who had spent a few vacation days in Venice, died upon returning to his hometown with unmistakable signs of the disease, and so it came about that the first rumors of the epidemic in the city on the lagoon made their way into German-language newspapers. The Venetian authorities replied that health conditions in the city had never been better, and took the most urgent measures to combat the illness. But probably foodstuffs had been infected, vegetables, meat or milk, for, denied and hushed up as it might be, death flourished in the narrow lanes, and the prematurely occurring summer heat, which turned the water of the canals lukewarm, was particularly conducive to its spread. In fact, it seemed as if the epidemic had experienced a revivification of its strength, as if the tenacity and fertility of the germs that caused it had redoubled. Cases of recovery were rare; eighty out of a hundred victims died, and horribly, because the disease was attacking with extreme virulence and often in its most dangerous form, called the "dry" form. In such cases the body was not even able to discharge the water that was excreted in massive quantities from the blood vessels. Within a few hours the patients dried up and, with convulsions and hoarse moans, choked on the blood that had become as thick and sticky as pitch. They were better off in the occasional instances when, after a slight indisposition, the disease took the form of a deep coma, from which they no longer, or just barely, awoke. At the beginning of June the isolation sheds of the Ospedale Civile quietly became filled up, hardly any space was left in the two orphanages, and there was frightfully heavy traffic between the quay of the Fondamente Nuove and San Michele, the cemetery island. But the fear of causing general harm to the city, concern for the recently opened exhibition of paintings in the Public Gardens, and anxiety over the tremendous losses with which the hotels, businesses and the entire multifaceted tourist industry were threatened in case of a panic and a boycott, proved to be of more weight in the city than love of the truth and respect for international conventions; these concerns induced the authorities to maintain obstinately their policy of silence and denial. The chief medical officer of Venice, a distinguished man, had resigned from his position indignantly and had been clandestinely replaced by a more compliant personality. The populace knew this; and the corruption of their leaders, along with the prevailing insecurity and state of emergency that the stalking death had brought forth in the city, resulted in a certain demoralization of the lower classes, an incitement to criminal and antisocial impulses, which took the form of intemperance, shameless behavior and a growing crime rate. In the evening one could see many drunken people, which was unusual; it was said that malicious riffraff were making the streets unsafe at night; muggings and even homicides occurred repeatedly: it had already been proved on two occasions that persons who had allegedly fallen victim to the epidemic had really been made away with, poisoned by their own relatives; and professional vice took on conspicuous, excessive proportions hitherto unknown here, and at home only in the south of the country and in the Orient.

The Englishman communicated the heart of the matter. "You would do well," he concluded, "to leave today rather than tomorrow. It can't be more than a few days before they declare a quarantine." "Thanks," said Aschenbach and left the agency.

The square lay in sunless sultriness. Unknowing foreigners sat in front of the cafés or, completely covered with pigeons, stood in front of the church and watched the birds swarming, beating their wings, shoving one another aside and pecking at the corn kernels people offered them in the palms of their hands. In feverish excitement, in triumphant possession of the truth, which had left an unpleasant taste in his mouth and a fantastic terror in his heart, the solitary man paced to and fro over the flagstones of the magnificent square. He was considering an action that would be cleansing and decent. After dinner tonight he could go up to the lady adorned with pearls and deliver the speech he was now sketching out word for word: "Please permit a stranger, Madame, to give you a piece of advice, a warning that is being withheld from you out of self-interest. Leave, and right away, with Tadzio and your daughters! Venice is plague-stricken." Then he could lay his hand in farewell on the head of that implement of a mocking deity, walk away and escape from this swamp. But at the same time he felt that he was infinitely far from seriously wishing to take such a step. It would recall him to his senses, it would restore him to himself; but a man who is beside himself dreads nothing worse than to become himself again. He recollected a white building adorned with inscriptions that gleamed in the evening light and in whose diaphanous mysticism his mind's eye had become absorbed; he then recollected the odd figure of that traveler who had awakened in the aging man a youngster's roving desire for faraway, strange places; and the idea of returning home, acting sensibly, sobering up and resuming his labors and his status as a master was so repellent to him that his face contorted into an expression of physical nausea. "They want people to keep quiet!" he whispered violently. And added: "I *will* keep quiet!" The consciousness that he was an accessory to the secret, and equally guilty, intoxicated him, just as small quantities of wine intoxicate a weary brain. The image of the afflicted and neglected city, confusedly present to his mind, kindled his hopes, inconceivable hopes that bypassed reason and were tremendously sweet. What was that mild happiness of which he had earlier dreamt for a moment, when compared with these expectations? What were art and virtue to him any longer in contrast to the advantages of chaos? He kept silent and he stayed on.

That night he had a frightening dream — if one can give the name of dream to an experience of both the body and the mind. Although it came to him when he was fast asleep, in complete independence of his will, and his senses were fully alert, nevertheless he did not see himself as a separate participant moving in a space external to the events; rather, their theater was his soul and they broke in from outside, violently overcoming his resistance — a profound, intellectual resistance — forced their way through, and, when they had passed, left his existence, and his lifetime's accumulation of culture, totally destroyed and annihilated.

The dream began with anxiety, anxiety and pleasure and a terrible curiosity about what would ensue. Night reigned, and his senses listened; for, from far away, a din was approaching, a hubbub, a blend of noises: a rattling, a blaring and a muffled thundering, along with shrill shouts of jubilation and an articulated howl on a prolonged *u*-sound — all of this interspersed with, and capped by, the eerily sweet tones of a deeply cooing, brutally insistent flute, which bewitched the body in a shamelessly importunate manner. Yet he was aware of a phrase, obscure, but characterizing all that followed: *"The foreign god!"* A smoky glow flickered up, and he recognized mountain country, similar to that around his summer house. And in the uneven light, from the wooded heights, between tree trunks and moss-covered boulders, there they came rolling and plunging down in a whirlwind: human beings, animals, a swarm, a raving horde — and flooded the mountain slope with bodies, flames, tumult and a reeling round-dance. Women, stumbling over the excessively long skin garments that hung from their belts, shook tambourines above their heads, which were thrown back in a groan; they brandished torches, which emitted a spray of sparks, and naked daggers; they held hissing snakes, grasping them by the middle of their bodies, or held up their breasts with both hands as they advanced screaming. Fur-girt men, with horns above their brows and shaggy body hair, bowed their necks and lifted their arms and thighs, sounded bronze cymbals and beat furiously on drums, while smooth-skinned boys goaded he-goats with foliage-encircled staffs, holding tight to their horns and letting themselves be dragged along by their leaps, shouting. And the god-possessed people howled out the call that consisted of soft consonants with a prolonged *u*-sound at the end, a call sweet and savage at the same time, like no other ever heard: it resounded in one place, bellowed into the air as if by stags, and was taken up in another, by many voices, in riotous triumph; with this call they incited one another to dance and fling about their limbs, and they never let it die away. But the deep, luring flute tone penetrated and dominated it all. Was it not luring him, too, as he resistingly experienced this, summoning him with shameless persistence to the festival and enormity of the utmost sacrifice? Great was his dread, great his fear, honest his endeavor to defend his world to the last against the stranger, the enemy of the sedate and dignified intellect. But the noise, the howling, multiplied by the echoing mountainside, grew, took control, escalated into overpowering madness. Odors befuddled his mind: the biting smell of the goats, the scent of the gasping bodies, an odor like that of stagnant waters, and still another smell, a familiar one — sores and a rampant sickness. His heart rumbled to the drumbeats, his brain was in a whirl, anger seized him, delusion, numbing lust; and his soul desired to join in the dance of the god. The obscene wooden symbol, gigantic, was unveiled and uplifted: then they howled their watchword with even less restraint. Foam on their lips, they raged, stimulated one another with lascivious gestures and groping hands, laughing and moaning; they poked the goads into one another's flesh and licked the blood from their limbs. But the dreamer was now with them, one of them, a slave of the foreign god. Yes, they were his own self as they flung themselves upon the animals, tearing and killing, swallowing scraps of flesh that were still smoking, while an unbridled coupling began on the trampled, mossy ground, as an offering to the god. And his soul tasted the lewdness and frenzy of extinction.

The afflicted man awoke from this dream enervated, shaken; powerless now, he belonged to the demon. No longer did he shun the other guests' observing glances; he did not care whether he was arousing their suspicions. Anyway, they were escaping, leaving; numerous cabanas were empty; there were many unoccupied tables in the dining room, and in the city a foreigner was only rarely to be seen. The truth seemed to have leaked out; despite the tenacious conspiracy of the interested parties, it seemed impossible to avert the panic any longer. But the woman with the pearl jewelry stayed on with her family, either because the rumors did not reach her or because she was too proud and unafraid to give in to them: Tadzio remained; and Aschenbach, in his naïveté, felt at times as if flight and death might remove all surrounding interference by living people, and he might be left alone on this island with the beautiful boy—yes, when, of a morning by the sea, his eyes rested heavily, irresponsibly, fixedly, on the desired one, when, at the close of day, he pursued him, shorn of dignity, through narrow streets where, unacknowledged, that foul death stalked, his monstrous wish seemed like a real hope to him and morality seemed to be null and void.

Like anyone in love, he wished to please his partner, and was bitterly worried that this might not be possible. He added youthful, cheerful details to his wardrobe, he wore precious stones and used perfumes, he spent a long time on his toilette several times a day and came to meals adorned, excited and tense. When he saw the sweet youngster who had stolen his heart, he was disgusted by his own aging body; the sight of his gray hair, of his pinched features, plunged him into shame and made him lose hope. He felt an urge to freshen up, to restore himself physically; he frequently visited the hotel barber.

Covered with the hairdressing gown, leaning back in the chair under the ministering hands of the chattering man, he was tortured as he looked at his reflection in the mirror.

"Gray," he said, with distorted mouth.

"A bit," the fellow replied. "And all because of a little negligence, an indifference to external things, which is understandable in important people, but is nevertheless not altogether praiseworthy, especially since it is just those people who should be free of prejudices about what is natural and what is artificial. If certain individuals' moral objection to the cosmetic art were to be logically extended to the care of their teeth, they would give quite a bit of offense. After all, we are only as old as our mind and heart feel, and in certain circumstances gray hair can be a greater untruth than the correction of it, which they disdain. In your case, Sir, you have a right to your natural hair color. Would you permit me to restore to you what is rightly yours?"

"How so?" asked Aschenbach.

Then the eloquent man rinsed his customer's hair in two different fluids, a clear one and a dark one, and it was as black as in his youth. Thereupon he formed it into soft waves with his curling iron, took a step backwards and surveyed the head he had been treating.

"All that's lacking now," he said, "is to freshen up the facial skin a little."

And like someone who hates to finish what he is doing, who is unable to satisfy himself, he proceeded from one treatment to another with a constantly renewed, animated officiousness. Aschenbach, resting comfortably, incapable of resistance, and in fact with hopes aroused by what was going on, saw in the mirror how his eyebrows were arching in a more well-defined and symmetrical style, how his eyes were growing longer, their brightness enhanced by a slight painting of the lids; looking farther down, he saw a lightly applied, gentle carmine appear where the skin had been brownish and leathery; he saw his lips, which had just been anemic, now pouting in a shade of raspberry; he saw the furrows in his cheeks and around his mouth, the wrinkles around his eyes, vanish beneath cream and the breath of youth — with beating heart, he caught sight of a youngster in his prime. The cosmetician was contented at last, and, in the way such people have, he thanked his customer with obsequious courtesy. "I just did my little bit to help," he said, putting a final touch to Aschenbach's outer man. "Now, Sir, you can fall in love without hesitation." The bewitched man left, dreamily happy, confused and fearful. His tie was red, his broad-brimmed straw hat sported a multicolored band.

A warm storm wind had sprung up; it rained only occasionally and sparsely, but the air was humid, dense and filled with the smell of decay. Fluttering, clapping and whirring sounds assailed his ears and, feverish beneath the rouge, he felt as if wind spirits of an evil breed were stirring about in space, monstrous birdlike creatures of the sea that rummage through the condemned man's meal, gnawing at it and befouling it with filth. For the sultriness took away his appetite, and he was haunted by the idea that his food had been poisoned by contagious matter.

One afternoon, on the trail of the beautiful boy, Aschenbach had penetrated deeply into the tangled lanes of the sick city. His sense of direction failing him, since the alleys, waterways, bridges and small squares in this labyrinth were all too much alike, and no longer sure even of the points of the compass, he was concerned above all not to lose sight of the ardently pursued image; and, forced to exercise a degrading caution, flattening himself against walls and taking cover behind the backs of people walking ahead of him, for some time he was unaware of the weariness and exhaustion that the emotion and never-ending tension had inflicted on his body and mind. Tadzio was walking behind his family — he usually let the governess and his nunlike sisters go ahead of him in narrow places — and, sauntering alone, he turned his head at times and sent a glance of his peculiarly hazy-gray eyes over his shoulder to make sure his lover was still following. He saw him, and did not give him away. Intoxicated by this knowledge, lured onward by these eyes, made a laughingstock by passion, the enamored man stealthily pursued his unsavory hopes — and finally found himself cheated of a sight of them after all. The Poles had crossed a bridge that had a short, high span; the height of its arch concealed them from their pursuer, and when he had stepped onto it in his turn, he could no longer find them. He looked for them in three directions, straight ahead and on both sides of the narrow, dirty quay, but in vain. Enervation and weakness finally forced him to give up the search.

His head was burning, his body was covered with sticky sweat, his neck was trembling; a thirst he could no longer endure tortured him; he looked around for any kind of refreshment he could find on the spot. In front of a little greengrocer's shop he bought some fruit, strawberries — overripe, soft merchandise — and ate some as he walked. A small, deserted square, which looked as if it had been placed under a curse, opened up before him; he recognized it, it was here that, weeks earlier, he had formulated the plan of escape that had come to nought. On the steps of the cistern, in the middle of the square, he sank down and leaned his head against its stone rim. It was quiet, grass grew between the paving stones, garbage was scattered around. Among the weather-beaten houses of varying heights around him was one that resembled a palazzo, with Gothic-arched windows, behind which dwelt the void, and small balconies adorned with lions. On the ground floor of another house was a pharmacy. From time to time, hot gusts of wind carried the smell of carbolic acid to him.

He sat there, the master, the artist who had attained dignity, the author of "A Miserable Man," who in such exemplarily pure form had renounced bohemianism and the murky depths, had abrogated his sympathy for the abyss and had vilified vileness; the man who had ascended the heights; the one who had overcome his learning and outgrown all irony, who had grown accustomed to the obligations imposed by the confidence of the masses; he whose fame was official, whose name had been ennobled and whose style boys were exhorted to take as a model — he sat there, his eyes closed; only occasionally did a mocking and embarrassed sidewise glance escape from beneath their lids and quickly conceal itself again; and his slack lips, cosmetically heightened, shaped isolated words out of the thoughts, the strange dream-logic, of his half-slumbering brain.

"For beauty, Phaedrus, take note! beauty alone is godlike and visible at the same time, and thus it is the path of the sensual man, young Phaedrus, the artist's path toward intellectuality. But do you believe, my dear boy, that anyone for whom the path to the intellect leads through the senses can ever attain wisdom and the true dignity of a man? Or do you believe instead (I leave the decision to you) that this is a path of dangerous charm, truly a path of error and sin, which necessarily leads one astray? For you must know that we poets cannot travel the path of beauty without Eros joining company with us and taking over the lead; yes, even though we may be heroes after our fashion and moral warriors, we are still like women because passion is what exalts us, and our longing must remain merely love — that is our pleasure and our shame. Now do you see that we poets cannot be wise or dignified? That we necessarily go astray, necessarily remain dissipated adventurers of the emotions? The master's pose of our style is a lie and folly, our fame and honorable status are a farce, the confidence the crowd has in us couldn't be more laughable, and education of the people and of youth by means of art is a risky enterprise that ought to be prohibited. For, how could a man be suitable as an educator when he is born with an incorrigible natural penchant for the abyss? We may deny the abyss and acquire dignity but, no matter how we try, it attracts us. Thus, we may perhaps renounce knowledge, which is a dissolvent; for knowledge, Phaedrus, has no dignity or severity; it knows, understands and forgives, without self-discipline or form; it sympathizes with the abyss, it *is* the abyss. Therefore we decidedly reject it, and henceforth our only concern will be for beauty — that is, for simplicity, greatness, a different kind of severity, the 'new naïveté,' and form. But form and naïveté, Phaedrus, lead to intoxication and desire, they may even lead a noble man to horrifying crimes of the passions, which his own beautiful severity rejects as being detestable; they lead to the abyss, they, too, lead to the abyss. They lead us poets there, I say, for we are unable to soar upward, we are only able to commit extravagances. And now I am going, Phaedrus; as for you, stay here; and only when you see me no more, depart in your turn."

A few days afterward, since Gustav von Aschenbach was feeling indisposed, he left the Hôtel des Bains at a later hour in the morning than usual. He was suffering from certain attacks of dizziness which were only partially physical, and which were accompanied by a violently increasing anxiety, a feeling of inescapability and hopelessness; and it was not clear whether that feeling related to the outside world or to his own existence. In the lounge he noticed a large quantity of luggage waiting to be carried out; he asked a doorman who it was that was leaving, and was given the name of that Polish noble family, which he had secretly expected to hear. He heard it with no alteration in his sunken features, but with that brief raising of the head with which one casually takes cognizance of something one had no need to know; and then he asked: "When?" The answer was: "After lunch." He nodded and walked toward the sea.

It was dreary there. Over the wide, level body of water that separated the beach from the first long sandbar, shuddering ripples ran from the near to the far distance. An autumnal mood, a feeling that it had outlived its time, seemed to weigh upon the once so colorfully animated, now almost deserted, pleasure ground, on which the sand was no longer kept clean. A camera, apparently without an owner, stood on its tripod by the edge of the sea, and the black cloth spread over it flapped in the chilly wind with a slapping sound.

Tadzio, with three or four playmates who were still left to him, was moving about on the right in front of his family's cabana, and Aschenbach, a blanket over his knees, resting in his reclining chair about halfway between the sea and the row of cabanas, was watching him once again. The game, which was unsupervised, because the women were probably busy with the preparations for departure, seemed to be disorganized and was getting out of hand. That stocky boy in the belted suit with black, pomaded hair, the one called "Jaschu," taunted and blinded by sand thrown in his face, forced Tadzio into a wrestling match that ended quickly with the fall of the beautiful, but weaker, boy. But, as if, at the hour of parting, the servile emotions of the inferior were transformed into cruel brutality and a desire to take revenge for a long period of slavery, even then the victor did not leave the underdog in peace, but, kneeling on his back, ground his face into the sand so persistently that Tadzio, already out of breath from the fight, was in danger of suffocating. His attempts to shake off his human burden were convulsive, at moments they stopped altogether and recurred only in the form of twitching. Horrified, Aschenbach wanted to leap up and save him, when the violent boy finally released his victim. Tadzio, very pale, raised himself partway and sat there motionless for several minutes, leaning on one arm, his hair tousled and his eyes growing dark. Then he raised himself to his feet and slowly walked away. They called to him, at first cheerfully, then in alarm and imploringly; he didn't listen. The blackhaired boy, who probably started to regret at once that he had gone too far, caught up with him and tried to make friends again. A gesture with one shoulder dismissed him. Tadzio walked down diagonally to the water. He was barefoot and was wearing his striped linen suit with the red bow.

At the edge of the water he lingered, with lowered head, drawing figures in the wet sand with the toes of one foot, and then entered the shallow water close to shore, which at its deepest point did not even wet his knees, walked farther out, pushing forward indolently, and reached the sandbar. There he stood for a moment, his face turned toward the horizon, and then he began to pace the long, narrow stretch of exposed ground, moving slowly toward the left. Separated from the mainland by wide waters, separated from his companions by a caprice of his pride, he walked with streaming hair, completely isolated and devoid of human ties, out there in the sea, in the wind, with limitless haze behind him. A few times he stopped to look into the distance. And suddenly, as if recalling something, as if through some impulse, he placed one hand on his hip, swiveled the upper part of his body in a beautiful contrapposto to the stance of his feet, and looked over his shoulder to the shore. The observer sat there as he had once sat when the gaze of those hazy-gray eyes, transmitted from that threshold, had first met his. His head, leaning on the back of the chair, had slowly followed the movements of the boy who was walking far out there; now it rose, as if to meet that gaze, and fell onto his chest, so that his eyes looked up from below, while his face took on the limp, intensely absorbed expression of deep slumber. But it seemed to him as if the pale, charming psychagogue out there were smiling to him, beckoning to him; as if he were raising his hand from his hip and pointing outward, floating before him into a realm of promise and immensity. And, as he had done so often, he set out to follow him.

Minutes went by before people hastened to the aid of the man who had slumped sideways in his chair. He was carried to his room. And, before that day was over, a respectfully shocked world received the news of his death.

A Word About the Translation

THE ORIGINAL German text of "Death in Venice" makes special demands on any translator. The author, a literary elitist and a master of German prose, not only used every grammatical resource of his language in a virtuoso fashion; he introduced many rare words, created paradoxical juxtapositions of terms, and indulged in very long, complicated sentences. The richness of his verbal imagination and the subtlety of his thought are everywhere in evidence. In many instances, a very literal translation reads like gibberish in English, and the translator is forced to resort to a paraphrase in order to convey the intended message. Thus, no two English translations, even of equal quality, will ever resemble each other closely. Unfortunately, there is also much latitude for divergences in basic quality.

The present translator is aware of the existence of five prior English versions: those by Kenneth Burke (1925; the very first), H. T. Lowe-Porter (1930), Erich J. Heller (1970), David Luke (1988) and Clayton Kolb (1993). The Heller and Kolb translations were not readily available, and have not been consulted.

Most of the Burke translation is serviceable and neatly expressed, but the work as a whole is vitiated by a large number of careless errors and hilarious misapprehensions, beginning in the very first sentence, in which Burke informs us that the year 19— threatened Europe with very bad *weather* (!).

The translation by Lowe-Porter, with which most older readers are familiar, has been severely but justly impugned by Luke, in the introduction to his own version, for its errors, omissions and undue transpositions. I would add that frequently, especially in the second half of the story, she tends to abridge the text sentence by sentence, offering a succulent extract instead of the full rich feast. Her elegant English prose makes her translation by far the most delightful and readable of the

63

three I have consulted, with numerous admirable verbal formulations — but at a great cost to completeness and a true representation of the original. She has taken a text as challenging to a German reader as Henry James can be to us, and reduced it to the cozy domesticity of, say, Somerset Maugham.

Luke's version, which advertises itself as an unsurpassable *ne plus ultra*, is indeed scrupulously accurate, its vocabulary almost always remarkably well chosen, but it is still the work of a mortal, not a god. One may find it a little stiff and stuffy, one may consider its verse equivalents of Mann's already "purple" hexametrizing as overdone; and there are some puzzling small omissions.* Nevertheless, I am pleased to state that, if all other versions were to disappear in some cataclysm or *Götterdämmerung*, the world would be most fortunate to have Luke's.

The present, brand-new, translation, which is scrupulously complete, tries to be as literal as possible while still preserving proper English (modern American). It also tries, wherever humanly possible, to preserve the comparative length of the original sentences and, within each long sentence, to transmit the informational quanta in the same general sequence as the original (that is, to keep the beginning at the beginning, the end at the end, and so on). Every attempt has been made to communicate to the reader of English the same impression of architectural stateliness or flickering nervousness that a German reader derives from threading his way through the labyrinthine sentences of the original. And the sharp contrast when a short, pungent sentence follows!

Although I sincerely hope that the present translation will afford pleasure to the reader, I confess that I see it as an analytic translation, or X-ray of the original text, rather than one that, for better or worse, creates a totally new synthesis, with gleaming epidermis, out of the component parts. With very rare exceptions, mentioned in the Commentary, I have used English equivalents (rather than introducing Italian or other names and phrases) wherever Mann chose to keep to German; I am convinced that there isn't a single accidental word in the entire German original.

---

* In the first chapter alone, there are three small omissions of which I find at least the first and third irritating: (1) Luke fails to say that the strange man's shirt was a sport shirt (this links up motivically with the street musician's sport shirt in the last chapter); (2) he doesn't say that the strange man's vantage point in the portico of the mortuary chapel was "elevating" as well as "elevated" (perhaps not so important); and (3) he doesn't include the phrase indicating that the spontaneity by which an author gives pleasure to his readers can only be achieved if he himself is deriving pleasure from the act of composition.

Commentary

THE YEAR

ALTHOUGH there was hardly a year in the decade and a half before the First World War that didn't threaten the security of Europe, it is clear from other sources that Mann's "19—" refers to 1911. Thus the specific crisis involved is the Second Moroccan Affair, in which Germany sent a warship to the Mediterranean in response to French occupation of the cities of Fez and Rabat.

THE MODELS FOR GUSTAV VON ASCHENBACH

Mahler. Aschenbach's first name and physical characteristics were borrowed from the Austrian composer, who died (in Vienna, not Venice; Wagner had died in Venice) in May 1911 while Mann was vacationing on Brioni. Mann had met Mahler briefly in September 1910 when the composer visited Munich to conduct the world premiere of his Eighth Symphony. Mann stated afterward that Mahler was the first truly great man he had yet personally encountered. Aschenbach has nothing else to do with Mahler in particular or composers in general, except that his maternal grandfather was a Bohemian conductor, like Mahler.

Hauptmann. There are a few traits of the playwright and novelist Gerhart Hauptmann in Aschenbach's makeup. Hauptmann was about the same age at the time, and was widely considered the dean of living German writers. He was of Silesian birth (though born in Ober-Salzbrunn, not in Liegnitz, the "L." of the story), and in the years just preceding 1911 he had turned away from his early Naturalism and championing of the proletariat toward a Greek-tinged mythological vitalism. And yet, without the shadow of a doubt, Aschenbach is mostly Mann.

Mann. Mann himself lived in Munich, possessed a villa in the Bavarian

Alps (at Bad Tölz, birthplace of the eminent physician/novelist Hans Carossa), had a foreign mother who brought creative blood into a bourgeois family, shared Aschenbach's methodical working habits and had reached a kind of impasse in his writing. The astute critic's characterization of Aschenbach's weakling heroes had been made, word for word, about Mann's protagonists. Even stranger to relate, all four books cited in the second chapter as the chief works of Aschenbach's maturity, with the very same titles, had been planned and then abandoned by Mann himself! (The title of the novel *Maya* — *Maja* in German, *māyā* in Sanskrit — means "illusion"; in Hindu and Buddhist philosophy it connotes man's sensory belief in the reality of the three-dimensional multiplicity that surrounds him, cloaking the true transcendent oneness of the universe; Schopenhauer had used the term.) Mann also really wrote an elegant brief essay on the Lido beach, just as Aschenbach does (Mann's subject: Wagner). For, indeed, the vacation described in the story, Brioni in May and Venice in June, was taken in 1911 by Mann, who derived numerous incidents from his actual experiences, not least of which was his encounter with a real-life Tadzio. Naturally, Mann preserved his decorum and his wits, or we would never have had the story. And the cholera was in Palermo, not Venice. (Nor was Mann ever made a nobleman by a German ruler.)*

ASCHENBACH'S CAREER

The second chapter of the story makes the greatest demands on everyone. Although it seems almost intrusive, and may tempt some readers to skip it, it is an integral and essential component of the narrative. The trouble is that here Mann seems to be writing for his immediate contemporaries — in fact, for that handful among them who avidly followed every literary trend and were thoroughly familiar with the current professional jargon of book reviews and avant-garde esthetics. A brief, "chronological" abstract of Aschenbach's career may be helpful: A nobody from the provinces, he made a mark early by his great powers of expression. At first he floundered because his thirst for fame was still stronger than his individual voice or viewpoint. Soon he became popular in two ways: for the average, naive reader, his stories were picturesque and beautiful; for the emancipated youth of the nation — dissatisfied with the rampant industrialism, capitalism, militarism and imperialism, and desperately seeking spiritual leaders among creative artists — he was an *enfant terrible*, revealing the secrets of the artistic life and

---

* Prior to the First World War, within the German Empire there were still several semiautonomous rulers of varying rank, chief of whom was the King of Bavaria.

casting doubts on its sanctity. Later, in constant response to new trends, he ceased to pay homage to the scientific, psychologically oriented naturalism and realism of the outgoing generation and came down strongly in favor of both the emotional side of man's nature and a sanctimonious morality. His heroes, somewhat like himself, did not possess the initial advantages of position, wealth or good looks, but made their way in the world by their brains and their ardent sense of purpose. As Aschenbach grew even older and even more successful, he polished his style till it shone and became established as a master of prose style, fit for schoolbooks.

THE TOPOGRAPHY

The circumstantial exactness of the locales, familiar to Mann's readers, makes the events of the story even more uncanny.

Munich. The Prinzregentenstrasse, an elegant park, museum and embassy thoroughfare in the center of the city, runs from the royal palace gardens eastward to the river Isar (and beyond). Immediately to the north of the westernmost part of the street is the large park known as the English Garden (Englischer Garten), within which was located the Aumeister, a forester's house with a restaurant. The "meadow" in which Aschenbach continues his walk (still northward although he is supposed to be turning homeward) is the Hirschau, alongside which the Northern Cemetery (Nördlicher Friedhof) is situated. The Byzantine-style mortuary chapel was the work of the architect Hans Grässel, built in 1896–99. The cemetery was the terminus of a trolley line. Föhring is a suburb across the Isar. Schwabing is a section of town (noted at the time as an artists' colony) west of the English Garden and north of the city center.

Between Munich and Venice. Trieste (belonging to Italy since 1918) and Pola (now Pula; on the Istrian peninsula, now Istra; part of Yugoslavia after the First World War) were still in the Austro-Hungarian Empire at the time of the story; hence, the Austrian guests at the resort island offshore from Pola (not named by Mann, it is Brioni).

Venice. The ship crossing the northern Adriatic from Pola first passes the Lido (at first, Mann identifies it merely as "the island of sea-baths"). The Lido is one of a north–south archipelago of long, narrow islands forming a natural breakwater between the Adriatic (the beach is on the side facing the open sea) and the Venetian Lagoon. Just north of it is the strait or channel called the Porto di Lido (in the story, "the narrow strait that is named after it [the Lido]"). The Public Gardens (Giardini Pubblici), where the bersaglieri were drilling (light infantrymen with picturesque uniforms), are at the southeastern tip of the city's main island. The ship continues into the Canale di San Marco and approaches the very heart of the city, stopping opposite St. Mark's Square (Piazza di San Marco) and the adjoining Piazzetta, with its two freestanding columns topped by statues (a lion on one and St. Theodore, or Todaro, on the other). The position of the ship affords views of the Bridge of Sighs (Ponte dei Sospiri), the Doges' Palace (Palazzo Ducale) and St. Mark's Cathedral (Basilica di San Marco) behind it, the vista ending at the Clock Tower (Torre dell'Orologio), which is built over an archway leading into the Merceria, the main shopping street.

Later, when Aschenbach reluctantly attempts to flee, he continues west of the San Marco complex, following the sinuous Grand Canal (Canal Grande) under the Rialto Bridge (Ponte di Rialto) for its full length up to the Railroad Station (Stazione Ferroviaria). In the English travel agent's description of the epidemic, mention is made of the Ospedale Civile ("Civico" in Mann's text, but in this case I have made the tacit correction), in the northeastern part of the main island, near the very long quay known as the Fondamente Nuove, from which boats leave for the cemetery island of San Michele.

On the Lido, where most of the story takes place, the two hotels mentioned really existed, although the Excelsior was actually the Excelsior Palace, and Mann unfailingly refers to the hotel where Aschenbach stays in German words meaning "Sea-Bath Hotel"; in this case, to avoid awkwardness and to help indicate how real much of the story was, I have used its actual (French) designation, the Hôtel (with circumflex, please!) des Bains.

THE POLISH NAMES

Aschenbach was probably able to recollect some Polish because he came from Silesia, a Slavic (later, specifically Polish) region that his German ancestors conquered (see the reference to this in the fifth paragraph of the second chapter). Tadzio is a nickname for Tadeusz (Thaddeus); Tadziu is the vocative case of Tadzio. (Polish is one of the languages possessing this special case in the declension of nouns — including proper names — used when directly addressing, or calling to, a person or thing.) To preserve Mann's mystique of u-sounds, I have kept the name of Tadzio's friend in the very form that he used, "Jaschu" (to be pronounced "Yah'shoo"), always keeping it in quotation marks. Despite some earlier translations and even some learned commentaries, this is not a form of Jascha, which is the Russian nickname for Yakov (Jacob), but is actually Jasiu, the Polish vocative of Jaś (Johnny), the nickname for Jan (John). The first name of the real-life Tadzio, who identified himself long after the story appeared, was Władysław, (Ladislaus); nickname, Władzio, with vocative Władziu. The real first name of his stocky, dark-haired friend was Janek.

LEITMOTIFS AND SYMBOLISM: GENERAL REMARKS

Throughout his career, Mann made use of leitmotifs (like the musical ones in Wagner's operas): words and phrases that characterize a person, situation or idea and recur periodically to identify the new situation with preceding ones (naturally, it is only after a recurrence that one can recognize the earlier occurrence as a motif). Thus his stories need to be read very closely and attentively. In addition, his characters and situations are often emblematic or symbolic of some underlying thought. In "Death in Venice" — partly in response to literary trends of the day — he was for the first time employing a largely mythological symbolism, based in this case chiefly on ancient Greek mythology. To trace through the whole story all, or even a large number, of the leitmotifs and symbols occurring in "Death in Venice" would be a herculean task and would spoil the reader's own enjoyment. Instead, I have selected the three following examples, in order of increasing subtlety:

(1) It is fairly obvious that there is a strong connection between the strange man in Munich, the superannuated dandy from Pola, the surly gondolier and the leader of the street musicians, whom I shall here refer to as A, B, C and D, respectively. None of them "belong" in their surroundings: A isn't Bavarian, B isn't young, C isn't Italian and D isn't Venetian. A, C and D all have red hair and death's-heads (very little in the way of nose and lips). All have something striking about their hats (the material, the rakish angle, etc.); A and D both wear sport shirts; and so on. B's rouge and red tie prefigure Aschenbach's subsequent beauty treatment. They are all symbols of decay and death, and to varying degrees they all represent the Dionysian principle (see the following section) in their foreignness and unruliness.

(2) The word "tiger" appears three times in the story. When Aschenbach first feels the urge to travel, he sees in his imagination a landscape like that of the Ganges delta; the climax of this vision is the frightening epiphany of a tiger in the thicket. When he calms down and makes realistic travel plans, he decides he need not go "all the way to the tigers." This is high irony, for eventually the tigers come to him, in the form of cholera: the third mention of tigers is in the description of the worldwide spread of the disease from the Ganges delta. All this ties in with the Dionysian principle as well, because (in the version of the myth that Mann chiefly adheres to) Dionysus came to Greece from India, and tigers drew his chariot. (Moreover, the intricate waterways of Venice are like the tangled channels of the Ganges delta.)

(3) In the first chapter, a clever conversationalist compares Aschenbach's life-style of hard work to a tightly clenched fist that never opens into a loosely dangling hand. Yet, at the very close of both the third and fourth

chapters, under the influence of his infatuation for Tadzio, his arms and hands hang loosely.

THE CLASSICAL REFERENCES

General Remarks. Why did Mann choose Greek mythology and philosophy as the allover symbolic frame of reference for the story? None of Aschenbach's books are about the ancient world, and Venice first attained importance only in Byzantine and medieval times. The probable answer is threefold: (1) Aschenbach is by this time a "classic writer" (and in German literary history, classicism is strongly associated with Greco-Roman influence), who is said to represent "the European spirit" (and in the view of many, ancient Greece is the fountainhead of that spirit); also, in the story he is made to recollect what he learned about Greece in school. (2) The Italian surroundings reminded Mann of the ancient high civilizations of Europe, which were inseparable from the Mediterranean. (3) Since his story was about a man's passion for a boy, Mann's thoughts were irresistibly drawn to the European culture in which *paiderastía* was an accepted social practice, extensively reflected in literature.

Although Mann strove to appear as a paragon of erudition, archival evidence indicates that it was only after deciding to use Greek mythology and philosophy that he boned up on it, referring to traceable German-language translations and compendia. At any rate, it is important to note that his classicism is seen through the prism of Schopenhauer, Wagner and Nietzsche.

Absolutely essential to one's understanding of the story is the distinction Nietzsche draws in *Die Geburt der Tragödie* (The Birth of Tragedy) between two polar strands of the Greek religious and creative experience: the Apollonian strand, with the sun god Apollo standing for the bright, dignified side of human nature and endeavor (optimism, rationalism, civic pride, noble forms of worship — reflected in such literary forms as the Homeric epics and Socratic philosophy), and the Dionysian strand, with the wine god Dionysus standing for the dark, rebellious recesses of the soul ("intoxication," antisocial dominance of the emotions, savage chthonic religion — reflected in the heady art of music and the Athenian tragic drama, which was originally a musical form). Aschenbach has developed into a thorough, official Apollonian; his "natural" enemy is Dionysus the dissolver, symbolized in the story by the four grotesque characters who prophetically cross his path.

The following part of the commentary is devoted to individual explanations of the classical references in the story, in the order of their appearance.

Page 1: *Motus animi continuus* (a constant agitation of the mind). The classical references begin, unobtrusively enough, in the first paragraph with an alleged quotation from Cicero. The eminent Mann editor T. J. Reed has reported that this phrase is nowhere to be found in Cicero's writings, but was borrowed by Mann from a passage in Flaubert's published correspondence.

Page 2: The stranger's broad, straight-rimmed hat has been compared with the *pétasos* worn by the god Hermes as summoner of the souls of the newly dead; and his iron-tipped stick has been compared with the *thýrsos*, the wand carried by devotees of Dionysus.

Page 12: The goateed man in the inner cabin of the Pola ship has been compared with a satyr, one of the half-human, half-goat followers of Dionysus. In his obvious concern to convince Aschenbach of the attractions of Venice, he is another one of the mysterious figures who seal the writer's fate. The rowdy clerks on the main deck have been compared with noisy Dionysian revelers.

Page 16: The mysterious gondolier, who disappears as abruptly as the stranger in Munich, is not only a Dionysus figure and a death figure; as a surly boatman, he also resembles Charon, who ferries the souls of the newly dead across the river Styx in the underworld. His laconic "You will pay" is the most ominous bit of irony in the story. It is amusing to note that, in the 1913 Baedeker for Northern Italy, tourists are warned: "for visits to distant islands only gondolas with numbers should be engaged"; obviously, unlicensed gondoliers were a fact of life!

Page 18: Aides: a poetic form of Hades, god of the underworld.

Page 18: The boatload of importunate musicians also represents Dionysus' noisy crew.

Page 20: At his very first appearance (and repeatedly thereafter) Tadzio is associated with Greek statues, particularly the series depicting a seated boy extracting a thorn from his foot. Later, his arms are described as "chiseled." His untrammeled (though instinctively graceful) "Greek" behavior is contrasted to the repressed medievalism of his sisters.

Page 23: "Phaeacian" (I have willfully added "happy-go-lucky" to the text so that readers who don't remember every detail of their Homer will not be stopped dead in their tracks). The reference is to the *Odyssey*, in which Odysseus washes up on the island of the Phaeacians, who live for pleasure since their land is fertile and they have no troublesome neighbors. The quoted line (corresponding to VIII, 249 of the *Odyssey*) is translated here literally from the German line that Mann cites (from the 1781 translation by the poet Johann Heinrich Voss). My translation of the full two-verse sentence from the Greek (the king of the Phaeacians is speaking) would be: "Always to us the banquet is dear, and the cithern and dances,/Raiment frequently changed, and the steaming bath and the bedroom."

Page 23: Eros is the Greek god of love, usually depicted as a handsome youth. Parian marble, desirable statuary stone, came from the Aegean island of Paros.

Page 26: The advice to Critobulus, the son of his devoted pupil Crito, was given humorously by Socrates after Critobulus kissed the son of the playboy/adventurer Alcibiades (who had been a favorite of Socrates). This advice is reported by Socrates' pupil Xenophon in his *Memorabilia* (I, 3).

Page 33: The opening of the fourth chapter, contrasting in tone and style with all that has come before, is a conscious piece of "fine writing" of which Mann was quite proud. His prose here tends to become metrical, even falling into perfect dactylic hexameter, the meter of Homer (my translation suggests this quietly here and there). And, indeed, this is like a Homeric hymn to the sun god Apollo. At this point in the story Aschenbach, the professed Apollonian, is in practically complete possession of himself and enjoying himself no end on the Lido. His appreciation of Tadzio, which is not yet out of bounds, exhilarates and uplifts him in a legitimately lyrical ecstasy. *Póntos* = "sea" in Greek.

Page 36 (the two paragraphs beginning with "Icon and mirror!"): The concept of the sun redirecting us from the intellectual to the sensory plane is derived from Plutarch's treatise *Erotikos*. The concept of mental elevation from a beautiful object to the external idea of Beauty itself is thoroughly in line with Plato's teachings; in fact, Aschenbach's "sin," as both man and artist, is that he was ultimately satisfied with Tadzio's body itself and did not use it as a mere springboard for loftier elucubrations. In this passage, I have boldly translated as "anamnesis" a German word that means merely "recollection"; I am convinced that in this context it refers to Plato's theory (derived from Pythagoras and expounded in the dialogue *Meno* and elsewhere) that, in the process of learning, the soul recalls data from prior existences; so that, for instance, a child prodigy has inherited the soul of a great scholar. The word "enthusiasm" in this passage (and a few other places) should be understood etymologically as *en-theos-iasmos*, the state in which a god is inside a person, possessing him.

The description of the sacred grove in which Socrates instructs Phaedrus is based closely on Plato's own text near the beginning of the dialogue *Phaedrus*; Achelous is a river god. But some of the erotically tinged, sophistical philosophy that follows is derived from the dialogue *Symposium*.

Semele, the mortal daughter of a king of Thebes in Greece, loved by Zeus, king of the gods, was tricked by the goddess Hera, Zeus's jealous spouse, into requesting that Zeus visit her bed not in the disguise of a mortal but in all his divine glory; when he was compelled to do so, she burned up. Zeus rubbed her ashes into his thigh, from which Dionysus was later born. Mann has done something dangerous here: the image of Semele burning because of love is apt and delightful, but it is part of an older myth about the origin of Dionysus that locates this event right in Greece, although the rest of the story is inextricably connected with the later rival myth of that god's origins in India. To be sure, this later myth, hinted at in Euripides' play *Bacchae* and extensively developed after the Asiatic conquests of Alexander the Great, attempts to reconcile the stories by claiming that Dionysus made a far-flung raid from Greece into India, and was merely returning from there.

Page 37: Mann derived Eros' love of idleness (at second hand) from Plutarch's *Erotikos*, where it appears as a citation from a lost play of Euripides.

Page 38: It was Zeus's attendant eagle that bore the beautiful Trojan shepherd boy Ganymede up to heaven for his master's pleasure. Ganymede later waited on the gods' table. Here, Kenneth Burke's translation has the eagle carry off a stag (*Hirt* mistaken for *Hirsch*)!!

Page 39: The comparison with a gamecock is, once again, from Plutarch's *Erotikos*.

Page 40: Eos, goddess of dawn, arises daily from the bed she shares with her husband Tithonus, who was given the gift of immortality but not that of eternal youth. Thus she is on the prowl; three of her conquests are named in the paragraph. Her brother is, of course, Apollo, driving the sun chariot.

Page 40: Poseidon, god of the sea, was ritually associated with horses and bulls. Although it is not the true explanation of this association, Mann seems here to be equating the horses with the waves and the bulls with the roar of the sea. "Panic life" refers to the nature god Pan, a licentious hybrid of man and goat. Hyacinth was a beautiful boy loved by both Apollo, who "forgot his oracle, his bow and his cithara," and the wind god Zephyrus, who killed the boy with a discus out of jealousy. The dying boy was metamorphosed into the flower that bears his name.

Page 42: Another young beauty who became a flower was Narcissus; in love with his own good looks, he drowned trying to mate with his reflection in a pool.

Page 46: "The eros that had seized hold of him" is, of course, the homoerotic variety.

Page 47: The street singers are another manifestation of Dionysus' wild, unrespectable retinue, and their chief is one of the leading Dionysus/Death figures in the story. His mockery is like that of Death in old pictorial sequences of the Dance of Death, which has echoes in such different literary works as Poe's "The Masque of the Red Death" and Leroux's *The Phantom of the Opera*.

Page 48: The Greeks associated pomegranates both with fertility and with death; Persephone, the abducted spouse of Hades, could no longer return to the upper world of the living after eating a pomegranate.

Page 55: Aschenbach's dream is the antithesis of the sunny Apollonian idyll that opened the fourth chapter. Here Dionysus irrupts horribly into his world as a foreign conqueror, followed by his raving Satyrs and Maenads (male and female devotees, respectively), and forces a complete capitulation. The Dionysiac wild vocalic call is associated in Aschenbach's mind with the shouts of "Tadziu" he has heard on the beach.

Page 58: The "wind spirits . . . birdlike creatures" are the Harpies, who in the legend of the Argonauts come to befoul every meal of the seer Phineus, by the Black Sea, as punishment for offenses against the gods.

Page 62: Aschenbach's final vision of Tadzio is as a *psỹkhagōgós*, or *psỹkhopompós*, one who leads the souls of the newly dead to the world beyond — a role usually assigned to the god Hermes.

MISCELLANEOUS

Page 6: Schiller's disquisition is the long essay *Über naive und sentimentalische Dichtung* (1795), often considered the incomparable pinnacle of German esthetic thought.

Page 8: Saint Sebastian, said to have been martyred in the late third century for his Christian activism, is usually depicted in art as a handsome young man with an expression of fortitude or bliss, even though he is being riddled with arrows.

Page 14: The poet "who had in the past seen the domes" was August von Platen (1796–1835), a notorious homosexual.

Page 16: "Au revoir, excusez . . . bonjour" is French for "Good-bye, excuse us . . . good day."

Page 19: The translation retains the German (and European, in general) way of counting storeys. What Americans often call "the first floor" is "the ground floor"; what they call "the second floor" is "the first floor"; and so on.

Page 32: "Pas de chance, monsieur": "Hard luck, Sir!"

how to start a home-based

Children's Birthday Party Business

Amy Jean Peters

Guilford, Connecticut

BLANDING LIBRARY
REHOBOTH, MA 0276

To buy books in quantity for corporate use
or incentives, call **(800) 962–0973**
or e-mail **premiums@GlobePequot.com**.

Copyright © 2009 by Morris Book Publishing, LLC

ALL RIGHTS RESERVED. No part of this book may be reproduced or transmitted in any form by
any means, electronic or mechanical, including photocopying and recording, or by any information storage and retrieval system, except as may be expressly permitted in writing from the
publisher. Requests for permission should be addressed to The Globe Pequot Press, Attn: Rights
and Permissions Department, P.O. Box 480, Guilford, CT 06437.

Library of Congress Cataloging-in-Publication Data
Peters, Amy Jean.
 How to start a home-based children's birthday party business / Amy Jean Peters.
   p. cm.
 Includes bibliographical references.
 ISBN 978-0-7627-4938-6
1. Children's parties—Planning. 2. Birthday parties—Planning. 3. Home-based businesses—
Management. 4. Consulting firms—Management. 5. New business enterprises—Management.
I. Title. II. Title: Home-based children's birthday party business. III. Title: Children's birthday party
business. IV. Title: Birthday party business.

GV1205.P48 2009
793.2'10681—dc22

                                                                            2008039475

Printed in the United States of America
10 9 8 7 6 5 4 3 2 1

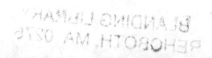
BLANDING LIBRARY
REHOBOTH, MA 02769

For Chet and Max, whose birthdays inspire.

"I think I can, I think I can."

—*The Little Engine that Could*

Contents

Acknowledgments

Thank you to the many folks who lent a hand in the creation of this book, including Laura Lenahan, Leslie Bullock, Lili Foggle, Heather Howard, Michelle Kaufman, Darlene LaFontaine, Nancy Lavin, and Shannon Ludwin. And, of course, thanks always to my three guys, Peter, Max, and Chet Sims.

Introduction

"I used to have home parties, but never again. I always hire someone to plan and run my children's parties," says Darlene LaFontaine, a very capable mother of three. Very capable, yet she finds herself flummoxed when it comes to even the thought of planning her children's birthday parties. I began weighing the idea of starting my own birthday party planning business as I heard this sentiment echoed again and again. Parents, for varied reasons, were finding it more and more challenging to plan and hold successful home birthday parties. Citing everything from wear and tear on their homes, to inability to provide engaging activities, to the expense of do-it-yourself parties, parents conveyed feelings of frustration when planning and holding home-based birthday parties without help.

So, six years ago, I donned my birthday party hat, hung out my shingle, rolled up my sleeves, and went to work planning children's birthday parties. Ever since, it has been a whirlwind of excitement. I've planned hundreds of successful parties, for children of all ages from toddlers to teens. These parties have ranged from simple, at-home affairs for a handful of children bobbing for apples and painting watercolors to over-the-top events for dozens with elaborate entertainment for the birthday child and friends as well as for the adults. All have presented their unique challenges and all have brought their own unique rewards. It is a colorful, always evolving field that continues to grow and develop at a brisk clip.

It Is a dynamic field that I've found to be somewhat impervious to economic downturns. In fact, from a $250,000 fete for a seven-year-old Florida girl, complete with helicopter rides, to $100,000 first birthday parties as reported in the *New York Times*, this era is fast proving to be the gilded age of children's birthday parties. It has become the norm in many geographic areas for the cost of children's birthday parties to average between $200 and $400. Likewise, there is a certain "keeping up with the Joneses" attitude many parents share when it comes to planning their child's birthday celebration. If the next door neighbor had a pony, then perhaps their child will have two ponies!

And, like LaFontaine, more and more these parents are turning to event consultants to plan their children's birthday celebrations, making this the ideal time for you to think about hanging out your shingle, too.

The ideal candidate for a home-based birthday party business is a person who enjoys working with children and is enthusiastic, energetic, and organized. The ideal candidate needn't worry about putting on a clown nose or pulling a fluffy white rabbit out of a hat. Rather, organization is the key to creating a successful business.

It is possible to start a healthy home-based children's birthday party business with a shoestring investment. Within months, a children's birthday party planner can turn a profit. I was able to develop my business on a relatively small budget and found myself in the black almost immediately after opening my doors for business and planning my first event.

From soup to party nuts, this guide outlines in friendly, accessible language everything you will need to know to start your own party planning business, including creating a savvy business plan, sourcing supplies, designing a unique and engaging logo, creating positive word of mouth, holding a dynamite first event, producing a user-friendly Web site, designing an ideal home office, and more.

Back to Darlene LaFontaine. The straw that broke the camel's back and led her to hire event planners for her children's birthday parties?

"My last at-home party was a disaster. I thought I had every base covered when I had eleven boys over. We organized a football game in the yard. Then it was time to come in for cake and when they trooped into the house all I could smell was dog doo as they ran through the house and tracked it everywhere, through the upstairs and down to the basement for the games I had set up there. This, of course, was my worst nightmare—despite my efforts of casing the yard before the party. Worse yet, we didn't even have a dog then! I've never looked back. Every year since, I've hired children's birthday party planners to coordinate my kids' parties. Every party has been a success and, honestly, I've spent less than I did when I planned them myself."

Read on to learn more about planning children's birthday parties and to discover everything you need to know to start working in this rewarding field.

Happy Birthday Party Business to You!

Why Now Is the Moment

Blow out the candles and make a wish! If your wish is to become a children's birthday party planner, the timing couldn't be better. The children's birthday party business is booming and there are virtually unlimited possibilities for organized, enthusiastic, creative individuals to create a lucrative niche in this exciting field.

A quick Internet search reveals the energy in this area. There are more than 850,000 children's birthday party blogs, filled with discussions about the what's, where's, when's, why's, who's and how's of planning a successful event. In fact, there are more than 300,000 blogs directly addressing first birthdays and how best to celebrate them. In the majority of these blogs, parents are looking for help in planning their child's event. You are the help they are looking for!

Likewise, MTV's *My Super Sweet 16* has been a phenomenal hit, focusing viewers' eyes on over-the-top teen birthday celebrations, including parties on the famed *Queen Mary*, docked off of California's perennially sunny coast, and swank soirees held at the nation's Rock and Roll Hall of Fame in Cleveland. For these celebrants, no gift is too grand—even a Porsche isn't considered over the top!

Top Five Reasons People Hire a Party Planner

As my business has developed, I have listened to and tracked the primary reasons parents hire me to plan their children's birthday celebrations. As your business develops, you will want to keep your ears open as well so you can craft your business to meet the needs of the parents in your area.

1. *Freedom to Enjoy the Party*

   This is often the single most important reason parents turn to event planners: They don't want to miss out on the party. Parents who plan and organize their own parties are often so busy scurrying about while they organize games, cook pizza, and slice cake that they miss out on their child's excitement and joy at being the star of the day. Hiring a party planner enables the parents to interact and enjoy the day and the event.

2. *Planner's Expertise*

   This may seem self-evident. Of course, parents depend on your expertise, but it is a point that can be so obvious as to be obscured. Parents are paying for your expertise and the bar will be higher than that of a parent-run, home-based birthday party. You must be organized and detail-oriented. As a party planner, you will know how to pace the party, how to most efficiently plan activities and serve food, how to handle any meltdown situations, and more. Parents will rely on you for this.

3. *Not in My Backyard*

   Many parents do not want to have their children's birthday parties in their homes or yards. Parents often do not want the mess, fuss, and clean-up involved with holding children's events at home.

4. *Not Enough Hours in the Day*

   We live in a busy world and many parents are too busy to plan a children's birthday party. Even a simple, at-home party can involve hours and hours of work—buying and sending out invitations, picking up or baking a cake, creating games and activities, selecting decorations, and filling goody bags. It can be daunting. As your business takes flight, you will be able to do these activities with your hands—practically—behind your back.

5. *Party Insurance*

   This is ultimately why anyone chooses an event planner. You are, in essence, an assurance that the event will be successful in every way. Parents count on you to plan an engaging, well-engineered event. This can be intimidating as you start out, but also exciting. It is a thrill to pull off a successful event, one at which parents and children leave with smiles on their faces.

Notes from the Field

Ask an established party planner if you can observe or, better yet, help at one of her events. Choose a planner who will not be in direct competition with the business you are planning to create—you don't want her to think that you are stealing any proprietary information! Plan to arrive in time to watch or assist with setup and stay through clean-up. This is an ideal way to help gauge your compatibility with the characteristics needed to be a top-notch party planner. By helping at an event, you will see first-hand the high level of energy needed to produce a successful event. You'll also experience the pace of a typical party—fast! From the first guest's arrival to the distribution of the much-clamored-for goody bags, successful kids' birthday parties move along at a quick and energetic clip.

More and more, busy parents in dual-income households are turning to professional birthday party planners to create the perfect birthday events for their children. From yoga sessions to sushi-making workshops, children's birthday events run the gamut.

Parents are willing to pay for this expertise with tabs for children's parties commonly running upwards of $500. In fact, mega-retailers like FAO Schwartz are able to command tens of thousands of dollars for a single party! Greeting card giant Hallmark estimates that parents spend $600 million each year on children's birthday cards, gift wrap, and party ware. This is an apt indicator of the health of the children's birthday party market.

Birthday Party Traditions from around the Globe

As you develop your birthday party business, you will want to consider traditions of other countries. If you live in an area with a large immigrant population, it is particularly important to consider their customs and to incorporate these beloved customs into the day's special events.

Some customs brought to us by other countries have become part of our traditional birthday celebrations, as well. For instance, many birthday children in this country ask for colorful and festive piñatas at their parties. This tradition came to us from our neighbor to the south, Mexico.

Key Characteristics of a Children's Party Planner

Consider these important characteristics of a successful children's party planner. Then answer yes or no to each of the questions posed in the list.

- *Are you organized? Yes or No*

  This, perhaps, is the most important attribute. Pulling off a successful party is not a rabbit-out-of-a-hat magic trick. A successful, engaging event means careful, thoughtful organization. From addressing and mailing the invitations to providing matches to light the birthday cake, this job requires thorough organization.

- *Do you pay attention to every last detail, no matter how small? Yes or No*

  This key characteristic dovetails with organization. An otherwise successful event could be sabotaged if the event planner forgets to pack the princess-themed tablecloth. Parents are paying for your special care.

- *When the going gets tough, are you able to maintain a smile? Yes or No*

  Remember, you will be working with children. Even if the birthday child is crying (and this will happen), you will need to maintain a positive attitude. Your smile projects a positive energy. When the unexpected happens at a child's party, remember to turn any frown upside down and keep on smiling.

- *Are you flexible? Yes or No*

  This is a vital component for creating a successful birthday party business. Perhaps you've planned a party for ten but then—surprise!—fifteen children arrive for the event (this will happen, too!). You need to keep your virtual toolbox at the ready and be equipped for these situations. Maybe your caterer doesn't arrive or the chocolate ice cream cake turns out to be vanilla. Be flexible and keep smiling.

- *Are you good with children? Yes or No*

  Do you really like being around children? Children with their wonderful passions and enthusiasms can also be unpredictable. The child who couldn't live without a pony party may decide, on the day of the party, to turn up her nose at the ponies. You will need to help reignite her enthusiasm. Children's birthday parties are often noisy and move at a pace different from that of adult parties. Are you comfortable being alone with children?

■ *Are you self-motivated? Yes or No*

As with all home-based businesses, self-motivation is essential. You won't have a boss calling to prompt you to print business cards and to distribute brochures. Motivation falls squarely on your own two shoulders.

■ *Do you have a high energy level? Yes or No*

Make no mistake about it. Your energy level will in large part dictate the energy level of the children's party. A dour, lackluster event planner leads to low energy at the party. Remember that smile. Likewise, you will need this high energy level to ensure successful marketing efforts for your growing business.

■ *Are you a good listener? Yes or No*

Successful event planners know how to listen—and, in some instances, to listen between the lines. What is your client really looking for? Be sensitive to your clients' words and thoughts.

■ *Do you know how to juggle? Yes or No*

Not literally—you don't need to run away with the circus. Rather, you may be called upon to focus on more than one task at a time. During the party, for instance, you may need to supervise the serving of pizza while ensuring that who gave what gift is being recorded as each is being opened.

■ *Are you an enthusiastic salesperson? Yes or No*

Part of your work as a successful party planner will be to sell your business and your ideas. Party planners who rise to the top of their field are confident in their planning abilities and willing to talk up their products and their services. Party planners need to network and solicit business, selling clients on their creativity and energy.

■ *Are you creative? Yes or No*

Successful event planners are able to "think outside the box." This ability ensures high-energy, unique events and also allows for creative problem solving, an absolutely essential tool in the event-planning business.

Birthday celebrations first originated hundreds of years ago in Germany. We can also credit the Germans with our tradition of blowing out the birthday candles before making a wish. German birthday celebrations continue today and are called *kinderfeste*. "Kinder" means child and "feste" means party or festival. Since these first kinderfeste hundreds of years ago, many other countries have adopted different customs to celebrate children's birthdays. They include:

- *Argentina*. Unlike the U.S. custom of a sweet sixteen, Argentina's children celebrate a fabulous fifteen by dancing the waltz.
- *Brazil*. In this South American country, the birthday celebrant receives a tug on the earlobe for each year of age.
- *Canada*. In some parts of Canada, our neighbor to the north, the birthday child's nose is rubbed with butter or grease. It is believed that the greased nose makes the child too slick for bad luck to stick.
- *China*. In this Asian country, noodles are served for the birthday meal because they symbolize a long life.
- *England*. In merry old England, fortune-telling cake is served. Objects are cooked into this special birthday cake. For instance, if a slice of cake contains a coin, the recipient of that piece will be rich.
- *Germany*. In this country, where children's birthday parties originated, the candles on the cake are lit at breakfast and left lit all day. As it is also celebrated in the United States, when the candles are blown out in one try, the celebrant's wish is granted.
- *Israel*. Here, the birthday child sits in a chair that grown-ups raise in the air, moving it up and down to correspond to the child's age.
- *Japan*. This is a day for new clothes. The birthday child wears an entirely new outfit.
- *Mexico*. Festive piñatas fashioned from crepe and tissue paper are a part of this country's birthday celebrations. The piñatas are loaded with goodies and hung from the ceiling. Once they are cracked open, all of the children share the piñata's bounty.
- *Russia*. There is no birthday cake here. Russian children prefer pie for their special day.
- *Vietnam*. In this Asian country, everyone celebrates birthdays on New Year's Day. The country does not acknowledge the exact date a person is born.

Self-Assessment

Are you ready to put on your festive birthday hat and jump into this exciting field? Take the time to carefully consider these questions. Creating a children's event-planning business is exciting and often exhilarating, but it also requires commitment, in terms of time, energy, and finances. Make sure that this is the field for you before you put on that birthday party hat and set out to create your new business.

Are You Ready to Make a Commitment?

Assess your life and consider whether you have the time to plan and create a business. It can be all-consuming to develop a new business. Be sure you have the time to commit to this development. If you don't have the time to build the foundation for your business, you may be setting yourself up for disappointment as your new business likely will not thrive.

Are You Passionate about This Field?

Event planning is a whirl of excitement and brings wonderful returns, in terms of both pay and job satisfaction. Yet, it is also a field that involves a certain level of stress. Expectations are high. Parents are paying you to develop a perfect birthday party for their child. Most parents don't allow for a very wide margin of error when they are paying a planner for her expertise.

Are You Comfortable Working with Both Adults and Children?

This is critical for your success because this job requires that you enjoy interactions with both parents and with children. This is a somewhat unusual skill set requirement. You will plan the event with the adults and then need to ensure that both parents and children enjoy the event, which is sometimes easier said than done.

Are You Confident Enough to Be Your Own Boss?

This question is not as straightforward as it seems. Sure, most of us dream about being our own boss, running the show. However, being your own boss takes a great degree of discipline. Who is going to tell you to put your nose to the grindstone when you don't feel like working? Self-employed party planners need to have focus and drive and to feel comfortable making business decisions. As the leader of your company, you will make myriad decisions regarding everything from determining who makes the best birthday cakes (in terms of both good taste and budget) to how to finance your company.

Are You Ready and Able to Finance Your New Business?
It takes money to make money. Don't jump into a new business without a willingness to make a financial commitment. You'll only set yourself up for frustration if you are unable to finance your business dreams.

If you are committed, passionate, and enjoy working with both adults and children, planning children's birthday parties can be a lucrative and energizing business choice. And, the reward of a child's big grin after a successful event is a special one, indeed.

Challenges of the Field
Now it's time for the tough news. As described above, planning children's parties offers many opportunities for those hoping to make a career transition or to re-enter the work force. There are a few—though not insurmountable—potholes.

These potholes, described below, can all be patched. Starting a new business takes energy but also patience and the willingness to work through these challenges. As you start your business, it is imperative that you honestly assess these challenges. After all, you won't be able to tackle these issues until you identify them. Just as your doctor won't prescribe an antibiotic until she has identified your illness, you can't resolve your challenges until you label them. Finally, don't let that bugaboo, procrastination, derail your plans. Some folks, when faced with challenges, tend to put off what should be done today.

A Matter of Geography
It is a simple matter of doing the math: Event planners in more populous areas will have a broader pool of clients from which to draw. If you live in a rural area, there will be fewer opportunities for event planning. Also, if you live in an area that has been affected by an economic downturn (the closing of a local manufacturing plant, for instance) your growing business may be affected. If you are starting a children's event-planning business and find yourself affected by an economic downturn or a small population pool, you can turn to the Internet to broaden your business. This will be discussed in depth in Chapter 11.

Not Enough Hours in the Day

The schedule for children's birthday party planners can also be challenging, especially for mothers with young children. Children's birthday parties are often held on weekend afternoons, making it necessary for event planners with young children to find childcare arrangements. Keep in mind, too, that an event scheduled to run from 1 p.m. to 3 p.m. will require you to be on-site for at least an hour before and after. (This would be an absolute bare minimum and applies only to very small parties. Usually, you will need to spend more time on-site the day of the event.) There is no getting around it: event planners often need to spend weekend time away from their families, since parties are most often held on weekends.

On Your Own

Some event planners occasionally feel isolated. It is paradoxical that in a field focused on party giving, a great deal of the legwork is done solo. You will spend many hours doing office work and, in your home-based office, the going can get lonely. I find, though, that the blend of office work and on-site work forms a happy balance.

Depending on Others

As a party planner, you will be dependent on subcontractors—caterers, photographers, disc jockeys, and the like—to come through for you. Chapter 5 offers a detailed discussion addressing the use of subcontractors and ways to ensure successful relationships with these subs. There will be times, however, when a sub will fall through. Perhaps a caterer will forget the chicken tenders, or the cake will arrive late. You will not only have to solve these problems when they arise, but also do so with calmness and as much good cheer as you can muster.

Getting the Word Out

Overall marketing efforts will be addressed in Chapter 10. Although there are both many traditional and innovative ways to market your growing company, you will find that one of the most effective (and, happily, free) methods is through word of mouth. As the old adage goes, you are only as good as your last event. Of course, word of mouth takes time to grow and build. You will need to stage several events to get the ball rolling, and this can be frustrating for new event planners, eager and ready to get their businesses off the ground.

"I Mean Business"

A final challenge is creating your own mental framework, as well as that of family and friends, signaling that your party planning business is just that: a business. Too often, novice party planners think of their businesses as a hobby. This is not an effective mind-set. In order to generate the energy and enthusiasm necessary to launch your new career, you must focus on the development of your new business, which includes writing a business plan and orchestrating financing.

Opportunities in a Rapidly Growing Area

It is difficult to overstate the optimal conditions for creating a successful children's event-planning business. From over-the-top first birthdays to sweet sixteens and every year in between, parents are turning more frequently to event planners. In this keeping-up-with-the-Joneses world we live in, there is definitely a feeling of keeping up with the baby Jones, as parents opt to hold more elaborate birthday parties for their children. This means more opportunities for enthusiastic, creative, passionate individuals working to create the job of their dreams in this lively field.

Whether you are newly retired and looking for a fresh challenge or a young mother looking for a flexible work schedule, this career affords you the opportunity to create your own niche. You can create a thriving business, planning only a dozen or so events per year. Or, you can opt to hold an event or more every week. This field is infinitely flexible, making it ideal for most.

Additionally, a children's event planner can develop a business on a virtual shoestring and see financial returns almost immediately, making it an optimal business opportunity for anyone eager for a quick return.

Launching a children's party planning business also affords an ideal launching pad for creating an even larger event-planning business. Many niche event planners, such as those who start their careers planning only children's events, go on to plan other types of events as their businesses flourish.

Birthday parties are special days, and children eagerly anticipate their birthdays for months. As Lewis Carroll so aptly wrote in *Alice in Wonderland*, "There are three hundred and sixty-four days when you might get un-birthday presents and only one for birthday presents, you know."

Frequently Asked Questions

Should I quit my full-time job in order to start this business?

This must be determined on a case-by-case basis. In my case, I couldn't afford to quit my job as an art teacher when a friend and I decided to launch a children's birthday party business, Art Escapade Birthday Parties. (My friend subsequently left to become a public school teacher. She used the flexibility of our party planning business schedule to complete a master's degree in education). As the business launched, I chose a part-time model and, as it grew, I decreased my hours as an art teacher. In this way, there was no financial hardship for my family. If you are financially able to forgo the pay from your current job, you may consider leaving to start your birthday business. However, even if it is not a financial hardship to leave your current job, you may want to avoid closing the door to your current job just yet. You may dip into the children's birthday business and find that it isn't your cup of tea.

Do I have to be a magician or a clown or some other type of entertainer to be successful?

This is probably the question I am asked most often by those hoping to start a children's birthday party planning business, and the answer is a clear and definite "no." In fact, clowns and magicians are a dime a dozen compared to good party planners. Key to successful party planning is the ability to manage myriad details, stay focused, and maintain a high level of organization. Pulling a rabbit out of a hat is not a qualification.

Do I need a certain degree to launch my business?

There is no special degree necessary to launch your new business. There are event-planning degrees and certifications (see Appendix) but most children's birthday party planners step into the field drawing on their own backgrounds. Many of the most successful planners I know and have worked with are stay-at-home moms (who, often, have planned successful parties for their own kids) and retirees who raised their own children. These women and men have efficiently managed households and they bring this expertise to their party planning businesses.

From Princesses to Ponies: Finding Your Niche

Congratulations! You've given yourself time to reflect and assess. You've decided the children's birthday party planning business is a good fit and you are ready to develop a business in this field. Now comes the time to start making some important decisions about the type of event-planning business you will develop.

The information in this chapter will help you to determine whether you would prefer planning and hosting the parties yourself or would you be better served using outside consultants. For instance, would you be willing to plan a pool party at the local recreational facility or a skating party at the local skating rink? If so, you will need to involve other professionals at these facilities.

This chapter offers guidelines for defining your business mission and choosing a business model. Will you focus on only one party type, developing a very distinctive niche? An example of this business model would be a party business focusing solely on princess-themed parties. Or, do you want to develop a more broadly based party planning business, one that offers a variety of themes and venues?

There are benefits to both models. By planning events at various venues and developing assorted themes for parties, you may be able to attract a larger pool of clients since your services will be suitable for both genders and all ages. However, this wide scope can become somewhat diluted and a bit of a marketing challenge, whereas marketing oneself as the "Queen of the Princess Parties" is a very clear hook that is very appealing to countless little girls.

This chapter will offer advice and pose questions, helping you to develop the best business model for your current situation. "Current" is key here

Services Provided by Children's Birthday Party Planners

Depending on the type of birthday party business developed, you will be called upon to provide a wide variety of services. Don't be scared off by this list. Some party planners choose to keep their businesses small so they don't need to offer all of these services. As your business grows, though, you may find yourself happily expanding the number of services you offer:

- Invitations
- Décor, from balloons to piñatas and custom banners
- Birthday cakes
- Catering
- Entertainment such as magicians, "mad" scientists, skateboard experts, or beading artists (beading parties are popular with the tween set)
- Photography
- Videography
- Inflatables, including the ever-popular moon bounce
- Disc jockeys
- Tents
- Special lighting or sound equipment
- Staffing
- Party gifts, usually the highly sought-after (at least by the young set!) goody bags
- Flowers (not a common request for kids' parties but one that will occasionally crop up)
- Linens (again, not as common at informal kids' parties, but a service that will likely be required at a larger, more formal party)
- Thank-you notes

because, often, event planners change the model of their businesses as their life situations change. Many event planners throw their birthday hats into the ring when their kids are young. As their children grow, some of these event planners choose to grow their party planning businesses as well.

Notes from the Field

For my event-planning business, Art Escapades, I've used my background as an artist and event planner, combining these skills to create a successful art- and craft-themed birthday party business. This model enabled me to start my business with a small investment in marketing materials, home office supplies, and art materials. Rather than using a variety of venues, I created an Art Escapades birthday party room at a site away from my home. I decided it was important to create a site separate from my home. At the time of Art Escapades' launch, my children were small, and I felt it would be too complicated to hold parties at a dedicated room in my home. My mantra of "always keep it professional" came into play here. I did not want my children to disrupt the birthday parties as they were occurring, so, instead of putting temptation right under my kids' noses, I opted to hold parties elsewhere. As my business has grown, I have also chosen to take my parties to other venues when clients request it. Holding children's parties at other venues has been a wonderful and exciting challenge. Although the majority of the parties I plan are held at the Art Escapades birthday party room, my business has evolved to a new level, allowing me to expand to other venues.

Choosing Where to Conduct Parties

The next step is to determine the ideal location at which to hold children's birthday parties. In general, there are three options: conducting parties at one designated space that you have created specifically for this purpose, as I originally did; holding parties at a variety of off-site venues, ranging from bowling alleys to skating rinks; or holding parties at the homes of your clients. Of course, you could also choose more than one of these options. For instance, you might create a designated party space as well as being open to planning parties at other venues.

Creating Your Own Space

Many party planners make the choice to create a dedicated space that is always stocked and prepared for parties. Perhaps you have a room in your basement that is light-filled and appropriate for parties (remember, this party space needs to be festive so if you choose to fix up a basement room, make sure that you provide plenty of light—natural,

A Caveat

When choosing the types of parties you will plan, don't be tempted to use trade-marked names such as Thomas the Tank Engine, SpongeBob SquarePants, or Pirates of the Caribbean in any of your marketing materials. Owners of these trade-marks keep an eye out for fraudulent uses of their trademarked names and do not look kindly on those who use them without permission.

if at all possible, or artificial. Try to steer clear of fluorescent lighting. It tends to be harsh and the slight flickering of fluorescent lighting can actually bother some children.

You may also choose to investigate your town's resources. For instance, many locales offer space in their community centers for a nominal fee. The downside of renting space at a local community center is lugging your supplies back and forth, since most centers do not have on-site storage. A clear advantage, though, is separating your work from your home life, a factor that some event planners find critical. Some churches and synagogues also offer space for community events as do some public libraries.

Off-site Venues: Are They Right for You?

For some children's party planners, holding parties at varied venues is ideal. Are you this type of planner?

1. *Are you comfortable holding events at a broad array of venues, from rock-climbing facilities to zoos, children's museums, pizzerias, and more? Yes or No*
2. *Are you comfortable with the idea of working with a wide array of suppliers and vendors? Yes or No*
3. *Is your schedule flexible enough that you are able to spend time traveling to various venues, both for vetting and for the actual event? Yes or No*
4. *Are you comfortable negotiating contracts with a wide variety of vendors? Yes or No*

If you answered "yes" to all of these questions, you are a candidate for holding parties at a variety of venues. Your affirmative responses indicate that you would enjoy the excitement and challenges of holding parties at assorted sites.

Tips for Creating an Inviting Party Space

- Choose a cheerful, bright paint color to liven up the walls
- Hang piñatas, streamers, garlands or other colorful items
- Install a small refrigerator for juice boxes, ice-cream cakes, and water bottles
- Install a wardrobe with shelving that can be used to house all of your supplies, from paper towels and napkins to a first-aid kit
- Cover the table with colorful contact paper. Don't use the contact paper of yore—light blue flowers and pale calicos, for instance. There is a new generation of contact paper with surfaces like chalk board (kids can doodle with chalk while they wait for their cake) or a memo board surface (to be used with dry erase markers). When purchasing dry erase markers, check the package to be sure it is labeled "non-toxic." There are several brands of dry erase markers and not all are safe for children to use. Remember, too, that your tables and chairs need to be kid-sized. Small children are apt to tumble off full-size chairs.

A Variety of Venues

If you have opted to plan events at a variety of venues, you will need to develop parameters for these businesses:

- *How far are you willing to travel to plan and hold a party?* Be reasonable about this. Don't feel pressured to say "yes" to planning a party at an aquarium a hundred miles from your home if you are not comfortable with this choice. Remember, especially if you have childcare to arrange, that traveling a hundred miles each way every time you visit the site (for planning and for the actual event) is time-consuming and expensive when you take into consideration gas and wear and tear on your car.
- *What is your comfort level?* You must feel absolutely comfortable in a given venue. For instance, would you be comfortable planning a paintball party, a popular option with adolescent boys? Perhaps you have two left feet and wouldn't be comfortable out in the paintball trenches. Remember, a party

planner is flexible. Perhaps an extra paintball player is needed to make the teams even—and you're the player! If you are not comfortable with a client's suggested venue, recommend another venue that offers a similar experience. Or, if the client resists that change, opt out. Not every initial consultation with a prospective client will end in a signed contract.

■ *Does the venue have all required insurance?* In case of an accident, would the venue have adequate coverage? Insurance will be covered in greater depth in Chapter 3. You will need to protect yourself with appropriate insurance as well, but it is vital that you confirm a site's insurance coverage is appropriate and adequate. Ask to see proof.

■ *Does the venue have a solid reputation?* This point is absolutely critical as you build the foundation of your children's event-planning business. You may be the best children's party planner on the planet but if you hold an event at a venue that is sub-par, your event, most likely, will be sub-par as well. As you develop your business, you will create relationships with other vendors as well as other party planners. Through this word-of-mouth grapevine, you will develop a bank of invaluable knowledge about local vendors and venues. If a client suggests a venue that has received less than glowing reviews, you will want to share this information with your client. A word of caution: Be factual and accurate in reporting a venue's shortcomings. Just as you are developing your successful business based largely on your reputation, so are the area's venues. Don't malign a vendor or venue without good information at your fingertips to support your claims.

Parties at Your Clients' Homes

If you opt for this route, remember that your client is entrusting you to care for their home as you would your own. Although, at first glance, this may seem the easiest option in terms of logistics and expense, it comes with its own drawbacks. If you are asked to plan a Frisbee golf party for fifteen five-year-old boys, you are not only responsible for creating an engaging Frisbee event, but also you are responsible for the safety of the children and of your client's home. Key to this is organization. You must be thoroughly organized to pull off parties at your clients' homes. This means showing up on time with your toolbox—virtual and real—full and at the ready.

Conversely, holding parties at clients' homes takes the onus off of you to provide a space and, especially as you develop your business, is financially beneficial since you will not need to make an initial investment in creating your own party room.

You will need to invest in storage boxes and bins that are easily transportable. These will serve as your party on wheels, with contracts, notes, candles (always carry extra birthday candles!), first-aid kit, and more at your fingertips.

Who Is the Audience for Your New Business?

As well as selecting a site or sites at which to conduct parties, you will need to target an audience for your services. If you are planning princess-themed parties, your target, primarily, will be young girls. If you opt for sports-themed parties, you will target boys more directly than girls.

Chapter 10 outlines strategies for reaching this target audience. It is important as you begin developing your business that you consider the population you hope to target and determine if there is a market for your services. If you live in a small town with only five thousand residents, you may need to broaden your scope. Offering only pirate parties will mean limiting your pool of clients to the handful of young boys—and a few adventurous girls—who might opt for a pirate-themed party. Conversely, if you live in a larger city, specialization could be an important key to your success. Perhaps there are successful children's party planners in your city who offer more generalized services, with a variety of themes. If this is the case, then specializing could help you to create your own brand and niche.

Weighing Part-Time and Full-Time Options

One of the chief benefits of event planning is its extreme flexibility in terms of creating part- or full-time career opportunities. As owner of Art Escapades, I have adjusted the number of parties I orchestrate based on other commitments in my life. When my children were very young, for instance, I chose to take on fewer clients. As my children have grown, so too have the opportunities for growing my business.

Planning children's birthday parties is not only a creative and dynamic opportunity, but it also allows for extreme flexibility in so many ways. Perhaps you decided to start your business on a smaller scale, holding parties only at a dedicated space in your home, and planned on a small, part-time salary. It is always possible, and, indeed, often desirable to adjust your company as your life and lifestyle change. Perhaps you begin the business while employed part-time outside of your home. As you develop your children's birthday party business, you may choose to retire from

Take the time to carefully reflect and to assess your current situation. This is an opportunity to consider your career and financial goals and to determine the time you are willing and able to commit to your new business.

1. *How many hours per week do you plan to devote to your new business?* Be realistic! If you are already the head of your local PTA, in charge of the town library's book sale, and a volunteer at the community's senior center, you may not have many hours left to devote to your business. That is perfectly fine. You can still create a thriving business without a tremendous time commitment. However, do not plan on a full-time salary if you have only ten hours per week to devote to children's birthday party planning.

2. *How big is your community?* I grew up in a small, rural town with a population hovering around three thousand. Simply stated, there are not as many party planning opportunities in smaller communities. There are ways to use the Internet to expand outside of your small community (more about this in Chapter 11) but, at least initially, you will want to carefully consider the population of your local area.

3. *What are your financial goals?* Are you hoping to earn $200 a month to help pay for your kids' piano lessons? Or, are you hoping to earn enough to pay for a big family vacation? Or, do you envision a business that will generate a full-time salary for you? If the latter, you will need to plan on devoting full-time hours to your developing business.

your part-time job and to grow your children's birthday party business into a full-time proposition. Likewise, you may decide to scale back a full-time birthday party business when your life becomes busy with other tasks.

Specialization

You've started to formulate plans for your new business, from choosing a venue to planning for a part- or full-time model. It is also important to hone in on your area

What Your Clients Say

As you develop your business, remember to be a good and careful listener. We all like to think that we are attentive when listening to our clients, but sometimes, in the flurry of our busy business days, we listen with one ear instead of two. I have found that by focusing—no multitasking!—and noting my clients' concerns, I have been able to maintain and grow my business.

As Lili Foggle, a suburban mother of two, says, "I'm an over-the-top kind of girl and I like to throw an over-the-top party." To this end, Foggle is willing to shoot the moon in terms of budget when it comes to planning her kids' parties.
"I'm able to do it and I like to do it. My mom did it for me when I was growing up and I really want to create parties that are fun for my kids and their friends."
Foggle has enlisted a variety of children's party planners over the years—from pony party experts to karaoke leaders—but says that having a detail-oriented party planner is key.

"The party planners who receive repeat business from me are the ones who do absolutely everything, from writing down the names of the children and the gift they gave to arranging all of the food. All I have to do is show up, have fun at the party, and watch the kids enjoy themselves."

Heather Howard, mother of three young girls, cites the convenience and ease of hiring a children's birthday party planner.

"It's just so much easier to hold my kids' birthday parties away from home. Then, there is no clean-up before and after. And, I like having someone else in charge of entertainment. Then, when it is time for the kids to leave, you are not trying to kick people out of your comfortable home. It is just time to go—the venue is closing or moving on to another event."

These two women make a key point. Whether you choose to specialize or to be a general planner, whether you develop your own party space or conduct parties at clients' homes, your success will be based on your ability to outline and fulfill all of the details involved when planning a successful children's birthday party.

of specialization. As I wrote earlier, my background in art and event planning made creating a children's birthday party business focusing on art and craft parties a clear-cut choice. Likewise, you may have a skill that lends itself perfectly to an area of specialization. Perhaps you were once a baker. Cookie- and cupcake-baking parties are very popular, so you could use your expertise to create a party business focused on creating sweet and whimsical baked goods. Or, maybe you live on a farm and raise ponies. Your expertise would make you an ideal candidate for pony- and horseback-riding parties, another popular party theme for kids today.

Keep in mind, though, that to create a successful business, you do not need to have a specific area of expertise, such as baking or art. Rather, as outlined in Chapter 1, you must have energy and organizational skills to create a top-flight party planning business.

A Checklist of Popular Party Themes

One of the pleasures of planning children's birthday parties is the diversity of themes. Although you may develop a very specific niche, it is still important for you to keep abreast of trends and popular party themes.

To stay on top of these trends, you will need to do some sleuthing. Keep an eye on the television schedule and take note of the shows kids are watching. From PBS to Nickelodeon and Cartoon Network, all of these stations air shows that provide inspiration for children's birthday parties. PBS's *Sesame Street,* for instance, remains a popular theme for the young set while Cartoon Network's *Yu-Gi-Oh* series provides the catalyst for many boys' parties.

Take a stroll through your local mall. This is another rich lode for party themes. What are the kids wearing, for instance? Tween girls like beading parties. Check out what the teen girls at your local mall are wearing for what's hip.

Bookstores also provide fodder for staying current. Speak with your local bookseller about what is flying off the shelves. For instance, Harry Potter parties have remarkable staying power, as do American Girl Doll parties.

When you have an opportunity, go right to the source and ask children what types of parties they love. I've found that an absolute perennial favorite is the bowling party. Kids five years and up love to party at the bowling alley. (Note to those of you who worry about gutter balls: bowling alley staff kindly put up sides on the alleys to keep stray balls from inevitably going into the gutters.) The list provided here shows current themes. You may find that the list varies a bit based on geography. For instance, horse-themed parties are always a popular staple in the southern part of the United States. Beach parties, for obvious reasons, are a hit in areas with access to beaches. As you read through this list, consider which themes might be most popular in your area. Also assess which themes are of particular interest to you as you develop your company.

As mentioned earlier, keep in mind that many of these themes are trademarked and legal eagles at companies like Disney and Nickelodeon keep a close eye out for trademark infringement. It is fine to plan a SpongeBob SquarePants party using themed products (such as plates or party hats) that have received the okay from Nickelodeon's legal department. It is, however, not kosher to run advertisements proclaiming that you are the "Queen of SpongeBob SquarePants Parties." Basically, as a rule of thumb, don't plan on using trademarked names in your advertising and promotional pieces unless you have permission from the trademark holder.

- American Idol
- Astronaut
- Barbie
- Barney
- Batman
- Baseball
- Beach Bonanza
- Blue's Clues
- BMX
- Bowling
- Bratz
- Care Bears
- Cars and Trucks
- Cat in the Hat
- Cheetah Girls
- Circus
- Cowboy or Cowgirl
- Dinosaur
- Disney Princess
- Dogs
- Dora the Explorer

- Elmo
- Farm Animals
- Fashion or Dress-Up
- Firefighter
- Football
- Hannah Montana
- Harry Potter
- High School Musical
- Ice Skating
- Justice League
- Karate
- Knights
- Kung Fu
- Little Mermaid
- Luau
- Mickey Mouse
- Movies
- NASCAR
- Olympics or Sports Games
- Painting
- Pirate
- Pizza Party
- Pokémon
- Polly Pocket
- Ponies
- Robots
- Rockets
- Rock Climbing
- Roller Skating
- Safari
- Scooby Doo
- Sesame Street
- Shrek
- Skateboarding
- Sleepover

- Soccer
- Spiderman
- SpongeBob SquarePants
- Sports
- Star Wars
- Strawberry Shortcake
- Superman
- Sweet Sixteen
- Swimming
- Taekwondo
- Tea Party
- Teenage Mutant Ninja Turtles
- Thomas the Tank Engine
- Tie Dye
- Trains
- Transformers
- Treasure Boxes
- Unicorn
- The Wiggles
- Wild Horses
- Winnie the Pooh
- Yu-Gi-Oh
- Zoo Animals

Frequently Asked Questions

Am I limiting my business's possibilities by not considering outside venues, instead planning parties at only one designated location?

Not necessarily. At first glance, using a variety of venues would seem to imply an ability to draw from a broader swath of the population. If you host parties at venues ranging from horse stables to ice skating rinks and art museums, you are broadening your appeal in one way. However, I have found that many successful party planners, by focusing on one area and one venue, can refine and perfect their parties, building tremendous word of mouth and large client volume. This has been true for my business, Art Escapades. Most of the parties I plan are held in a room I designed specifically for art-based birthday parties. And, as the name implies, the activities at the parties are art- and craft-based. By keeping my scope narrow, I have created a well-oiled machine. As my business grows, I occasionally have customers who ask me to plan an Art Escapades party at another venue—a private home, a recreational center, an art museum, a natural history museum, or other locale. I enjoy the challenges of planning these off-site parties, as well. Although my niche at first glance might appear somewhat narrow, I have found that it has not limited my ability to draw in clients and to continue to grow my business.

To help get my business started, should I offer to plan a birthday party for a friend's child without charging?

Although different experts offer different opinions about this, I urge you to resist the temptation to jump-start your business with a freebie. There are too many possible perils. First and foremost, you must always treat your business as a business and not a hobby. Business owners are paid for their services. And, who is to say that after hosting a free event for one friend, another friend won't ask you to do the same for her? This would be an awkward position to find yourself in. Also, I have found that planning parties for friends' children offers numerous pitfalls. Friends might expect extra services or have higher expectations. And, if a problem does arise, the friendship could be damaged. As I grew comfortable planning parties, I took on friends as clients but only when I felt I had all of the necessary tools to guarantee a successful event.

BLANDING LIBRARY
REHOBOTH, MA 0276

Setting Up Shop at Home

Creating a Work Space

It is time to plan and create your home work space. This space is not the area in which you will hold birthday parties. Rather, it will be your office base, the site from which you contact and work with clients and vendors, complete your billing, create marketing materials, and complete the other desk work necessary for your successful event-planning business.

A Dedicated Work Space

First and foremost, your home office must be a dedicated work area. In other words, don't set up your folder files and note cards on the kitchen counter or on top or your washer and dryer. Your office space must be professional and organized. As business and lifestyle dynamo Martha Stewart points out, "life is too complicated not to be orderly." Don't hinder your own progress by being disorganized.

Your work space need not be large. Perhaps you will set up a desk at one end of your living room, or, if you are an empty-nester, you could convert a bedroom into an at-home office. It is possible to convert a large walk-in closet into a cozy office space. Remember, too, that you will be meeting clients in this work space so make it as polished as possible.

Large, chain office supply stores offer excellent prices on attractive office furniture as well as free or discounted shipping. Likewise, large retailers can offer high style furniture at low cost. And thrift stores are often a good source for office furniture, too. Be sure, though, if buying furniture second-hand, that it is sturdy. No wobbly legs! Remember, too, that you will spend long hours in your office chair, so don't skimp when selecting the right seat. Ideally, the

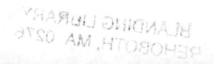
BLANDING LIBRARY
REHOBOTH, MA 02769

Tip Top Organization

Ask any successful business owner and most will put their ability to stay organized at the top of their list as a key to business success. In order for your business to stay on track, you need to maintain order in all areas of your life including:

- **Home:** When working from home, it is critical that you keep all of your non-office home space as tidy as possible. It is hard to focus on the party planning work at hand when you have a sink full of dirty dishes or a couch covered with laundry waiting to be folded and put away. Likewise, when clients visit your home office, your tidy home will reflect your professionalism.

- **Office:** A messy desk is a sign of an unorganized business owner and party planner. Make sure that your desk and office space always look tidy and smart. Keep paper to a minimum. For instance, make it your rule of thumb to sort your mail as it comes in—no languishing piles. Put junk mail right into the recycling bin, bills to be paid into your bill file, and personal correspondence in the appropriate files.

- **Family:** Working from home means staying on top of your family's organization as well. If you have an early morning meeting, for instance, you might want to pack the kids' lunches the evening before. Keep a family schedule on your refrigerator, showing where you and your family need to be during the week. This clear communication keeps everyone in the loop.

- **Time:** Oh, the elusive nature of time. It seems there are never enough hours in the day. In fact, with a bit of careful organization, you'll find that there usually is ample time. Do you need to finish a proposal? Set your alarm clock an hour early so you have time to thoughtfully complete the proposal. Meeting with a client twenty miles from your home? Leave twenty minutes early to ensure that you arrive on time. Nothing can ruin a business faster than failing to arrive punctually.

- **Health:** We don't always think of health when considering organization, but we should. Too often, with our busy lives on the go, we forgo healthy meals or forget to take our daily multivitamin. Make sure to keep yourself and your family healthy by creating wholesome meals, managing time so everyone in the family is getting enough sleep, and scheduling in time for exercise, even if exercise means a short ten-minute walk.

Notes from the Field

Teach your family to respect your office space. Don't let your teenagers put their feet on your desk or your toddler eat Cheerios there. Impart to your family the serious nature of your business and encourage them to treat your office space with care.

chair will have an adjustable height feature as well as adjustable armrests. Make sure the chair swivels.

To add polish to your desk and office, consider an attractive lamp. This is practical (you will be doing lots of paperwork at your desk and will need good lighting) as well as inviting to your clients. A vase with fresh flowers also signals to clients that you take the care to think about details such as brightening your work space with fresh flowers.

A colorful rug adds a homey touch to your work area. A rug also absorbs sound, another plus. Even if your office is set up on a carpeted floor, consider layering a rug over the wall-to-wall carpet. The rug needn't be expensive. Many big-box retailers sell handsome rugs at very reasonable prices. Just as the fresh flowers show your attention to detail, so, too, will the rug.

You may want to display framed photographs of successful birthday parties you've planned. Be sure to get the okay from your clients, however, before displaying photos from their children's birthday parties. Most of your clients will be pleased to say "yes," but you must check before using photos of parties you have planned in any of your marketing efforts.

A bulletin board is also useful, both for pinning important messages and for displaying photographs and news clippings about your business.

Buying Office Equipment

You will need to make an investment in office equipment. This initial investment could be relatively modest if you take inventory of the equipment you already own. For instance, you may already own a computer and printer that will suffice as you first set up shop.

Choosing a Computer

If you already own a computer, you may opt to use it for your new business. However, if it is a computer shared by six different family members, you may need to invest in a second computer! Desktop computers use sophisticated software to make all aspects of your business—from creating proposals to billing and marketing—a cinch. Computers are also affordable. A complete system, including hard drive, monitor, mouse, modem, and printer, can be purchased for $1,500. With careful shopping, this price can be even lower.

Many event planners spend a good deal of time in their cars, driving to different sites and meeting with clients. For these planners, a laptop computer might be a good choice since it is portable and offers greater flexibility. Laptop computers are available beginning at about $500.

The Perfect Printer

Keep an eye out for sales at big-box retailers. Printers, complete with copying and scanning functions, can be purchased for well under $100. Plan on purchasing a printer with the copying and scanning options. If you are planning a bulk mailing, it is worthwhile to have an outside print shop complete the copying for you. However, for smaller jobs, it is essential to have a copier available at your home office. The scanner function on your printer will also prove invaluable. You will use it to scan in photos or logos for marketing pieces.

Fax Machines

You will find that a fax machine is also an invaluable piece of office equipment for sending information to clients and to the vendors and suppliers with whom you will be working.

Although some computers have a fax already installed, many event planners find it beneficial to have a separate, dedicated fax line. By using a dedicated line, your computer doesn't have to be running for you to send or to receive a fax. Fax machines begin at about $100.

Telephones and Answering Machines

Don't skimp when it comes to purchasing a phone and setting up a home-office answering machine. Buy a cordless phone that has the useful speaker function. Likewise, automatic redial, memory dial, caller ID, and a mute button are useful tools. You may also choose to purchase a phone with a headset so your hands will be free to type notes into your computer. Phones with all of these functions begin at about $50.

Don't be tempted to use your family answering machine for your business use. Instead, use an answering machine dedicated solely to your business. You do not want a client's first impression of you and your business to be anything less than top flight. A prospective client may not find your toddler's voice on the answering machine professional or cute.

When creating a message for your answering machine, be sure to include the name of your business, your name, and when you will return incoming calls. Also, be sure to ask the caller to leave contact information. For instance, is it better to call back using the caller's land line or her cell line? My answering machine message is, "This is Amy Peters at Art Escapades Birthday Parties. I will call you back as soon as possible, so please leave the best numbers at which to reach you. Thanks, and have a great day." Happily, answering machines are not a big expense. They are available for $20 and up.

If you are a recent retiree or stay-at-home mom hoping to plan and hold only a handful of birthday parties each year, perhaps six or fewer, you may choose to forgo the expense of a separate phone line and answering machine, finding that your business budget simply can't accommodate the cost. If this is the case, then leave a professional-sounding message on your home answering machine. Use the format described above but omit your business name from the message.

Often, voice mail is better than an answering machine. Most telephone service contract providers offer voice mail for a nominal fee. Advantages include the ability to check messages while you are out as well as directing your clients' calls directly to

Notes from the Field

Never put a client on hold. Your answering machine or voice mail will take care of any incoming calls that might arrive while you are on the other line. Prospective clients will not appreciate being told to hold. Instead, focus and listen to their requests and then check for messages on your answering machine or voice mail.

Internet Tip

Consider custom postage stamps for all of your mailings. At www.zazzle.com you can design your own postage stamp. As you develop your brand, you will want to emblazon all of your marketing materials, including stamps, with your custom-designed logo. You want people to make the connection between your business and your logo. Accomplish this by using your logo as frequently as possible.

the message center rather than to a busy signal. Frustrated clients, met with a busy signal, may not bother to call back.

Finally, get rid of the annoying call-waiting feature. Your clients can hear the bothersome clicks as other calls come in. And, these clicks may be distracting to you as you ponder who is trying to reach you.

Cell Phones

Because you will be spending a lot of time outside your office, you will want a reliable cell phone and cell phone service provider. Compare prices with cell phone service providers in your area. Make sure you buy a plan with adequate minutes, as it is likely you will use your cell phone frequently. Cell phone providers love it when their customers go over the allotted number of minutes—they charge big bucks for these extra minutes.

Buying a cell phone can be expensive, but some service providers give a free phone to customers who sign a one- or two-year commitment. Be sure that you are willing to take on this commitment, though. There are penalties for early termination of cell phone contracts. Sometimes, it is more prudent to simply buy the phone outright and not be beholden to one service provider.

Make sure that you have client, vendor, and supplier numbers in your cell phone's memory. When you are on-site and the caterer has not arrived with the birthday cake, you need to have instant access to the caterer's number.

Some party planners opt to use their cell phones as their primary business phones. In this way, they separate their family phone from their business. One clear advantage is that your cell phone is portable and always available. This same advantage can prove a liability. It is challenging to troubleshoot a catering problem on your cell phone while also trying to negotiate city traffic. Reception can also be an issue. Although less of an issue in urban areas, there are still areas in the country where cell phone service is patchy. If you live in a populous area with reliable cell phone service and you feel comfortable using a headset while using your phone, then you might consider a cell phone as your main business line. Finally, in many states it is illegal to use a cell phone in a car unless the user has a headset. It is wise to buy a headset. It leaves your hands free for safe driving.

Postage Solutions

As you develop your business, you may choose to lease or buy a postage meter. Another convenient option is to buy postage online from providers such as www .stamps.com and www.usps.com. At sites like these you can download software that allows you to print postage directly onto labels.

You will also need a postal scale. Basic postal scales begin at $10 and are available at office supply stores.

The Paper Trail

Stationery is an important decision, as well. Because your stationery will represent you in your absence, you want it to make a professional impression. For this reason, buy the best stationery that you can afford. Rather than sending letters on inexpensive copying paper, choose a better grade of paper. Office-supply stores can print stationery for you with your letterhead. You will want to include your logo on absolutely every piece of marketing material, from your business cards to your Web site, so don't have your stationery printed until your logo design is complete (Chapter 4 includes a discussion on logo design and importance).

While you are at the office supply store, stock up on pens, pencils, sticky notes, paper clips, a stapler, a tape dispenser, and other miscellaneous goods.

Selecting and Purchasing Party Supplies

You will need to acquire a basic stock of party supplies. Don't shoot the moon; buy supplies sparingly at first while you determine the scope of your business.

As you schedule parties, you will buy the items needed. For instance, for your first pirate-themed party, you will buy the appropriate items (such as hats, goody bags, and piñatas). You don't want to fill a closet with theme-related items. The party that

Paper Trail Checklist

Don't be caught short upon your return from the office-supply store. Starting a new business means buying an assortment of office supplies including:

- Pencils
- Pens
- Paper clips, assorted sizes
- File folders
- Ruler
- Pencil sharpener
- Sticky notes, assorted sizes, including lined pads
- File boxes or filing cabinet
- Bulletin board for news clippings, photographs, mission statement
- Dry erase board, often helpful during client presentations
- Stapler and staples
- Plastic covers for client proposal packets
- Lined paper and copier paper
- Tape, both transparent and masking types
- Mailing labels
- Name tags
- Envelopes, assorted sizes for mailing statements as well as for mailing 8½ x 11 client proposals
- Large three-ring binder
- Three-hole punch, important for preparing your portfolio

Generic Birthday Party Supply Checklist

You should create a basic stock of non-themed, generic items, including:

- Transparent goody bags
- Paper tablecloths
- Paper napkins
- Party hats
- Blowers
- Plates and plastic cutlery
- Streamers in assorted colors
- Goody bag treats (more on this in Chapter 5)

At your fingertips, you will want everything necessary to put together a party in a hurry. I have had parents call on a Thursday for a party on Sunday! For these parents (although, happily, most parents plan ahead), you'll need to keep this basic stock of generic supplies on hand.

is hot this year may not be so hot next year, and you don't want to burden yourself (and your budget) with excess inventory.

The appendix lists sources for buying children's birthday party supplies. Many online vendors provide good values and professional service. However, it may be beneficial to your growing business to develop relationships with local party-supply vendors. They are likely to offer volume discounts if your business requires that you buy in bulk. Also, they could prove to be a tremendous marketing asset, displaying your brochures in their shops and spreading the news to customers about your party planning abilities.

Zoning Issues

Always check local zoning regulations before opening up shop in your home-office site. Zoning regulations are established at the local rather than the state level so a home-based business that passes zoning muster in one town may not pass in the

Notes from the Field

Keep an emergency toolbox with you at all of your events. This toolbox has proved invaluable to me. I use a real toolbox—purchased at my local hardware store. It holds:

- Paper
- Pen
- Box of tissues
- Cell phone charger. (My cell phone ran out of juice at a critical moment. From that day on, I have kept a spare charger at the ready.)
- Matches (for lighting birthday candles)
- First-aid kit
- Disposable camera (many parents, in their rush to get out the door, forget their cameras at home. You'll be their hero when you pull one out of your emergency toolbox.)
- Disposable cleaning wipes for tidying up spills
- Antibacterial hand cleanser
- Cake knife
- Plastic spoons and forks
- Business cards
- A glue gun (you'll be surprised at the many ways in which a glue gun can save the day!)

next town over. Anticipate concerns of your neighbors. Conduct business in a quiet and unobtrusive manner. Don't plan to put out signs. Bear in mind that outdoor signage and increased traffic volume are two issues that lead to zoning regulations barring home-based offices. If you plan to hold parties at your house, be scrupulous in checking the zoning regulations regarding parking. Some cities don't allow on-street parking during certain hours. Most likely, you'll be able to establish your office

Internet Tip

For more information about business licenses, contact the Small Business Administration (SBA) at www.sba.gov.

at home, but before moving ahead be sure to check with local government officials to confirm all zoning regulations.

To contact local zoning officials, call your town clerk's offices or use a computer search engine to see if zoning regulations are posted online.

Applying for Licenses

As your business grows, you may need to apply for and buy a business license. Check with your town clerk's office for the parameters of your town or city's rules regarding business licenses. Business licenses are usually available for a nominal fee and are renewed annually.

It may be tempting to set up shop without checking zoning and license regulations. Don't give in to this temptation! It is always better to be on the safe side and to educate yourself about your municipality's ordinances regarding zoning and business licensing. It would be frustrating to develop a thriving business only to then have a legal tussle because of inadequate research or paperwork on your part.

Choosing Insurance

Be sure to check with your insurance agent regarding your insurance coverage. It is imperative that you have adequate coverage, both to protect your office and office supplies and equipment as well as to provide liability coverage for yourself, for any people you might employ, and for party attendees.

Your current homeowner's or renter's policy may provide adequate coverage. If not, inexpensive riders can be added to your policy to offer you and your business full insurance coverage.

It is possible to buy inexpensive insurance through online sources, but I recommend working with an agent you trust. You do not want to get caught short on your coverage.

Keeping It Professional

This chapter has covered some of the more technical nuts and bolts of developing a children's birthday party business. Covering all of these issues as you develop your business is essential for your business's success. View these fundamentals as the foundation of your business. Take the time to complete all of these steps—from meeting with an insurance agent to sourcing the best office supplies—in order to avoid frustration or, worse, failure down the line.

There can be a temptation with a home-based business to be too casual. This often leads to a business collapse. Keep your attitude and your home office professional. The children's birthday party business is energizing, lively, and fun but it also demands professionalism and organization.

Frequently Asked Questions

How can I convince my kids that my office is out of bounds?
You must draw a firm line in the sand on this issue: absolutely no children allowed in your work area. If your office were off-site, kids would know that trampling through with muddy feet and dropping cookie crumbs are no-no's. Kids must learn that the same is true of your home office. It is for your professional use only. Brook no exceptions and you will find that your children come to accept and respect your professional space.

I am planning to keep my party planning business small, perhaps only five events per year. Do I really need to invest in insurance?
Yes, yes, and, again, yes. In particular, you must arrange for liability coverage. If you have planned a party at which a child slips and injures herself, you must make sure that you are financially protected. Without liability insurance, you risk your business as well as your personal finances.

04 Ready, Set, Start

The Nuts and Bolts of Establishing Your New Business

This is an exciting moment in the creation of your children's birthday party business. You've made important decisions about the design and scope of your business and now you are ready to move on to the next steps. I call these the "nuts and bolts" steps, as they are literally the steps needed to bolt and hold your company together. Without this planning, your company's chances of success are diminished.

In this chapter, we'll focus on writing a business plan and on completing all of the research and planning involved in creating this powerful business plan. This research is exciting as you will discover trends, track growth, make professional contacts, and learn about your competition as well as find and target the audience for your new business.

According to the United States Small Business Association, a whopping 50 percent of small businesses fail within the first year. They fail, according to the SBA, in large part due to poor planning. Many people developing home-based businesses neglect to plan, create, and write a business plan. This is a critical mistake. Don't think that you can "wing it." A comprehensive and thorough business plan will help you to delineate your goals and your growth. This chapter outlines the steps and research involved in creating this successful business plan.

Research, Research, Research

There is no such thing as too much research. The more you know, the better able you will be to create a thriving business. You're excited about the possibilities of your new birthday party business but will you find the same enthusiasm in your community? Who will use your services? Are there other party planners already working in your area? Will your business duplicate their efforts? How is the economy playing a role in the children's birthday party business? What are the current trends in the children's birthday party business? How are these businesses financed? You get the idea! Before starting any business, there are many questions to research and answer. I can't overrate the importance of this research. Interview any successful business owner, and she will tell you that research before opening a business is absolutely key to success.

Another common mistake is being a bit careless about recording the information you unearth. As you delve into your research, you will learn volumes about the children's birthday party business and business development in general. Don't store these volumes in your head! As you research, keep careful notes. This is too much information to commit to memory.

Gumshoe Guru

Start your research by going back to basics: old-fashioned, gumshoe investigating! Not only is this kind of research valuable, the gathering of it is energizing as you meet folks involved in the children's birthday party business.

Don't give in and use the phone for this sleuthing. Instead, visit your local party supply stores in person and ask about the children's birthday party market. Don't interrupt the manager while she is working with other customers. When she has a spare moment, begin by explaining that you are developing a children's birthday party business. You'll want to establish that you are not setting up a competing business. Once you've made this connection, ask if you could interview her about current trends. If the answer is yes, then find out if this is a convenient time or should you return at a better time? Once you've established an ideal time for this conversation, ask about what party themes are popular, where parents opt to hold parties, and what new trends she is seeing in the birthday party business.

Likewise, a trip to the local grocery-store bakery could prove useful. What types of cakes are most often requested? What size cakes are ordered (an indicator of the size of a child's birthday party)?

Survey parents about their thoughts and needs with regard to their children's birthday party celebrations. This information will be helpful in formulating your business plan, allowing you to craft a plan that matches the needs and expectations of the parents.

Sample Parent Survey

1. Do you have birthday parties for your children at home or outside of the home?
2. Do you or would you be willing to pay for a party planner?
3. What do you think is a reasonable budget for a child's birthday party?
4. How many children do you invite to your children's birthday parties?
5. What types of parties do your kids like? For example, do they like parties with a sporting theme, such as bowling or soccer?
6. How do you find out about party options?
7. What has been the most satisfying birthday party experience you and your children have had?

It will also be helpful to check in with children's birthday party facilities, such as ice-skating rinks, bowling alleys, art centers, and zoos. Again, explain that you are not setting up a competing business. Rather, you are developing a business that will bring revenue to their businesses. Once you have made this clear, you will likely find that these venue owners and managers will be glad to share information with you about their facilities and their usefulness.

Keeping an Eye on the Competition

Who else is on the birthday party planning playing field? You will need to gather accurate information about your competitors. This will help you define your niche. If, for instance, there is a party planner who has created a successful business planning music-based birthday parties, you will probably want to avoid competing directly with her. In other words, if a specialization or niche is already filled, try to find another area, especially if you live in a relatively small town or city. Two party planners with the same specialization may be one too many for an area with a small population base.

Let Your Fingers Do the Walking

You can find your competition by searching the local phone book. As you develop your business, the phone book will prove invaluable. It is interesting that in this age of computers and ever-advancing technology, a simple tool, such as the phone book, still remains vital. As you find your competition in the yellow pages, you may want to interview some of these party planners as well. If you opt to develop an arts-based birthday party planning business, then an owner of a sports-based birthday party planning business will probably be willing to speak with you about the children's birthday party market. In fact, he may welcome your entry into the field since a synergy is often formed when a field grows. That's why car dealers often line up their dealerships on the same road, one after another. The belief is that this clustering create a buzz and means bigger sales for all of the car dealerships. The same can hold true in other businesses, as well.

Surfing for Leads

You will also be able to track your competition using the Internet. Go to your favorite search engine, such as Google or Yahoo!, and then type in keywords such as "children's birthday party planner," and your state and town. A list of your local competitors will appear on your computer screen.

More Detective Work

Next, you will need to resort to more old-fashioned gumshoeing as you search for your competitors. Some party planners rely almost entirely on word-of-mouth promotion and don't even bother with a phone book listing. This is not recommended for your business. Word-of-mouth promotion is free and fantastic, but a phone book listing is also essential.

As you find your competitors by networking with local merchants involved with children's party planning (caterers, bakers, entertainers), plan on visiting your competitors in person rather than over the phone. It is always useful to put a face with a name. And an in-person visit will enable you to do this.

Creating a Niche

You've completed your research and it is time to solidify your business's niche. Perhaps you had planned on "mad scientist" parties but, through your research, have discovered that another planner has very successfully taken this market. If this is the case, choose another niche. Unless you live in an area with a rather large population, you are taking a risk going head-to-head with a successfully established niche planner.

If you are planning to hold parties at varied venues with varied themes, you still need to determine a niche. Will you be the party planner with the most competitive prices? If, for instance, you found through your research, that parents felt over-charged for planning services, this might be a fantastic way to develop a successful company.

Some successful event planners develop a niche as budget-minded party planners. Just as a savvy contractor can save you money on a building project, a successful children's birthday party planner can create real savings for her clients by buying party supplies in volume, negotiating with vendors, and developing a rapport with other suppliers. Although the niche for my business is art-based, many clients tell me at the end of their children's parties that I saved them money, as well. "It would have cost me more to do this at home," is a common refrain from parents.

For your company to have an optimal chance at success, it needs to be unique in some way. Using your research, find a way to differentiate your company from the competition. You will need to have an answer to this question before writing your business plan.

Naming Your Business

Don't underestimate the importance of this step or the power of your business name. A business name should convey professionalism, creativity, clarity, and more. Add to this the fact that an ideal business name is unique and is composed of only a few words. Don't be intimidated by these parameters, though. Instead, view your business name as one of your most valuable marketing assets, one that will serve as a first impression of your birthday party planning business.

Noting Your Niche

Perhaps most essential when choosing a business name is clearly stating your business's niche. Live Animal Adventure Birthday Parties clearly states that this birthday party business will entertain the children with living creatures. Likewise, Priceless Pony Parties tells your audience that you plan pony parties. By using the word "price-less" in your name, you convey a feeling of uniqueness.

Some new business owners are tempted to give their business a name that will ensure an early listing in the phone book—AAAA Parties!, for instance. Don't do it. This name tells your audience nothing about the nature of your business. If you feel

> **Notes from the Field**
>
> Many event planners begin their search for the perfect name with a brainstorming session. Gather a group of friends and, if possible, people associated with children's birthday parties—caterers, bakers, photographers. Create a non-threatening environment and remember that every idea is a good idea. Don't insist that participants take turns. Write down all of the ideas on large paper taped to the walls so everyone can see their ideas as they flow. Serve refreshments, encourage everyone to think of "blue sky" names, and enjoy this creative process.

that you must land an early spot in the phone book, consider AAAA Priceless Pony Parties. However, this gives a less professional finish to your business.

Keep It Short

You want your audience to remember your business name, so stay away from cumbersome names and tongue twisters. Consider the blockbuster retailer Target. One simple word, as well as their brilliant bull's-eye target logo, conveys mountains of information about the retailer. You'll want to choose a business name consisting of no more than half a dozen words. Remember, a name you may find clever—Susan's Savvy Celebration Solutions, for instance—really does not convey the nature of your business or roll easily off of the tongue.

Keep Your Options Open

You may decide to hang out your birthday party shingle with a focus on princess parties, leading you to consider a princess-themed business name. This is apt in that the name clearly delineates your niche. However, the name may become limiting if you choose to expand your business. Perhaps you will opt to take on pirate parties as well, to increase the audience for your services. If so, a name like Happily Ever After Princess Parties won't float.

This can be a conundrum for new business owners who aren't sure how their new businesses will develop and expand. If you think the scope of your business might expand, choose a business name that won't limit this expansion.

Don't be misled into thinking that changing your business name midstream is an easy task. Your business will establish itself largely through word of mouth. You don't want to build up invaluable word-of-mouth marketing only to have it disrupted by renaming your business. Also, as will be outlined below, there is paperwork to be filed and trademark searches to complete when naming a business. Simplify your life and choose a business name that you plan to keep throughout the life of your business.

It is also advisable to avoid using your name when naming your business. Unless you already have a reputation for party planning, your name will not add to the value of the business name. And, if at some point down the road you decide to sell your business, a new owner would probably not want your name attached. Likewise, a geographic moniker can be limiting to your business growth. As you use the Internet to market your business, chaining yourself to an earthbound location—like "Seattle's Silly Science Sessions"—can be limiting.

Don't Be Silly!

Yes, the children's birthday party business is about having fun and celebrating festive occasions. However, don't convey a sense of silliness in your business name. Parents, who will be hiring you, are looking for a levelheaded and good-natured party planner and a silly business name will not reflect these important qualities.

Avoid Over-the-Top Jargon

Try to avoid words like "magnificent," "amazing," "remarkable," and "out of this world," for instance. These types of words are too hyperbolic and don't really reflect anything about your business. Remember, you only have a few words and a few seconds to make an initial impression on your potential audience. Use powerful words that convey information about your business.

Internet Tip

For answers to frequently asked trademark questions, check out www.uspto.gov, an amazingly useful site for understanding sometimes tricky trademark issues.

Trademarking Your Name

You've done it. You've found the perfect name for your new business. But wait! There is another essential step. You will need to ensure that the name you have chosen has not already been trademarked by another business. Do this research at the United States Government's Patent and Trademark office Web site, www.uspto.gov.

Consider if your new business name is similar to an existing trademarked name. A couple in Elizabethtown, Kentucky, decided to open a store named Victor's Secret. Needless to say, lawyers at Victoria's Secret were not pleased and the couple had to rename their business.

You should also consider trademarking your name and logo. Trademarks can apply to business names and to logos, such as Nike's famous swoosh and Coke's uniquely shaped bottle. On the one hand, you may plan to keep your business small and feel that obtaining a trademark is an unnecessary hurdle. If you have any thoughts of expansion or of one day franchising your birthday party business, plan on applying for and obtaining a trademark. As with obtaining the necessary licenses and permits, it is best to build a solid business foundation from day one, and that includes appropriate trademark appropriation.

You should budget at least $1,000 for this trademark process. This will include attorney's fees for a thorough trademark search as well as for the application process. This also includes the $325 payable to the United States Government to be included with your trademark application. Remember the old adage, it takes money to make money? You may feel hesitant to spend this much money up front, and if you are quite certain your business will stay small and very local, a trademark is probably not critical. If, however, you have any thoughts of developing a larger business, consider speaking with an attorney about the prudence of obtaining a trademark.

Finally, many states require registration of your business name. This is often done through the county and is known as filing a DBA (doing business as) statement.

Creating Your Unique Logo

Your logo carries as much weight as your name and, like your business name, it must convey a sense of professionalism. Although there are inexpensive software design programs available for home computer users, plan on hiring someone to create your logo. A less-than-professionally produced logo is not the message you want to send to prospective clients.

Internet Tip

Some party planners opt to use an online source when designing a logo. One of these sites, LogoWorks (www.logoworks.com) offers logo design packages beginning at $299. This price includes ten custom designs for you to preview and enables you to be an active participant in the design and revision process. Another plus: it is possible to complete your LogoWorks logo in one week. Another site, TheLogoLoft (www.thelogoloft.com), offers a package priced at $239. While creating your logo with TheLogoLoft, you will be working with in-house designers to create your custom logo. If you opt to design your logo using an online site, choose a service that uses in-house rather than freelance designers. In-house designers tend to produce higher-quality work. Also, use a site that offers assistance via the phone. Sometimes, it is difficult to express via e-mail your thoughts about the design of your logo. Make sure that the design company you choose offers a phone help line.

Choose your designer carefully. Look at the logos she has created for other clients before hiring her. Be sure to talk about the fees for her services up front. Another word of caution: do not use clip art. The clip art birthday hat icon you think is perfect? Well, a lot of other party planners will think it is perfect, too, and might use it for their logos. You want your logo to be unique and an expression of yourself and your sensibilities. Like your business name, your logo will appear on every piece of your marketing materials, from your business card to your Web site.

Consider some of the iconic logos that have been so successful: McDonald's arches, Nike's swoosh, Apple Computer's apple, Target's bull's-eye, and Shell Oil's shell. These logos act as mnemonic devices, helping us to remember the companies these logos represent. Most likely, when you see yellow arches, your mind thinks of McDonald's. Likewise, Nike's swoosh brings to mind sports and athleticism. Make your logo contemporary and catchy.

Crafting a Compelling Mission Statement

Wait, there's more! Don't feel bogged down by these steps. Instead, view all of these processes as exciting building blocks in the formation of your company. And, the

Mission Statement Checklist

- *Be concise.* Try to limit your statement to one sentence. If you can't synthesize your mission into one sentence, perhaps your vision is not yet clear about exactly what type of birthday party business you are developing. Look at it this way: If NASA can boil down its work into one sentence, the rest of us can, too!

- *Choose words carefully. Because you are limiting your mission statement to one sentence, careful and thoughtful word choice is key.* Don't throw in extraneous words like "amazing," or "unique." You have to explain, through your statement, why your business is unique. In keeping it short, it is better to jump right in with your statement rather than beginning with "Our mission is . . ."

- *Be specific.* Don't write a general mission statement like this: "To give a fun-filled birthday party to all ages." This is too general and does not describe your niche, your target audience, or how you execute your business.

- *Consider what will be the most important aspect of your business.* Is it the theme you've developed? The price point? The location? Make sure that this is highlighted in your statement. Perhaps you have done your market research and realize that there is a need in your area for parties planned with smaller budgets in mind. If so, you want to highlight this in your statement.

- *Use an appropriate tone.* In other words, this statement should be professional but not too stiff and uptight. After all, as a children's birthday party planner, you are in the business of fun.

- *Edit, edit, edit.* When you think you've honed and refined all you can, check once more. Don't throw in extra adjectives or articles. Say more with less.

- *Say your mission statement out loud.* This is important. If your mission statement sounds stilted or somehow unnatural, tweak it so it rolls more easily off the tongue.

- *Post your mission statement.* Voilà! When your statement is crafted, print it out and post it in your work area. This statement should inspire you every day.

Internet Tip

Think about the businesses you admire and do business with. Use the Internet to check their corporate Web sites to read their mission statements. It is likely that you will find compelling and succinct mission statements. Successful companies are almost always reflected in their apt mission statements.

more you think about the steps and questions posed in this chapter, the closer you will be to opening the doors to a very successful business.

A mission statement succinctly outlines the goals and mission of your business. Consider Web search-engine giant Google's mission statement: "Google's mission is to organize the world's information and make it universally accessible and useful." Or NASA's statement: "To explore the universe and search for life; to inspire the next generation of explorers ... as only NASA can." Birthday party venue provider Chuck E. Cheese sums up its mission in this way: "To bring families together in a wholesome environment for fun, games, and kids."

All of these mission statements are only one sentence long. Don't let your mission statement ramble on. It should be memorable and if it is too long-winded for you to remember, it is likely that others won't remember it, either.

Mission statements are often called vision statements because they reflect the vision of the business, the business owner, and the business employees. It is helpful to keep the idea of vision and looking forward to the growth of your business as you craft your statement.

Selecting a Business Structure

You will need to determine the best business structure for your new venture. Be sure to give this selection careful consideration. The type of business structure you choose has ramifications for your growing company. Different business structures have different implications for protection of personal assets, tax issues, the ease with which you would be able to sell your company or take on partners, and more.

By choosing a business structure, you will help to define the vision for your company. For instance, if you initially opt for a sole proprietorship, you will begin to develop a business based on the idea that you will be solely in charge. Likewise, if you choose a partnership model, you will develop a company based on a model of shared responsibility.

Sole Proprietorship

As the name suggests, this structure is straightforward and often appropriate for new business owners. As the sole, or only, owner of your business you will assume responsibility for all profits and all losses. It is relatively easy to set up a sole proprietorship. You will need to file a DBA, as discussed above, and open a checking account in your business's name.

The downside to this model is that a significant business loss could wipe out your business as well as your personal funds. For this reason, as your business grows, you might consider other business structures.

Partnerships

There are two types of partnership structures: general and limited. General partners share fully in the running of the business. In other words, if you and a friend choose to develop the business together as equal partners, the two of you will form a general partnership. Both partners will share in the profits as well as be responsible for the business's losses.

A limited partner plays a different role. A limited partner may contribute financially but not be part of the day-to-day operations. A limited partner would receive a share of the profits based on her financial investment. This more complicated business model is probably not the ideal model for a relatively small birthday party business.

Limited Liability Company

This business structure is a relatively new option with the first limited liability company (LLC) having been formed in Wyoming in 1977. LLCs combine the tax structure of a partnership while offering protection for the business owner from personal liability. This structure also protects each partner's personal interests. Limited liability companies are managed by members or managers. A business owner can be a member or manager. LLCs are authorized by state governments, so regulations vary from state to state.

LLCs are the most popular business structure for small business because they combine the best benefits of partnerships and incorporation. If you opt for an LLC, you will need to obtain the necessary paperwork through your secretary of state's office. Cost of forming an LLC varies from state to state, with some states charging as little as $40 and others charging $900.

Incorporation

Forming a corporation is more complicated, as it involves establishing a business as a totally separate legal entity from the business owner. Few event planners, as they first set out, choose to incorporate as it is expensive to establish and the company must pay corporate taxes. An advantage to incorporation is the protection of your personal assets. Most event planners find that an LLC is a better choice as it offers the protections of incorporation without all of the cumbersome paperwork and legal work needed to form a corporation.

You may find that, over time, you will change your structure. Many business owners upon setting up shop choose to structure as sole proprietorships. If you have any doubts about the best business structure, consult with a lawyer.

Writing a Business Plan

Don't be intimidated by the prospect of writing a business plan. It is actually an exciting and dynamic process allowing you to hone and refine your business ideas. When writing your business plan, you will essentially be answering a series of straightforward questions. By breaking the writing process down into these incremental steps, it becomes very manageable. When you finish writing your business plan, you may—especially if writing is not your strength—want to have a professional editor look it over and add polish. Since you will be using your business plan if you seek financing from a bank, you won't want spelling errors or grammatical jumbles. Don't pay someone to write the plan for you, however. It is better to have your voice and personality reflected throughout the plan since this voice is a representation of your company.

What Is the Overall Vision and Plan for Your Business?

This section is called the executive summary, and a summary is exactly what you will aim for in this part of your business plan. In this first segment of your business plan, you will sum up all that follows—your goals, your competition, your plans for marketing and growth, for instance. In your finalized business report, this section appears first. However, you may want to write the other sections of your business plan first and then summarize what you have written.

What Is Your Business Going to Offer?

This is, again, a straightforward question, asking you to describe your new company's services. Be specific here. Don't write, "My goal is to start a children's birthday party planning business." This is too general. Explain what your product is, why it is unique, and what are the opportunities for you to grow a business like this. In this section you will also detail the business structure you've chosen (a sole proprietorship, for instance).

Who Is Your Competition?

You've already done your research. Clearly delineate your competition and why your business will succeed in the face of this competition. Explain how the niche you've chosen will find success in your town or city and why.

Who Are Your Customers?

This question is as vital as defining your competition. It also affords you the opportunity to consider if your area has the customer base you need to succeed. Whenever possible, use numbers and statistics. Look at local census and economic information to build a solid, fact-based business plan.

How Will You Market Your Business?

Do you plan to advertise in your local yellow pages, create business cards, or build a Web site? A detailed discussion of marketing will follow in Chapter 10, telling how to create powerful marketing tools. For your business plan, you need to outline a basic structure for your marketing goals. Again, be as specific and offer as many details as possible.

When Will All of These Things Happen?

This section of your business plan functions as a timeline for your developing business. Discuss your target date for holding your first event, your target date for launching a Web site (if you plan to launch one), your goals in terms of timing for growth, and other time-specific goals. This is very helpful for you in terms of framing your business, as well. By filling in this timeline, you will have a more transparent map of the timeframe for your company's projected growth.

Notes from the Field

Successful event planners report that they took the time to reflect and to answer these questions before writing their business plans. Answering these questions first will help direct you as you write your plan:

1. What type of children's birthday party services will you provide? Try to clearly define your business. Think about what your specialization will be.
2. Who are your customers? Consider realistically the market for your birthday party services.
3. How will you reach these customers? You may produce the best birthday-party widget ever, but if you don't market your business, it will not be successful.
4. How will you finance your business? Perhaps you are planning to start relatively small and already have most of the equipment you need on hand. If you have larger goals in mind, how will you finance these objectives?

Who Will Manage Your Company?

As a small business owner, you will be the primary manager for your company. Small business owners often rely on other professionals to help keep the ship right. These include lawyers, accountants, and other consultants. If you plan to use any of these professionals, outline their use in this section of your business plan.

How Will You Finance Your Company?

Again, be clear and specific. If you plan to finance using a line of credit you already have (for instance, a line of credit on your home), describe the interest rate on the line of credit, the amount you plan to borrow, and your plans for repayment. If you plan to borrow from a friend or family member, outline the same basics—interest rate, amount borrowed, and repayment schedule. Remember, keep it all official and professional.

Appendices

You're almost finished. You've probably found that by treating your business plan as a question and answer exercise, it has been a manageable and enjoyable process, creating excitement for your new venture. In this final section, you will attach any spreadsheets or other numbers that are relevant as well as copies of any necessary licenses and permits.

Financing Your Business

As I've already written, a children's birthday party planning business can be launched successfully with a small budget. However, all businesses take some funding to get off the ground and, as the old saw tells us, "you have to spend money to make money." Now that you have a business plan in hand, it is time to make decisions about how you will finance your company.

Structuring your finances is a critical step in the creation of your business. From using your credit card to approaching a local bank for a small business loan, there are multiple ways to finance a business. As you consider the possibilities, maintain realistic expectations at the fore. Keep emotion out of your financial equation. Starting a business is a thrilling and exhilarating time. Don't get caught up in the excitement and find yourself in financial straits due to over-borrowing or bad financial planning.

Your Own Resources

If your plan is to start small—planning only one or two events per month—then it is prudent to take stock of the equipment you already own. Most households already have at least one computer. Perhaps, at least as you start out, you will decide to use the computer you already own. Similarly, although a top-quality digital camera ultimately will prove invaluable to your marketing efforts, you may choose to put off buying a camera until your business is creating a profit.

Friends and Family

Friends and family may offer to help in financing your business. If you accept their help, make it official and work out a plan for repaying their generosity. If your mother-in-law tells you she doesn't want to be reimbursed, plan on reimbursing her anyway. Things can get sticky if loans between friends and family are not repaid. Don't jeopardize your business or personal relationships by neglecting to keep things professional when it comes to money, friends, and family.

Credit Cards

Be very cautious if you choose to fund your business launch with credit cards. Interest rates on these cards can top out at more than 25 percent, so if you are unable to pay off your balances in full quite quickly, you should try to steer clear of this option. When you factor in high interest payments, you may find that any profits you've made are quickly wiped out.

There are many hungry credit card companies, hoping for your business, so these companies are often willing to negotiate better terms than the ones offered in their marketing materials. Call the companies' toll-free numbers and speak directly to a customer service representative to negotiate the best interest rate possible.

Home Equity Loans and Other Credit Lines

Sometimes we are too quick to consider home equity loans a source of "free" money because interest rates tend to be low and the approval process is often quick and quite lax. As with using credit cards, I advise caution. However, home equity loans at a low interest rate are a better source of funding than credit cards. If you opt for a line of credit, negotiate with the lender for the best rate and take out only the dollars needed. Be prudent. If the bank offers a $10,000 line of credit, use it sparingly. Perhaps you will only need to tap into the line for $1,000 to launch your business.

Bank Financing

If your dream business involves launching an event-planning business with the goal of earning a full-time income, then the infrastructure costs of creating that business will be higher as well. If this is your goal, bank financing may be the financial path for you.

When approaching bank loan officers, a thoughtful, well-researched business plan is essential, so do not contact these officers until you have this business plan firmly in hand. When considering a bank with which to do business, consider a locally owned bank, as they are often more willing to work with small and local businesses than the big chain banks. And, shop around. I have found a wide variance in the different packages that financial institutions create and offer.

A Timeline for Opening Your Birthday Party Business

Opening a business takes time and thought. Don't plan on holding your first event until you have covered all of the steps necessary to open your business. A realistic timeframe is to allow three month's time from the moment you conceive of your birthday party business to the exciting time when you and your client sign on the dotted line of a contract. You won't hold your first event until this period is over. For instance, if the first event you plan is a small party for twelve children at a local bowling alley, you could easily plan this party in a month's time. However, if your first party is an event for fifty guests with catered food, a clown, a face painter, and a strolling musician, then you will need several months to plan and develop the event.

Month 1

- Begin envisioning the model for your business. Start thinking "outside the box" about all the possibilities for your company
- Take these visions and begin research: What niche will work in your area? Who will your clients be? Who is your competition?
- Develop a name for your company
- Develop a logo for your company
- Start work on your business plan
- Arrange to hire accountants and lawyers if you are planning to use their services
- Create a powerful mission statement

Month 2

- Complete work on your business plan
- Arrange financing
- Buy office supplies and set up your home office
- Set up a birthday party site (not necessary if you plan to hold parties at rented venues)
- Have stationery, letterhead, business cards, and any other printed materials designed and printed
- Start spreading the word about your new business by telling friends and colleagues, as well as posting your business card or brochure on community bulletin boards. At this point, be wary of spending money on advertising
- Send a press release to local newspapers, regional magazines, or local television affiliates, describing your new business. Remember to outline what makes your birthday party business unique

- Meet with colleagues who work in the children's birthday party field, including disc jockeys, magicians, company managers who rent inflatables, caterers, and bakers. Let them know you are opening a birthday party business

Month 3

- As prospective clients call, arrange a time to meet
- Using information gathered on the client questionnaire (see page 60), create proposals, including event details as well as costs involved
- Have contracts prepared for you and your clients to sign, showing the agreed-upon event details

The Finish Line

By completing all of the steps outlined in this chapter, you have built a strong and durable foundation for your new business. It is sometimes tempting to gloss over or to skip some of these steps, but for a business to succeed, it is important to follow through on all of these nuts-and-bolts logistical issues.

New Business Checklist

Before you plan and hold your first event make sure you have:
- ❏ Selected a name for your business and applied for a DBA
- ❏ Crafted a compelling, memorable mission statement
- ❏ Chosen the best business structure for your business, keeping in mind that as your company grows, the business structure can change
- ❏ Applied for any necessary licenses
- ❏ Checked with your local authorities to confirm that your business is within the town's zoning code
- ❏ Arranged financing for your business
- ❏ Written a thoughtful, thorough business plan

All checks? Good for you. You are ready to plan your first event!

Inventor Thomas Edison received almost 1,100 U.S. patents over the course of his life for everything from the phonograph to the incandescent light bulb. His recipe for success was straightforward and applies to any new business owner: "The three great essentials to achieve anything worthwhile are, first, hard work; second, stick-to-itiveness; third, common sense." Stick to all of the steps in this chapter and your business will be off with a flourish.

Frequently Asked Questions

Why do I have to choose a business structure?

It is inviting to start a business without choosing a business structure. After all, you might think, I am only planning an event a month, so I won't have any problems keeping all of my financial ducks in a row. These ducks won't line up as well if you don't choose a business structure at the onset of your business's launch. The business you launch now may grow ten- or twentyfold over the years and it is critical to have a business structure in place. You might plan to simply fold the small amount you anticipate earning initially into your personal accounts. Don't do this. It is a fool's errand to think that you can avoid paying what is due to the IRS. Choose a business structure, maintain separate bank accounts, and keep things on the up and up from the word go.

I am still uncertain about choosing a business structure. Is there any source for free professional advice?

One of the best resources for anyone launching a new business is SCORE (Service Corps of Retired Executives). These self-described "counselors to America's small businesses," offer free online and face-to-face advice to new business owners. These retired professionals also offer mentoring services. From tax tips to financing and managing your business, these experts provide an invaluable service at no charge. See www.score.org for more information.

Hanging Out Your Shingle

Preparing for Your First Party

Congratulations! Your birthday wish has come true and you have completed all of the necessary steps to throw open the doors to your new business. And, by completing all of the steps outlined in Chapter 4, from researching your competition to creating a powerful mission statement and writing a thoughtful business plan, you have proven that you have the organizational skills to keep your new business buoyant. This is an incredibly exciting time for most new business owners as they plan their first event.

Remember, you are only as good as your last event, a mantra that will be echoed throughout this book, so take care when planning your first birthday party. I was recently reminded of this when I spoke with Maura Cutler, a mother of three, who chose to hire a children's party planner to help with a recent birthday celebration.

"I chose party planners who specialize in bringing animals to homes—like Angora bunnies and guinea pigs. Well, the party was a success until the end, when the people I'd hired packed up and left—but forgot their six-foot snake in our house. My mother-in-law discovered it and she is deathly afraid of snakes. It was a disaster, and I won't use this company or recommend them to anyone else," explained Cutler.

Only as good as your last event? This company is out of luck, then.

Start Spreading the News

It is time to spread the good news about your developing business. Chapter 10 offers in-depth advice for marketing your business, from creating eye-catching and powerful business cards to creating a yellow pages advertisement that really works.

When you first throw open your doors (literal and figurative!), networking will prove to be one of your most effective strategies. In other words, tell everyone you meet that you are the proud new owner of a children's birthday party planning business. Tell your friends over coffee, mention it at your church or synagogue coffee hour, let your friends know on a girls' night out at the movies. You will be amazed—I know I was—at the number of moms who will express interest in taking you up on your services, ASAP!

Shannon Ludwin, a busy mother of two, describes why she and other moms are so eager to take on extra help when it comes time to plan their children's birthday parties.

"Kids' parties are so challenging to plan these days, because it seems like the parties I used to have when I was small—the trusty pin-the-tail-on-something game, a cake shaped like Scooby-Doo and a little goody bag—don't entertain kids for very long. Also, having no plan or activity creates stress for me, too, because I don't want kids just running aimlessly through my home looking for things to do. I want something that is enjoyable for them, and with small children, they like to run, move, build, paint, color, or be involved in something that keeps their attention. So, plans, activities, and art projects seem to work very well because they can be tailored to the ages."

Ludwin sums up the feelings of so many parents. It is challenging to create a birthday party environment that will engage the children in a safe and creative way. That is where you and your expertise come into play!

Remember, though, as you tell friends and acquaintances about your new business that it is a business. Don't offer to help a friend without being compensated. This is a professional service you are offering and, often, new business owners must remind themselves not to be underpaid for their services.

Likewise, as you plan your first event, be sure to keep everything "official." In other words, have your client—even a good friend—fill out all of the paperwork, beginning with a client questionnaire. This ensures that you are all on the same page regarding venue, theme, cost, and so on. This paper trail will prove invaluable as your business grows. You may think, as you plan your first party, that you can store all of the details in your brain. Think again. Write down absolutely everything in an organized fashion.

What is the name of the birthday child? _____

How old will s/he be? _____

What day is the actual birthday? _____

What are the names of his/her siblings? _____

How many children will attend the event?_____

How many adults will attend? _____

What are the ages of the children? _____

Are there any special accommodations to be made?
For instance, are there allergy issues to be considered? _____

_____

What is the theme for the event? _____

What is the venue for the event?_____

What date is the event? _____

What is the start time? _____

The end time?_____

Who is sending invitations—you or the client? _____

What is the entertainment? _____

What type of decorations will there be? _____

What type of food is to be served? _____

What is the budget? _____

This documentation will help to protect you if a client is dissatisfied for any reason with the final event. Perhaps the client specifies only purple balloons and then complains later that she wanted rainbow balloons. Simply pull out the original client questionnaire showing that the client asked for purple balloons. This record system is also useful for parents who use your services year after year—and, as successful party planners know, clients return again and again to organized, resourceful party planners.

Avoiding Common Early Mistakes

New business owners can save themselves a lot of heartache by avoiding the most common mistakes. Yes, the failure rate of small businesses—50 percent within the first year—is alarming. Still, according to the Small Business Administration, taking straightforward actions to avoid early missteps will help to ensure the success of your business.

According to experts, there are ten common mistakes that business owners make. As the adage goes, know your enemy. Consider these common mistakes and conquer them rather than letting them conquer your fledgling business.

1. **Procrastination**

   We all fall prey to this at one time or another, putting off the task that is a bit daunting. Don't make this mistake with your small business. This is particularly important when creating your business foundation. For instance, don't procrastinate about arranging adequate insurance for your business or applying for the appropriate licenses.

2. **Lack of Professionalism**

   Always remember to be polished and professional in all of your business dealings. This includes creating and distributing the highest-quality business card you can afford, and crafting a professional message on your answering machine. Every facet of your new business is a reflection of yourself. Make that image professional. A prospective client who calls and finds the phone answered by your two-year-old will probably not choose to use your services, having encountered a lack of professionalism on this first phone call.

3. **Underestimating the Competition**

   Be truthful in your assessment of the competition in your area. If someone else has already captured the market for princess parties, then you need to develop another niche. Don't trust that your services will succeed in a market already successfully dominated by another planner. You need to differentiate yourself from your competition.

4. **Growing Too Rapidly**

   This is a challenging conundrum for new business owners. As the calls start to roll in, some new business owners are too eager to say "yes" to every proposed event. Don't stretch yourself too thin as you grow your business. If you take on too many parties and are unable to adequately plan and staff them, your reputation could take a beating. Growing a business might require taking on additional employees, a process that takes time and careful thought.

5. **Not Enough Money**

   My mantra, as I developed my business, was that an event-planning business can be launched on a combination of a shoestring budget and a passel of imagination. "Shoestring" does not mean that you won't need to invest any money in your company. You will need to buy the basics, so don't face inevitable disappointment by launching your business without a financial plan and financial backing.

6. **Poor Management**

   Poor management is the bane of many small businesses. Some new business owners continue to treat their fledging operations as hobbies rather than businesses and fail to oversee and manage all of the details involved in running a business. I can't overstate how vital it is to keep thorough records of everything—from every dollar you spend, including the $1 spent on a box of paperclips, to the type of cake the birthday girl prefers. Optimal management will result in more clients returning to you for your expertise as well as bringing in new clients as the good word of mouth spreads.

7. **Disorganization**

   When a prospective client arrives at your office, you won't want to fumble through files looking for the appropriate forms. Likewise, on the day of the party, a client won't appreciate misplaced juice boxes. Clients are paying you to be organized. My clients often cite organization as a primary reason for hiring me. They expect me to remember the cake knife, the party hats, and the goody bags so they don't have to worry.

8. **Wrong Location**

   Perhaps your office is in the wrong location. If you live in an off-the-beaten-track location, you might need to consider renting an office space elsewhere. Location could also refer to your small town or city. If you are planning to launch a full-scale business, you need to have the population base to support these plans.

9. **Opening for the Wrong Reasons**

   Unfortunately, some at-home business owners hang out their shingles for the wrong reasons. Perhaps they view party planning as "easy money" and hope to earn money without earning the trust and respect of clients. Don't open an at-home business on a lark. To be successful you must be fully committed to the idea and the work involved.

10. **Undercharging**

This was particularly challenging for me when I first began planning events. I thought, mistakenly, that by charging less I would find more clients. Don't make this mistake. Yes, you are in this for the joy of party planning but, ultimately, to make your business work you need to profit. There is the adage, "you get what you pay for." Remember this when you price your events. Your client wants a quality event. Don't set prices so low that you need to cut corners or, at the end of the day, you find that you have earned nothing—or even lost money—after spending many, many hours planning a successful event.

Your First Event

Not only are you only as good as your last event, but also your reputation will be bolstered—or brought down—by your first event, so it is imperative that you plan your first event with attention to every last detail.

You will begin the process of planning by meeting with the parents of the birthday child. Schedule a time to sit down with the parents. Don't conduct this initial consultation via the telephone. It is important to develop relationships with your clients. It will result in a better event because you will have a deeper understanding of your clients' desires.

Internet Tip

Consider offering a cup of tea or coffee or a glass of soda water. This shows a sense of hospitality and grace. Serve the coffee and tea in mugs adorned with your logo. At Web sites such as www.discountmugs.com, you can purchase customized mugs for less than $1 each. Always, you need to be mindful of branding your business—in other words, of creating your business's personality. Part of doing this includes using your logo often.

Event Checklist

Week before the birthday party:

- Contact venue for final confirmation; double-check date and party start and end times.
- Contact any entertainers and confirm their arrival time.
- Contact any caterers and confirm delivery or pickup times.
- Contact any inflatable suppliers and confirm delivery and pickup times.
- Confirm number of attendees.
- Arrange and confirm any extra staffing needs.
- Schedule for pickup and delivery of any rental items.
- Make sure to check quantities of all party favors.
- Make sure that you have all décor items.
- Confirm you have adequate quantities of all paper goods
- Create goody bags.

Day before the birthday party:

- Make sure your birthday party toolbox is stocked.
- Gather all of your supplies together (from décor items to paper goods and goody bags); if possible, pack them in your car a day early.
- Make final confirmation with party venue.
- Make final confirmation with parents of birthday child.
- Pick up any necessary rental supplies.
- Make sure to have small bills for tipping any delivery people.

Day of the birthday party:

- Double-check that you have loaded all necessary supplies—make sure that your cell phone is charged!
- Arrive at the venue early. It is always better to be on the early side when preparing for a child's party.
- Set up for the party.

During the birthday party:

- Greet all guests professionally. Make sure that your setup work is complete so you can focus on the guests.
- Tell the party attendees where to put the presents and their coats, and then direct them to the first activity.
- If you are providing the entertainment, make sure you are prepared and organized. I do all of the prep work for my art-based birthday parties before arriving at the party venue.
- After all of the guests have arrived, begin official party activities. Make sure that all of the children know one another. Often, party attendees go to different schools or might even live in different towns. Have the children introduce themselves. Perhaps, use an ice-breaker, asking the children to tell their names and their favorite type of candy or favorite color. Kids love this kind of list.
- Create the flow of activities. Perhaps the parents want cake first and then the entertainment. Make sure that the children transition from one step to the next.
- Maintain order. Yes, kids can get pretty revved up at a birthday party. However, I have found that as long as this energy is channeled and the kids are made aware of the expectations regarding behavior, maintaining control is not too challenging. As kids arrive and introduce themselves, I introduce myself, too, and outline the rules of the party. I do it in a good-natured way, acknowledging that everyone is at the party to have fun. However, as I point out, everyone will have more fun if the rules are followed. Frankly, I have found that 99.9 percent of the time, kids are delighted to comply.
- Serve any food the parents have asked for. For larger parties, you will need to hire help. For small parties, where the parents have asked for only cupcakes, it is easy enough for you to serve the kids.
- If the parents have asked that presents be opened at the event, oversee this. Do this in an orderly fashion—no ripping open packages willy-nilly! Note all gifts for thank-you cards to be sent later.

- Make sure to have a final activity after the primary entertainment, cake, food, and present opening are complete in case any time remains.
- Make sure that the kids leave in an orderly fashion.
- Help the birthday party parents take the presents to their car. I find that large, sturdy garbage bags are useful for this.
- Thank them for using your business.
- Throughout the whole event, keep smiling. Your smile shows your enthusiasm and care. It's not always easy to smile, especially when the birthday-party child is in tears because her best friend, at the eleventh hour, couldn't attend. It's not easy but it is important!

After the birthday party:

- Follow up with the parents, making sure that they were satisfied with everything. If not, listen to their concerns.
- Bill your clients.
- Contact the outside venue (if you used one) for their feedback.
- Check with any outside caterers or other entertainers for their feedback.
- Make notes of any concerns you might have—note both the best elements of the day as well as any worrisome bits.

If your client is meeting you at your home office, make sure to schedule the meeting when your kids are in school or you have other childcare arrangements. Also, don't answer your phone while meeting in person with a client. Your answering machine or voice mail will pick up calls for you. Remember, this is a business and you want to convey a sense of professionalism.

Begin by filling out a client and party information questionnaire (a sample is included in this chapter). You will use this information to complete a proposal, so make sure that the information you include on the client information form is thorough and accurate. You will need to find out:

- **Birthday child's name and age.** First and foremost, find out the name of the child. Then, use the child's name throughout the rest of this first meeting. Small things like this—using the child's name rather than using the generic "your child"—help elevate your business to a more professional level.

- **Date for event.** Consult your calendar when writing down the date and time. I recently attended a dinner party on a Friday evening. The caterer, when initially meeting with the host and hostess, dutifully wrote down "February 8," because that was the date given to her by the host and hostess. Unfortunately, the host and hostess were looking at the previous year's calendar—which indicated that the eighth fell on a Friday, the day preferred by the couple giving the party. Unfortunately, when the caterer returned to her office and wrote down the details of the job and entered the event onto her calendar, she placed the event on Saturday the eighth because the current year's calendar indicated that the eighth would fall on a Saturday. End result? The caterer did not arrive, thinking the party was occurring the next evening. Our lovely hostess went scurrying off in her yellow Volkswagen Beetle to buy prepared food at the local grocery store. This is a gentle parable, reminding all of us to dot every "i" and to cross every "t." Even the smallest detail is significant.

- **Venue for event.** If you are a planner who holds events in only one space, this will not vary from event to event. If however, you use a variety of venues, note the client's preference here. If the client requests an event at a busy venue, ask for alternate party dates and/or alternate venue sites.

- **Number of attendees.** Some birthday parties, particularly for tots, include both adults and children on the guest list. Be sure to note the number of adults and the number of children who will be attending. Don't be the party planner who brings only juice boxes, forgetting to bring a carafe of coffee or other beverage appropriate for adults.

- **Type of food and drink to be served.** Children's birthday parties run the gamut in terms of refreshments. Some parents prefer to keep it simple, opting to serve individual cupcakes and leave it at that. Other parents want the whole nine yards: pizza, chips, fresh fruit, juice, and water, as well as refreshments for the adults. Make sure that you get a clear sense of the parents' desires.

- **Type of preferred activities.** What types of activities do the parents and the birthday child want at the event? Really listen to your client. Kids often have very specific ideas about their parties. If it's a pirate party, the birthday child might want everyone to wear matching hats and eye patches. If it is a princess party, the party princess might not want anyone but her to wear a tiara. Children frequently have a vision of what their perfect party will look like. Listen closely. Paying attention to these details will help you to rise above your competition. Be realistic, too, about the viability of the activities. Owning an arts-based birthday party business, I've had many creative requests. Some, though, simply aren't possible given the ages of the children. For instance, I had a request for two- and three-year-olds to build hinged marionettes, complete with complex dowel-and-string controls. I gently redirected the mom to a more appropriate activity, sock puppets, and the party was a wonderful success. This is a fine line, a sort of negotiating skill that you will continue to develop as you meet with clients. You must listen to their ideas and considerations and then carefully and diplomatically redirect them if necessary. I've also had requests for three-hour birthday parties for three-year-olds. It is, of course, possible to entertain this young brood for three hours, but it takes very careful organization and extra expense.
- **Budget.** The all-important question of money. Parents sometimes have grand visions without the understanding that grand visions often require grand budgets for their execution. Although I've touched on this earlier, it bears repeating: do not undercharge. Undercharging can result in business failure. This is a business and your goal is to make money. It is tempting when you first hang your shingle to cut the prices for your services. Don't be tempted. Charge a fair rate that will cover your expenses and pay what you determine is a satisfactory wage (Chapter 6 offers guides for determining this rate).

With this information, you will be able to create a proposal for your client. A proposal is a clear plan outlining the purpose of the event, the venue, the age and number of attendees, the event theme, event activities, food and drink, goody bag stuffers, decorations, and the cost (broken down into categories).

I like to present a proposal in a colorful folder (found at office supply stores) with my card affixed to the front. In this folder, I include a sheet with testimonials from past clients as well as a photograph from a recent event. I also include a complete breakdown of the services I will provide for the client—from arriving early at the venue to make sure that everything is ship-shape (I've arrived at many venues only to find myself vacuuming a room that hadn't been adequately cleaned following the previous event) to sending thank-you's after the event. In my efforts to maintain an open and honest line of communication with all of my clients, I break down all costs. For instance, I show the amount to be spent on decorations, the amount for food, and the amount for entertainment all on separate lines rather than lumping them all together. In this way, a client is able to see where her dollars are being spent.

From Cakes to Party Hats, Finding the Right Suppliers

According to party-supply giant Hallmark, $600 million is spent annually on items for kids' parties. These items include invitations, party hats, paper plates, and napkins, for instance. This is an impressive figure and gives some sense of the size of your market. When it comes to holding and planning children's birthday parties, many parents find that they have deep pockets. Given the market for these goods, it is also no surprise that many vendors, hoping to take their share of the birthday party pie, sell birthday party supplies.

Online and Chain Store Suppliers

The appendix for this book lists many online vendors. Online vendors offer some advantages including, often, low prices because of their high-volume sales. Additionally, because these online vendors often have massive warehouses, the range and variety of party supplies is frequently quite vast. If, as your business develops, you find that you need large numbers of supplies—for instance, party hats by the gross—then an online vendor may offer the best values.

If you live in a more populated area, you are probably within driving distance of a store that is part of a chain of birthday party supply stores.

Keeping It Local

Conversely, a local vendor may charge marginally more but there are pros to spending the extra pennies. It can prove invaluable to forge a relationship with the owners of these local "mom and pop" shops. Owners of party supply stores can help you to promote your business by displaying your cards and brochures, and they are often able to keep you up to date on current party trends. If you see certain themed items in the half-price bin at your local party store, it's a good indicator that a once-hot party theme has grown lukewarm.

To find local party supply stores, whether part of a chain or locally owned, look in your area's yellow pages under "party supplies."

Big Values at the Big-Box Stores

Big-box retailers are also useful for sourcing party supplies. When visiting these chain stores you'll find many aisles chock-a-block with useful products. Most big retailers have a section devoted to party supplies and offer the typical fixings for goody bags such as inexpensive plastic trinkets and cellophane bags. Often, I find other areas of these stores more useful. I regularly check the toy section at a big-box retailer near my home. I look for clearance toys that could be used in goody bags. Likewise, I keep an eye on the houseware department for colorful, plastic cups and dishes as well as festive tablecloths. By buying supplies at these big-box stores, I often save my clients money. A piñata that costs $15 at a local party supply store is often only $8 at the big-box vendor. A big-box vendor won't offer the variety that a party supply store will, but it can prove useful for more generic party supplies as well as for maintaining budgets, both yours and your client's.

Odd Lot Opportunities

Odd lot stores are another good source for reasonably priced supplies. As the name suggests, the merchandise at these centers is variable as the stores pick up odd lots cast off from manufacturers and retailers. Most of the merchandise is closeouts and overstocks, so what is in the store one day may not be there the next. Odd lot stores offer tremendous values and often are good sources for paper goods as well as goody bag treats. When shopping at an odd lot store, proceed with some caution. Often, paper goods sold at odd lots stores are overstocks and not simply tired or out-of-fashion merchandise. Sometimes, though, when a hot trend goes flat, the licensed goods end up at an odd lot store. To protect yourself from buying dud merchandise, don't stock up on paper goods with a tie-in to a movie, television program, or other current trend unless you already have a party planned at which you will use the merchandise.

Creative Customizing

Customized birthday treats are growing in popularity for both children's and adult's parties. From birthday banners to hats, candy, napkins, T-shirts, and CDs, the sky is the limit when it comes to customized treats. Online retailers offer competitive pricing. Key, if using customized items, is allowing time for the products to be made and delivered. According to Birthdayz by Shindigz (www.birthdayzbyshindigz.com), customized CDs require two weeks' production time plus a time allowance for shipping.

Customizing can add an extra layer of flair and fun to a child's birthday party, and customization doesn't have to break the bank. Compare prices at the various online customizers (listed in the Appendix) or use a local customizer.

Fantastic Food

As the event planner, you may or may not be responsible for the food. My event-planning business, Art Escapades, offers food as an "add-on." In other words, I market my business focusing on developing a creative project to engage young hands and minds. At a typical party, this project and all of the accompanying steps takes about one and one half hours. I have found that about half of all parents prefer to supply their own food. The other half asks for me to plan and serve the food. As you develop your business, you likely will spot a similar trend. Unless the party is a fête for a hundred at a local country club, food tends to be more casual at children's birthday parties. Casual does not mean sloppy or careless. Kids attending birthday parties care about their cake and clamor for its arrival.

Notes from the Field

Food allergies are quite common, so it is important to ask if any of the children attending the party have any allergies. At many of the parties I plan, a child has an allergy and is unable to eat the main birthday cake. Allergies to peanuts are especially prevalent. Find out in advance if a child has an allergy, then make sure to provide that child with a treat she can eat. It's no fun for a kid to miss out on eating birthday cake, so be sure to take this extra step and provide an allergen-free treat. The child will thank you as will your clients for taking this extra step.

Don't plan on getting too fancy, though, according to advice from Manhattan-based Herban Gourmet catering owner Leslie Bullock.

"As a caterer, I've come to realize that, from a food perspective, it's best to keep it simple and familiar. This is no time for the parent to bring out an extravagant or unusual food theme. Kids are very honest, and if they don't like the chocolate raspberry ganache cake that mommy picked out instead of the Disney-themed white cake from the store, they'll let you know! Same goes for gourmet grilled pizzas, lamb kebabs, and smoked salmon on potato pancakes. Stick with chicken tenders, hamburgers, and pizza."

In fact, for some children's parties, she prepares the gourmet pizza and lamb kebabs for the parents, noting that she is seeing a trend of children's birthday parties morphing into simultaneous adult parties. While the parents nosh in one room on high-end food, the kiddies are entertained in the next room by the magician or other entertainer or activity.

Bullock emphasizes that the children's food—chicken tenders, hamburgers, and pizza—be top-notch, though, because the food is a reflection of the quality of your business.

Take the Cake

Unless you want to get the permits required to set up a commercial kitchen, plan on buying birthday cakes at local bakeries and grocery stores. In my business, I find that many parents and children request themed cakes from our local branch of a large chain grocery store. This is an easy and reliable solution. There is no surprise in the taste, quality, or price of these cakes.

Cupcakes are another current craze, with kids and adults practically swooning for them. They are an elegant birthday party option since they are, by their nature, in an ideal, single-serving size. Grocery store bakeries will often create themed cupcakes, as well. Birthday kids also like iced cookies, decorated with their initials or their ages.

Local bakeries can also be a reliable and useful resource for your business. Like the local party-supply vendor, a friendly baker can help spread the word about your new business. And, it is good to think about spending locally, as well. As caterer Leslie Bullock cautioned, though, don't focus on the bakery's fanciest tarts and tortes. Kids like their cakes in a classic form.

Notes from the Field

Over the years, as part of my ongoing research for my event planning service, I have surveyed hundreds of local children about their cake preference. Number one choice? Marble cake from the local grocery store!

The Perfect Slice

It's a rock solid fact. Kids love cheese pizza. If you are looking for a sure-fire recipe for hungry kids, add one slice cheese pizza, one juice box, and one cupcake. Ahhhh . . . kiddy perfection. Most grocery stores' deli departments make fresh, made-to-order pizzas at a reasonable price. If you choose this option, you will need to have a method for keeping the pizzas warm while the party progresses (it is almost always best to eat at the end of the party—eating first is messy and often distracts the children from focusing on the business at hand: celebrating the birthday child). Although grocery store pizzas may be more economical, an easier option may be delivery by a local pizzeria. Of course, if you live in a more rural area, a pizzeria delivery van may not be an option! However, even in many small towns, a local joint will deliver pizzas at a specified time. Be sure to tip the pizza delivery person as you would a waiter: 15 to 20 percent with a minimum tip of $2. Build in a bit of wiggle room, too. If you plan to have the children eating pizza by 4 p.m., have the pizzas delivered by 3:30 p.m. This allows for time to call the pizzeria if the pizzas don't arrive on schedule.

The Ubiquitous Juice Box

Juice boxes at today's kids' birthday parties are de rigueur. In fact, kids consume billions of these sweet beverages every year. Save yourself time and money by stocking up on lots of these colorful boxes at a big-box store that offers pricing near wholesale. You may want to limit your purchasing to white juices—apple and white grape—if you are concerned about staining carpets.

While you are buying juice boxes, also stock up on bottled water. Buy the smallest bottles possible, since kids tend to drink only a bit. In many areas, it is possible to buy small boxes of water, similar to juice boxes. You may choose to buy large bottles and pour water into cups. I caution, though, that sometimes, in the heat of the party moment, it is simply easier to have bottles or boxes to distribute.

Fancy Feast

You will plan parties that involve more than cheese pizza and cupcakes, although these parties will most likely be less common. For these events, you will need to have networked and researched caterers who will work with you to ensure a successful event.

Find these caterers by first thinking about successful events you've attended. Who catered these events? Why were these caterers memorable? Likewise, if you have been to an event with less than yummy food, take note of these caterers and put them on your "don't call" list. Just as you are building a business based in large part on word-of-mouth marketing, caterers do the same. Which caterers in your area have good word of mouth?

Of course, in every aspect of your business, you will want to compare prices. This helps you to keep your prices competitive with other planners and your clients will certainly appreciate your efforts to maintain a reasonable budget. In this case, though, the lowest price is not always the best route. For instance, if you are serving chicken fingers with an assortment of sauces, the caterer with the lower prices may be serving pre-frozen fingers as opposed to fresh chicken fingers. Clients who ask for more elaborate food will care about these distinctions. With this in mind, make sure that when soliciting estimates from caterers you are comparing apples to apples. In other words, let the caterer know that you are requesting fresh, all-white-meat chicken fingers. Don't assume that she will know.

You will also want to be very clear in determining who will supply the necessary dishes. When it comes to chicken fingers—a finger food—paper plates would suffice. For parties with more elaborate food, you will need dishes, cutlery, serving utensils, and linens.

The All-Powerful Goody Bag

"Goody bags" are two words that can strike fear into the hearts of even the most intrepid parents planning birthday parties for their children. As all moms and dads know, the goody bag can make or break a party. You may have clowns, stilt walkers, jugglers capable of keeping twelve balls of fire in the air—but, as the party winds down, if you fail to produce a goody bag that suits the party goers, hue and cry can, and probably will, break loose.

As Nancy Lavin, a mother of three puts it, "Goody bags? That's why kids go to birthday parties." Not to put too fine a point on this issue, children love birthday parties for many reasons, including their amazement at fire-juggling entertainers. However, it is true that children have come to expect a goody bag at a party's close.

Who can blame them? It seems that American culture has become obsessed with goody bags. Adults like to receive them at parties as well. And, some of the goody bags being bandied about at adult parties are so valuable that the Internal Revenue Service had to put out a special statement addressing their rules regarding goody bags and taxes.

"The Commissioner of the Internal Revenue Service today wished the Academy Award nominees the best of luck at Sunday's presentation, but he reminded celebrity recipients of the six-figure goodie bags that they qualify as taxable income and must be reported on tax returns."

"As the world watches the glamour and glitz of the Academy Awards, it's important to keep in mind that movie stars face the same tax obligations as ordinary Americans," said IRS Commissioner Mark W. Everson. "We want to make sure the stars 'walk the line' when it comes to these goodie bags."

Everson makes a good point—news reports about the "official" Oscar gifts that will be given to stars place the value at more than $100,000. These amazing caches of loot include handheld electronic devices, diamond jewelry, free stays at plush resorts, and more.

Happily, kids haven't set the bar quite this high for their goody bag treats. It is important, as you plan a party, to work closely with the parents to determine their vision of the goody bag. Be clear about budget and expectations when developing goody bags. Ask parents for specifics. Do they want candy and toys? Do they want the goody bag items to tie in with the party theme? How much are they planning to spend per goody bag?

A final and important note: Don't be too lavish when planning goody bags. In an era of McMansions, parents might ask for McGoody bags as well. In my experience, when parents have asked for absolutely over-the-top goody bags, some parents of party attendees have been embarrassed by the excess. As one parent recently whispered in my ear, "Oh no! This goody bag cost more than the present my child brought for the birthday child." Don't put party guests in this awkward position.

Goody Bags Go Green

A happy turn in the world of party planning is the opportunity to make an event "green" or environmentally friendly. This trend is becoming more and more evident when it comes to goody bags, as well. More and more, parents are asking me to steer clear of landfill-clogging cellophane bags and, often, the cheap plastic toys that, in the blink of an eye, go from a partygoer's goody bag straight into the garbage.

If parents are eager to plan a green party, consider using cloth or paper bags rather than plastic. Opt for wood toys rather than plastic. If choosing plastic toys, opt for a higher quality toy that won't instantly make its way to the circular file. As a general rule of thumb, cheaper is often not better when it comes to goody bags. I had to learn this the hard way after stuffing goody bags with rainbow colored plastic spring toys. They looked great and the kids loved them—until they tried to use them. They didn't work. I would have been better served to buy the real McCoy, a metal Slinky. At about $2 apiece, a junior Slinky is fun and reliable. The rainbow spring toys, at $1 each, were cheap—and worthless. Kids didn't even bother taking them home from the party.

The Feel-Good Goody Bag

Some kids are opting to give a goody bag that does good! One child, who was interested in nature and animals, gave contributions in the name of each partygoer to the World Wildlife Foundation. After an animal themed party, all partygoers received certificates showing their contribution to the World Wildlife Fund as well as a stuffed animal representing an endangered species. The stuffed animals were purchased at a big-box chain store for $3 each. A $5 contribution was made in the name of each child. In this way, each child had something to carry home (a stuffed animal) and a reason to hold their head high (making a contribution to help save endangered animals).

I am seeing this trend slowly pick up speed. Just as some kids are asking that, in lieu of gifts, a donation be made to a worthy organization, some children are doing

---

Internet Tip

For an array of interesting and inexpensive craft ideas suitable for goody bag treats, check out Oriental Trading at www.orientaltrading.com. From make-your-own paddle ball games to color-your-own Frisbees, this site offers reasonably priced projects that engage children.

the same when it comes to goody bags. Making a gift to a charity is an important lesson for all, children and adults. Parties with a focus on giving rather than getting result in tremendous positive energy and good feelings. Of course, everyone likes to receive presents, and I am not suggesting complete abandonment of goody bags, but it is interesting to consider a goody bag for a good cause.

The One-Item Goody Bag

Another popular trend is the one-item goody bag. Many parents, tired of sorting through all of the plastic tchotchkes that come home from other children's birthday parties, ask me to provide one quality gift for each birthday party attendee. In another twist, some clients have asked that each party recipient receive a book. This is a popular choice because the book can tie in with the party's theme and be reasonably priced (children's paperbacks start at about $5).

After a soccer party, each party attendee might receive a soccer ball. After a kite-flying party, each child might go home with his own colorful kite. Often, buying one gift of a better quality is less expensive than filling a cellophane bag with items that will be quickly discarded.

The Personalized Goody Bag

Personalized treats are all the rage when it comes to kids' birthday parties, not only in terms of the décor (personalized banners, for instance) but also for the goody bag stuffers. For the tween set, I have ordered customized lip gloss. Younger kids enjoy craft boxes personalized with their names. Customized candy is also a favored goody bag treat. See the appendix for sources.

DIY Goody Bag

The do-it-yourself (DIY) phenomenon is everywhere—from checking yourself out at the grocery store to knitting your own sweater. I've seen the same trend when it

---

It's All in the Name

Note that in some areas of the United States, goody bags are referred to as "loot bags." The same idea, only with a different name.

Smart Tip

Kids love taking photographs, so plan on having a few disposable cameras at the ready. Encourage kids (and their parents) to take candid shots. Often, these spontaneous photographs turn out to be family favorites because they capture the happiness and energy of the event. Internet sites like www.camerasforall.com offer personalized disposable cameras beginning at about $5 per camera.

comes to goody bag treats. Some of my clients are asking for me to plan an activity during which party attendees will create their own take-home treat. Perhaps kids will paint their own little treasure chest for storing diminutive odds and ends. Or, kids might make their own sand art bottles. In this way, the goody bag treats add to the life of the party.

Say Cheese, Please!

Some parents will ask that the event be photographed or videotaped. Photography is a highly skilled art so you will want to do your research before hiring a photographer or videographer. Word of mouth is a good place to start your search. Just as you are building your business largely on word-of-mouth marketing, so do good photographers. Ask at local bakeries for the names of the photographers who are frequently asked to shoot wedding photos (bakers will know these names since they are often at the church, synagogue, or other reception site setting up the cake when the photographer is there taking shots). Ask friends who have hired photographers. Search through your local yellow pages or check online at www.ppa.com (Professional Photographers of America, Inc). If you make contact through these venues, be sure to do a thorough reference check. Ask the photographer for names of clients to whom you can speak. Of course, look through her portfolio, as well.

Make sure that your client's photography preferences are clear, as well. Some parents will prefer candid shots while others will want more posed images. Also, do the parents have a preference for black and white versus color photography? Candid shots, often done in black and white, are currently the trend. In a style called photojournalism, these photographers shoot only events as they unfold, never asking for contrived or posed photos. If your client is expecting posed shots of friends and family, this is not the type of photographer to hire.

A final caveat: Just because a photographer is your area's ace wedding photographer does not mean she will bring the same expertise to photographing a children's birthday party. Make certain that the photographer likes children and understands how to work with children.

Keeping the Beat

Parties with disc jockeys (DJs) are popular for teens and tweens. It is particularly true with DJs that you get what you pay for. You will find that some DJs offer to host an event for a few hundred dollars while others will charge upwards of $1,000. As a rule of thumb, plan on spending between $100 and $300 per hour.

A good DJ can absolutely make or break a party, so be sure to do a thorough reference check. Again, finding a DJ through word of mouth is best although there are several associations that will help guide you to DJs in your area. Before hiring a DJ, ask to attend one of his events.

DJ Checklist

Before signing on the dotted line, make sure that your DJ:
- *Is insured and has liability coverage.* Ask to see proof.
- *Will agree to a written contract.* Don't hire a DJ—or anyone for that matter—based on a handshake. Always insist on a written contract. This protects you as well as the DJ.
- *Will play requests.* Amazingly, some DJs won't. Also, be clear about the type of music to be played, ensuring that music appropriate for kids is all that he is spinning.
- *Will dress appropriately.* This is less important for informal children's parties but I have been to elegant weddings only to have the DJ show up in scruffy jeans.
- *Will allow enough time for setup.* Unfortunately, this has been an issue in my business: DJs showing up late, not allowing time for setup. This makes teens impatient and the paying parents grumpy.

Working with Your Client

Congratulations. You are ready to hold your first event. You should pat yourself on the back for completing all of the steps leading up to this moment. Laying the groundwork for a new company is challenging. Kudos to you for building a solid foundation.

Finding Your First Client

Getting that first client on the hook can be a bit challenging, but it will happen. I found that posting fliers about my party planning business proved to be the most effective way to find clients when I first opened up shop.

Many town libraries have bulletin boards on which you can post news about your company. Plan on creating a flier with your phone number listed on tabs at the bottom. Then, prospective clients can pull off one of the tabs and have your phone number at the ready. Many towns also have community centers with bulletin boards where you can post your news.

Along with posting fliers around town (always check with the library or community center before posting your flier), tell everyone you know about your new business. As I wrote earlier, tell friends, neighbors, business associates—anyone and everyone.

You can also consider an advertisement in your local newspaper (more on this in Chapter 10). However, I find that for fledging businesses, the best bet is word of mouth and posting fliers.

Connecting with Your Client

As outlined earlier in this chapter, when you first meet with your new client you will fill out a worksheet, outlining the client's needs and desires. From this information, you will generate a proposal detailing all aspects of the birthday party—from the type of activities planned to the cake flavor, the goody bag treats, any customized decorations, and more. The proposal also breaks down the cost of the party for the parents of the birthday child. Once you and your client have signed the proposal and contract, get ready to plan!

Planning Your First Event

You've done your legwork and research, so planning and holding your first children's birthday party will be a veritable piece of birthday cake! As is echoed throughout this book, pulling off a successful party is primarily about organization and attention to detail. To avoid any unhappy birthday surprises, do not leave anything to chance. Using the birthday party planning checklist included in this chapter will help to ensure a happy day. I rely on this checklist for all of my party planning.

Do not underestimate the time it will take you to set up for the party. The birthday child's parents will not appreciate arriving at the party only to find that the tablecloths aren't on the tables, the balloons and streamers aren't festooning the room, and the goody bags are not made! Leave plenty of time to travel to the site (I always allow extra time for a flat tire—you never know!) as well as ample time once you arrive.

Once at the site, keep your cell phone and checklist handy as you calmly work, either at your dedicated space or with the professionals at an outside venue. Predetermine with the parents what time they plan on arriving. I encourage parents to arrive near the start of the party. If they arrive too early, while I am still setting up, it can be a distraction and add stress.

Expect the first guests to arrive early. Unlike adult parties, where folks tend to show up fashionably late, kids show up on time—or early. Greet everybody with a smile and be prepared to direct children to where they should hang their coats and place their presents. Make sure, too, that you dress appropriately for the big day. You are a professional, so no sloppy jeans or sweatpants. It is okay to be casual at a casual kids' party (khakis and a crisp shirt) but not messy.

The timeline for each party will vary. If you are holding an event at an ice-skating rink, for instance, you will want to have an activity to engage the children while they are all arriving. Once all of the kids get to the rink, the professionals there will likely instruct the children about selecting skates, ice safety, and other rules of the ice. After the allotted skating time has passed, you will be responsible for ensuring that the children return rented skates and make their way to the facility's party room. There you will oversee the activities you've arranged with parents. Perhaps parents have asked for another activity or for pizza to be served.

Crowd Control

For many novice party planners, the chief concern is keeping control of the birthday attendees. I know that when I began planning parties, I worried about this as well. Happily, I have found that kids, though keyed up, tend to behave well at birthday parties when the parameters for behavior are clearly outlined.

- **Set the tone.** As children arrive, let them know what you expect. For instance, I might greet the children by saying, "Place your birthday gift here, hang your jacket on the hook in that corner, and then please sit while we wait for everyone to arrive. There are markers and paper at each seat. Perhaps you would like to make a birthday card for [birthday child's name]." In this way, the children are clearly directed. When the children aren't guided, they tend to become a bit wilder. Have a plan.

- **Be prepared.** The kiss of death for a birthday planner is lack of preparation. Don't plan on blowing up balloons while the children arrive. You will be distracted and chaos is likely to ensue. When the children begin arriving, be "on" for them. In other words, greet each child personally, asking his or her name. Smile and look directly at them. These sound like small things but they add up to big results: good behavior.

- **Don't be afraid to discipline.** You are in charge of this event, so don't be afraid to discipline a child who is misbehaving. At the end of the day, the parents will thank you for this. Conversely, if you let a child misbehave and disrupt a party, the parents will be frustrated with you. Be gentle in your discipline. I try to take a positive spin when trying to calm down a child. "Megan, I know you are excited because it is Nancy's birthday but it is time to sit down and help the birthday child celebrate her day." Usually, a gentle intervention such as this will work well. If not, I (very) occasionally have to ask a child to take a time out. In virtually every instance, after a time out, the disruptive child will behave. After all, no one wants to spend the party in time out. Again, parents expect you to take these actions. I have spoken with planners who are afraid to discipline—and their events can spiral out of control.

- **Have a plan.** I develop and plan more activities than I anticipate needing. You have to be prepared for kids who sing "Happy Birthday," eat cake, and open presents in ten minutes flat! The events you thought would fill thirty minutes have whizzed by in a third of the time. What do you do with the remaining twenty minutes? Sometimes, I pull out face painting supplies. I am not an expert face painter but have found that kids love even basic face painting, such as whiskers and a triangular nose, turning them into a cat. I have been to children's birthday parties where, after the clown leaves and the cake is eaten, there is nothing for the kids to do but get wound up and

Notes from the Field

Always confirm with parents whether they want their child to open presents at the party site. Parents often have strong opinions about this. Some feel it is important to open gifts at the party site so the children giving the gifts will have the opportunity to see the birthday child receive them. Other parents don't want present giving to become competitive—a who-gave-the-biggest-gift sort of competition—so they opt to open presents at home with just family.

go crazy. Make sure you have enough activities to fill the party's time span. Again, your clients expect this. They are paying you to fill the time.

These basic guidelines have served me well. Kids, generally, are happy to be asked to a party and want to please. Be amiable, firm, and prepared when it comes to keeping kids happy, safe, and well behaved.

Developing References and Referrals

Make it your mantra: you are only as good as your last party. In this word-of-mouth business, you must always keep this in the front of your mind. Another way to keep your eye on the prize: Would you be satisfied if the party you just planned and held was in honor of your child's birthday? If the answer is anything other than "yes," you need to reflect and retool.

The All-Important Reference

Part of the word-of-mouth process is creating references. When you first develop a new contact with a client, she will probably ask for references. A reference is a person who can speak about your abilities and skills and help to differentiate you from your competition. You will want to have a list of several references. Don't ask your sister-in-law to be your reference. Ask professional contacts as well as clients for whom you have planned successful children's birthday parties. Professional contacts will include party supply store owners, caterers, bakers, photographers, videographers, disc jockeys, and others who have helped you to throw a great event. Don't assume that your favorite caterer will act as a reference. Always ask first before

Birthday Party Planning Checklist

This checklist covers everything you will need to consider for the party you are planning. Some items won't apply to every party. For instance, you may or may not be arranging food or having custom decorations made. This checklist is a powerful tool. If, as you plan, you are able to provide checkmarks for every applicable line, your party will almost certainly prove successful. I rely on this checklist for every party I plan. It ensures that I dot every "i" and cross every "t" and helps to reassure me that on the day of the party there will be smooth sailing.

- Reserving a venue
  - Do you have a signed contract with the venue?
  - Did you call the venue to confirm the day before the party?

- Mailing invitations

- Arranging entertainment
  - If you arranged entertainment, did you check references and receive a signed contract?
  - Did you confirm with the entertainment the day before the party?

- Arranging for a photographer or videographer
  - If so, did you check references and receive a signed contract?
  - Did you confirm with the photographer the day before the event?

- Arranging catering
  - If so, did you check references and receive a signed contract?
  - Did you confirm with the caterer the day before the event?

- Setting up pizza delivery
  - If so, did you confirm the day before the event?

- Hiring a DJ
  - If so, did you check references and receive a signed contract?
  - Did you confirm with the DJ the day before the event?

- Arranging for a birthday cake
  - Did you confirm the day before the party that the cake would be ready for pickup or delivery?

- Renting inflatables
  - Did you confirm the inflatables the day before the event?

- Buying and renting decorations
  - Did you buy or rent any tablecloths?
  - Did you arrange for any customized decorations?
  - Did you arrange for any special displays, like cotton candy machines or popcorn machines?
  - Did you arrange for balloons?

- Creating goody bags
  - Did you purchase goody bag treats?
  - Did you fill the goody bags and double-check your numbers, ensuring that you have one for each child at the party?

- Arranging for floral arrangements
  - If so, did you check references and receive a signed contract?
  - Did you confirm with the florist the day before the event?

- Arranging for any rentals, such as tables, chairs, or glassware
  - If so, did you confirm the rentals the day before the event?

- Confirming the number of party attendees

- Purchasing themed party supplies
  - If so, have you checked quantities?
  - Ordering custom items
  - If so, have you confirmed that spelling of the birthday child's name and quantities are correct?

- Stocking your emergency toolbox

- Readying your cell phone
  - Did you charge your cell phone?
  - Did you program your cell phone with all applicable names—from the caterer to the clown?

- Arranging childcare
  - Did you arrange for childcare for your children?

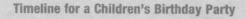

Timeline for a Children's Birthday Party

This timeline is a guide for planning your first event. However, the lead time for planning children's birthday parties is highly variable. For instance, a party for ten kids at the pool is a snap compared to a sweet sixteen for a hundred guests, complete with a DJ, videographer, and catered food. As you plan more parties, you will learn to adjust this timeline. As you begin, though, this timeline provides a good rule of thumb for allowing enough time to complete all of your planning.

Three months before the birthday party:

- Meet with parents and complete parent questionnaire
- Using this information, complete proposal, including budget, activities, number of guests, and venue
- Begin sourcing vendors (such as caters and photographers, if necessary)

Two months before the party:

- Confirm guest list and mail invitations
- Confirm all outside vendors and suppliers
- Order any custom or personalized items

One month before the party:

- Purchase goody bag supplies
- Purchase paper goods

One week before the party:

- Confirm number of attendees
- Reconfirm all outside vendors, suppliers, and caterers
- Touch base with the parents, addressing any of their concerns and letting them know that you are all set for their child's party

having a new client check with a reference. Some business owners and individuals prefer not to give references.

Along with creating a stable of persuasive professional references, you will develop a group of clients who are willing to speak to your prospective clients about your party planning abilities. Following a successful event, call the client and ask if she will act as a reference. Don't ask at the party site. Wait until you make your post-event phone call, something you will do after every event. Choose clients who will be articulate and comfortable speaking to your prospective clients.

The Power of the Referral

Referrals are an invaluable way of creating a thriving birthday party planning business. When a current client refers you to a new client, this is called a referral. In other words, you plan a party for Susie, and then Susie's parents, appreciating your expertise, refer you to Jennifer and her parents.

There are various ways to gain referrals. You can be direct and ask your client to refer you to one of her friends or acquaintances for a possible business contact. If you choose this route, don't ask every client you work with. Gauge your clients. Some will be willing to pass your name along to friends while others will not. Some experts suggest that you ask only 20 percent of your current clients for referrals.

As with references, don't ask at the party site. Wait until your follow-up phone call to ask for any possible referrals. Be honest with yourself, as well, and ask for referrals only from clients who received an absolutely top-rate party. Let's face it: you will plan parties with a few bumps in the road—a pizza delivery made too late or a clown who turned out to be more scary than funny. As a party planner, you are a problem solver and you will mend these bumpy patches, but these clients are probably not the ones to ask for referrals

When it comes to referrals, you get what you give. Go the extra mile for clients from whom you are asking referrals. And, remember to thank your clients for referrals with a thoughtful, personalized thank-you letter, as well as considering a small discount on a future event.

Documenting Your Successes

As your business develops, it is essential that you create a portfolio of your party success. This will be a valuable marketing tool when you meet with new clients.

A three-ring binder works well for your portfolio, since it enables you to take out pages for photocopying if necessary. Choose a classy three-ring binder. Check at a local stationery store or online for a suitable binder.

On the cover of your binder, place your logo and company name. Likewise, the first page inside the binder should have your company name, logo, and mission statement. Use good quality paper for this portfolio rather than plain copier paper. Sheet protectors are also a good idea; they allow you to insert the pages and handle them frequently without damaging or fraying them. Pages in sheet protectors are also easily photocopied.

Inside the binder, include photographs from successful events. Remember to receive permission from clients before using the photos. Most clients will be flattered that you've asked and pleased to agree. Also include a brief, bulleted description of the event, which includes the type of event (first birthday, for instance), the venue, the number of attendees, and any details that made the event special and unique.

To make this presentation even more persuasive, ask clients for testimonials that can be included with the photographs and bulleted description. This is a powerful message, demonstrating visually and verbally that you created a successful event.

You will also want to include any newspaper or magazine clippings that have featured your business. Chapter 10 will include a discussion describing how to write press releases to help ensure coverage by local newspapers and magazines. Also note any television coverage of your business.

Don't be afraid to toot your own horn. As poet Walt Whitman so aptly put it, "If you done it, it ain't bragging." View your portfolio as one of your most powerful marketing tools. Keep it up to date and fresh, adding pictures from your most recent events. Have fun with this tool and let it reflect the energy and personality of your party planning business.

Internet Tip

In this age of scrapbooking, it is possible to create vivid, imaginative pages with a minimum of effort. At www.addictedtoscrapbooking.com, more than three hundred birthday-themed items are offered for sale—stickers, stamps, and other embellishments that will add to the creative presentation of your portfolio.

Frequently Asked Question

I've completed all of the steps you've described for developing my business. Now, I have my first children's party scheduled. Unfortunately, I am feeling a bit nervous about "running the show." Any advice?

This is a common feeling and one that should not alarm you. Holding your first children's birthday party is exciting but can also cause a case of the butterflies. Even now, many years into my party planning business, I still feel that rush of adrenaline, or nerves, right before an event. Experts say this rush of adrenaline is a good thing as it brings a high level of energy and alertness, and prepares us for the busy pace of a children's party. If you have done all of your prep work—and it sounds as if you have—then your party should go off without a hitch. As I have written throughout this guide, organization is key. Make sure that you have checked every applicable item on the birthday party checklist provided in this chapter. All checks? You are good to go. And, as Dr. Seuss so eloquently put it, "Will you succeed? Yes you will! (98 and $3/4$ percent guaranteed.)"

Managing Your Money

You've developed and held your first successful event, creating loads of positive energy and excitement about your new enterprise. You've also taken the time and the care to build a rock-solid foundation for your business, focusing on all of the building blocks, from creating a business plan to designing a dynamite logo.

Once you've successfully completed all of these steps, now is the prime moment to focus on finance, projecting a growth curve for your new business as well as developing systems for monitoring and maintaining your finances.

Don't be afraid to manage your money. Too many small businesses, according to the Small Business Association, fail because of financial mismanagement. Mismanagement includes overspending on initial inventory (don't buy too many birthday hats until you know you will need them!); insufficient capital to successfully launch your business; use of personal cash for business, or vice-versa, using business monies for personal use; incomplete recordkeeping; inaccurate billing; and more.

How Much Do You Hope to Earn?

Varied earnings potential is absolutely one of the benefits of this exciting field. You can develop a business with the expectation of holding one event per month, planning to earn a bit of "fun money." Or, you can develop the business into a full-time occupation with full-time earnings. According to U.S. Department of Labor statistics, the average compensation for an event planner is $50,000. Event planners in urban areas often make well beyond this figure.

Smart Tip

Keep business and personal expenses separate. Have separate bank accounts and credit cards for personal and business use. This will ensure tighter financial management as well as proving essential at tax time when you begin to sort out what your business owes to Uncle Sam.

Be realistic about your goals and your ability to commit the time needed to develop your business. And, be realistic about your financial needs. If it is imperative that you contribute $25,000 to your household budget, know that it can take years to build up volume for an event-planning business. You can't plan on full-time earnings during your business's formative years.

Likewise, full-time salaries require full-time commitments. Unfortunately, some folks developing home businesses think they can get away with working fewer hours than they would at a typical nine-to-five office job. Think again. Developing an at-home business requires dedication, time, and commitment.

Being Realistic about Creating a Budget

Although a children's birthday party business can be launched on a relatively small budget, there are some costs you will have to incur. As I discussed earlier in the book, there are ways to keep costs down. Use a computer you already own, for instance. Some costs, though, simply can't be avoided.

Rent or Mortgage Payments

Since you have set up an office in your home, you won't need to worry about adding a new rent payment on top of the rent or mortgage payment you already make. In fact, an in-home office space counts as a tax deduction (although don't try to pull a fast one on the IRS by pretending your home office is bigger than it is. The IRS considers the home-office tax deduction a red flag when choosing who to audit).

Phones

Although initially you may opt to use your home line, as your business grows you will want a phone line dedicated to your business. This adds to the sense of

- Monthly rent or mortgage payment $ _____
- Monthly land line phone expense $ _____
- Monthly cell phone expense $ _____
- Monthly utilities $ _____
- Monthly transportation costs $ _____
- Monthly postage costs $ _____
- Monthly wages $ _____
- Monthly insurance costs $ _____
- Monthly online service fees $ _____
- Miscellaneous expenses $ _____
- Budgeted monthly total expenses $ _____

professionalism (teach your kids not to answer your business line!) and will also help you keep your financial records square. Shop around for the most competitive plan. Many phone company sales representatives will negotiate a better deal when asked to do so. Also, if you bundle services—for instance using the same supplier for both your phone line and your Internet connection—you might be able to negotiate a better price.

You will want to conduct the same negotiations when choosing a cell phone package. You absolutely do not want to use more than the number of minutes allotted by your plan. Cell phone companies often charge a king's ransom for these extra minutes. Don't skimp on the number of minutes in your plan, as it is likely you will rely heavily on your cell phone for conducting business.

Utilities

With an at-home office space, you won't take on extra utility costs. However, as your business grows, if you opt for an off-site office, factor in any utility costs—gas, electric, oil, water—that are not covered by the building's owner (if you are a renter).

Transportation

With high gas prices, you will need to factor in the price of fuel for your car. Or, if you live in an urban area and plan on using mass transportation, factor in these costs. Be sure to keep track of the miles you log in your car or the dollars spent on mass transit; these may be a deductible expense at tax time. Be honest—don't write down the miles spent driving the kids to art class or soccer. Keep a mileage log in your car. Use a small notebook and jot down mileage and dates. Your accountant will thank you at tax time.

Office Supplies

Be sure to include the money you spend buying paperclips, stationery, and other office supplies in this category. New business owners often don't factor in some of these smaller expenses, not realizing that all of these small expenses can result in a rather large final tally.

Postage

You will be mailing promotional materials as well as proposals and statements to your clients, and postage will take a bite out of your budget. With the advent of the Internet, some of your promotional efforts will take place via the Net, obviating the need for postage. Nevertheless, sometimes good old snail mail is simply the best—or only—way to go.

Wages

As you take on staff, you will need to figure employees' wages into your budget calculations. Many children's birthday party planners choose not to hire any full-time employees. Rather, they might rely on college kids, stay-at-home moms, and retirees looking for a few extra hours of work in a lively environment.

Insurance

As discussed in Chapter 3, you will need to ensure that your new business is adequately insured and work with an insurance agent to set premiums and to set up any necessary riders. Include insurance costs when you calculate spending. If you have an annual premium, simply divide by twelve and add that amount to each month's budgeted expenses.

Online Service Fees

Include the cost of your online provider when you estimate your monthly spending. You may choose to buy a package from your telephone service provider if it provides incentives to customers bundling their services. You may receive a better deal on both your phone and Internet packages if you buy both from the same provider.

More Expenses

The items listed above cover the basic expenses for which you will need to budget, particularly those of a new business. As your business expands, other expenses may crop up including fees for certified public accountants and attorneys; fees for Web site hosting; costs to cover attending event-planning trade shows; advertising and marketing costs; expenses for maintenance on your office site; and repayment on a line of credit. Other miscellaneous expenses need to be considered as well. For instance, I recommend that all children's party planners read Martha Stewart's *Good Things for Kids* magazine. This is a wonderful resource, filled with creative ideas for hosting children's events and for entertaining children. The cost of this magazine should be considered a professional expense.

Pricing Goods and Services

Now that you have budgeted for your expenses, you need to consider income and how you will price your services. This is not as straightforward as it might sound, as party planners in different regions make use of different models to negotiate their fees. Striking the balance between charging enough, but not too much, for your services can be a challenge. You will need to mark up for labor and materials costs enough to earn a satisfactory profit.

Charging a Percentage

For large-scale parties, many party planners add 10 to 15 percent to their costs. For example, if you buy balloons for a client's party at a cost of $200, you would charge $220 to your client (adding on 10 percent). Or, if the caterer charges $800, you will charge your client $880. In other words, if the cost of the event totals $5,000 (and kids birthday bashes do reach into this stratosphere), then you will charge your client from $5,500 to $5,750.

At first glance, a profit of $500 to $750 looks satisfying. But, party planner beware. How many hours did you spend planning the party? How many miles did

Use this form to estimate your costs when planning a party. This will help to ensure that you charge your client the right fee. Some of these fees may not apply to the party you are planning. For instance, if you hold parties at clients' homes, you will not be incurring a venue rental fee. Note, this list does not include your daily overhead costs such as utilities and phone service. It is important to note this because the total cost as reflected on this form does not include your fixed costs. Once you total all of these costs, you will either need to add a percentage to cover the fixed costs and your hourly fee, or determine a fixed price per child as described in this chapter.

- Venue rental fee $ _____
- Food costs $ _____
- Decoration costs $ _____
- Entertainment costs $ _____
- Photographer costs $ _____
- Videographer costs $ _____
- Inflatable costs $ _____
- Paper goods costs $ _____
- Customized favor costs $ _____
- Transportation costs $ _____
- Total $ _____

you rack up on your car? How many hours of childcare did you pay for to enable you to leave your kids at home while you ran the event? What about your other overhead, including phone bills and utilities? After paying all of these costs, what is left as profit? Do your math and make sure that you are charging a percentage that is fair to your clients and enables you to make a profit.

For each of these items, list a per-month cost in the first blank and a year-end total in the second blank. This is an important projection to make because many new small business owners underestimate their expenses, leading to a disappointing start. By charting your expenses, you will be able to more appropriately and accurately bill your clients to cover your fixed costs. Finally, don't forget to factor in miscellaneous expenses (for instance, the cost of buying fresh flowers once a week for your at-home office). These expenses can add up, as well.

- ■ Online service fees $_____ $_____
- ■ Insurance $_____ $_____
- ■ Wages $_____ $_____
- ■ Postage $_____ $_____
- ■ Office Supplies $_____ $_____
- ■ Transportation $_____ $_____
- ■ Utilities $_____ $_____
- ■ Land Line Phone $_____ $_____
- ■ Cell Phone $_____ $_____
- ■ Miscellaneous $_____ $_____
- ■ Totals: $_____ $_____

The Flat Fee

For smaller parties, plan on charging a set fee per child. For instance, if you are the owner of a teddy bear tea party business and conduct parties in your clients' homes or your designated space, you may choose to charge a flat rate of $25 per child. This fee includes the cost of party goods—hats, goody bags, tea supplies, a teddy bear for each child, cake—as well as covering your business overhead. If the parents ask for add-ons—pizza and chicken tenders—for instance, you would adjust the per-child rate. As with the percentage billing model outlined above, be sure to do the math. Does the $25 per child cover your costs and still leave you with a reasonable profit?

Another factor in pricing your services is to consider your geographic region. Prices in the populous Northeast tend to be substantially higher than in the South, for instance.

Frequently Asked Question

Do your clients prefer flat fee or percentage billing?

I have found that the majority of clients prefer flat fee billing. I think this is because the parents I work with feel reassured that the price is set and that there will be no nasty billing surprises at the end of their child's birthday party. It is true, in fact, that it is easy for planners and clients to do the math when a flat fee, say $40 per child, is the agreed-upon charge. It leaves little wiggle room—which, often, is a good thing.

07

Tracking Your Money

The Bottom Line

You've created a list of projected expenses, developed a budget, and determined your financial goals. Now, as you get your business up and running, you need to make sure to keep track of your money. And, of course, keep an eye on the bottom line. As a business owner, you must work to develop a budget and track finances in a way that ensures your company's profitability. As I wrote in Chapter 6, too many of us are afraid of bookkeeping tasks, finding them daunting. Think of financial recordkeeping as little more than basic addition and subtraction because that, in fact, is the truth.

Careful recordkeeping is key to your business success. It is important for you to understand how the money in your business is flowing—how much is flowing out to pay expenses and how much is flowing in to cover these expenses. Obviously, a company that doesn't generate enough income to pay all of its expenses won't survive long.

When commenting on the early days of Wal-Mart, the company he founded, Sam Walton said, "If you can't make your books balance, you take however much they're off by and enter it under the heading ESP, which stands for Error Some Place." Obviously, Wal-Mart would not be the giant it is today if his accounting team continued this mysterious ESP system of bookkeeping. You shouldn't plan to rely on ESP as an effective recordkeeping method!

Help Is on the Way

Don't be afraid, though, to ask for financial help. As with all things in life, it is wise to know when to ask for help. As businesses grow, most owners choose to take on expert financial help. A certified public accountant (CPA) can help you with your financial paperwork. CPAs can be found through the yellow pages or at Web sites like www.cpadirectory.com. Ask friends and business associates for recommendations as well. Make sure to choose a CPA who is familiar with and has experience with home-based businesses. The guidance of a CPA will also be helpful at tax time.

Make sure when choosing a CPA to sit down with her to make sure that your working styles are compatible. This is a professional with whom you will be discussing sometimes sticky financial issues. Make sure that the CPA you choose is a good listener and someone with whom you feel comfortable.

Confirm your payment arrangements when hiring a CPA. Will she charge a flat fee (for instance, a set fee for preparing a basic tax form)? Or, will she charge by the hour? What about telephone consultations? Between the two of you, lay out a framework for payment.

Key Financial Statements

For those of you who plan on tucking your earnings into a piggy bank, think again. There are three key financial documents with which you will want to become familiar. For those of us who are not math whizzes, these statements can sound intimidating but they shouldn't be. In fact, they are simply charts showing how money is earned and spent.

Profit and Loss Statement

Also know as a P and L, this is a very straightforward document. It outlines what you are earning and what you are spending or losing. At the end of your business day, the profits need to outweigh the losses. These documents can be generated on a monthly or quarterly basis. Generally, it is better, as a new business owner, to generate the statements monthly.

These statements will help you to identify just how much money you are actually making. Often, these statements offer some surprises. Perhaps, for instance, you didn't realize that your phone bill was taking such a big bite out of your profits. If this is the case, perhaps it is time to research and find a more competitively priced phone plan.

Profit and loss statements also help to track trends. After generating a year's worth of statements, you can start to chart the busiest times for your event-planning business. You may find that your birthday party business is busiest at a certain time

Profit and Loss Statement

Projected monthly income	$ _____
Projected monthly expenses	$ _____
Phone, land line	$ _____
Phone, mobile	$ _____
Utilities	$ _____
Postage	$ _____
Wages	$ _____
Advertising	$ _____
Insurance	$ _____
Accounting services	$ _____
Legal services	$ _____
Office supplies	$ _____
Transportation	$ _____
Loan repayment	$ _____
Internet service	$ _____
Web hosting service	$ _____
Party supplies	$ _____
Miscellaneous	$ _____
Total expenses	$ _____
Anticipated monthly net income	$ _____

of the year—summer, for instance, when children are out of school and it is possible to have parties at outdoor locations.

Balance Sheet

A balance sheet is a snapshot of your company's financial condition at a given moment. This document outlines your assets, your liabilities, and your capital. These are generated monthly, quarterly, or annually. As your business grows, this document will prove increasingly valuable.

Cash Flow Statement

As the name suggests, this statements tracks the flow of your business's cash, including the money spent on operating your business, investing in your business, and financing activities of your business. In other words, any movement of cash is documented on these statements. These statements can be generated monthly, quarterly, or annually. I find that this statement gains more importance and relevance as your business grows.

Financial Software

If all of this sounds overwhelming, take a deep breath and relax. With a bit of common sense and some basic computer software, it is not too challenging to create and maintain financial statements.

QuickBooks by Intuit (www.quickbooks.intuit.com) is a popular software choice for small business owners managing their finances. This user-friendly software allows you to create invoices, write checks and pay bills, track inventory, and more. It also interfaces with other frequently used software like Microsoft Word and Excel. QuickBooks offers integration with many online banks, enabling users to quickly download statements. Another plus: information from QuickBooks can be imported directly into income tax preparation packages like Turbo Tax. It may seem easier to simply use pen and paper and, in fact, in your business's infancy, you may choose this route. However, the chance for errors is greater if you are doing your financial statements without the benefit of a computer checking your math!

Billing Your Clients

When a client signs an agreement with you, she is agreeing to the terms of payment described in the contract. Perhaps you ask for a 50 percent deposit due at signing

Invoice Checklist

- Your business name
- Your business logo
- Your business phone number
- Business e-mail
- The word "Invoice" or "Bill" near the top
- Date
- Invoice number (no two of your invoices should have the same number)
- Payment terms (e.g., due upon receipt of invoice or due within thirty days)
- Customer name
- Customer address
- Description of goods and services provided and cost of these goods and services
- Total amount due
- Payment types accepted (check, credit card, etc.)
- Consequences of overdue payments (you may choose to charge interest if payments are not made with a certain timeframe)

with the balance due within thirty days of the birthday party finish. The agreement should make clear the expectations for payment.

Do not hand your client a bill at the close of their child's birthday party. Let them relax, enjoy the moment, and not worry about pulling out a checkbook. Instead, when you next return to your desk for bookkeeping, create an invoice for your client. The invoice checklist here provides a framework for billing your clients.

Most likely, you will create your invoices with an online program, a good choice since these programs will double-check your math. After you print out the invoice, write a personal note. It can be simple—a brief thank you and your signature. Your clients will appreciate even this small gesture. According to research done by an associate professor at the School of Hotel Administration at Cornell University in New York state, waiters and waitresses who write "thank you" as well as their names on restaurant-goers' bills, receive significantly higher tips. I am not suggesting that you are looking for tips. Rather, this study shows that people respond positively to a personal touch, no matter how small.

Make sure that your invoice has the same terms of payment outlined in your planner/client contract. For instance, if the agreement stipulates that you will charge interest after ninety days, then echo this language in your invoice.

When a Client Doesn't Pay

Happily, it is a one-in-a-blue-moon situation when I have had a client unwilling or unable to pay a bill. I anticipate that you will find the same—parents plan and want to pay for your services in a timely fashion.

If you discover yourself in a situation with a difficult client, take a deep breath. Sometimes, clients simply misplace bills. Or, perhaps you receive a check that bounces. Again, give your client the benefit of the doubt. Offer your client the opportunity to write another check or to pay with cash. I think that it produces less stress on all sides to be calm and cool when collecting payment from a recalcitrant client. Be friendly, show respect, and in almost every case you will be paid for your services.

If a client refuses to pay, find out why. Was she disappointed with one of the services you provided? Does she feel that you reneged on one of your contractual obligations? Is she financially unable to pay? If your client is short on cash, work out a payment plan, perhaps allowing her to pay a monthly payment until her account is paid in full. If, even with a full arsenal of negotiating skills, you are unable to resolve a financial dispute, seek advice from your attorney.

Making Cents

Critical to your business success is tracking the flow of your money—what you are earning and what you are spending. This shouldn't be intimidating. Careful—and, not necessarily complicated—recordkeeping will help you to keep airtight financial reports. These records will help you to develop plans for growing your company as well as proving invaluable at tax time.

Finally, you cannot sustain a company unless the income exceeds the outflow of cash. As Thomas Jefferson, the third president of the United States and the primary author of the Declaration of Independence, so aptly put it, "Never spend your money before you have it."

Frequently Asked Questions

Should I itemize my bills?

Some event planners itemize, others do not. I choose to itemize all of my clients' statements. I have found that clients appreciate the transparency of my billing system. I outline each cost—the cost for the birthday cake, the caterer, the customized goody bag treats. My clients tell me that they prefer an itemized bill and, in terms of my recordkeeping, it is helpful for me to have itemized bills on file for all of my clients.

I am really not confident about my computer skills. Is it okay to do my bookkeeping in old-fashioned ledgers?

I was intimidated by computers when I first threw open my business's doors but, thanks to amazingly easy-to-operate software like QuickBooks, my fear of bookkeeping disappeared faster than a New York minute. I do know of party planners who keep records the old-fashioned way, but I really recommend learning a basic financial software program. It is too easy to make a basic addition or subtraction error when using pencil and paper. A software program catches math snafus instantly.

08

Managing Your Taxes

Oh, my. Even Albert Einstein had trouble with his taxes, opining that, "the hardest thing in the world to understand is the income tax." According to the National Federation of Small Businesses, 47 percent of all small business owners feel unable to understand the tax code. There is no question that tax time can be tricky. Happily, though, there are straightforward steps you can take to ease the crunch at tax time.

One of the first steps is to determine if you need an Employer Identification Number (EIN) when paying your taxes. This is a number assigned to you by the Internal Revenue Service (IRS). You will need this number if you have employees or if your business is incorporated. If not, you can use your social security number when filing your business taxes. Log on to www.irs.gov to obtain an EIN. There is no charge if you obtain your number through the IRS Web site. Be cautioned that other Web sites offering to assign EINs will levy a charge for their services.

Recordkeeping to Ease Tax Time Stress

The absolute best gift you can give yourself in terms of reducing tax-time stress is to keep thorough and detailed records. Above all, always keep your personal and business accounts separate. Don't be tempted to use your personal ATM card for a business purchase or vice versa. By keeping these accounts separate, you will be able to use the statements generated by your bank at tax time.

Tax Deductions: A Baker's Dozen

1. Home office
2. Office supplies
3. Office furniture
4. Other equipment
5. Software
6. Mileage
7. Insurance
8. Travel, meals, entertainment, gifts
9. Retirement contributions
10. Social security
11. Telephone expenses
12. Child labor (Often, small business owners are allowed to deduct income paid to their own children. If you are a small business owner with a teen looking for work, then this might be a useful deduction.)
13. Subscriptions

Take a moment to look at the Small Business Tax Deduction Checklist included in this chapter. This checklist makes clear the necessity of good recordkeeping. From the cost of taking a client out for a cup of coffee to the miles you rack up on your car traveling to appointments, all of these expenses may qualify as legal deductions, but you must have documentation (receipts and records) in order to qualify for these helpful deductions.

Tracking Deductions

As you track expenses, keep this straightforward framework in mind: If you bought an item specifically for your business, then it is almost certainly a deduction. Following this guide, a second phone line, installed in your home and dedicated to your business, is a deduction. On the other hand, a phone line that is used primarily by your kids to plan play dates is not a business expense. Stationery with your business logo? Absolutely a legitimate business expense. Stationery emblazoned with your name that you use for both business and pleasure? Not a legitimate deduction.

Your system for keeping receipts doesn't need to be fancy. In fact, it can be downright old-fashioned. File folders, or even shoeboxes, can fit the bill. The key is organization and staying on top of the process. Don't let receipts pile up.

Small Business Tax Deduction Checklist

Although small business owners often dread paying their dues to Uncle Sam, there are ways to reduce your tax bill. Many small business costs are deductible.

- *Employee wages and most employee benefits.* Obviously, this deduction won't apply if you are running a one-woman show, but as your business grows, you may choose to take on employees. If so, this deduction will be a benefit to you.
- *Interest on business loans.* If you have taken out financing to fund your growing company, the interest on these loans is an allowable deduction. Note, though, that interest on a credit card is not an allowable deduction.
- *Real estate taxes on business property.* Just as real estate taxes on your home are deductible, so, too, are taxes on an off-site business property. If you have a home-based office, then a percentage of your real estate taxes can legally be deducted.
- *State, local, and foreign income taxes assessed to your business.*
- *Business insurance.* Any additional policies you have taken out to cover your business should be considered an allowable deduction.
- *Advertising and promotion costs.* These costs can prove to be sizable, making this an important deduction.
- *Employee education and training.* Event planners often complete certification programs, which are tax deductible.
- *Education to maintain or improve your own required business skills.*
- *Legal and professional fees.* The fees you pay to the lawyers and other professionals who help with your business can be deducted.
- *Utilities.* For an at-home office site, a percentage of the total utilities cost can be deducted.
- *Telephone costs.* This includes any dedicated telephone lines, whether land lines or cellular lines.
- *Office repairs.* Leaky roof needs to be replaced? Keep the receipts so you can deduct this cost at tax time.
- *Automobile expenses.* If you use your car extensively for your business, a portion of that expense is deductible.
- *Meals, travel, and entertainment.* These expenses may be deductible if they relate specifically to your business.

Notes from the Field

As you earn money, you must set some aside for your taxes. If you anticipate owing more than $1,000 in taxes by the end of the year, you must make quarterly payments to Uncle Sam. These four payments are due the fifteenth of January, April, June, and September. Use IRS form 1040-ES to help calculate the amount you owe. You will also use this form to submit your payment to the government.

Instead, file receipts as soon as you have them in the appropriate box or file. I keep a file for every month. Other party planners prefer quarterly files, which are helpful for paying quarterly estimated taxes. Most receipts have the merchant's name already printed on them. If not, note the merchant's name. If it is not immediately evident what the receipt is for, then make a note of that as well. I like to paperclip the receipts in date order by type. In other words, I clip all of my office supply receipts together in date order; my utility bills are clipped together separately, again in date order; any receipts for entertaining are clipped separately, in date order, and so on.

By filing receipts as soon as they are in my hand, I am able to make this process quick and easy. It's a breeze to find documentation when tax time rolls around.

Hiring a Professional to Help with Your Finances

As your company grows, I recommend that you hire a professional to help you with your finances. It is money well spent. A savvy financial expert can save your company money. According to the National Federation of Small Business, a whopping 88 percent of small business owners hire a professional to help them file taxes and to make determinations about allowable tax deductions.

When choosing a financial professional, consider your needs. Do you want someone to prepare monthly financial statements or are you looking for a professional to take care of your finances only at tax time? If you are looking for year-round advice, you will want to consider hiring a certified public accountant (CPA). If you are looking for help at tax time, either a CPA or an enrolled agent (EA) will fill the bill.

Keep in mind, as you begin your search, that not all CPAs and EAs are created equal. To find an accountant, ask other friends and colleagues for their

2008 Estimated Tax Worksheet
Keep for Your Records

1	Adjusted gross income you expect in 2008 (see instructions below)	**1**
2	● If you plan to itemize deductions, enter the estimated total of your itemized deductions.	
	Caution: *If line 1 above is over $159,950 ($79,975 if married filing separately), your deduction may be reduced. See Pub. 505 for details.*	**2**
	● If you do not plan to itemize deductions, enter your standard deduction from page 1.	
3	Subtract line 2 from line 1	**3**
4	Exemptions. Multiply $3,500 by the number of personal exemptions. **Caution:** *See Pub. 505 to figure the amount to enter if line 1 above is over:* $239,950 if married filing jointly or qualifying widow(er); $199,950 if head of household; $159,950 if single; or $119,975 if married filing separately	**4**
5	Subtract line 4 from line 3	**5**
6	**Tax.** Figure your tax on the amount on line 5 by using the **2008 Tax Rate Schedules** on page 5. **Caution:** *If you will have qualified dividends or a net capital gain, or expect to claim the foreign earned income exclusion or housing exclusion, see Pub. 505 to figure the tax*	**6**
7	Alternative minimum tax from **Form 6251**	**7**
8	Add lines 6 and 7. Add to this amount any other taxes you expect to include in the total on Form 1040, line 44, or Form 1040A, line 28	**8**
9	Credits (see instructions below). **Do not** include any income tax withholding on this line . .	**9**
10	Subtract line 9 from line 8. If zero or less, enter -0-	**10**
11	Self-employment tax (see instructions below). Estimate of 2008 net earnings from self-employment $_____ ; if **$102,000 or less,** multiply the amount by 15.3%; if **more than $102,000,** multiply the amount by 2.9%, add $12,648 to the result, and enter the total. **Caution:** *If you also have wages subject to social security tax, see Pub. 505 to figure the amount to enter*	**11**
12	Other taxes (see instructions below)	**12**
13a	Add lines 10 through 12	**13a**
b	Earned income credit, additional child tax credit, and credits from **Forms 4136, 8801 (line 27),** and **8885** .	**13b**
c	**Total 2008 estimated tax.** Subtract line 13b from line 13a. If zero or less, enter -0- . . ▶	**13c**
14a	Multiply line 13c by 90% (66⅔ % for farmers and fishermen)	**14a**
b	Enter the tax shown on your 2007 tax return (110% of that amount if you are not a farmer or fisherman and the adjusted gross income shown on that return is more than $150,000 or, if married filing separately for 2008, more than $75,000)	**14b**
c	**Required annual payment to avoid a penalty.** Enter the **smaller** of line 14a or 14b . . . . . ▶	**14c**
	Caution: *Generally, if you do not prepay (through income tax withholding and estimated tax payments) at least the amount on line 14c, you may owe a penalty for not paying enough estimated tax. To avoid a penalty, make sure your estimate on line 13c is as accurate as possible. Even if you pay the required annual payment, you may still owe tax when you file your return. If you prefer, you can pay the amount shown on line 13c. For details, see Pub. 505.*	
15	Income tax withheld and estimated to be withheld during 2008 (including income tax withholding on pensions, annuities, certain deferred income, etc.)	**15**
16a	Subtract line 15 from line 14c	**16a**
	Is the result zero or less?	
	☐ **Yes.** Stop here. You are not required to make estimated tax payments.	
	☐ **No.** Go to line 16b.	
b	Subtract line 15 from line 13c	**16b**
	Is the result less than $1,000?	
	☐ **Yes.** Stop here. You are not required to make estimated tax payments.	
	☐ **No.** Go to line 17 to figure your required payment.	
17	If the first payment you are required to make is due April 15, 2008, enter ¼ of line 16a (minus any 2007 overpayment that you are applying to this installment) here, and on your estimated tax payment voucher(s) if you are paying by check or money order. (**Note:** *Household employers, see instructions below.*)	**17**

Instructions for the 2008 Estimated Tax Worksheet

Line 1. Adjusted gross income. Use your 2007 tax return and instructions as a guide to figuring the adjusted gross income you expect in 2008 (but be sure to consider the items listed under *What's New* that begins on page 1). For more details on figuring your adjusted gross income, see *Expected AGI—Line 1* in chapter 2 of Pub. 505. If you are self-employed, be sure to take into account the deduction for one-half of your self-employment tax (2007 Form 1040, line 27).

Line 9. Credits. See the 2007 Form 1040, lines 47 through 55, or Form 1040A, lines 29 through 33, and the related instructions.

Line 11. Self-employment tax. If you and your spouse make joint estimated tax payments and you both have self-employment income, figure the self-employment tax for *each* of you separately. Enter the total on line 11. When figuring your estimate of 2008 net earnings from self-employment, be sure to use only 92.35% (.9235) of your total net profit from self-employment.

Line 12. Other taxes. Use the instructions for the 2007 Form 1040 to determine if you expect to owe, for 2008, any of the taxes that would have been entered on your 2007 Form 1040, lines 60 (additional tax on early distributions only), 61, and 62, and any write-ins on line 63, or any amount from Form 1040A, line 36. On line 12, enter the total of those taxes, subject to the following two exceptions.

Exception 1. Include household employment taxes Form 1040, line 62, on this line only if:
● You will have federal income tax withheld from wages, pensions, annuities, gambling winnings, or other income, or
● You would be required to make estimated tax payments (to avoid a penalty) even if you did not include household employment taxes when figuring your estimated tax.

If you meet one or both of the above, include in the amount on line 12 the total of your household employment taxes before subtracting advance EIC payments made to your employee(s).

Exception 2. Of the amounts for other taxes that may be entered on Form 1040, line 63, do not include on line 12: tax on recapture of a federal mortgage subsidy, uncollected employee social security and Medicare tax or RRTA tax on tips or group-term life insurance, tax on golden parachute payments, or excise tax on insider stock compensation from an expatriated corporation. These taxes are not required to be paid until the due date of your income tax return (not including extensions).

Line 17. If you are a household employer and you make advance EIC payments to your employee(s), reduce your required estimated tax payment for each period by the amount of advance EIC payments paid during the period.

-4-

Internet Tip

When you have a CPA or EA's name in hand, you should check their organization's professional Web sites to ensure that they are licensed. For information on CPAs, log onto the National Association of State Boards of Accounting at www.nasba.org. For information on EAs, log onto National Association of Enrolled Agents at www.naea.org.

recommendations—word of mouth is a good way to find any professional. Surf the Web, as well, since many accountants have Web sites outlining their areas of specialization.

When you arrange your first meeting with a CPA or EA, make sure that you have organized paperwork in hand. Financial professionals are not paid to sift through unsorted papers and receipts. It is your responsibility to hand organized files, paperwork, and receipts (as described above) to your CPA.

At this first meeting, make sure that the CPA or EA has experience working with small business owners. Be sure to confirm her fee. Is it a flat fee? A per-hour fee? What about phone calls—how will they be billed? Finally, make sure that you feel comfortable working with this person. It is imperative that you feel confident in this person and comfortable working through sometimes prickly financial situations with her.

Audit Advice

If the Internal Revenue Service (IRS) opts to audit your company, you will want to have a paid professional, such as a CPA or an EA, to assist you.

The IRS has ramped up its efforts to audit small businesses, suggesting that small businesses are often in non-compliance with the tax code. Don't be one of these businesses. Be scrupulous in your recordkeeping and honest in your accounting. Then, when the IRS requests an audit, you can provide all of the paperwork necessary.

The IRS will be primarily interested in revenue. Make sure that all of your revenue is deposited into a business account. Do not put business income into a private account. The IRS also considers barter income. For instance, if you provide a service to the caterer who then provides you with free cheese pizzas, the IRS considers this as income.

The IRS will also be interested in reviewing your expenses. So, if you submit expenses for taking clients to dinner, you must provide a receipt indicating that you did, indeed, pay for that dinner.

Supply your accountant with all of the necessary paperwork and have her meet with the IRS. It is generally better for you to stay away from the audit. If you do choose to attend the audit, be respectful and polite. The IRS agents will not appreciate any difficult attitudes.

Financial and Recordkeeping Software

There are literally hundreds of types of software available for managing your finances. Some, of course, are head and shoulders above the others in terms of quality. To find the best software, ask other event planners as well as friends for their recommendations.

I find that QuickBooks products work very well and are extremely user friendly. These products allow you to track inventory, expenses, and sales; generate statements and invoices; create financial statements; download credit card and bank transactions; import tax forms; generate payroll; and more. QuickBooks products start at about $100. Microsoft's Excel software is another popular option.

When it comes time to select financial software, choose a product that fulfills your needs. Perhaps you simply want a program that will produce basic financial statements. Or maybe you are planning to hire employees and will need software that can help to track and generate payroll. Assess your needs, and then find a user-friendly software package. Many companies offer a free trial use of their software, allowing you to discover first-hand if the product will work for you.

The bottom line when it comes to finances is careful recordkeeping. Unfortunately, too many people neglect to keep these records. The process is not difficult and, if done daily or weekly, not time consuming. Don't be afraid to manage your money. Your business depends upon your close eye.

Frequently Asked Question

I am planning to use a paid tax preparer, rather than a CPA or EA, to prepare and file my taxes. Is this a good idea?

Although paid tax preparers tend to charge less than CPAs or EAs (and therefore are a tempting choice), I would recommend paying the few extra dollars to secure the services of a tax professional other than a paid preparer. Although the majority of paid tax preparers are on the up and up, there is no system for checking their backgrounds. Also, keep in mind that a paid tax preparer—such as those employed during tax season by large tax-preparation companies—is not legally able to represent you during an IRS audit.

Choosing a Legal Eagle

When your new business first takes flight, it may seem hard to envision the day that you will need legal advice—but, as your business grows, that day will dawn. A lawyer can give you advice about the ideal business structure for your company, words of wisdom about creating contracts for clients and vendors, suggestions for negotiating a solid lease, and information about complying with local zoning laws, among other things. In a word, the advice of a good lawyer is invaluable.

When to Hire a Lawyer

Although this is a decision that differs from company owner to company owner, I recommend finding an attorney sooner rather than later. Once you find yourself in legal hot water, it is too late to be looking for an attorney. Finding an attorney takes time and care. Don't wait for an emergency to find the right lawyer to help your growing business.

Many small business owners tell me that not having an attorney actually costs them more than having an attorney. For instance, one children's party planner reports being strong-armed into a seven-year lease with many restrictive stipulations—if she had had an attorney, she would have consulted with her and realized there were alternatives to that unfortunate position.

I recommend finding a lawyer as you launch your business. This is not to say that you will need to shell out big bucks for your legal counsel. It is simply better to get your legal ducks in a row so when the time comes that you need legal advice, it will be at the ready.

Why You Need an Attorney

Although you may think that you can navigate the legal channels on your own, there are many instances when an attorney will prove invaluable. Attorneys will provide important counsel when you are:

- Negotiating rental agreements
- Applying for a business structure, such as an LLC or incorporation
- Creating vendor contracts
- Creating client contracts
- Dealing with any liability issues
- Reviewing financial paperwork
- Applying for business licenses and permits
- Reviewing zoning ordinances
- Reviewing trademark and copyright issues
- Reviewing contracts provided to you by outside vendors and venues
- Organizing the eventual sale of your company
- Completing legal documents needed for franchising

Choosing the Lawyer Who Is Right for You

To find a lawyer, begin by asking other small business owners to make recommendations. The legal field has become very specialized, so you will want to hire a lawyer who deals with small businesses on a regular basis. When you have compiled a list of highly recommended attorneys who specialize in dealing with small businesses, make initial contact with these attorneys over the phone. This will give you a sense of their styles and whether these styles are a match with yours. After you've made these initial phone contacts, choose one or two attorneys to meet with in person.

Some attorneys charge an hourly fee. Make sure that, if this is the case, you know who is doing the work. For instance, you may be quoted a $300 per hour fee, covering a senior lawyer's fees. Ensure, then, that paraprofessionals or junior lawyers are not doing the work. If they are, you should be charged a smaller per hour fee for their hours. It is important to find out how you will be billed for phone calls, as well. A few minutes on the phone with your lawyer can result in a rather large legal bill. Consider the lawyer who charges $300 per hour. A thirteen-minute phone call, rounded up for billing purposes to fifteen minutes, equals $75 of billable time!

Client/Attorney Checklist

When meeting with these attorneys and making your choice consider the following criteria:

- *Do you like the attorney? Yes or No*
  This may sound so straightforward as to be ridiculous but, in fact, too many clients feel needlessly intimidated by their attorneys. Remember, you are the person doing the hiring and choosing, and you should feel as you would when you hire any other employee. You should feel comfortable and at ease speaking with your attorney.
- *Is the attorney's office conveniently located? Yes or No*
  Again, sounds straightforward, but you should choose an attorney with an easy-to-access office site. Driving thirty miles each way to meet with an attorney probably doesn't make sense, especially if you have to arrange for childcare to do so.
- *Do you know the attorney's area of specialization? Yes or No*
  You will want to choose an attorney whose practice focuses on small businesses. Lawyers' specializations can be rather narrow—from estate law to divorce law. Choose a lawyer whose expertise matches your needs.
- *Does the attorney work for a big firm? Yes or No*
  Big firms, with their larger overhead, tend to charge higher per hour rates. However, big firms often have more lawyers in each area of the law. In other words, more lawyers are available for your specific small-business needs.
- *Do you know who will be doing the work? Yes or No*
  Some large firms have paralegals and associate lawyers who do much of the daily "grind" work. If this is the case, are you comfortable with that arrangement? If not, you will probably want to consider a smaller firm where you will consistently be dealing with the work of one attorney.
- *Do you know how you will be billed? Yes or No*
  This, of course, is key, as legal bills can skyrocket. Often, lawyers will charge a flat one-time fee for straightforward legal situations, such as forming a limited liability corporation. If you are quoted a flat fee for a service such as this, make sure that this fee includes disbursements (things like overnight mailing of packages or filing fees due to the state).

This agreement is between Art Escapades Birthday Parties (hereafter referred to as PLANNER) and Rabbit Hat Magic (hereafter referred to as VENDOR).

Event date: June 13, 200X

Event arrival time: 2:30 p.m.

Event start time: 3:00 p.m.

Event end time: 5:30 p.m.

1. VENDOR agrees to provide:
   One hour of magic for ten children with all necessary props. The VENDOR agrees to arrive punctually and to perform an act appropriate for children. The VENDOR agrees to show proof of insurance.

2. PLANNER agrees to provide:
   An individual on-site to act as a liaison for the VENDOR as well as convenient parking.

3. Fees
   The PLANNER agrees to provide $150 to the VENDOR for the one-hour magic show.

4. Terms
   PLANNER shall pay VENDOR a deposit of 50 percent at the signing of this agreement. The balance will be due at the completion of the party on June 13, 200X.

5. Cancellation
   If the VENDOR cancels for any reason, he or she will forfeit the 50 percent deposit. If the PLANNER cancels for any reason, he or she will not ask that the deposit be returned.

6. Force Majeure
   This agreement is automatically canceled if the event is interrupted by an act of God, by war, or by strikes.

7. Hold harmless and indemnification
   The PLANNER and VENDOR agree to hold one another harmless from negligence and to mutually indemnify.

8. Acceptance of full agreement

This agreement, plus attachments, constitutes the full agreement. Any changes to this agreement must be approved in writing by both PLANNER and VENDOR. Those parties affixing signatures below agree to accept the terms and conditions of this agreement.

VENDOR _____   DATE _____

PLANNER _____   DATE _____

Other attorneys will ask for a retainer. For instance, you pay the firm $1,000. Then, as you need legal services, the attorney will draw from this escrow account. If this is the arrangement made, then it should be clearly stipulated (in writing) that if the relationship between you and the lawyer does not continue, the money still in this escrow account will be returned to you.

Written Agreements and Contracts

You will need to become familiar with using written agreements and contracts, both with your clients as well as with the vendors with whom you work. Even when planning a small party for a friend, it is best to keep things legal and on paper. This helps avoid any painful misunderstandings. It can be inviting to simply proceed on a handshake, but to do so is to go ahead with some peril.

Some folks find the idea of legal contracts intimidating. You shouldn't feel this way. A contract is a wonderful tool and at its essence it outlines what services you will provide at what price—simple as that! The sample contracts shown in this chapter indicate just how straightforward a contract can be. The contracts shown are quite bare-bones, and for more complicated events a more involved contract will be required. However, even in a more complicated form, a contract states each party's responsibilities in fulfilling an agreement.

By clearly outlining your obligations in a contract, you help to ensure that your client will not experience any nasty surprises or disappointments at the birthday

Notes from the Field

Many children's party planners find Quicken's contract software useful for creating contracts. Quicken Legal Pro 2008 offers 140 form and contract templates and is available for as little as $29.99. See www.quicken.com for more information.

party. These contracts are legally binding, as well, and could be used if your client took any legal action. Don't be alarmed by the thought of legal action. The majority of party planners find clients reasonable and fair, but for those who aren't, be sure to have a signed contract in hand. Consider the case of Elana Glatt, a New York City bride, who found instant fame (or, perhaps, infamy is more like it) by suing her florist for $400,000. Why? Glatt's wedding flowers (hydrangeas, which cost a whopping $27,000) were the wrong color and caused her wedding day to be ruined. The court will use the written agreement, signed by Glatt and the florist, to help resolve this thorny legal tangle.

You may choose to create your own contract using legal contract software or simply creating your own contracts from scratch. If the contract is complicated or involves a large amount of money, you might want to have your attorney review it upon completion.

Remember that contracts are confidential. You may feel like sharing some of the details with a colleague, but don't. The arrangements made are strictly between you and your client or vendor. Do not share this information.

Legal Advice When Interviewing and Hiring Employees

As your birthday party planning business grows, you may need to hire additional staff. There are a number of ways to accomplish this. First you need to assess your needs. Do you need an extra pair of hands to help you pass out slices of cake and to clean up after the party is over? Or, do you need someone to take on more complicated tasks such as scouting locations and vetting vendors? For the former, you might opt to hire a teenage neighbor. When I need an extra pair of hands, I sometimes turn to my teenage son to help out. He is reliable and enjoys assisting me. I do pay him for his time, though. I urge you to pay everyone who helps with your event, even if it is a nominal sum.

Contract Checklist

When you create contracts, make sure that you are able to check "yes" for the following questions:

- *Did you call it a contract at the top of the document? Yes or No*
  Make sure that you have the word "contract" front and center. This seems basic (and it is) but a document without the word "contract" may not necessarily be as watertight as one with the word used prominently.

- *Did you spell all names correctly? Yes or No*
  Again, this may sound too basic to be believed, but you would be surprised at the number of misspelled names I have seen in contracts. Check and double-check the spelling of any names and businesses included in the contract. If you are dealing with a vendor, be sure to include their business structure (LLC, for instance).

- *Is the writing straightforward and free from jargon? Yes or No*
  I think this is why so many people are frightened when hearing the words "legal contract." They picture a dense document jammed with legalese. Your contract should use everyday language and steer clear of long and complicated sentences.

- *Is the contract directed to the right person? Yes or No*
  An event planner friend just found herself in a pickle because she had a contract directed to—and signed by—the wrong person. The speaker she had arranged for a conference was not aware of the contract and didn't show up! This provided a very stressful lesson for my event-planning friend about the importance of directing the contract to the person responsible.

- *Did you spell out the details? Yes or No*
  Maybe the parents think you will be showing up with the birthday cake—when you have no intentions of doing so. Spell out every detail in your contract. Who will arrange the pizza delivery and payment? Who will arrange for the clown? The face painting? The setup and clean-up? Put everything in writing.

- *Did you specify payment amount and payment plan? Yes or No*
  Be sure to not only include the amount to be paid but the time at which
  it should be paid. If you ask for a 50 percent deposit, make sure to note
  this in the contract as well as noting the date that the deposit is due. Also,
  outline when final payment is due.
- *Have any modifications been made in writing? Yes or No*
  Be sure to make changes to the contracts in writing. Perhaps, at the signing, the parents decide to serve cupcakes instead of cake. Make sure to
  make a hand-written note of this on the contract. Then, both parties should
  initial this modification. It is best, when signing contracts, to have each
  party initial every page, as well. That way no one can claim to have missed
  a page when reading through the contract.
- *Have you delineated how the contract can be terminated? Yes or No*
  Although the vast number of contractual obligations are fulfilled without a
  hitch, occasionally a contract does need to be terminated. You need to outline a process for this termination. For instance, you might want to ask that
  a letter be submitted if the contract is to be terminated. You will also need
  to outline financial ramifications of a termination. Will you return all of a
  client or vendor's deposit? What is the timeframe for termination? You will
  need to make these considerations to safeguard your business's financial
  health. If you are planning a large children's birthday party, you will need
  to provide a financial outlay well in advance. You must ensure, through the
  contracts, that you are not left in a financial lurch.

Temporary Employees

Many party and event planners turn to temporary employees to help with big
events. This is particularly true if an event planner conducts only a handful of large-
scale events each year. These planners do not need to keep extra employees on staff.
Rather, they can turn to these temporary employees when the need arises.

To find temporary employees, agencies such as Kelly Services (www.kellyservices
.com) or Manpower (www.manpower.com) are dependable resources. These agencies
refer employees to you. You then pay the agency who, in turn, pays the temporary
employee. Using these services can also save you bookkeeping headaches since you

will not be responsible for paying these employees' benefits or for withholding tax or social security monies. Rather, the temp agency is responsible for taking care of these things, easing the paperwork on your end. You will pay a bit more per hour than you would if you hired the employee directly, but, in this case, it is money well spent.

Hiring Friends and Family

As I wrote above, my teenage son is willing and cheerful about helping out at children's birthday parties, so he is a good choice for me when the party is small and I need help doing small tasks—pouring water, passing out paintbrushes, helping the children wash their hands. I always pay him and treat him with the same respect I give to anyone who works for me.

Employee vs. Independent Contractor

An important consideration as you begin staffing your business is whether you will be utilizing employees or independent contractors. Temporary employees, as outlined below, do not fall into the same category as employees since you will not be responsible for their benefits or for paying into their tax and social security.

- When hiring an employee, you clearly delineate the hours to be worked; independent contractors, who often work for many different organizations, are sometimes not available for all of the hours needed.
- When hiring an employee, you have more leeway in terms of a perfect personality match since you will be drawing from a broad pool of candidates. When using an independent contractor, you will have less control.
- When hiring an employee, you will be responsible for any employee benefits, such as vacation pay or sick leave; an independent contractor will be responsible for their own benefits.
- You can hire an independent contractor for a very specific task, such as editing a newsletter. I know a children's party planner who hires an independent contractor to spend twenty hours per month writing and editing her marketing materials. By opting for this independent contractor, she can hire someone with a specific area of expertise for just a few hours per month.

Reaching Out to Potential Employees

There are a number of ways in which to reach out to prospective employees.

- *Start spreading the news.* Once again, so many vital elements in the event-planning business come down to word of mouth. Let folks know that you are looking for employees. Let your colleagues at the party supply store, the women in your weekly coffee group, and the members of your PTA all know that you are looking for employees. Over and over again, I have found this an effective way to find and hire good employees.

- *The big power of the small classified.* Consider a classified ad in your local newspaper. These inexpensive ads can draw good applicants to your pool of potential clients. Remember to include your logo in the ad, specifics about the qualifications you are looking for in any employee, the hours needed, and any benefits. If you need weekend help, then be sure to include that in your ad. You want to convey as much information as possible to potential employees.

- *The draw of the Internet.* One of the major developments in terms of finding employees is the advent of Craigslist (www.craigslist.org). This online advertising site offers free ad placement (except in a handful of major cities such as New York, Seattle, San Francisco, and San Diego, for instance) and reaches an enormous, worldwide audience, tracking more than 4 billion hits per month! Almost 20 million new classifieds are posted each month. Because of its broad scope (Craigslist targets more than five hundred U.S. cities) it is important that you target your audience when placing your free classified. This easy-to-use and accessible Web site guides you through the straightforward process of posting your online advertisement.

Keep this in mind if you turn to family and friends to help out. Although your best friend may chime in and offer to help dish up ice cream at your next event, make sure that you make a formal arrangement with the friend. Tell her when she needs to arrive to help with setup and how long clean-up and post-party issues will take. Make sure to negotiate her wage. Nothing can spoil a friendship faster than a business dealing gone sour. Don't use friends or family without compensating them. I really can't say this too many times or in too many ways. Be good to your buddies and family!

Having issued this caveat, friends and family can be a wonderful asset to your business. I have enjoyed working with friends at events who have brought their positive energy and good cheer with them as they support me in my efforts.

Interviewing Potential Employees

You've put out feelers and received resumes and cover letters from a variety of prospective employees. Now, it is time to start sorting through this pool of applicants. This first sorting process will be the easiest. You will have three piles: "yes," "no," and "maybe." Into the "no" pile go all of the applicants who don't have the appropriate qualifications. You will be surprised at the number of folks who apply willy-nilly to any employment advertisement—even when their qualifications are not even remotely similar to those requested in the advertisement! Put these applicants directly into the do-not-pass-go "no" pile.

Similarly, the "yes" pile will sort itself out quite easily. These are the applicants with the qualifications you've outlined. As well, these people will have written a thoughtful and succinct cover letter to accompany their resumes. Pay attention to small details. If an applicant misspells your name in the cover letter, then she is probably not a person who will pay attention to detail. In other words, not a good children's party planner.

More complicated is sifting through the "maybes." These are applicants who can't quickly be relegated to the "no" stack or promoted to the "yes" pile. These might be applicants who have most of the required experience or have some other quality that draws you to them. Be careful not to let emotion cloud your vision. For instance, just because the person grew up in your hometown or attended the same grade school, that does not make this person an ideal candidate. It is easy to let emotion (simply liking a candidate) blur our vision about that person's actual qualifications for the job.

Once you have sorted your applicants into three stacks, you will make initial contact with those in the "yes" pile through a brief phone call. Make sure that you call the applicants at the time and number they've outlined—you don't want to catch a future employee at an awkward time, such as during her regularly scheduled weekly meeting with her current boss!

Notes from the Field

It is illegal to ask any questions about an applicant's age, race, gender, religion, marital status, or parental status. Don't be tempted to ask an applicant if he or she is going to have childcare issues—this is an illegal question and could get you into hot water.

Once you have a prospective employee on the phone, tell her that you have enjoyed reading through her letter and resume and find out if she is still interested in the job. If she is, set up a time for an interview.

The Interview

Interviews, whenever possible, should be face to face rather than over the phone. Sometimes this simply isn't possible, but for the best results, aim to meet in person. Dress professionally for this interview. Just as you expect applicants to put their best foot forward when meeting you, remember that the interview process is a two-way street. Your prospective employees will want to see that you run a professional, tight ship.

When the applicant arrives, have her fill out a formal job application. Job application forms are available at office supply stores, or you can use the sample provided in this chapter. Don't create your own form. Protect yourself and use a form that complies with state and federal laws regarding discrimination.

Be sure that the applicant feels at home and comfortable before starting the interview. Show her pages from your portfolio to help her get a sense of who you are and how you run your business. Perhaps offer her a cup of tea or seltzer.

Ask all applicants the same roster of questions. In this way you will be ensuring a level playing field. Take notes as the applicant responds (let her know you will be taking notes so she is not surprised by this). You may think that you will remember her responses even without taking notes, but it is likely that you won't remember everything accurately. You are likely to blur interviews among different candidates if you don't take adequate notes during each interview.

It is important to ask what I call "situation" questions. For example, ask, "What would you do if the pizza delivery person never arrived?" rather than asking, "Do you handle stress well?" I've found that most people think they handle stress well (or, at least say they do during a job interview). By asking these situation questions, you will find out not only if the applicant is prepared to deal with the stressful situations that can occur at kids' parties but also if the applicant is a creative problem solver.

Make sure the applicant truly likes working with kids. Even if an applicant has had success working with event planners who conduct parties for adults, this same applicant may be less at ease at children's events. Again, instead of the straightforward, "Do you like working with kids?" (to which virtually 100 percent of your applicants will say "yes"), ask "Tell me about your work with children."

As you formulate interview questions, steer clear of "yes or no" questions. These don't offer the applicant an opportunity to easily describe her experiences. Likewise, these questions don't afford you the best tool for discovering if the applicant is a good fit for your company. Consider some of these questions:

1. What are some of the challenges you've faced in past jobs and how have you handled these challenges?
2. What is the work accomplishment of which you are proudest?
3. What is it like working for your current supervisor? What are her strengths and weaknesses?
4. What are the most rewarding aspects of your current job? The least rewarding?
5. Why are you leaving your current job?
6. What characteristics do you look for in a supervisor?
7. Describe any improvements you've made in your current job and give specifics.
8. Describe a customer complaint and how you resolved it.
9. Why should I hire you?
10. Do you have any questions for me?

At the close of each interview, let each applicant know your projected timeframe for hiring: when you will be letting interviewees know about your decision. Try to follow this timeframe. We've probably all been in a position in which we're waiting to hear if we have been hired for a job. It can be a nervous wait!

Please use black or blue ink and print when filling out this form. Answer all questions and sign and date the form at the bottom.

Personal Information:

First Name _____

Middle Name _____

Last Name _____

Street Address _____

City, State, Zip_____

Phone _____

Are you eligible to work in the United States? Yes or No

If under 18, do you have an employment/age certificate? Yes or No

Have you been convicted of, or entered a plea of guilty, no contest, or had a withheld judgment to a felony in the past five years? Yes or No

If yes, explain:_____

_____

_____

_____

Position Available:

Position Applied For_____

Days Available _____

Hours Available _____

What date are you available to start work? _____

Education:

Please list school name and address, the diploma or certificate received, and the date of graduation:

_____

_____

_____

Please list any skills, training, awards, or other qualifications:

_____

_____

_____

Employment History:

Start with your most recent employer.

Employer _____

Address _____

Supervisor _____

Phone _____

E-mail _____

Title _____

Responsibilities _____

_____

From _____ to _____

Salary _____

Reason for leaving _____

Employer _____

Address _____

Supervisor _____

Phone _____

E-mail _____

Title _____

Responsibilities _____

_____

From _____ to _____

Salary _____

Reason for leaving _____

Employer _____

Address _____

Supervisor _____

Phone _____

E-mail _____

Title _____

Responsibilities _____

_____

From _____ to _____

Salary _____

Reason for leaving _____

May we contact your present employer? Yes or No

References:

Please list three references, providing name, address, and phone number.

_____

_____

_____

I certify that the information contained in this application is true and complete. I understand that false information may be grounds for not hiring me or for immediate termination of employment at any point in the future if I am hired. I authorize the verification of any or all of the information listed above.

Signature _____

Date _____

Making the Hire

After the interview process is complete, take the time to carefully review your notes. Sleep on your decision, too, and be sure that you aren't simply hiring the applicant you like the most (of course, it is important to like the applicant) but also the applicant who is most qualified.

Call the applicant to offer your congratulations and to offer her the position. Your pick might ask to have time to consider your offer. You should always agree to this, assuming the applicant is asking for a reasonable amount of time to think over her decision.

When she accepts, you will need to put the offer in writing and ask her to sign it. This is basically a contract ensuring that she is sincere about taking on this new role. In the letter, outline the parameters of the job: start date, salary, benefits, and so on. This will help to negate any future misunderstandings.

Top Ten Qualities in a Children's Party Planning Employee

Of course, depending on the job you are filling, you will look for different qualifications. If you are looking for an editor to create your quarterly newsletter, you will need to find an able writer and editor; if you are looking for a graphic designer, you will want to search for a designer who creates images that suit the style and message of your company. These specifics aside, any employee you hire should possess as many as possible of the following qualities:

1. Detail-oriented
2. Organized
3. An effective time manager
4. Creative
5. Customer-service oriented
6. Budget-minded
7. Self-motivated
8. Good listener
9. Positive attitude
10. Enjoys working with children

Once you have a signed contract with your new employee, it is imperative that you let the other applicants know that you have chosen someone else. This can be done with a phone call or a letter. Many business owners neglect to contact these other applicants. Don't be one of these business owners. Put yourself in the applicants' shoes. It is not a good feeling to be left hanging. Let these folks know about your choice so they can continue with their job hunts. As your business expands, you may want to hire one of these other applicants. Make sure to keep the good karma flowing by keeping them in the information loop.

Training New Employees

There is nothing more frustrating than being hired for a job and then being ignored! I've been in this position, waiting for training that never arrives. Make sure that you welcome your new employee and show her the ropes. If you have hired her as a graphic designer, create a chart showing the design materials you will need and when you will need them. If you have hired her to help at the actual events, show her sample timeframes of parties and what your expectations are for her.

Be a Good Boss

Reflect on your own work experience. I would venture to go out on a limb and say that we all prefer the boss who occasionally brings in coffee and donuts, offers us the opportunity to leave early on a sunny summer Friday, or distributes movie passes to the local theater. Be this kind of boss. Treat your employees well and they will do the same for you. Remember, you get what you give in life!

Back in Chapter 5, I wrote about word-of-mouth marketing and how important it is to have employees who help with this positive word of mouth. Your employees can be wonderful advocates if you are a fair and honest leader. To paraphrase Theodore Roosevelt, the best boss is the one who has enough sense to pick good employees to do what she wants done and enough self-restraint to keep from meddling with them while they do it! Choose employees carefully, train with care, and treat them with respect.

Frequently Asked Questions

I can't afford to hire a lawyer but I need legal advice. What can I do?
Many states offer innovative approaches for providing low- or no-cost legal counsel. In California, for instance, Tele-Lawyer offers advice, via the phone, from veteran

lawyers for $3 per minute. Most issues are resolved in ten minutes or less. Use your computer search engine and type in the name of your state and the words "inexpensive legal help" or "low-cost lawyer" to see if your state offers any of these innovative options. Web sites such as www.legalzoom.com are also helpful, providing low-cost, straightforward legal advice about basic issues such as contracts, creating a business structure, and hiring employees.

A friend has asked me to plan a party for her daughter. She is reluctant to sign a contract, saying she wants to keep it "all between friends." What should I do?
Planning parties for friends' children can be a sticky business, made more so when a friend is reluctant to sign a contract. Explain to your friend that the contract is as much a protection for her as it is for you. The contract ensures that she gets what she is paying for and provides her with solid event insurance—ensuring that you will follow through on your obligations.

Even after all of my careful efforts to choose the right employee, it is not working out. What can I do?
Unfortunately, even the best laid plans can go awry. If you are frustrated with an employee, try to pinpoint the reasons why. Is she routinely late for work? Is she making personal phone calls on company time? Is she making careless mistakes? Make a written record of these infractions. Make sure that you are holding up your end of the bargain by being a good communicator. Have you been clear in outlining her job responsibilities? Has she received adequate training? Are you being a fair boss? If you answer "yes" to all of these questions, it may simply be an untenable working relationship. Before terminating an employee, you must give her verbal warnings for unsatisfactory work performance. If you must terminate an employee, do so in person—not via the phone or e-mail—and do so with respect and a calm manner. Keep it all professional.

10 | Start Spreading the Word

Letting Everyone Know about Your Business

As your business grows and you begin to plan more events, you will want to focus on marketing your business. Marketing efforts cover a broad swath—everything from word-of-mouth buzz to creating interactive Web sites. In fact, in a nutshell, any outward face of your company—from the aromatic tea you serve in a customized mug imprinted with your logo at the initial meeting to the way you present yourself at the event to the writing of press releases—is a part of your marketing and advertising plans.

Marketing is all about creating a brand. Think of some of your favorite companies. There is one national food-store chain known for a quirky blend of products and excellent service. Customers love the Hawaiian-shirt wearing store staff, the fresh flowers artfully displayed inside the entrance to each store, the focus on organic products, and the attention to detail. I know lots of folks willing to drive more than a hundred miles round trip to buy their groceries at these stores. A willingness to travel so far, when most of us have grocery stores much closer to home, is a testament to the power of branding.

Through your marketing efforts, you will need to differentiate yourself from your competitors as well as develop customer loyalty. Don't make the mistake of thinking that your clients aren't noting your efforts. At initial consultations with prospective clients, I offer tea, coffee, and seltzer water. I offer a variety of flavored coffees, tea sachets (rather than tea bags), and seltzer water poured from a glass bottle rather than from a plastic liter bottle. Over the years, I've had many clients tell me that this attention to detail drew them to my company rather than to one of my competitors. By focusing on the small details and spending a bit more (just pennies, really), I helped build a strong business.

Creating a Marketing Plan

Just as you created a business plan to help you define the trajectory of your new business, a marketing plan will enable you to position your new business and to market it to a targeted audience. And, just as with your business plan, a marketing plan can be easily produced if you focus on five key questions. Because you have done your research, answering these questions thoughtfully should be a relative snap.

1. *What is the purpose of your marketing plan?* For new business owners, the purpose is to let prospective clients know that you are the new kid on the block. As your company grows, the purpose of your marketing plan will shift. No longer will you need to promote your new business; rather, your marketing plan will focus on client satisfaction and reaching new customers.

2. *What is the current situation for your new business?* In other words, who are your competitors and your target audience, and what is the state of your finances? It is helpful to break this down into four parts (often called a SWOT analysis): list your (S)trengths, your (W)eaknesses, your business's (O)pportunities, and (T)hreats to your business.

3. *What are your objectives?* If your sights are aimed at creating and planning five events a year, you probably won't need a fancy Web site or extensive advertising. In fact, this would probably prove to be financial sabotage. Running even a handful of ads could erode your entire income.

4. *What are your tactics?* This chapter will outline possible marketing tactics, from placing ads in local newspapers to creating an effective business card and creating radio advertising spots. You will need to determine which will work for you. For instance, does advertising in your local newspaper make good sense—are the rates affordable and the circulation broad enough to make these ads worthwhile?

5. *What is your budget?* Money talks and, when it comes to marketing plans, it talks loudly. Simply put, running ads, creating brochures, and creating direct mail campaigns adds up to big bucks. Don't sink your new business by overspending on marketing.

Advertising

Virtually every business uses some type of advertising. Simply stated, advertising is a means by which to persuade consumers to use your services rather than those of one of your competitors. In this Internet era, options for advertising have become more complex. Once, running an ad meant calling your local newspaper advertising representative and having the staff there design and produce your ad. Now, with so many easy-to-use design software packages available, many small business owners opt to create their own ads—and to place these ads in media ranging from newspapers and magazines to the sides of city buses.

Newspaper Advertising

Running ads in your local newspaper remains a viable option for many small business owners. In particular, when you first open for business and are still in the process of creating word-of-mouth buzz, running a few ads can provide a wonderful springboard for the launch of your business.

To run an ad, you will need to call your local newspaper or newspapers and ask to speak with an advertising representative (or, as they are usually called, ad rep). This person will work with you to plan a schedule for your ads as well as assist you in creating a budget for your advertising plans. Remember, your rep is a sales person and probably receives a commission based on sales. Because of this commission-based pay, she will be eager to schedule as many ads as possible. Be careful: advertising costs can become overwhelming to new business owners. Be firm about your budget and if the advertising costs seem prohibitive, let your rep know. Often, reps have the leeway to negotiate a better rate. Package rates (for instance, running one ad per week for four weeks) may result in a better column inch rate. Similarly, some papers offer free color to clients buying advertising packages.

When it comes to advertising, bigger doesn't always mean better. Instead, it is important that your ad be positioned in a key spot. Ask for a right-hand

Notes from the Field

Consider placing an ad on the side of your car. That's right—on your own four wheels. Customized magnetic signs are available for under $50 and can be produced in less than a week. Make sure to include your logo when you have your magnetic sign produced. These magnetic banners can easily be applied and removed.

page. Research shows that the readers' eyes tend to fall to the right-hand pages first when reading the paper. Make sure that your ad will not be buried in the classified section and that, if it will be grouped, that it is placed with other like businesses. In other words, you don't want your advertisement promoting a children's birthday party business to be stuck in the middle of a group of automobile dealers' advertisements. These points are key because a two-column-wide by four-inch-deep advertisement can be tremendously effective when placed properly. However, this same advertisement could be money thrown away if it is not placed with care.

Along with placement, it is essential that your ad convey professionalism and the specifics of your business. As I mentioned above, there are many accessible software packages that enable laypeople to produce professional-looking ads. You will have to gauge your own comfort level when using this software. If you don't feel up to creating your own ads, then don't. A poorly produced and carelessly written ad will damage your new business.

Choose the words for your ad carefully. Think of the advertisements that draw your eye. Most likely, they are not cluttered with words and images but rather are easy to read and clear in the information they present. Consider using bulleted points to delineate the ways in which your company is unique and the features that separate you from the competition.

Make sure to include contact information. I have seen too many ads in my own local paper in which new business owners have forgotten to include their basic contact information! Of course, you will need to include your logo in the ad. Make it your mantra to include your logo on every piece of paper associated with your business, from all of your advertisements to your business cards and your invoices.

Advertising on the Internet

Some home-based business owners find that Internet advertising helps bring potential clients to their Web sites, a valuable marketing aid. I caution new business owners to use care when placing ads on the Internet (and in traditional media, as well), as advertising costs can quickly skyrocket.

One inexpensive placement to consider is your local municipality. Many towns and cities offer inexpensive space on their Web sites. Contact your town hall to look into this option. This can be a very good source of promotion for your business, as you are directly targeting the audience within your town or city.

As your company grows, you might want to place an advertisement on a popular Web search site such as Yahoo or Google. GoogleAdWords (www.adwords.com) offers a popular option, enabling your ad to pop up on the right-hand column of the screen when certain keywords are typed into the search field. In other words, if you run a pony party business in Missouri, then you might request that your ad pop up when someone using the Google search engine types in "pony, birthday party, Missouri." When the searcher sees your ad, she can opt to click on it, leading her to your Web site. You pay only for the number of clicks on your ad—not for the number of times it appears on the Google Web page. This type of advertising is more appropriate for bigger party planning businesses and for businesses with updated and engaging Web sites up and running.

Television Advertising

For new businesses, this option can be too expensive. However, as your party planning business grows, television advertising may prove to be a valuable avenue for reaching new customers.

There are two costs incurred when placing advertisements on television: the cost of producing the advertisement and the cost of placing the ad. Creating an advertisement can be done on a relative shoestring. Some production agencies will create a thirty-second spot for less than $1,000. Some local television stations will agree to produce the commercial for you, if you agree to buy advertising space on their channel.

We all hear the stories of sky-high per-minute costs for ad spots aired during big events like the Super Bowl—where the placement of one sixty-second commercial can cost millions of dollars. However, in local markets, you may be able to place an advertisement for well under $100 as some local stations charge $5 or less per every thousand viewers you reach.

Television advertising is not for the party planner with a small business model. If your goal is to hold half a dozen parties a year, then, clearly, television advertising is not necessary. However, if you are planning to grow your business into a full-time endeavor or plan on franchising, television commercials could be an ace in the hole for creating new markets for your business.

Movie Theater Advertisements

Advertising on movie theater screens before the film starts to roll has become big business. In fact, as revenues from ticket sales have declined, movie theater owners have become more and more dependent on the income they earn from running commercials before the show. Many business owners find that this is a powerful use of advertising money, since the commercials play to a captive audience—a captive audience of almost 1.5 billion in 2007. Once moviegoers find their seats, they usually stay put until the movie starts.

As with buying television spots, costs for placing an ad on a movie theater screen vary broadly. Buying a national spot means big bucks, but if you are buying a spot at your local cinema targeted at your town or city, you will find more affordable rates.

Remember to include your logo in any onscreen advertising, whether on television or at your local cinema.

Radio Advertising

Some party planners find radio advertising a powerful tool for promoting their businesses. Depending on the time and length of your advertisement, you may receive a rate of $5 or less per thousand listeners. These listeners are in their cars, on their way to work, or running errands, and, like the folks in movie theaters, are a captive audience.

Some local radio stations may be willing to produce the ad for you at low or no cost. If you have a popular disc jockey on a local radio station, you may want her to read the copy for your ad. This is an attractive option.

Advertising on Social Networking Web Sites

It is the dawn of a new age and, as a result, party planners who specialize in events for teens—paintball and rock-climbing parties, for instance—find clients by opening accounts on popular social networking Web sites like Facebook (www.facebook.com) and MySpace (www.myspace.com). There is no charge to open these accounts. Both MySpace and Facebook offer a classified advertising option at no charge to its users. The audience on these Web sites is vast. Facebook alone has 60 million active users and these users average 500 million searches per month!

Advertising in Direct Marketing Mailings and Publications

You're probably familiar with direct mail books; they arrive in my mailbox with amazing regularity. These booklets offer businesses a chance to reach a wide range of customers at a nominal price. For instance, you may be able to target 10,000 homes for $99.

Checklist for Creating a Successful Advertisement

Creating a powerful advertisement takes time and attention. You will want to take the care to make a persuasive advertisement, as this will be the first encounter many of your prospective clients have with you. You will want to ensure that your ad is an apt indicator of the quality and professionalism of your business.

■ *Have you written a powerful headline? Yes or No?*

If you don't hook a reader with your headline, it's unlikely she'll continue to read the copy in the rest of your ad. You might opt for a newsy headline, especially when your business first opens: "Introducing a Children's Birthday Party Planning Business" or "Available for the First Time: Fairy Princess Parties." Another option is an intriguing headline: "Celebrate Your Child" or "Create Magic for Your Child." This type of headline tends to make the reader curious and to draw her in to read the rest of your ad. Don't stint on taking the time to write a crackerjack headline.

■ *Is it persuasive? Yes or No*

Is your copy effective in persuading a prospective client to contact you? To be persuasive, you need to offer specifics: what type of business it is, and the details of your party planning business. This is your opportunity to differentiate yourself from your competitors. It is also effective to offer a testimonial from a client (obviously not possible if you haven't yet held your first party). Just as most of us check to see who has given two thumbs up to a recently released movie, readers of your ad will likely find a testimonial from a past client very persuasive.

■ *Is your ad running in the appropriate place? Yes or No*

Although I have already recommended running your ad in a local newspaper, this is not always the best choice. Most regions have parenting and children's magazines, listing programs for children ranging from music and art classes to summer camps and children's birthday party planning providers. Your advertising dollars might be better spent placing ads in these child-focused publications. Do your research before placing an ad. Ask your ad rep for a media kit. This kit will include copies of the newspaper or magazine and details about the magazine or newspaper's circulation, as well as rates for running advertisements. Some parenting and children's magazines are placed free of charge in doctor's offices, at the entrance to libraries, and near the checkout lines at grocery stores. This could be very beneficial to your business. Also, the shelf life of a weekly newspaper is limited—readers tend to look through the paper and then put it into recycling. Magazines are often given more attention and aren't recycled quite as quickly.

- *Did you ask for appropriate placement? Yes or No*
  All of the hard work you've spent creating your ad could be derailed if the folks at the local newspaper or magazine don't place the ad in the correct position. Make sure to have a discussion with your ad rep, ensuring, for instance, that your ad won't be buried at the bottom of the classified pages amidst a group of ads touting tag sales.

- *Do you have a method for tracking your ad's efficacy? Yes or No*
  This tracking, also called keying, helps if you are running advertisements in more than one publication. Keying enables you to find out which readers are referring to your ad. To do this, you need to consider adding a promotion or incentive, a different incentive in each ad. Perhaps, you will offer a free initial consultation or a discount on the birthday cake. Make sure that the incentive is meaningful enough that a client might be compelled to call for a consultation but not so big as to break the bank.

If you choose to place an advertisement in one of these books, such as AdBook Direct or Valpak, you will want to be sure that you can measure your ad's efficacy. In other words, offer a distinct promotion or discount, only available through this direct mail book advertisement.

News Features and Press Releases

Placing news stories in your local newspaper is a fantastic—and free—method for promoting your business. Generate press releases whenever you have news to report about your developing company. For instance, you will want to write and submit a press release to your local newspaper when you first hang out your shingle. As your company grows, you will have opportunities to generate other releases. Let your local newspaper know if your business changes location, when

Notes from the Field

One party planner I interviewed discovered—too late—that using a direct mail book was too effective. Her business, specializing in creating stuffed animals, was overwhelmed by the number of calls. She was not able to respond to all of the calls and she agreed to plan too many parties. In the end, bad word of mouth shut down her business. If you plan to advertise in a direct mail book, be ready to take on the extra volume of business that might come as a result of this promotion.

you celebrate a milestone (planning your hundredth event, for instance), or expand your business.

One caveat: All press releases must have a news "hook." In other words, don't expect a newspaper to run your press release if there is no news angle. Only submit press releases when you have important information to share.

Submit your press releases to the editor's e-mail address. Usually, newspapers list e-mail addresses on their mastheads, but if your local paper doesn't list these addresses, call the paper for the editor's name and e-mail. Submit your press release directly to the editor as an attachment. In your e-mail cover letter, introduce yourself, state the purpose of your e-mail, and indicate that you will follow up on this initial correspondence. This e-mail note should be no more than a few lines in length.

E-mail the editor again after a week or so if you have not had a response, confirming that she received your e-mail and attachment. Editors often appreciate a gentle reminder like this—but don't nag. It is now in the editor's hands to make a decision about running your press release.

Sometimes, editors are intrigued enough about a press release to run a feature-length story. If this happens, congratulations! Feature pieces often include photos and interesting background stories. If the editor decides to generate a feature-length piece based on your press release, she will probably have a reporter contact you for an interview. A photographer may accompany the reporter, as well. Don't be nervous about this opportunity to be interviewed. It is a fantastic chance to promote your company and to get the word out. Have fun!

Press Release Checklist

Press releases should follow a certain format, as shown below.

FOR IMMEDIATE RELEASE

Most press releases have the words "FOR IMMEDIATE RELEASE" typed across the top. If, for some reason, the release needs to be held, type the date of release, in all capital letters, across the top of the release.

CONTACT:

Contact Person

Company Name

Phone Number

Fax Number

E-mail Address

Web Site

HEADLINE

Make sure to write a compelling headline. If you don't hook the editor with your headline, she may not bother reading the rest of your release. Don't use unnecessary words—be succinct and to the point. If this press release is announcing the opening of your business, then an appropriate headline would be "Introducing a New Children's Birthday Party Planning Service Specializing in

_____." This informs the editor that you are launching a new business and lets her know your niche and how this differentiates your business from others.

CITY, STATE, DATE

The first paragraph of your release should open with something called a "dateline." This is simply the city, state, and date of your release. These words should be in capital letters at the beginning of the paragraph.

BODY TEXT

Follow the dateline with a powerful sentence, following up and augmenting the information in the headline. A good press release answers who, what, why, when, where, and how. Make this your rule of thumb. When you have completed your press release announcing the opening of your business, are all of these questions answered? For instance, have you explained who you are, what your business is (be specific—how are you different from your competition?), why you have opened your business, when it opened, where it opened, and how you opened it?

When you are satisfied that these questions are answered, type "END" at the bottom of your release, indicating to the news editor that the press release does not continue to another page. Brevity is beauty when it comes to press releases, so aim for five hundred words or fewer.

Finally, always write releases in the third person. In other words, "Cinderella Smith is the owner of a new children's birthday party planning business," is correct. "My name is Cinderella Smith and I just opened a children's birthday party planning business," is not correct.

Newsletters

In this age of blogging, text-messaging, and interactive Web sites, newsletters may sound a bit quaint and old-fashioned. I have found, however, that a well-crafted newsletter produces wonderful results. Newsletters can be distributed via e-mail (more on this in Chapter 11) but old-fashioned snail mail is effective as well. Making them available at various points of purchase works well, too.

As with all of your marketing materials, make sure that your logo is displayed prominently on every page. And, remember to keep the "news" in newsletter. Your clients are busy and want to find engaging, useful information in your newsletter.

Your newsletter should contain information pertinent to your business—a new location, new hours, milestones reached, awards received. It could also offer more generalized information about the children's birthday party business—for instance, trends that are on the rise as well as trends that are on their way out. You might try offering a promotion in your newsletter. Just as offering a promotion can help you to track the efficacy of your advertising, you will be able to track the effectiveness of your newsletter by keeping a record of the number of clients who ask about the newsletter promotion.

You will need to determine the frequency of your newsletters. I find that quarterly works well. A monthly newsletter can become burdensome—for you to produce and for your clients to read. Additionally, it may be difficult to create enough news to fill a monthly newsletter.

You will also need to make decisions about your newsletter's circulation. Will you send it only to existing clients or will you send to a broader base? If you choose to send to a broader audience, you will have to keep in mind the added production costs you will incur by creating more newsletters, increased postage costs, as well as buying or creating an effective mailing list.

If you choose to buy a list (see Appendix for sources), you will need to determine the demographics before purchasing the list. Mailing lists can be generated based on myriad characteristics, ranging from income level and gender to the presence of children, education level, hobbies, geography, and more.

List prices vary, depending on the supplier. Typically, though, plan on spending about 10 cents per name on your list, so a list of 250 will cost $25. Some lists are available for one use only, while others will be available for a prescribed length of time— one year, for example. When buying lists, consider a company's reputation. Creating mailing lists is a complex task and you want to choose a company that keeps its lists up to date and free of spelling errors.

Direct Mail

As the name suggests, direct mail marketing involves mailing brochures or other marketing materials to a targeted audience. The mailing piece could be as simple as a single-color postcard or as elaborate as a full-color, glossy brochure. The audience for your direct mail piece could be small—250 or so—or a cast of thousands.

If you opt to create a direct mail piece, you will need to carefully consider the type of mailing list you will purchase. As described above, you will want to tailor a mailing

Notes from the Field

Successful event planners report that they have the most success with direct mail campaigns sent at quiet times. In other words, avoid direct mail campaigns that land in potential clients' mailboxes near holidays. Overwhelmed by mailboxes stuffed with holiday catalogs and solicitations, a lot of this mail can be too easily overlooked. Make sure that all of your direct mail pieces have a classy, uniform look. And, of course, always include your logo.

Direct Mail Cost Checklist

You will incur the following costs when you conduct a direct mail campaign:

- *The cost of creating the mailing piece.* Whether simple or elaborate, you will incur a cost for creating this piece. Factor in not only the cost of printing the piece but also the cost of designing it, especially if you are hiring an outside graphic designer.

- *The cost of buying a mailing list.* Plan on spending several hundred dollars on this list. If you plan to send to only 250 people, consider that a response rate of 1 percent is considered a success. That means you will have, as a result of your campaign, 2.5 potential clients contact you. This does not necessarily mean that they will hire you to plan their child's birthday party. In other words, if you are going to invest energy in a direct-mail campaign, consider a broader universe of names when buying a list.

- *The cost of postage.* Postcards are your most economical mailing choice but, at approximmately 39 cents per stamp, a direct mail campaign involving 1,000 postcards results in a whopping $390 in postage!

- *The cost of doing business.* If you offer a special promotion in your direct mail piece (a 5 percent discount on your services, for instance) you will need to factor this in as a cost. A party that would normally net $500 for you will only net $475 when you factor in the 5 percent discount.

list to reach a very targeted audience. You might want to buy a list focusing on two-income families with children present and limit the list to your geographic area. Or, if you specialize in princess and tea parties, you might want to have a list compiled that does not include parents who have only male children. It is critical that you spend time developing your list in order to help ensure success for your direct mail campaign. A direct mail response rate of 1 percent is often considered a resounding success, so carefully weigh the costs of the campaign against the possible benefits. Consider how many parties you will need to plan in order to recoup the cost of the direct mail campaign.

A Walk through the Yellow Pages

An obvious choice for a small business owner is to place an ad in her local yellow pages. This ad doesn't need to be large, but it should include your name, logo, and contact information. It should also include a line that specifically describes your business's niche. Unfortunately, since phone books are produced annually, you may be out in the cold for the larger part of a year if you open your business just as a new directory lands on your clients' front steps.

Many areas have more than one business directory or yellow page offering. Two such books are delivered to my doorstep, for instance. Having competing directories can be good news for you, enabling you to negotiate a lower rate for your advertisement. If you are able to afford listings in both, then do so. If not, compare prices and circulation and select the best choice. Advertising contact information is listed inside your phone book.

When creating your yellow pages advertisement, be sure to include your cell phone number as well as your land line. If your cell phone is your business line, then list only your cell number.

In the meantime, you will probably want to list your business on Internet yellow pages. More than 80 percent of Internet yellow pages users contact a business they find online, making it an easy point of entry. These listings offer flexibility, since they can be changed frequently. You may start with a small line listing and as your business grows, develop a larger ad presence. There are several Internet yellow pages providers. This is helpful to new business owners since the competition among these companies leads to lower advertising rates for you.

Notes from the Field

When creating and placing your first advertisement in the yellow pages, don't opt for a color advertisement. These advertisements tend to be very expensive and, research shows, ineffective. The color does not draw more eyes to your ad. In fact, because the color is printed on yellow paper, the colors tend to be washed out and faded and generally not appealing.

The Power of Word of Mouth

After jumping through all of these advertising and marketing hoops, the circle comes back to word of mouth or buzz advertising. Good buzz is the best advertising that money can buy—but, of course, good buzz can't be bought. It has to be cultivated and developed over time.

According to a recent Neilsen BuzzMetrics survey, the word American consumers most closely tie to advertising is "false." Americans, rightly so in many cases, have grown cynical about advertising. In contrast, this same survey revealed that 78 percent of respondents trust the recommendation of a friend. This is word-of-mouth advertising at its best and most powerful.

Although it may seem that you cannot wield much influence when it comes to creating good buzz, there are five important steps you can take to help ensure good word of mouth:

1. *First and foremost, offer good service.* Not only are you only as good as your last event, you are only as good as the level of detail you offer. Go the extra mile. Remember the tea I serve at initial consultations? These gestures help create good will, and your customers appreciate the extra TLC. I remind myself before every event to follow the "rule of two As—be accommodating and adaptable." I think this is what elevates a good party planner into a great party planner: the ability to accommodate requests and adapt to surprises or unexpected requests, often right on the spot.

2. *Keep a positive attitude.* Be positive about your company, even if a party goes off with a bit of a hitch. Have an open conversation with the client about any problems and arrange for compensation, such as a reduction in the bill. Keep open lines of communication with your employees and treat them fairly. You do not want them spreading any negative news about your business. Explain the importance of this to your employees and encourage them to approach you directly about any problems they perceive. Then, when they do approach you, really listen to their thoughts and comments. After all, they are "in the trenches" on party day and may have witnessed something you didn't see.

3. *Let your customers know you care.* Do this by mailing your quarterly newsletter and by mailing a birthday card to the child in subsequent years— even if the parents have not hired you to plan their child's party. This

shows your attention to detail and your level of care for your business and your clients.

4. *Mix and mingle.* I'll talk more about this later in the chapter, but it is important to network with other professionals in your field, including party planners, caterers, bakers, DJs, florists, and entertainers. Let these other professionals get to know and respect you. Then, when asked to make a recommendation to one of their clients, your name will be front and center in their minds.

5. *You get what you give.* Just as you are working to create this good buzz, so are the other folks in your field. Make sure that you are spreading the good word about your colleagues in the event-planning business and the good word will come back to you, as well.

Making and Distributing Brochures and Business Cards

Don't skimp when preparing these marketing materials. For some of your clients, your brochure and business card will be the first contact they have with you and your business. You will distribute your cards and brochures at party supply stores, caterers, bakeries, and entertainment centers, so these materials will represent you in your absence.

A Professional Business Card

I find my business card to be one of my most persuasive marketing tools—small but mighty. I recommend a tri-fold business card. When folded, it has the same dimensions as a typical business card so it can easily be tucked into a wallet or purse. However, using a tri-fold card enables you to include lots of information about your business, including:

- The name of your business
- Your name
- Your contact information, including phone number, fax, e-mail, and Web address
- Your logo
- A bulleted list of your specialties
- The types of payment you accept—for instance, do you accept credit card payments?

Notes from the Field

When asking local merchants to display your business cards and brochures, be sure to supply them with plastic racks for your cards. By providing these display stands, you ensure that your materials will be displayed in a professional and tidy manner.

- A photo of yourself
- A testimonial from a client

Office supply stores offer design software at their sales counter for creating business cards and other office stationery. You can design your business card yourself, using a popular design software such as InDesign (www.adobe.com). Big-box office supply stores print business cards for a reasonable fee. In fact, one of these chains recently introduced a thirty-minute business card option. From design to printed card—voila!—in just thirty minutes.

Make sure to use a clean, crisp typeface that is easy to read. It can be tempting to choose a script typeface but these can be harder to read. Don't try to cram too much information onto your cards. Keep your bulleted points brief and limit each point to a few words. Finally, don't use a point size that is difficult to read. Aim to keep all of the type at 10 point or larger.

Buy the best cardstock you can afford, and remember to keep all of your printed materials—from your stationery to your invoices and business cards—in the same style and tone. All of these materials help to create your brand or, in other words, your professional image.

An Effective Brochure

Your brochure should include all of the elements of your business card. Don't try to cram too much information into your brochure. Less can be more, and open and airy design is more appealing to the eye than an over-filled design. In your brochures, you will have room for additional testimonials from clients as well as for photographs from events you have planned. Be sure to get the okay from clients before using photos from or testimonials about their children's parties.

Your brochure does not need to be on glossy stock and in full-color. Rather, an effective brochure can be printed with black ink on high-quality 8½ x 11-inch paper. I recommend a tri-fold brochure. The 8½ x 11 paper, once printed on both sides, can be folded to measure 3¾ x 8½, a common brochure size.

Use the same color and style stock that you used for your business card, as you want all of your promotional pieces to be similar in style and tone. Big-box stores offer competitive pricing for printing and folding your brochures. These office supply chains also sell the plastic stands for displaying your cards.

Networking News

In real estate it's all about location, location, location. In the event-planning business, it's often about contacts, contacts, contacts. You will want to focus early in the development of your business on creating a strong network of colleagues. Not only will these colleagues prove invaluable in helping you to brainstorm through any problems that might arise, but they will be essential in helping you to get the word out about your business.

Although there are national organizations for event planners, small-scale children's birthday party planners will often be better served by attending local and regional meetings. These meetings are held by groups like the chamber of commerce and local convention and visitors bureaus. You should plan on joining your local chamber of commerce. For a modest annual fee, you will receive abundant publicity, including, in many cases, exposure on the chamber's Web site (www .chamberofcommerce.com).

A Few More Ideas!

When it comes to advertising and marketing your company, try to keep your mind open to any idea. The goal of all of your efforts is to promote your business and to earn the trust of your clients.

Perhaps you've noticed that a billboard at the edge of your town has been vacant for the past year. Odds are, then, that the billboard's owner would cut a good deal in order to fill that billboard space. It can't hurt to ask.

Another children's party planner has found success by offering a promotion when she sends her invoices. By offering a future benefit—a discount on a party yet to be held—she builds good will, even as she is billing her clients.

Another successful planner wears an eye-catching custom T-shirt promoting her business when she takes her kids to the beach or shops at the local grocery store. This has generated new business for her.

Yet another planner tells me that placing an old-fashioned sandwich board outside her downtown office has brought in many new customers. She purchased an inexpensive sandwich board from an online source (www.displays2go.com), but you could create your own with two pieces of plywood. It is interesting that in our high-tech world, basic advertising techniques, such as a sandwich board, can still be so effective in generating traffic.

I've generated new business by volunteering my services at fund-raising events for local non-profits. I have also given seminars about the children's birthday party business and created new business in that manner.

Marketing your business takes time, energy, commitment, and cash. All of this must be backed up by a grade-A product. As advertising guru Jerry Della Femina so aptly puts it, "There is a great deal of advertising that is much better than the product. When that happens, all that the good advertising will do is put you out of business faster."

Frequently Asked Question

I have a very limited budget. Where do you recommend I spend my advertising and marketing budget?

Start by paying for a listing in the traditional paper yellow pages, delivered free of charge to the ends of driveways and to front stoops of apartments across the country, as well as for a listing on an online yellow pages site. To find your local yellow pages, both online and traditional paper-bound options, type "yellow pages advertising" and the name of your state in the search line of your preferred search engine. This will allow you to research the various choices available to you as well as to compare prices. You should be able to find rates beginning at just a few dollars per month. Remember, too, that word-of-mouth advertising is free, so from the moment you launch your business, begin creating good buzz. For example, visit your local party supply store with festively decorated cupcakes for the staff. Tell them about your new venture and about your plans for developing a business. Networking and forming bonds with other folks involved in the children's birthday party business is free and makes excellent business sense.

The Power of a Provocative Web Site

In the course of the past decade, computer use has soared with more and more Americans plugging in to their computers. According to comScore, an Internet marketing research company, there are 700 million Internet users spanning the globe. There are more than 150 million Internet users in the United States alone, an amazing number considering that the entire U.S. population numbers about 300 million. This means that one out of every two Americans has access to and uses the Internet! According to numbers provided by the Pew Internet and American Life Project, 73 percent of all adults use the Internet. Given these numbers, it is evident that creating a Web site to market and develop your business makes good sense.

Creating a Persuasive Web Site

There are several steps involved in setting up and creating a Web site. If you are a relative novice to the technological world, don't be intimidated by this process. It is exciting to launch a Web site and it can lift your business to a new level.

Selecting a Domain Name

First things first: what will be your Web site name? Of course, in an ideal world, you would simply use the name of your business, for example, www .perfectponyparties.com. Unfortunately, if you typed this name onto the search line of your Internet explorer, you would find that someone else has already acquired this domain name.

Be prepared to try several different names or combinations of words and letters in order to create a unique domain name. For instance, if the name of

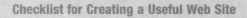

Checklist for Creating a Useful Web Site

Make sure, when creating your Web site, that you are able to answer "yes" to all of the items on this checklist. By doing so, you will help to ensure that you do not unintentionally sabotage your Web site.

- *Is the type on your Web site legible? Yes or No*

  Okay, this may sound too obvious to be believed but, unfortunately, many novice Web site designers opt for a typeface that is too small, too ornate (script typefaces often fall into this category), or set against a dark background color, rendering it virtually impossible to read. Don't get too fancy with your typefaces. Straightforward is the best road to success.

- *Is there valuable content on every page? Yes or No*

  Don't waste your viewers' time. On average, according to industry numbers, folks spend less than one minute on a Web site. This means that your Web site has to be immediately persuasive so your viewers stay longer than sixty seconds. Make sure that your home page is attractive and engaging and features your logo.

- *Is your menu immediately evident? Yes or No*

  There is nothing more frustrating than trying to navigate a Web site that doesn't have a menu that can be easily accessed. Put your menu on either the left- or right-hand side of the screen rather than at the bottom of the page. Don't make visitors to your Web site struggle to find your menu.

- *Have you compressed image files? Yes or No*

  Make sure, when building your site, that you compress any image files. If you do not compress these files, users will have to wait longer for your screen to appear. Some users will be too impatient to wait and will simply move on.

- *Is your contact information easy to access? Yes or No*

  Again, seems straightforward, right? I am reminded again and again, as I search through Web sites, that many web designers overlook this routine matter. If finding contact information brings to mind that proverbial needle-in-a-haystack search, then the Web site is sure to fail.

- *Is your Web site well organized? Yes or No*

  Don't make your readers jump through hoops to find the information they are looking for. At the very top of your Web site, be sure to clearly state your niche and any other information that makes your business unique. Perhaps you have an exclusive agreement with a local caterer. If so, note that near the top of your first Web screen page. Don't make your Web site too long. Remember that sixty-second window I wrote about? You don't have long to convince the viewer that you are the ideal children's party planner. Keep the copy directed and focused on telling your viewers about exactly the type of services you provide.

- *Is your Web site navigable with a minimum of clicks? Yes or No*

  Nobody likes to be burdened by too many clicks. The typical browser wants your screen to pop up on her computer with the information clearly evident. Don't use a lengthy introduction that requires the Internet user to "click to skip." Take your viewer right to the heart of the content of your Web site. Along these lines, don't use pop-up windows, blinking lights, or scrolling type. These often come off as amateurish and cheesy.

- *If you use external links, do you check regularly to make sure they are all still active? Yes or No?*

  If you use external links (these are links to other Web sites, often featured in blue type within the body of a Web site), make sure to see that these links remain active. For instance, within your Web site, you might want to place a link for your viewers to read about trends in the children's birthday party business, or you might want to direct them to a link with catering ideas. Regularly check to be sure these links remain active.

- *Is your Web site up to date? Yes or No*

  If you ignore every bit of advice above, don't ignore this final point. The kiss of death for any Web site is to be outdated. In fact, as I researched this book, I revisited some Web sites I had used and enjoyed in the past only to find them in need of being dusted off. Links were inactive, holidays that had long since passed were still being promoted, and pricing was out of date. These sites, ones that I had planned on including in the Appendix of this book, a source of promotion for these sites, are no longer included.

These businesses may still be viable, but the message sent to viewers by an outdated Web site is that the company owners are overwhelmed or uncaring—either way, these are negative messages. I always tell prospective business owners that, while a Web site can bring new customers to your business, if you are unable or unwilling to keep your site up to date, don't bother to create a Web site in the first place. It's better to use more traditional forms of promotion—such as newsletters and yellow pages advertisements—than to have a creaky, out-of-date, unappealing site.

your company is Parties for Fun and that domain name is taken, you might try "Parties 4 Fun." However, be careful not to make your name too complicated or too long. You want your domain name to be easily recognizable and memorable.

Once you have created a unique domain name, double-check this by accessing a site such as VeriSign (www.verisign.com). Enter your domain name on this site to ensure that no other business has already registered that domain name.

Once you have ascertained that your domain name is up for grabs, you will need to register it. A comprehensive list of accredited registrars can be found at www.ICANN.com. Do be sure to choose an accredited registrar when registering your domain name. Unfortunately, there are a few less-than-honest companies out there, perpetuating registry scams.

Domain registry is relatively inexpensive—around $10 per year. If you are ready and willing to register your domain name for multiple years, you may be able to pay even less. Some registries will offer you the option of a private or public registration. Private, although a bit more expensive, is the better choice as it will help protect your personal identity, as well as—usually—reducing the amount of spam you will receive.

If, upon the completion of your registration, your Web site is already made, within four to eight hours the domain name and your Web site will be up and running. If your Web site is still under construction, park your new domain name with the registry company.

Finding a Web Site Host

To make your Web site available twenty-four hours a day, you will need to find a Web site host. There are well-known Web site hosts such as Microsoft Network

Questions to Answer on Your Web Site

Visitors to your Web site will be looking for answers to specific questions. Remember, these browsers typically spend only seconds perusing a Web site before moving on, so make sure that your answers to the following questions are clear and straightforward:

- *How can I get in touch with you?*
  This is key. You must put your contact information front and center. There is nothing more frustrating than being unable to quickly find telephone and e-mail contact information.
- *How much do you charge?*
  Although some party planners are hesitant to put prices on their Web sites, I have found that some prospective customers won't contact a children's birthday party planner if no indication of price is included on the Web site. You might want to use language rather than numbers to indicate your pricing policies. In other words, you might write, "reasonably priced parties from a top-notch planner."
- *Can you plan the whole party, from soup to nuts?*
  Note on your Web site if you offer complete children's birthday party planning services, from finding a DJ to catering the all-white-meat chicken fingers! If you don't offer all of these services, write that you "specialize in [party theme here] parties," describing your niche.
- *Do you have references?*
  It is important to include references or testimonials on your Web site. Include customers' kind words about some of the children's birthday parties you have planned and developed in the past. Be sure to check with your clients before quoting them.
- *Do you prefer to meet in person, via the phone, or via e-mail?*
  Let your customers know your preferred method of corresponding. It is usually better to plan a first consultation in person, but sometimes, due to schedule or geography, it makes more sense to make the initial consultation via the telephone.

Notes from the Field

Occasionally, a domain name is registered by two different parties. Make sure
to keep all documentation regarding your domain registration so if there are ever
questions about who was the first to register, you will have all of the necessary
paperwork at the ready. Important documentation includes the date of your registration (print out the registry's confirmation) and any payments you make for your
domain registry.

and Yahoo! Web Hosting, but there are also scores of lesser known hosts who offer competitive pricing. Be careful, though. Sometimes low price can mean low ser-vice. Make sure that the host company can offer answers to basic questions such as how often the site goes down and how long it takes to fix these glitches; how many incoming lines the server has; what level of customer support the company offers; and how many sites are hosted by the company. You won't want prospective customers to be frustrated when they are unable to access your Web site due to a less-than-reliable Web host. For this reason, some of the big players such as Yahoo! might make sense for your growing business. In fact, Yahoo! boasts an admirable 99.9 percent server uptime.

There are other factors to consider when selecting a Web host. Key among these is technical support. Choose a Web host with 24/7 technical support. And, make sure that they truly offer this support by e-mailing the tech support center at 2 a.m. on a Saturday night. Do you receive an immediate response? Sometimes, companies that advertise 24/7 service are less than honest.

Make sure that the Web host you choose offers secure server (SSL) feature. This will be critical if you decide to take credit card payments via your Web site. The SSL fea-ture ensures your customers that their credit card transactions are safe and secure.

Also, consider carefully the Web host's reliability. Never choose a company with less than 99 percent reliability. Consider that a Web host down even 1 percent of the time is not ideal. Don't frustrate your clients with a less-than-reliable Web host.

Some Web hosts tempt customers with promises of huge memory banks of 200 MB or more. Most Web sites require 5 MB or less, so don't pay for something you don't need.

Internet Tip

Several Web sites offer reviews from customers, rating various Web site hosts. These sites include cost comparisons as well as outlining the different features each host company provides. Two to try are www.top-10-web-hosting.com and www.hostingreviewsbyusers.com.

Of course, compare price, but as with so many things in life, when in comes to Web hosts, you get what you pay for. A Web host offering a $5 per month plan is probably going to prove less than ideal. Keep your customer in mind and choose a Web host that offers reliability and easy and quick access.

Some Web hosts offer discounts for customers signing up for quarterly or year-long packages. I would caution against these discount packages. Make monthly payments until you are sure that the Web host you have selected works for you and your business.

Constructing Your Web Site

Congratulations! You have a domain name and a Web site host. Now, you need to build your Web site. Some children's party planners leave the design of their Web site to graphic design professionals. On the plus side, these folks are experts at graphic design and will be able to construct a graphically appealing and eye-catching site. The downside? Web design comes at a cost, and children's party planners can expect to pay well upwards of $1,000 to have their site designed by a professional.

Some Web site hosts, such as Yahoo! Web Hosting, offer templates for Web site design. If you take this route, you could use Yahoo!'s template and plug in the important information about your business—contact information, logo, specialization, and so on. There are also myriad books and Web sites offering templates and advice for Web site building (see Appendix). If you feel comfortable working through the kinks and creating your own Web site, certainly give it a try. However, remember that your Web site may be the first impression prospective customers have of your business, so make sure that your Web site—whether designed by you or a graphic designer—is professional looking and always up to date.

Building a Blog Presence

Back in Chapter 1, I wrote about the vast number of blogs focused on children's birthday parties—a cool 850,000! Happily for those of us in the children's birthday party planning business, these blogs can afford a unique and free way to find new customers and to brainstorm with other children's party planners.

The word blog is a morpheme of web and log—weblog. The word blog is now used as a noun and a verb ("I am going to blog about children's birthday parties.") Evolved from online diaries, there are now more than 112 million blogs.

For some party planners I've interviewed, blogs offer a wonderful opportunity to meet (via cyberspace) and to work through problems, discuss new ideas, and to join up with others in the field. For event planners who sometimes feel isolated in their home offices, blogs can be the perfect remedy.

Using Online Sources

Frankly, it is rather astounding to have so much right at our fingertips. Not sure where to find clown noses? A quick Google search reveals 828,000 hits in 0.28 seconds. Gone are the days of calling around, being put on hold, and generally spinning one's wheels.

I tend to make many of my birthday party supply purchases locally, in part because of a "buy local" philosophy, but also to help keep connected with the buzz and trends in the children's birthday party planning business. However, there are

Internet Tip

eBay can be a fantastic source for birthday party supplies. A recent search turned up more than 20,000 listings for party supplies, many of them with the Buy It Now option (allowing eBay users to forgo the auction process and to buy the desired items instantly). One advantage to using eBay is their innovative feedback system. You can see, by clicking on the image you would like to purchase, the seller's feedback record. This record tallies positive, neutral, and negative responses. If you are not comfortable with the percentage of positive feedback, finding it too low, then choose another vendor. Simple as that!

times when it is simply more convenient or more economical to make purchases online.

Remember when you shop online that, just as with brick-and-mortar establishments, not all online stores are created equal. When I shop online, I look to see when the store was established. I also read the online store's "about us" section. This is often chock-a-block full of information, describing who owns the company, any newspaper coverage, the store's niche, and more. Also, I am always on the lookout for online sites with out-of-date graphics. These dated graphics send a signal that the store personnel are either overwhelmed (and unable to update their site) or inattentive to detail. Either way, it's best to avoid these sites.

E-mail Newsletters

E-mail newsletters can be a wonderful and inexpensive way to keep in touch with your customers. As with all of your marketing materials, make sure that your logo is displayed prominently on every page. And, remember to keep the "news" in newsletter. Your clients are busy and want to find engaging, useful information in your newsletter.

As with your snail mail newsletter, your e-mail newsletter should contain real news about your business. Of course, this newsletter is a way of promoting or advertising your business, but you want to give your readers a sense that you are sharing important information. Let them know when you have moved to a new location, changed your business hours, reached a notable milestone, or received a special accolade.

You can also use your newsletter to offer more general information about the children's birthday party business. Readers love lists, so this is a good opportunity to create trend lists. For instance, you might list the top ten children's birthday party themes or the top picks when it comes to selecting a cake for a child's birthday. People love lists of "ins and outs" as well, so consider including a list of what is hot and what is not.

Think about offering a unique promotion in your newsletter. Just as offering a promotion can help you to track the efficacy of your advertising, you will be able to track the effectiveness of your e-newsletter by keeping track of the prospective customers who ask for the e-newsletter promotion.

Ultimately, you are using e-newsletters to help maintain and deepen relationships with your clients. Make your newsletter so interesting that your clients look

Three Keys to e-Newsletter Success

1. *No more than 15 percent promotion.* Remember, this is a "news" letter, not an "advertising" letter. Make it newsy, showing your knowledge of the children's birthday party business.

2. *Keep it brief.* I try to limit my e-newsletters to five hundred words. I don't want to be relegated to the "read it later" list or, even worse, be struck down by the delete button.

3. *Do not send unsolicited e-mails.* Don't be a spam offender. Send your e-newsletter only to customers from whom you have received permission. Your customers will not appreciate unsolicited e-newsletters—aka spam. Most of my customers are pleased to receive quarterly newsletters. However, respect the wishes of your customers who prefer to be left off the list.

forward to receiving it. Think about the newsletters you receive (both in the regular mail and via the Internet) and consider the ones that are most effective. For instance, I receive an e-newsletter from an independent bookstore. I look forward to its monthly arrival and read every word of it. This newsletter has little overt advertising for the bookstore. Rather, the newsletter offers interesting lists of books, interviews with authors, and news about publishing trends.

You will need to determine the frequency of your e-newsletters. I find that, as with my snail mail newsletter, quarterly works best. None of us want to feel overwhelmed by too much information. By sending news four times a year, you will stay in the minds of your customers and potential customers.

Time to Boot Up and Log On

Although Thomas Watson, the chairman of IBM in 1943, famously said, "I think there is a world market for maybe five computers," we know now that to be a small business owner requires owning and using a computer. As you develop your business, you will determine the scope of its use. It is likely, as your company develops, that you will grow to use your computer for more and more functions and come to see your computer as a vital marketing ally. Use your Web site to offer free information to the millions of Internet browsers who turn on their computers to do research on everything from buying groceries to planning their children's birthday parties.

Frequently Asked Question

Why should I bother with a Web site when I am only interested in a local audience for my business?

This is a common mistake new business owners make, thinking that a Web site is directed at a global audience. In fact, whether you are marketing to a town of five thousand residents or to an entire state or country, having a Web site will help to promote your business. Many people now turn to the Internet rather than to the phone book to do research before buying a product, so it is important to have a useful, up-to-date, and information-filled Web site.

12 Onward and Upward

Growth and Trends

The children's birthday party business is a booming field and your business launch is timed perfectly to capitalize on this dynamic moment. According to the U.S. Department of Labor's Bureau of Labor Statistics, employment of event planners is anticipated, in the decade spanning 2006 to 2016, to rise significantly faster than average for the rate of other occupations. Although this language is a bit jargon-laced, the point to take away is that the business of planning children's birthday parties—and other events—is on the up-tick, good news for you and your blossoming business.

Growing Your Small Business

As your business grows, you will be faced with new choices and decisions. One of the most remarkable attributes of a home-based business is the possibility for tremendous growth. A children's birthday party planner who opens her business planning ten events per year may find herself, five years down the road, planning a hundred events per year.

Expanding Your Range of Services

You may be completely satisfied with your current level of business, and that is a fantastic position to attain. Many children's party planners opt to keep their businesses part-time. However, if you are ready to expand, you will have to make some choices about how to grow.

You may want to branch out into other areas of event planning. Many children's party planners eventually plan parties for adults, as well. As you plan children's parties, you will develop the skill set for developing adult parties, so it is a natural transition to move into the field of event planning for adult parties.

Children's Top Five Birthday Party Trends

Part of the thrill of this fast-paced field is the rate at which it changes. When it comes to planning children's birthday parties, what's hot can just as quickly be not. As this book rolls off to press, these are some of the hot trends. Have fun, as your business grows, keeping your eye on the "ins and outs" of your children's birthday party planning business.

1. *Green birthdays.* For many event planners, the buzzword is green, as more and more clients ask for environment-friendly birthday parties. From organic apple juice and all-natural cheese pizza to goody bag treats sent home in a reusable bag, the emphasis on environmentally savvy parties is likely to stay strong.

2. *Saying, "No, thank you" to gifts.* Complementing the green, environmentally friendly trend, more and more I am seeing children ask that, in lieu of gifts, donations be made to a favorite organization. Kids often like organizations that help animals—such as the World Wildlife Foundation. Also, post-Hurricane Katrina, I planned several events at which the birthday children asked that donations be made to the Red Cross in order to help New Orleans's Katrina victims.

3. *Make it custom, please.* Kids (and their parents) are requesting more custom decorations and giveaway goodies. From birthday banners with the child's name emblazoned on them, to customized tubs of lip gloss (for the teen and tween set), personalizing is a hit. Customizing has a surprisingly competitive price point and can take an "A" party to "AAA."

4. *Smile and say, "Cupcake!"* Kids love cupcakes, and these kid-sized mini cakes have become the sweet of choice at many kids' parties. Another popular sweet, in lieu of cake, are customized cookies such as those available at Beautiful Sweets (www.beautifulsweets.com). Children like these customized goodies. Some are iced with the child's name and age, while others are made to complement the theme of the party (for instance, in the shape of a bowling ball and pin for a bowling-themed party).

5. *A unified theme.* From the invitation to the cake decorations to the goody bag design, parents are asking for a unified design and theme. For instance, if the invitation has the child's name written in cartoon-type balloon letters, then the parents ask for this look to spill over into all of the other aspects of the design and décor.

> ## Top Ten Birthday Party Themes
>
> At the time I wrote this book, these party themes held the honor of top ten ranking, according to www.birthdaypartyideas.com, a Web site claiming to hold the "world's largest selection of birthday party ideas."
>
> 1. Princess parties
> 2. Pirate parties
> 3. Sweet sixteens
> 4. Tropical luaus
> 5. Scavenger hunts
> 6. Sleepovers
> 7. Tea parties
> 8. Fear Factor parties (based on the television show)
> 9. Dora the Explorer parties (based on the television show)
> 10. Beach parties

You may also choose to broaden your business by expanding your niche. If you have been the "Queen of the Princess Parties" for the life of your business, maybe it is time to take on another theme, which is particularly important if you want to grow your business.

You may also want to consider adding additional staff. One children's birthday party planner dressed herself as Cinderella and created a substantial business in a large urban area. Soon, demand outpaced her ability to arrive at every event in her magical coach. To continue growing her business, she hired and trained other performers to dress as Cinderella. Of course, great care must be taken to hire reliable, competent employees who will keep the reputation of your company untarnished.

Franchising Your Business

If you have created a unique and dynamic children's birthday party model, you may want to consider offering franchises of your business. Consider the amazing rise of the Build-A-Bear Workshop. Founded in 1997 by Maxine Clark, there are now almost four hundred Build-A-Bear stores in twenty countries. Although the stores in the United States, Puerto Rico, Canada, Ireland, and the United Kingdom are company

Growing Your Business Worksheet

As you consider raising your birthday party planning business to the next level, carefully consider and answer these questions. By doing so, you will help bring clarity to your desires and goals regarding expansion.

- ❑ *Are you ready for new challenges?* At a certain point, some small business owners get the feeling of "been there, done that," and want to stimulate and challenge themselves with new goals.
- ❑ *Are you ready and able financially to grow your business?* Expanding your business can involve big bucks. Consider the cost of hiring more employees or renting an off-site office space. Renting an off-site space involves more than paying your rent. You must factor in office supplies, office furniture, utilities, cleaning services, and more.
- ❑ *Do you need more employees?* Some small business owners find that at a certain point, it makes financial sense to take on a permanent employee rather than farming out a variety of odd jobs to independent contractors. Take time to do the math—are you paying more for your freelancers than you would for a permanent employee? If so, it might be time to hire.
- ❑ *Have you reached a revenue plateau?* Some party planners, like the Cinderella planner I described above, reach a revenue plateau. In other words, this planner simply couldn't be two places at once so her revenue or income stayed at a certain level. To overcome this, she took on employees to grow her revenue stream.
- ❑ *Can a larger version of your business do as well as the version you currently own?* This may be the single most important question to answer when considering growth. Some businesses do not thrive when they develop to the next level. If your business relies on your presence at every event, then, at a certain point, you won't be able to expand your business.

owned, the Build-A-Bear stores in fifteen other countries are franchise-owned. In other words, an investor paid Build-A-Bear Workshop for their business model, plan, and vision.

Chuck E. Cheese provides a similar model with more than five hundred locations in forty-eight states and five countries. As with Build-A-Bear Workshop, some of these locations are company-owned and some are franchises. Chuck E. Cheese provides franchise buyers with the opportunity to use their business expertise to open a successful business.

Before franchising your business, you will have to develop a proven track record at multiple locations. In other words, you will need to show that your business model works in more than one geographic region. This is important because many businesses are geographically or niche specific. Chuck E. Cheese and Build-A-Bear Workshop are two good examples of businesses that are not geographically specific. Folks just about everywhere love stuffed animals and pizza.

Another common mistake is hoping to franchise when business is not booming. Some small business owners look at franchising as a way to turn around a floundering business. But to draw franchisees to your business, you need to offer franchises when your business is doing well—and you must be able to document this success at multiple locations.

Also consider (honestly) if there is a concept like yours already in the marketplace. Build-A-Bear Workshop offered something unique to the marketplace when they launched their business in the late 1990s. To be a successful franchiser, you must have a unique product and be able to differentiate yourself from any possible competitors in the marketplace.

If you feel that you are ready to consider franchising your business, arrange to meet with your lawyer and begin discussions of the paperwork and costs involved.

Selling Your Birthday Party Business

Perhaps you have grown your business over the course of a decade or more and are ready for a change—a new opportunity or even retirement. At this point, some small business owners choose to sell their businesses.

To sell your business you have to be realistic about the business prospects. If profits are flat or nonexistent, you won't be able to sell your business. Work with your accountant to examine your profit and loss statements, cash flow statements, and other financial paperwork to track the trajectory of your business growth.

Perhaps your company's profits have grown at a steady rate of 5 percent every year since you hung out your shingle. This is powerful information to share with a prospective buyer.

A Blueprint for Building a Saleable Business

As you develop your business, you will likely have a projected arc of growth. You may hope to plan six parties during your first year of business, twelve the next, twenty-four the next, and so on. You may envision that at the end of this projected arc, you will sell your company for a profit. If this is your intent, then you will need to do certain things while developing and running your company to help ensure that sale.

- *Maintain accurate records from day one.* This point is critical. You must be able to show the continued and strong growth of your company. To do so, keep a complete paper trail, from your initial business plan to profit and loss statements and client referrals. All of this will be useful when it comes time to sell.
- *Develop a distinct niche.* This is a point returned to again and again throughout the book and, in terms of a successful sale, it is essential. To lure a prospective buyer, you need to clearly demonstrate your unique position in the children's birthday party business.
- *Maintain positive word of mouth.* This is another topic that is important at all times during the growth of your business—from bringing in your first client to finding a new pool of clients from which to draw. When you decide to sell your company, it will be imperative that the word of mouth surrounding your business is glowing. A prospective buyer will ask for references as well as do research of her own. For instance, she might check in at the local bakery. Make sure that you have developed a collegial and respectful relationship with the baker over the course of your business's life.
- *Show growth.* Your buyer will want to see the possibility for continuing growth in sales. People don't buy companies with the hope of staying even. Rather, these folks are looking for real growth. Create a graph showing your company's growth. This can be a powerful and persuasive visual when the graph shows a line going ever upward in terms of income and earnings.
- *Demonstrate that your business model can be moved to other regions.* A prospective buyer will appreciate a business model that is flexible and

A Checklist for Selling Your Birthday Party Business

If you decide to sell your children's birthday party business, you will need to cover all of the following bases for a successful sale:

- *Clean up your financial paperwork.* Make sure that you have all of your financial ducks in a row. By organizing your paperwork, you will be able to clearly illustrate your company's growth.

- *Create a business plan.* This doesn't need to be as involved or elaborate as your initial business plan but it should tell your company's story: when and where you began and how the company has grown. Show possible growth trajectories based on past growth of your birthday party business.

- *Work with your accountant to determine the fair value for your company.* Many small businesses fail to sell because they are incorrectly priced. Interestingly, sometimes the price is actually too low rather than too high.

- *Determine if you need to keep the fact that you are selling your company confidential.* It can—and often does—take months to sell a business. Some customers will be wary of using your planning services if they know you are in the process of selling.

- *Consider whether you would be willing to stay on as a consultant.* Sometimes, new business owners ask the previous owner to stay on as an advisor. You may or may not be comfortable with this role, so consider it carefully.

- *Be your own best promoter.* Even if you enlist a broker to sell your company, remember that nobody knows your business like you do. You are your company's best salesperson since you have built your party business through hard work and commitment. Don't be afraid to tell your story to sell your business.

- *Make sure to sell your company at the right time.* Just as it is not wise—or even possible—to sell a company that is barely limping along financially, be cognizant of economic conditions. If the economy has taken a downturn, then selling a business could be tricky.

can accommodate regional change. Does the model you have created in Dubuque, Iowa, have the same potential for growth in an urban area like Los Angeles? If so, this is a strong inducement to a buyer.

Your Wish Has Come True

Congratulations on creating a children's birthday party planning business. This is a lively, engaging, always growing field. A survey by Family Corner, an online source of parenting advice, puts the average cost of a children's birthday party at more than $200. When you consider that this is just the average, it is quite an astonishing number, putting the average cost in more populated urban areas closer to the $500 mark.

Michelle Kaufman, a New York City mother of one, considers $500 a bargain for the ease it provides on the day of her son's party.

"We used to do Jacob's birthday parties in Central Park ourselves and it was a huge pain because we would need to round up people to bring tables, chairs, decorations, and food—the whole works—to the park. So, we decided to start hiring and it has been so much easier. For the past several years, we've hired a children's party planner who specializes in soccer parties. She sends a group of people to coach and run the party. And, it all works like a top! I'll never plan my own parties again."

This is a common sentiment. Even in economic down times, folks tend to spend money on their kids and it provides a wonderful opportunity for all of us who enjoy working with children and planning their birthday parties. Birthdays are about celebrations and celebrating and it is a privilege and joy to be able to help children celebrate their all-important birthdays.

Frequently Asked Questions

I have more and more clients asking for me to create environmentally friendly—or green—events. Are there resources for planning these events?

The trend towards green continues to grow and suppliers are responding. For instance, Greener Printer (www.greenerprinter.com) is a certified green company offering custom printing on all recycled materials. Greener Printer also relies on wind-power to run its presses. Little Cherry (www.littlecherry.com) offers hundreds of tips for planning green: from using reusable, drawstring cotton bags for goody treats to filling the bags with toys made from sustainable wood sources to choosing party plates made from recycled stock. Finally, Eco Speakers, (www.ecospeakers .com) offers links to myriad Web sites offering tips to party planners for an eco-smart and eco-chic event.

I am thinking of expanding, beyond planning children's birthday parties. What are some of the other areas of event planning?
Having built a strong foundation planning children's events, you are positioned to successfully develop events in a wide range of areas, including—but not limited to!—planning award ceremonies, bar and bat mitzvahs, charity events for non-profits, conferences for businesses or colleges, fashion events, fairs, farmer's market events (events which are becoming increasingly popular), holiday or seasonal events, new product launches, seminars, sporting events, political fund-raisers, and store openings. Whew! It truly is an interesting array and one of the key reasons so many are drawn to event planning. There is enough variety to suit almost anyone.

Appendix

Birthday Party Supplies

From moon bounces to piñatas and everything in between, these online party supply stores offer a vast array of wares.

- Anderson's Giant Party Store, www.giantpartystore.com
- Balloon Time, www.balloontime.com
- Birthday Direct, www.birthdaydirect.com
- Birthday in a Box, www.birthdayinabox.com
- BirthdayZ by ShindigZ, www.birthdayzbyshindigz.com
- Celebrate Express, www.celebrateexpress.com
- Oriental Trading, www.orientaltrading.com
- Party Pro, www.partypro.com
- Party Supplies Hut, www.partysupplieshut.com
- Party Supplies World, www.partysuppliesworld.com
- Pinatas.com, www.pinatas.com

Customized Party Supplies

From customized banners to disposable cameras emblazoned with the birthday child's photo, customized supplies add extra flair to a child's birthday party.

- Balloon City U.S.A., www.ballooncity.com
- Cameras for All, www.camerasforall.com
- Custom Camera Collection, www.customcameracollection.com
- Marco Marketing Solutions, www.marcopromotionalproducts.com
- My M&Ms for Promotions, www.mymms.com

- Party 411, www.party411.com
- Personalized Party Favor, www.personalizedpartyfavor.com
- Personalized Party Favors, www.personalizedpartyfavors.com

Direct Mail and Mailing Lists

Goldsmith, Richard. *Direct Mail for Dummies*. New Jersey, IDG Books, 2002.

Mailing List Buying Guide, www.mailinglistbuyingguide.com; this useful Web site offers information about direct mail campaigns as well as guidance about companies offering mailing lists for sale.

Meisner, Chet. *The Complete Guide to Direct Marketing*. New York, Kaplan Business, 2006.

Good Reading

It is vital in any event-planning business to keep abreast of current trends. Make sure to track current books and magazines that will influence your work as a children's birthday party planner. Check your library or bookstore often for the most up-to-date books.

Developing a Niche

These books are useful as you choose and develop a niche for your birthday party planning business. I especially enjoy the Penny Whistle party guides. They are charming and inspiring.

Baltrus, Susan. *The Ultimate Birthday Party Book: 50 Complete and Creative Themes to Make Your Kid's Special Day Fantastic!* Colorado, Cook Communications, 2002.

Brokaw, Meredith and Gilbar, Annie. *The Penny Whistle Birthday Party Book*. New York, Fireside, 1992.

Brokaw, Meredith and Gilbar, Annie. *The Penny Whistle Party Planner*. New York, Fireside, 1991.

Hetzer, Linda. *Fifty Fabulous Parties for Kids*. New York, Three Rivers Press, 1994.

Krull, Sharron. *That Was the Best Birthday Party Ever: How to Give Birthday Parties Kids Will Never Forget*. California, Play Power, 1995.

Smith, Anita M. *Theme Birthday Parties for Children: A Complete Planning Guide*. North Carolina, McFarland & Company, 2000.

Vansgarg, Amy. *Hit of the Party: The Complete Planner for Children's Theme Birthday Parties. Pennsylvania, Diane Books Publishing Company, 2000.*

Warner, Penny. *Birthday Parties for Kids: Creative Party Ideas Your Kids and Their Friends Will Love.* California, Prima Lifestyles, 1998.

Warner, Penny. *Kids Party Games and Activities: Hundreds of Entertaining Things to Do at Parties for Kids from 2–12.* California, Meadowbrook, 1993.

General Event Planning Guides

Although none of these titles specifically addresses children's party planning, they do offer general and helpful advice for developing an event-planning business. When looking for useful guides, always check the book's copyright. Event planning is a fast paced and always changing field. Books that are more than five years old will probably be of little use.

Kilkenny, Shannon. *The Complete Guide to Successful Event Planning.* Florida, Atlantic Publishing Company, 2007.

Moran, Jill S., CSEP. *How to Start a Home-Based Event Planning Business.* Connecticut, The Globe Pequot Press, 2007.

Peters, Amy. *Start Your Own Event Planning Business: Your Step-by-Step Guide to Success.* California, Entrepreneur Press, 2007.

Inspiring Magazines

Although these magazines are not specifically directed at the children's party planners, I find they offer creative and interesting ideas that are useful for planning kids' events.

Family Fun Magazine: This publication offers advice on everything from creating the ultimate cupcake to designing games and activities for tots to teens. Subscriptions are $10 for ten issues and are available at www.familyfun.com.

Martha Stewart's Good Things for Kids: Crafts: This charming magazine offers ideas for creative craft and art projects. For more information, go to www.martha stewart.com.

Hiring Professionals

These are good resources when choosing to hire other professionals to help with your business. Check these Web sites to find lawyers and accountants in your area and to check their references.

- American Bar Association, www.aba.net
- American Institute of Certified Public Accountants, www.aicpa.org
- National Association of States Board of Accountancy, www.nasba.org

Training

For better or worse, there is no official certification for children's birthday party planners. For the better, because you don't need to acquire any specific certification to open your business. For worse, because if you are looking for training or certification, it can be a bit frustrating.

A good place to find informal training is at your local community colleges, which often offer classes in catering, food and floral design, web design, marketing, and other areas of interest to event planners. Community College School Guide (www .collegebound.net) offers information about community colleges throughout the country and the types of classes offered.

The two organizations below offer certification for event planners. This certification, while not specifically targeted to children's party planners, is still useful. Some clients look for a professional certification when hiring party planners. I have found, though, that typically, my clients do not look for or feel the need for certification.

Convention Industry Council, www.conventionindustry.org; this group offers the training to become a Certified Meeting Professional (CMP).
International Special Events Society, www.ises.com; this group offers certification as a Certified Special Events Professional (CSEP).

Small Business Development Help

Often you can find free, professional help in your community or at your fingertips when you access these Web sites:

- America's Small Business Development Center Network, www.asbdc-us.org
- Service Corps of Retired Executives, www.score.org

- Small Business Administration, www.sba.gov
- Small Business Development Center Network, sbdcnet.org

Trade Associations

I've found that networking locally has been the best way to grow and promote my business. Your local chamber of commerce will likely prove invaluable in helping you to network and to make important business connections (www.chamberof commerce.com). However, as your business grows you may want to attend the meetings of national organizations to learn more about event planning.

Event Planners Association, www.eventplannersassociation.com; the Event Planners Association offers legal and business advice as well as vendor resources and an online chat room for brainstorming with other event planners.

Useful Web Sites

www.birthdaypartyideas.com: This site claims title to listing "the world's largest collection of birthday party ideas." This Web site breaks the ideas into categories— "kids party ideas," "teen party ideas," and "adult party ideas," for instance. I find this site useful in helping to track party trends, as it typically keeps a list of the current top ten themes.

www.marthastewart.com: This Web site is simply loaded with inspiration. From how to set a festive table to designing child-friendly centerpieces and everything in between, this is a terrific source.

www.pbs.org/parents/birthdays/. This Web site, created by the crew at Public Broadcasting Systems, offers solid advice for children's party planners, including how to ensure that activities are age appropriate, how to determine the appropriate number of guests, how to develop child-friendly menus, and more.

Web Site Design

Lopuck, Lisa. *Web Design for Dummies*. New Jersey, For Dummies, 2006.

McFedries, Paul. *The Complete Idiot's Guide to Creating a Web Page*. Florida, Alpha Publishing, 2008.

Index